The
Unbridgeable
Divide

The Unbridgeable Divide

Alex Kimbell

Matador
12 Manor Walk, Coventry Road
Market Harborough
Leics LE16 9BP, UK
Tel: (+44) 1858 468828
Email: books@troubador.co.uk
Web: www.troubador.co.uk/matador

ISBN 1 899293 19 1

Cover: Illustration by Betty Williams
Pen and ink drawings by Ian Geddes and Carole Dunstone

Typeset in 12.5pt Garamond by Troubador Publishing Ltd, Market Harborough, UK
Printed and bound by Cambrian Printing, Wales

Matador is an imprint of Troubador Publishing

The
Unbridgeable
Divide

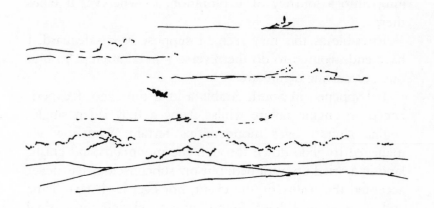

Chapter 1

I don't often dream.

At least I suppose I must, for they say even whilst the body sleeps a person's subconscious is ever active and once released from the realities of the day the unfettered mind is free to roam into the realms of beyond. In ancient times, people took great store of dreams; the Old Testament is full of related instances where dreams have had great significance, but these days, as with so many other aspects of our development, the art of interpretation has gradually been lost. Most people can remember fragments of dreams, especially when they first wake, but it is no longer fashionable to take them seriously, to query their meaning, let alone relate them to others.

Except for a select few. For there are those amongst us who have made a conscious study of dreams – not necessarily psychologists or those whose job it is to study the mind, but ordinary laypeople who out of curiosity have managed to develop the aspect further; so much that their subconscious becomes meaningful. With patience and dedication they can tune their mind to the stage whereby they can actually harness their subconscious, enabling them to jump into a journey of exploration, to wherever it takes them...

Enviable as this may seem, I suppose as a safeguard, I have endeavoured to do the reverse – in an attempt to blot out a reccurring nightmare.

It happened in South Arabia a long time ago: I experienced an engine failure whilst flying a fully laden single-engine aircraft over mountainous terrain. Somehow we managed to glide down through the mountains and crashland in a dried up wadi bed; but my subconscious has never accepted the reality of the event, nor ever let it rest. Time and time again I have found myself reliving those final moments of the descent, each time with the dream firmly in command. It relives and explores every tenuous avenue, all of which end in disaster. I have even attempted to override the situation by altering the facts ... a hidden knob and the engine bursts into life again – but to no avail. The dream always wins, often to counter with savage retribution by sometimes severing the control links leaving a lifeless control column and rudder pedals that flop uselessly to the floor...

But this was not what had woken me.

It was a person – or rather a presence that had forcibly penetrated my sleep. No nightmare; no terror leaving me wide-eyed and coated in sweat; instead an air of calm and gentleness prevailed. I lay in the bed and in the dim light picked out the unfamiliar surroundings of the room. The presence was still there, I could feel it lingering all around, but was unable to focus further. It was strangely familiar, as though we had brushed together before in some other time or space. But whether male or female I could not discern; perhaps souls travel unhindered by gender? I wish I knew more about these things. Gradually it began to fade. 'Don't go' I called out in my mind, 'don't go; who are you; why are you here...what made you come?'

I felt the presence smile, a knowing smile that again was

familiar, and began to flicker.

I tried my voice. 'Hello...' but it came out as a croak. 'Hello, who are you?' I called out loud.

But it had gone.

Chapter 2

I

I hadn't realized I was alone in the house and it took seven rings before I could reach the nearest phone, which was the one in the kitchen hanging on the wall.

Automatically I started to answer with my name, but then remembered it wasn't my phone, so read the number out instead.

'Mon Ami! C'est toi? It 'as been a long time... your father called into the shop and said you were 'ome on leave...!'

'Bernard! How good to hear you. How're things?'

'I am well. As well as can be expected ...'

Bernard, a Frenchman and an old flying friend of mine could best be described as the original entrepreneur. He'd first arrived in England during the latter part of the Second World War in order to learn to fly with the Free French. In between flying lessons he managed to find time to court a local girl – who's father also happened to own the one and only hardware shop in town. Not being one to let the grass

4

grow under his feet, nor for that matter to miss an opportunity, he soon became a familiar figure serving behind the counter, where he quickly learnt the business. His wedding coincided with his demobilization and with a ready-made job to walk into he decided to stay in England where he'd remained ever since. But that was as far as he had allowed himself to become Anglicised, for if anything his accent and mannerisms had become increasingly French over the years, greatly enhancing his profile as the archetype Frenchman abroad.

Beset by increasing ill health, his father in law gladly made the business over to his daughter and her capable new husband, but sadly never saw it grow to fruition for he died within two years of his retirement. This left Bernard the sole proprietor of a reputable and well-established business – which, by its location in the centre of town could be likened to Piccadilly Circus in London, where it is said if you stand for long enough, *everybody* you know will pass by at some time or other...

Under his vision the business flourished. He was a charismatic and colourful figure: one of nature's showmen, his forte being publicity (in which he always featured personally), together with a flair for original marketing – this long before the public had been brainwashed into absorbing the ever increasing levels of sophisticated advertising as later generated by commercial television. From the original hardware concept the store was opened up, soon to encompass lawnmowers and garden machines, a wide range of outside and country clothing and a saddlery. He ran out of space, so negotiated to buy the adjoining premises, before expanding further into kitchen equipment, pottery, an off-license specialising in French wines, a pet centre, garden furniture, indoor plants, a coffee shop – and so it went on, each department under its own colourful set of umbrellas, with French music playing softly in the background. The town had never seen anything like it and flocked there in ever-increasing numbers, for to be seen having 'coffee at Bernards'' was the in-place to be.

But no business can survive on publicity and marketing alone, and under Bernard's veneer of Gallic charm lay an astute businessman, whose first priority had been to install a sound foundation of financial management for his growing organization, as well as developing a knack of being in the right place at the right time.

Which was how I first met him.

I was looking at lawnmowers – or to be precise, at the large selection of second-hand machines that were displayed on a patch of lawn at the rear of the premises, each with a card on it saying that it had been tested and had a year's guarantee.

"Ow can I 'elp you, sir?' It was the man himself.

'I can't decide between these two lawnmowers. They both look to be about the same size, they have the same engine, they're roughly the same price...so whats the difference between them?'

'Eh-hue, what sort of lawn is it you 'ave to cut?'

'Well it's just grass...'

'Ow large is it; do you need a machine this size; is it a laid lawn or field grass and does it 'ave any trees in it?'

'Well it's a small paddock really – and yes, there are a few trees and the grass is, well, just ordinary grass – but certainly not up to bowling green standard...'

'If you 'ave trees, this is the machine you want; see, the grass collector is made from rubber and won't dent when you hit one! Also it 'as belt drive whilst this other one 'as chain drive; but they both work equally well. But, if it's a paddock you say, neither of these machines is really the one you want. You don't need to make any stripes' He thought for a minute and then grasped my arm. 'But, eh-hue, I 'ave just the machine for you – only it's not here at the moment. Just the thing for a paddock! Do you have thirty minutes, I will show it to you?'

'Oh, no need to go to any trouble, I'm just looking really...'

'Come, it is no trouble and this machine is just right for you. You will see...' He led me to his car.

'So, you 'ave a paddock, do you keep horses too – you 'ave been to our saddlery?' He asked as we drove out of town.

'No good heavens no, nothing so grand as that. It's only a small paddock – it used to be an orchard at the rear of my parent's house. I'm staying there at the moment. I'm just looking to see if I can find them something that would be easy to keep the grass down; otherwise it just grows into a wilderness. I do hope I'm not wasting your time...'

We drove on in silence and finally swung into the rear entrance of the local airport where he stopped in front of a hangar. And here it was I learned about his true passion. That ever since learning to fly with the French Navy, aeroplanes had continued to feature in his life. With a flair honed by business instinct, he bought and sold aircraft with impeccable timing, thereby not only managing to offset his flying expenses, but also creating surplus capital to purchase a succession of larger and more sophisticated machines.

As the hangar doors opened he saw my interest and it was then I told him that I was too was a pilot – and the small tractor lawnmower that had been the purpose of our visit remained forgotten in its corner. And so the first seeds of our friendship were sown, and in spite of an age gap of some twenty years, the friendship continued to blossom and bear fruit from a variety of different branches that were to develop over the years.

Thereafter, he graciously said I could fly whatever aircraft he happened to have in his hangar (so long as I covered the running expenses); an arrangement that would also suit him, for when buying and selling an aircraft it always meant a one-way trip, and if I was available and could be called upon to be a ferry pilot, he could then use two aircraft – when, of course, he would then cover the expenses!

Although I hadn't seen him for a number of years, I had little doubt that this was the reason for his call.

'Eh-hue your father said you were on 'oliday with nothing to do...' he continued, 'I 'ave an aircraft stranded at Dijon, which I 'ave to get back into this country by Wednesday – that's when the temporary export papers expire. So, today is Monday... I

7

can fly you to Dijon tomorrow – and we'll spend the night there, and then you can bring it back on Wednesday...?'

'Bernard – that's cutting it a bit fine isn't it?'

'It is the only time we 'ave. I was let down... it does not matter. You will do it?'

'Okay, so long as you don't try to sell me a lawnmower...'

'E-hue, you never did buy that one; I haven't forgotten! Good, eight o'clock at my 'anger then – and bring a toothbrush. Oh, I need your passport number... give it to me now over the phone, please.'

'Hang on, I'll just get it...' I retrieved it from my flight bag, where I keep it with my flying paraphernalia, and then without asking why, read him the number. He gave a grunt and then said 'C'iao' and hung up.

II

I went to bed early that night. It was odd being back in the room I'd had as a child, sleeping in the same old narrow bed that I'd last slept in some twenty-three years before. On the odd occasions we'd stayed when I was married to Annie, we'd always been put into the guest room with its large double bed; but now it was though the clock had been turned back and I was eighteen again, waiting to go to Sandhurst.

Nonetheless I still found it difficult to relax and completely switch off. After the hectic months in Ireland, where one always slept with an ear cocked open ready to be called out, the silence was almost too complete and in itself unsettling. Furthermore I was glad Bernard had rang; it would be good to fly with him again and spend a night in Dijon – and truth be known, however much good everyone said it was doing me, I was getting rather bored with the prolonged period of inactivity. For one thing, it allowed me to think too much, and I wasn't really ready for that. Now wasn't the time to think back: it was much easier to look forward and cope with life as and when it happened. To look back forced one to analyse the past... but then I'd always done that, and in many ways it was probably contributory to my present circumstances. Certainly with Annie, whose temperament had been the other extreme, and who never took a step without carefully thinking it through first. All she'd wanted was a normal married life; the security of her own home to bring up a brood of children and a husband who came home at five o'clock every evening. But that wasn't to be; instead she'd been pitched straight into the hurly-burly of army life, a husband who was away for months at a time, and where 'permanent' meant two years at the maximum. The stupid thing was, I'd known before we got married that she'd hate being a soldier's wife; it was totally contrary to her gentle nature and disposition – but it was pointless dwelling upon it now; that wouldn't turn the clock back, and at least we'd parted amicably and there were no hard feelings.

I smiled at the ceiling. The room had been painted how many times since I last lay here? Yet still the same old cracks had reappeared, wandering haphazardly towards the light fitting, under which hung the same old lampshade...

I turned the light out.

That's enough thinking... it's just what I said I wouldn't do, and there's no point in thinking about Annie now; it was all a long time ago – we'd both come out of it okay and life goes on. More important, if I'm flying in the morning I ought to get some sleep.

Like every other soldier I can usually put my head down anywhere and be instantly asleep. Except now my brain was too active; too full of thoughts, which if left would only multiply. There was only one other way: some people count sheep, but I try switching off each part of my body in turn. The minute your concentration wavers, you go back and start again. First, concentrate on your toes, relaxing each one at a time and then move up to your ankles and concentrate on them and when they're fully switched off you move up to your calves...

There was a light filtering through the curtains. Maybe it came from the solitary streetlight that was at the end of the drive, or more likely somebody had left the outside light on... but I wasn't going to get up and turn it off now. I remember, it used to shine in like that when I was a boy. Sometimes it flickered as though there was a branch of a tree waving in front of it, but I'd never bothered to investigate further in the morning. It was no longer important then. So still it flickered.

In the half-light I could make out the wardrobe at the end of the room... near where the apparition or whatever it was appeared last night. I'd been thinking about it all day but was no nearer to an answer. Had I just imagined it – could it have been a figment of my imagination? It had seemed so real; can the mind really conjure up a life-like presence like that? Like a genie out of a lamp? In a way it was frightening – not the genie itself, for there had been no threat there; it had only exuded a sense of calmness and peace... far more disturbing was the realization that my mind could be capable of conjuring such a vision – if that indeed was what I'd done? No, that was too much – too much to comprehend and anyway, highly unlikely. I'm just not that sort of person, so perish the thought. It must have been a dream, however real it seemed at the time.

But intriguing nonetheless... I suppose the only way to be certain would be to see if it happened again. Perhaps if I lie very still and concentrate... now, how far had I got? Arms. Start at the hands with the fingers...

III

He was there before me, pre-flighting a pretty Piper Twin Comanche that looked spanking new in red and white livery, although the registration letters on its tailfin belied its age and showed it was by no means a new aircraft. I helped him to push it out of the hangar and then wound the handle to close the hangar doors.

'Looks very smart, Bernard. What's the forecast like?'

'Eh-hue. I 'ave just 'ad it re-sprayed – and it is not a good job;

it cost nearly double than I thought it would! They said it was a job for specialists, as it needed special paint that was difficult to apply; but as far as I can see it's no more difficult than a car! Another time I will get a garage to do it...'

I secured the hanger doors and then joined him as he walked round the aircraft in a cursory pre-flight inspection, where seemingly he was more interested in pointing out the flaws in the paintwork than checking the aircraft. On completing the circle he stopped and looked up at the sky.

'The forecast? Huh, it is what you would expect for this time of the year in England – but, my friend, it will be better in *France*! Today is overcast, but the cloud base is not too bad – so we will fly VFR underneath. Tomorrow, who knows? They are forecasting a front to come through later, but per'aps we will miss it... put your valise and flight bag in the back,' he added, as he climbed into the left-hand seat.

'I think I 'ave just sold this machine to a man in St.Tropez ...' he continued as he primed the port engine '...naturally I included the cost of the spray-job in the price, I only 'ope 'e doesn't look too closely. Clear prop!' The port engine fired up and I hastily strapped myself in. 'So, on Wednesday I will fly on from Dijon and I will sell it to 'im...'

We taxied to the end of the active runway, and then waited impatiently whilst the needles of the engine instruments took their time to creep up the dials, Bernard drumming his fingers on the control wheel.

'I tell you my friend, *this* is an expensive aeroplane to run...' shaking his head as he completed the pre-takeoff vital actions, '...maybe for someone like *you*, a man of your means, but me? Huh, I would not 'ave another one; not for my private use. With two 160hp engines it cruises at about 'undred and sixty knots – that's only about ten knots faster than something like a Mooney with a single 180 hp engine. Admittedly this carries about 450 kilograms more, but 'ow often do you *use* the full capacity? This machine, with two engines, uses *double* the fuel and costs *twice* as much to maintain! Maybe it is all right for air-taxi work – people who can afford air taxis don't mind paying for two engines...' he gave me a knowing look with his piercing blue eyes '...I expect it makes them feel safer; but from an operating view, it is too *small* to be a twin and just doesn't make economic sense. Per'aps in America, where l'essence is cheap but... anyway, I will be *glad* to see the back of it and sell it to the man in St.Tropez.'

'So, what's our route?'

'Ah! Today we go direct! We 'ave two VOR's, so we may as well use them!' He thrust a chart into my hand. 'See, give or take a few degrees, from 'ere to Dijon is one-three-five magnetic, and there are VOR beacons nicely placed all the way!' He said this in a voice that inferred that he had had a hand in inventing the VOR and had personally had them installed on the direct route to Dijon. 'See, from 'ere we go to the VOR at Stapleford; that will take us just east of London Control Zone; then five degrees right onto one-four-zero will near enough take us straight through the beacons at Detling and Lydd. Then back onto one-three-five, across the Channel to the beacon at Abbeville. I'll call Paris then, and see if they'll allow us to cut the corner and route direct to Troyes – if they're not too busy and you 'ave a transponder, they usually give permission; but if not, we'll have to turn east,' he jabbed a finger onto the chart, 'and route to the beacon at Cambrai and then down to the beacon at Chatillon, west of Reims and on to Troyes – you see, keeping just east of their Controlled Airspace? After that, it is clear all the way to Dijon; beacons all the way, all we do is follow the needles...'

'What about Customs clearance?'

'Customs? Ah, I forgot it is a long time since you flew from 'ere. *Now*, by prior arrangement, we 'ave our *own* Customs facility 'ere. It is just a matter of a telephone call...' Again in a voice that inferred that the arrangement was strictly a personal one. 'So I 'ave already cleared us and the machine out, and filed a VFR plan.'

'Mmm. Shouldn't I have to show my face to Customs?'

'Non, non. C'est une formalité et, ah – it is no longer necessary. I telephoned and they 'ave all the information – including your Passport number...' he paused and gave me another knowing look. 'Also, eh-hue, I know this man – 'e is what you call a *good chap*. He's always in the shop... Ah, the engines are ready, we can go.'

Both temperature needles had barely reached their green sectors – but they had had their chance, and it was time to go. He released the brakes and with Gallic aplomb, swung onto the runway and opened the throttles.

'Bernard, you haven't told me what type of aeroplane you want me to fly back?' I asked, when we were settled on course with one VOR tuned to Stapleford and the other to Cranfield, giving us a continuous running cross bearing.

'Did I not? Huh, well, I'm afraid it will be a lot slower than this machine...'

'I see. Just how much slower?'

'It is a *French* machine – a Rallye Minerva. Do you know the type? But...' he fiddled with throttle levers, frowning with concentration '...but – ah yes, *this* aeroplane – the Minerva, it 'as the *large* 'undred and fifty 'orsepower engine in it, not that little engine they put in the Rallye Club, which otherwise looks much the same. Now *there* is an underpowered machine for you... No, this one 'as plenty of power – it's a proper *farmer's* machine; all metal, very strong and robust and it has a good short takeoff performance, which makes it good for fields. It has the leading edge slots that come out of the wing like a Tiger Moth. Eh-hue, and to fly...' he shrugged, '...it is not *spectaculaire* in any way... it is predictable and safe and it flies – well, as you would expect it to! But, this farmer who 'ad it, he fitted it with a fine-pitch propeller to get out of his fields – so even with the *large* engine, it does not make it go any faster, you understand? Short takeoff's yes, but otherwise...' he took both hands off the wheel in an emphatic gesture combined with another shrug to better demonstrate the point, '...it is slow, and if you try to make it go faster, it just makes a lot more noise! *Mais puis*, per'aps now it is getting a little long in the teeth – but it is still a *good* machine – I 'ad to take it in as a part-exchange.'

'Mmm, I think I've seen them about, but never looked at one close to. If it belonged to a farmer, did he go anywhere

13

in it – what level of instrumentation does it have?'

'Eh-hue! Instruments, now there... I 'ave *myself* fitted a brand new three 'undred and sixty channel VHF radio. The latest model – it only had an old Mickey Mouse crystal set before – but I left that in it as a backup, so now it 'as two!'

'Ah...well, that's good – so what else does it have? Any nav-aids – VOR, ADF, Markers?'

'Huh, what do you expect, a full panel? No, it just has the basic flying instruments, which were enough for 'im. He did not need expensive navigation equipment to fly from 'is farm and look at 'is fields. You can 'ave them fitted of course... but not in this one. But *you*, a professional army pilot will surely manage? You are used to flying with just a compass and a map...? Oh yes, it also 'as navigation and landing lights. They fit those as standard.'

'Navigation lights! Well *there's* something! I just hope I won't have to use them, especially on a limited panel... Ah well, I haven't done any eyeball flying in a fixed wing aeroplane for a long time, so I may be a bit rusty. It'll mean landing at Le Touquet and again at Lydd to clear Customs, I suppose?'

'*Naturellement!* That is the way we always used to do it. Anyway, the machine is not at Dijon, but at Darois – where there are no facilities, so you will 'ave to land at Le Touquet to get the exit papers stamped...'

We droned on our way. Bernard was a good pilot, with many hours experience that embraced a great variety of different aircraft, but I hadn't flown with him for a long time and had forgotten how he always gave the impression of being unable to relax in a cockpit. Instead of sitting back and allowing the machine to fly itself, he gripped the wheel with both hands, as though driving a car and rarely a minute passed without a minute adjustment to the trim or fine-tuning the pitch of one engine or the other. The aircraft had an autopilot and would have settled at the click of a switch, but autopilots were not Bernard's way: he preferred to fly hands-on.

Nonetheless, in spite of his earlier derogatory remarks, it was a sweet aircraft to fly in. Having flown helicopters for so long, I'd forgotten how elegantly a fixed wing aircraft flies by comparison. Instead of hanging forward in the straps whilst thumping through the air under the forced power of a rotor, our progress was smooth and effortless, transmitting an awareness and sensation of flight that somehow never materialises in a helicopter. It's difficult to describe, but at heart, I realized, I would always remain a fixed wing pilot; it was rather like coming home. I smiled at this newfound insight and took stock of all that was around. The cockpit was well appointed and logically laid out, as well as being comfortable and quiet; and unlike the interior of most military machines was uncluttered by the plethora of knobs and switches that relate to weapon-system arming panels, tactical radios, high-intensity searchlights, winching equipment and all the other things the army find necessary to install in a helicopter in order to fulfil a multi-purpose role. Also, unnecessary extravagance or not, it was a good feeling to be sitting between a pair of growling 160hp Lycomings as they effortlessly ate up the miles between the beacons, and one by one they slid on their way.

As we approached the French coast, Bernard changed frequency to Paris North Information and then waited for an appropriate gap in the mixture of French and heavily accented English transmissions that now flowed continuously into our headsets.

When commercial flying was in its infancy, it was unanimously agreed that English should be the common language used for all radio communication between aircraft and the ground. Flight Safety alone decreed that this was a fundamental requirement, and so English was universally adopted and thereafter recognised under International Aviation Law.

Except that is, to a Frenchman on his home ground.

I had first encountered this during my early flying training when converting from the light AOP 9 spotter aircraft to the relatively larger De Havilland Beaver. In order to fly liaison flights to destinations all over Europe, the Beaver was equipped with a cockpit full of instruments, including a Decca navigation system. This enabled the aircraft to be flown in all weathers and if need be, on the commercial Airways that interlink countries and cities throughout the world. If this was the way that commercial airliners managed to keep to their demanding schedules, then why not join them, for here was a readily available way of reaching ones destination with a degree of certainty! Moreover, one could always opt out at any time and continue to the obscurity of a military destination beneath the lower levels of the airways, so long as you had previously plotted and entered the information into the all-embracing Decca. Thus, the majority of the conversion course was devoted to brushing-up our Instrument Ratings to the exacting standards required to fly on the Airways, in order to take our slow-flying bush aeroplanes to the upper levels – to the frustration of controllers and delay to other users, both of whom were more accustomed to aircraft of a speedier nature in their exalted domain. The fact that we were military cut no ice whatsoever with the French controllers – indeed, the reverse appeared to be the case, an aspect not unknown to our instructors who, with Machiavellian deviousness, delighted in sending us to every conceivable destination that at some time or other would infringe French Airspace. If we could pene-trate French Airspace, they thought – or more to the point, if we could successfully hold our own when confronted by the despotic attitude of the average French Controller, we would be able to handle anything.

And so it proved to be, for on first encounter there seemed to be a conspiracy among the French to prevent others from understanding them. Give me a French newspa-per or a book and I can follow the story line well enough. I can also manage to hold my own in simple conversation, especially on a face-to-face basis when you can slow them down if necessary; but to hear them talk on the radio it becomes another language. To the untuned ear their voices become a continuous vowel sound where it's impossible to determine where one word ends and another begins. Occasionally a well-known word or phrase emerges from the background and you grasp at the straw: *Beacon Outbound* which gives you an idea of what is being said, but never enough to fully understand with a completeness that matters,

16

for invariably it is followed by more unending vowel burble and finally *très bien*. Très Bien? Now would that be the local colloquialism for 'Over', or hopefully even 'Out'? Would that be the end of the transmission, or will there be more to come? My first few attempts unwittingly interrupted an unfinished conversation, which caused a tirade of French and general confusion all round. After that I decided to err on the cautious side and wait a second or two before pressing the button to transmit... which pause caused the moment to be lost, and an open invitation for a new voice to chip in.

I was pleased to find that the others were experiencing similar difficulties and when we compared notes, none of us could figure out what there was so much to talk about? All that was required was confirmation of your position together with your in-flight conditions when you reached a compulsory reporting point on route – and which, when presented in the prescribed format should only take a matter of seconds, the very purpose being to free the air as quickly as possible. At least, that's how it always worked in UK airspace, with the comforting thought that should an emergancy ever arise, the system was designed to cope with it. Not so in French airspace, which I found out one day when flying a Beaver on Airways to Germany.

Our designated Flight Level was One-One-Five – or 11,500 feet, at which altitude we started to accumulate ice. The temperature gauge remained constant and the ice began to build, until we could no longer maintain our prescribed level. The usual non-stop flow of chatter was monopolising every moment on the radio and I waited for a break. At last one came and I pressed the button.

'Army Air 8797, is experiencing icing at Flight Level 115 and can no longer maintain altitude. Request a descent to FL.95?'

'Armee Air 8797, wait...' and then went on to talk to somebody else. Four minutes passed whilst we slowly lost altitude. Then: 'Armee Air 8797?'

'Nine-seven. Go.'

'Armee 8797. Say again your request?'

I reiterated our situation and also that we were IMC (Instrument Met Conditions) in cloud.

'Armee 8797. Wait.' We continued to descend, and lumps of ice were now being thrown off the propeller and banging against the fuselage. Another three-minutes conversation in French to another aircraft ensued, and then at last my Callsign.

'Armee 8797 is cleared to descend to Flight Level 95, call again at that level.'

'Nine-seven, roger... Ah, nine-seven is in fact passing through nine-five at this time, request further descent to Flight Level 75?'

'Armee 8797' in an exasperated voice. 'Wait, Out'.

Instead of recognising our situation and helping by offering to clear a path to a lower level, they were seemingly indifferent and content to follow, always two steps behind, until we finally fell out of the bottom level of the Airway and no longer under their jurisdiction. We limped on to our destination, slowly shedding our burden of ice in the warmer air close to the ground – and no doubt where everyone thought we belonged.

It was an unfortunate episode that angered me somewhat at the time; for when in difficulties, the least you expect is a degree of understanding, rather than total indifference from those who are there to help. But it also taught me a salutary lesson and one that would stand me in good stead on many occasions in later years when confronted by not only French, but Italian and Spanish speaking controllers, all of whom, given the chance, will immediately revert to their mother tongue in preference to English, regardless of the stipulations decreed by International Aviation Law! Had the icing incident occurred in UK airspace, the controller would have picked up the nuance of understatement and acted accordingly; but at the time I was still new to the game and had yet to make allowances, let alone realize that it is unfair to expect this level of understanding from an anonymous person speaking in a language not stipluatd by Aviation Law. I eventually learnt by listening to the professional approach adopted by airline pilots on the radio, who – whatever their nationality – prudently keep their exchanges as simple and concise as possible, thereby minimising any possible risk of misinterpretation. The other extreme would have been to declare an emergency, which undoubtedly would have gained instant attention – but it is against any pilot's better nature to do this, especially when the situation hardly warrants it, so in a no-win situation, best try to avoid it in the first place.

But listening to the mixture of vociferous chatter in the headsets now, did nothing to dispel my earlier prejudices or make me think that things had changed any for the better. Except for one difference: Bernard was a Frenchman, and as such, it was merely a matter of establishing the right credentials.

He jumped into the first available slot and started off in English, soon to be followed by a flow of voluble French. The controller answered, also in French – his tone suggesting that he was an extremely busy person, with a job that entailed far more demanding priorities than allowing him time to chat to any old passing aeroplane in transit. Bernard answered, his tone rising the required degree to register his end of the pecking order, whilst emphasising each point by beating the control column with his clenched fists. A heated exchange followed, with final submission from the controller, who spat out a series of numbers, before immediately transferring his attentions to another customer.

Bernard punched the numbers into the transponder and then activated the switch.

'Good, now 'e 'as us on 'is radar. We are cleared from Abbeville through 'is zone to Chatillon. I 'oped to route direct to Troyes, but they are busy – at least this is better than nothing – it cuts some of the corner...' He grunted with satisfaction and then re-tuned the second VOR accordingly.

'Numbers, numbers, numbers...' I said sadly, looking at the red digital figures displayed on the transponder and shaking my head.

Like a fish, he rose and took the bait.

'What is it, numbers?'

'Have you ever considered, everything in life is becoming

more and more dependent upon numbers? No longer are you a person with a name – just think how many numbers you are identified by: to a bank you are an account number, to an insurance company you are a policy number, you have a telephone number, a car number, a national insurance number, a passport number, a credit card number, a medical card number – just think about how many different numbers you have, the list is endless...'

'So, what is it you are saying?'

'Well, the only number I can ever remember is my army number, and in the army that does for everything. I remember years ago when I was first commissioned, I went into one of the old Co-operative shops – you remember, the forerunner to the supermarket, where everyone had a number for their 'divvy'? I'd never been in one before and I saw you had to join a queue in order to get out, and when it became my turn, the lady said "What's your number?" For a moment I was dumbfounded, then immediately snapped to attention and said "Four-Six-Three-One-Eight-Nine!"

"Coo" she said, "you don't come from round here, do you!" And I remember thinking at the time, if your name was no longer enough, instead of countless organisations identifying you by a different number, why not have one number that would do for everything and everybody? In this computerised age of ours it would be relatively easy to do, and how much easier life would be!'

He thought for a moment, whilst making a minute adjustment to the starboard pitch lever, which to my ear was already perfectly synchronised.

'Huh, I'm not so sure about that... what about the security aspect? All your eggs would be in the one basket! But I tell you what my friend, if that ever 'appens, I...' he took both hands off the wheel and pointed with both forefingers at his chest, '... I shall be Number One... and you? You can be Number Two!'

He gave me a roguish look and settled contentedly back into his seat. His answer delighted me; I'd expected a quick rejoinder and true to form he'd not only put his finger on the one weak spot, but also neatly bounced the ball back into my court. I could only think of one way to play it: 'Well Frenchman, if you are now Number One, and now that we're over your beloved France, what time have you arranged for the sun to come out?'

But the sun did not come out, and we remained under the grey overcast over the entire plain of northern France that stretches from the coast for 450 kilometres until it reaches the first high ground at the Plateau de Langres. Sixteen minutes later, and right on time, Dijon appeared under the nose.

IV

Some people believe that the ancient city of Dijon is only famous for its mustard; but ask any European pilot and they will tell you that first and foremost, Dijon – or more correctly Darois, the small satellite airfield some ten kilometres to the northwest of the city, is the home of Avion Robin, who manufacture a delightful range of light aircraft.

We touched down on the single runway at 12.30 and then unhindered by fences or other trivial restrictions, taxied off the field and onto the road that runs past the airfield, which we then followed for a short distance before swinging off to park on an apron directly outside the Avion Robin works.

'Eh-hue – we are just in time. Come follow me...'

I followed Bernard's stocky figure through a side door of the hangar, where he paused for a moment, twitching his nose like a bloodhound at first sign of the scent, before setting off on an unerring course towards the far corner, where a faint aroma of cooking was emitting from a door leading off.

Unlike its average English counterpart, the works canteen was a light and airy place with large windows that overlooked the field and altogether had the ambience of a well-run restaurant that had chanced upon aviation as its theme for decor. We made our way to a corner table, permanently reserved for the senior managers of the company, and where they gathered daily for an informal working lunch. Needless to say Bernard knew them all and made the introductions, before tucking a napkin under his chin and reaching for the menu. The talk carried on where they had left off, whilst they politely allowed Bernard time to consult the menu, after which he was drawn wholeheartedly into the discussion.

The talk flowed around me, and after a while I gave up trying to follow it and was content to sit back and watch the proceedings. From what I could gather the gist of the discussion was centred upon a proposal by Bernard, that he should become their recognised agent and distribute the full range of their aircraft throughout the UK; or more to the point whether their overall marketing strategy could or indeed, wished to encompass this development! They all had their own ideas on the subject, and at times the discussion became quite heated and with my handicap, I was only able to keep track of events by observing the body language of the participants together with their attitude and tone of voice.

Even so removed I found it interesting, especially as it was my first insight to a business discussion conducted by senior management of a company, and as such couldn't help comparing it to the more formal progression had it been held in a military environment, where rank and status is clearly visible. Not the fact that a visible rank structure dominates the proceedings by setting precedence or demanding automatic deference; for in practice the reverse is the case and indeed, actively encouraged. Junior members (who often have the brightest ideas) are invariably invited to speak first and at all times have an equal opportunity to expound or if necessary, argue their case. The difference is far subtler and designed to create an environment where any precedence will be for the subject in hand rather than deference to the rank of the individuals present. Moreover, the ambience created discourages any form of domination by individuals resorting to 'playground bullyboy tactics', which have no place whatsoever.

As an outsider, I was unaware of the position or any other acknowledged status of the people around the table, and whether – what in military circles could only be regarded as discourteous behaviour from one bullyboy in particular, would be tolerated by the others! Lunch stretched well into the afternoon, the discussion fuelled by numerous cups of coffee brought unbidden by the restaurant staff, then ended with an abruptness that was startling. One minute it was going full blast, each person vociferously talking over the rest, and the next they were all getting up with a scraping of chairs and shaking hands.

Whatever the outcome, Bernard was all smiles and seemingly unperturbed as he shook hands with everyone, before taking to one side a tall and lanky individual whom I'd noticed earlier from his habit of brushing aside his unruly mop of floppy hair that was forever falling over his heavily-framed spectacles, and had had the least to say than anyone else. I'd put him down as an engineer or designer, or in any event, someone not directly involved with the sales or marketing activities of the company.

'Mon ami, I am going to leave you with Julien 'ere... 'e is the chief engineer and speaks good English and has offered to show you round the factory – you would like to see how the aeroplanes are made? Ask 'im to explain about the wing design; that is the secret of the Robin's success! In the meantime, I – I 'ave, e-hue, *affaires* to attend to upstairs. After that, I will see to the refuelling of the aircraft – and I will also check the Rallye for you and make sure all is ready for the morning. So, I will catch up with you later and we'll go to the 'otel.'

I followed Julien into the main hangar where we climbed some metal steps to an upper level gantry that ran for the length of one wall, and from where we could view the whole of the main assembly line. It was an intriguing mixture of activities with both wooden and metal aircraft being assembled alongside each other. Carpenters were shaping and gluing wooden frames for fuselages and wings – the latter to be covered later by fabric in the traditional manner, whilst in

23

the next space sheet metal was being cut and riveted for the wholly different construction of metal aircraft. Leading off from the main body of the workshop were various rooms and annexes where ancillaries were stored and assembled and Julien told me that with the exception of engines and wheels, virtually every component was manufactured in-house. This even extended to the seats and upholstery, which were made up in an adjacent annexe by a group of ladies busily talking over the strains of music emitting from an old fashioned radio high up on a shelf, and periodically drowned by sudden bursts of whirring from their electric sewing machines.

The aircraft varied in size from two to six seaters, and whether metal or wood, all bore a strong family resemblance. They were all single-engine, low wing monoplanes with sleek rounded cockpits that faired aft into the fuselage, which was then set off by a distinctive swept tailfin – the common mark of their pedigree. Only the wings differed, the metal aircraft having straight conventional wings, whilst their wooden counterparts had wings that were straight for half their span and then bent up in a graceful sweep to the tip. This, Julien told me was the Jodel wing, originally designed in 1948 by Edouard Joly and his son in law Jean Delemontez for their Jodel (an amalgam of their surnames) D9 or Bébé. The Bébé was an extremely simple lightweight aircraft with a single seat open cockpit that had originally been designed for home construction. Simple to build and powered by a readily available 1600cc Volkswagen car engine, such was its popularity it became an instant success. So much that a two seat enclosed cockpit design – the D11 soon followed, again with the same distinctive cranked wing, for the secret of the wing lay in its unique shape: a clever combination of strength and aerodynamic efficiency, which gave the aircraft a weight carrying and performance advantage over similar types, as well as obviating the need for high lift devices such as flaps or leading edge slots, all of which are complicated and add weight.

This I could follow and certainly made sense for a simple lightweight machine. On a conventional wing, flaps have to have a precise linkage – normally concealed within the wing

24

structure, as well as strong fixing points; for they are positioned to let down from the trailing edge in order to increase the contour or aerofoil section of the wing.

When lowered, the increased contour creates more lift, which enables an aircraft to fly safely at slow speeds – especially useful when landing or taking off. But the penalty of a highly contoured wing is that it also creates an enormous amount of drag. Whatever size of engine used, the drag created by a wing of this shape will build up until it reaches a level whereby it will limit any further forward speed. Thus, on maximum or takeoff power an aircraft accelerates to its flying speed with ten or fifteen degrees of flap lowered. Once airborne and at a safe height, the flaps are gradually raised, flattening the contour of the wing, which then allows the aircraft to accelerate to its designed cruising speed. On attaining this, the power can then be reduced to a more economical setting, in which configuration the ratio of speed, drag, lift and weight are once again in equilibrium.

The Jodel wing I learned, managed to do all things: it was an intricate shape, the leading edge sweeping back for a couple of feet before straightening out to run parallel to the trailing edge for approximately half the span of the wing. There it swept up in an exaggerated dihedral, with the trailing edge tapering in to half its original chord length as well as having considerable 'washout' or twist built into that section.

Thus, slow speeds could be attained by reducing power and lifting the nose of the aircraft, which presented the whole of the wing area to the airstream as one continuous high lift, high drag ratio aerofoil – or the same as a conventional wing with flaps extended. To increase speed, instead of cleaning the wing up by retracting the flaps, one merely had to lower the nose and apply power: the resultant pitch down attitude negating the lift (and more importantly the drag) from the outer 'bent' sections of the wing as a result of their progressive washout. As the speed increased, so the point of centre of lift moved inboard, until the outer sections of wing became virtually redundant, there now being enough airflow over the inner stub sections to give the required lift.

'But what are these then?' I said, pointing to the underside of cranked wing on a nearby aircraft 'Surely those are flaps...?'

'Ah yes, that is progress... how best to explain?' Julien looked thoughtful for a moment and then shrugged. 'It is a long story... enough to fill a book, but I will try to give you an outline. From the little D9, Joly and Delemontez produced many different Jodel aircraft, all based on the bent-wing concept. They were all extremely pretty aeroplanes, streamlined and lightweight, which made them very fast. So fast and efficient, you could not land them – they just wanted to keep flying! So they added simple airbrakes – like a glider has, but under the wing, which killed the lift and allowed them land! Then in the late sixties Joly retired and Jean Delemontez teamed up with Pierre Robin and together they continued to develop these aircraft under a new company called Centre Est Aeronautique – which later was changed to the present name of Avions Robin.

'It was a successful partnership from the start, especially when they produced the DR 1050 – the D, by the way stands for Delemontez and the R for Robin – and this machine won many races, so they decided to develop it and produced the DR200 Series. They all had tail wheels, which made them very slippery, and a DR250 fitted with a 160hp engine could reach 160knots – not bad for a machine with a fixed-pitch propeller and a fixed undercarriage! Many different engines and sizes were used in the same airframe, the smallest being a 100hp Continental that was powerful enough to lift two adults and two children, and the largest a 180hp Lycoming – but that was a real handful and too difficult for the average private pilot, so only one was produced as an experimental machine; but it was a real racer! At the same time it was a logical development to replace the airbrakes fitted on the earlier models, with narrow chord flaps, which are as you see here. As you can imagine, the bent-wing concept together with flaps gives a hugely impressive envelope...'

He brushed the lock of hair away from his spectacles and tentatively led the way to the next machine in the line. At this stage it was just a framework and revealed the complexity of the internal structure.

'Each one is hand-built, piece-by-piece and as you see, it's very laborious! Anyway, by this time the Americans were fitting tricycle undercarriages to their light aircraft, which made them easier to land and overnight it became the fashion, so we decided to follow suite and developed the DR300 Series to take a nose wheel. Although they looked much the same as the DR200 on the outside, they were in fact very different – especially the wing design, which had a different aerofoil camber and improved the overall handling performance and stability – although that and together with the extra drag of the nose wheel made them marginally slower. And, like the 200 Series before them, they could be fitted with a wide choice of engine sizes...'

'So up to now all these aeroplanes had cranked wings and were made of wood – so what on earth made you start manufacturing metal aircraft with straight wings?'

He brushed his hair away from his spectacles again and looked at me bleakly for a moment. 'Ah, that is still another story. The metal ones are the HR Series – the H stands for Heintz, a Swiss engineer who joined us for a time. Although wood is still a practical material to make an aeroplane, in this day and age it is considered to be an outdated process – as well as having other drawbacks. For a start you need skilled labour, which is hard to find these days, as well as a good buyer who can select the right wood, for as you can imagine it's becoming increasingly difficult to obtain. Then, as I said just now, it's almost impossible to mass-produce anything in wood; every component has to be fashioned by hand, which is of course time consuming and expensive. So an obvious alternative was to consider a more conventional metal aircraft – and we managed to obtain a Government grant to fund the development... they liked the idea of a modern, all metal two-seat training aircraft. But it took a long time to get right; and in the meantime most of our customers were still attracted by the bent-wing concept as well as the proven and superior performance it offered – huh, and they did not care what the aeroplanes were made from!

We've got the metal HR's right now, and they are proving to be an excellent training aircraft, but we still sell more DR400's – that's our latest range of wooden aircraft...'

We moved on and looked at the engine-fitting bay, where one wall was lined with wooden crates containing engines of all makes and sizes. A DR400/160 Knight with its forward sliding canopy and slightly wider fuselage was next in line for an engine and a team of fitters were positioning a gantry with a newly unpacked Lycoming swinging underneath.

'Ah so there you are!' Bernard's voice came from the door. 'Eh-hue! Now *there* is a pretty little aeroplane...the 160 'orse-power Knight – to my mind the perfect marriage of engine and airframe. It is altogether a sweet thing to fly.' He made his way towards us and then paused in front of the machine. 'And look at the finish...now that's what I call a *proper* paint job! Oh yes, if only ...but then never mind: maybe 'e won't notice. Anyway, I 'ave seen to the Comanche and the Rallye – and I 'ave a car, and your valise is in it! You are ready now to go to the 'otel?' He turned and started to make his way to a black Citroen with red number plates that was parked outside.

I thanked Julien, who despite his business suit, was now heavily involved with the fitting of the engine, and followed Bernard out to the car, where he was impatiently revving the engine.

'So, what did you think of the factory?'

'Mmm, fascinating, especially the history behind the development! It makes me want to fly one – to see if this bent wing is all it's cracked up to be! But seriously, seeing that hive of industry makes me wonder what happened to our own aircraft industry? We've got nothing to compare... and there's obviously a market for light aircraft – especially on a worldwide basis; but the French and Americans seem to have virtually sewn it up between them!'

Bernard smiled and gave one of his Gallic shrugs whilst gesturing expansively with one hand as we drove at break-neck speed down the same road we had previously taxied the aircraft along. 'It is just the way things have gone... but if you think about it, even on a worldwide basis, the market for light aircraft is not very large. Not many people can afford a new one – besides, e-hue, the old ones never wear out! The Certificate of Airworthiness alone ensures that every three years they are torn apart and any worn or time-expired components replaced – so they go on forever!

'Anyway, now we go to the 'otel! It is only a small place, a family-run affair and not very far from 'ere. It is not expensive but very good and *très sain* – eh-hue, 'olesome! I 'ave stayed there many times before... then, after a short rest, we will go to a little restaurant I know nearby, where the food is very good. You will see...'

I have never been a great one for lunch, and given the choice will usually settle for a cup of coffee or at most a sandwich, else I find a compelling desire to sleep for the afternoon – especially after a glass or two of wine. And so it was now: for in spite of the mentally stimulating tour of the factory, my eyes were beginning to droop. The very thought of facing more food so soon made my eyes feel even heavier and I was thankful Bernard had included 'siesta' before the evening's activity. But then, this was France – where there was time for everything in its proper place.

V

'So my friend, we 'ave not had a proper chance to talk...'

We were settled in the corner table of a delightful country restaurant with a bottle of the local wine in front of us. It was obviously a popular place, for the dozen or so other tables were all occupied: mostly by large family groups with open, rosy faces and dressed in plain country clothes. Grandparents had pride of place, interspersed by children, kicking their legs under the table; all ages intent upon making the meal an occasion. Many of the families knew each other and talk flowed across from table to table, everyone craning to hear, with many interruptions and laughter.

I smiled at him and lifted my glass. 'Good place, this...'

'Why yes! I come 'ere many times. I often buy the aircraft that Avion Robin take in as part exchange when they sell a new one. That is 'ow the Rallye came to be left here. But now, I think maybe there is a market in England to sell their new ones – if, that is, I can negotiate a proper discount... but they are 'ard people to deal with.' He took a sip of wine. 'Now, my friend, what about you, what are you up to these days?'

'Mmm. I gathered that was what you were talking about over lunch. Me? Well, I've just finished my instructors course and I'm about to go back to Middle Wallop to teach soldiers to fly helicopters.'

'You – an instructor? Will you like that? I wouldn't 'ave thought it suited your temperament?'

A nearby table suddenly erupted into spontaneous laughter and then the joke or whatever it was, was passed on to all the other tables, which made it impossible to reply. As the laughter spread, with Bernard straining to hear, I thought about the observation he had made. Direct and to the point as usual, he'd hit the nail right on the head, for deep down, I knew I shouldn't have opted for the instructor's job and had only done so in order to keep flying, rather than being tied to a desk in a staff appointment – which at this stage of my career would have been the correct move to have made.

I'd transferred from my regiment into the Army Air Corps as a twenty-three year old subaltern in order to go flying, and although you'd expect the main role of the Army Air Corps to be just that, even if it meant teaching others to fly, this was not necessarily the case for a forty-two year old major at the critical stage of his career. For whatever regiment or branch of the army you belong to, and regardless of your experience to date – be it as a commander in the field, administrator, technician, regimental officer or whatever – if you wish to advance beyond the rank of major, or maybe half-colonel if you're lucky, your career plan should have included periodic postings to appropriate branches of the staff in order to gain practical experience and a working knowledge of the various systems and chains of command, which when put together make the army-machine function. Or in other words, know your way around the red tape.

Having 'been there and done it', then qualifies you to apply for Staff College, entry into which is not easy, for not only do you have to pass an entrance exam at an acceptable level and within a specified time-bracket, but also there are usually twice as many applicants as there are available places. This is the major stumbling block for the career soldier – and entirely necessary, for by now you are more than halfway up the rank pyramid, and if the pyramid is to keep its proper shape with a point at the apex, there has to be progressive fallout, else it becomes top-heavy. But not only is it necessary to gain entry to Staff College, the shape of your future career is then further determined on how well you pass out, for only the top echelon will be offered the worthwhile jobs. Then, having finally made it into the military fast lane, soldiering suddenly takes a different slant, for the human jungle being what it is, you unwittingly become a target to all those less successful, or who maybe see you as a threat to their own ambitions. Soldiering suddenly becomes political and you have to start watching your back – as doubtless happens in any other large organisation, the difference here being that hitherto the average soldier has been somewhat naïve about these matters!

Years ago I used to fly a major-general on a regular basis and once when sitting in his usual place beside me in the co-pilot's seat, he confided that the disparity between a major and a major-general was destined by a few bricks and the stroke of a few pens. Or to be precise, three bricks in the rank pyramid and the fairness of mind of your immediate superior when the time came to sign your annual confidential report! Many a good man has gone down simply by having more intelligence and ability than his boss, thereby becoming a potential threat... It was kindly advice and I daresay well meant to a young officer whom he saw doing a specialist job with the potential to use the advice to the best advantage; but at the time I had more pressing things on my mind and anyway, being practically at the bottom of the pyramid, it was hardly an immediate priority...

Until now!

In, of all the unlikely places, a provincial French restaurant and surrounded by noisy laughing people; which was hardly the time or occasion to focus ones mind on future career strategy – but then, was there ever a good time?

Thinking back, the only other time I had seriously questioned whether I should continue flying in the army as a career, had been nearing the end of my first flying tour in Aden: the subject of my reccurring nightmare, when I force-landed the Beaver into the dried-up wadi bed. But that hadn't been the end of it, for having survived the crash-landing we were then attacked by dissident tribesmen and the whole situation turned into what could have been a farcical clip from a wild-west film, with my passengers and I taking cover behind rocks and banging away at them with a motley collection of side-arms. Fortunately a Royal Marine fighting patrol came to our rescue just before we ran out of ammunition, but during the engagement two of the dissidents were killed – one of them, by me. You can tell yourself over and over again that in that sort of situation it's a case of either kill or be killed; but it made me realize it was a situation I never wanted to be in again: just because you wear a uniform, does it give you the right to kill? And as long as I continued to wear a uniform it would tempt providence; another situation would bound to happen at some time or place – for isn't that what soldiers are for? So perhaps now would be the time to chuck it all in, and if I wanted to continue flying, why not join a commercial airline?

Except, first I had to finish my tour – and bush flying Beaver's in that wild country was the ultimate elixir and one that any dedicated pilot would have given his back teeth for. Besides, there was still a war going on and there were never enough pilots, which left little time for meditation. And so time passed, and with it the incident faded, or rather was put away into that special box at the back of one's mind... and then, suddenly, my tour was up.

I needed a rest, they said. I'd been flying too much and a spell on the ground was now mandatory. The idea was not without its appeal, for I was beginning to recognise certain signs and mannerisms within myself that hitherto I had witnessed in others when nearing the end of their two-year period of daily combat flying. There's a name for it now: Post-traumatic Stress Disorder or Gulf War Syndrome; a result of chronic fatigue from living in a state of permanent stress; but the Gulf War was still to come and as such, PSD had yet to be diagnosed. Besides, I yearned for England, for green fields and fresh, clear, cold water.

Instead, I found myself down the road sitting behind a desk in the Joint Headquarters at Middle East Command, situated in the hottest, driest and dirtiest place imaginable – right in the centre of Aden.

'Ah good' the Brigadier said, 'at last, an officer with actual combat experience in this theatre, you'll be very useful and an invaluable member of the team...'

But I soon found that in any headquarters, a captain is the most junior rank – there just aren't any lieutenants listed on the establishment, so as junior, you rank as office boy.

I had a desk and an IN tray that the staff-sergeant clerk loaded every morning with an armful of files marked ACTION. The quicker you worked, the more files he brought in. And what was worst, you couldn't pass them on, for as the junior, I was the end of the line. Moreover, their content had no bearing whatsoever on the war we were engaged upon, and never even remotely called upon the 'useful combat experience' I had gained during the preceding two years. Instead I had to take ACTION on whether Mrs Corporal Wilkinson could bring her dog with her from Germany. And then ACTION on the behalf of Signalman Green – whom I had never met – in an on-going correspondence with our sister organisation in the Far East, arguing that he hadn't wilfully stolen his issue jungle green from that theatre, but had had nothing else to wear whilst in transit to the Middle East...

Six months went by and then I struck gold.

I don't know how it got into my tray, because it was actually addressed to the Royal Air Force, but in a joint headquarters, things have been known to go astray. Or maybe, since everyone wore the same desert khaki, the Chief Clerk thought I was in the RAF, on account of the wings pinned on my shirt.

The message was from HM Government to HQ Middle East Command asking whether a suitably qualified pilot could be spared for a six to twelve month secondment to fly their recently acquired twin-engine aircraft on Embassy liaison duties in South Africa?

This was too good to miss, especially when I learned that the aircraft was an old Series I, De Havilland Dove, recently retired from South African Airways and which, I reasoned, was well within my piloting capabilities. Indeed, although the request was obviously aimed at the RAF, no respecting Air Force pilot would want to be relegated to flying liaison duties in an insignificant and un-military aircraft such as a Dove... whilst I on the other hand, with an Instrument Rating and 2500 hours on Beavers, an aircraft only slightly smaller than a Dove, would make the ideal applicant... besides, how else could I escape from this dreary desk? So, tongue in cheek I applied for the job.

Three weeks later found me in Pretoria, walking round an ancient and somewhat battered Dove with a training captain from South African Airways. The Dove actually still belonged to them but was on some sort of government lease-loan arrangement, which meant they would still be responsible for maintaining it. It was still in their blue, white and silver livery, and you could still see where the crest on the nose and Suid Afrikaanse Lubbiens on the fuselage sides had been painted out. It...

'Eh-hue, they are a jolie crowd in 'ere this evening.' Bernard's voice brought me back with a start. 'Ah, *le garcon*! May I suggest we 'ave today's speciality of the 'ouse? It is always worth going for. Now, you were saying, you are to be an instructor on 'elicopters – what are they like to fly? Do you know, I have never even sat in one!'

I thought for a moment, wondering how best to reply and at the same time realising I would also be interested to hear my answer and whether it would help unravel some of the misgivings that were churning through my head.

'Um. Someone once defined a helicopter as being a complicated mixture of revolving parts that collectively defy gravity whilst trying to tear each other apart! Or at least, it was something like that... but seriously, it's difficult to explain – a helicopter is a machine and it flies, but it is not a *flying machine* in the same sense that a fixed wing aircraft is. They are at opposite ends of the flying spectrum, and neither can really do the other's job – at least not economically. Whereas a fixed wing aircraft has evolved into an express form of long-distance transport, a helicopter can best be described as a short-range flying platform. So instead of being an aerial bus-driver, I suppose a helicopter pilot is nearer to being a sort of crane-driver...'

I looked at him, but he merely returned my gaze, whilst his fingers were busy tearing lumps of bread, which he periodically dunked into his wine.

'Of course they're ideal for the army' I continued, 'they do everything – and a lot more besides, than the light aircraft they replaced. Where they win hands down is their ability to remain stationary in the hover and being able to ascend and descend vertically, which does away with landing strips and all the business of concealing them. Their other advantage is that they can fly in conditions that would normally ground a light aircraft. You can crawl along in limited visibility or fly in near gale-force winds... and this versatility makes them an ideal all-purpose tactical machine that can be based and operate in the frontline of any battle-field – so much that the new generation of helicopters armed with missiles are fast superseding the role of the tank.

'Then, there's the civilian market, where they are being put to more and more uses: fire-fighting, air ambulance, search and rescue, police surveillance, aerial crane, re-supply to oilrigs, executive air taxi...but then you know all this.

'Maybe, but I want to 'ear what you think. As I say, I 'ave never even sat in one, let alone operated one'

'Well, The down side is that helicopters are expensive.'

'So? What are you bothered about? You do not have to pay for the petrol!' He dunked some more bread, expertly popping it into his mouth with a sucking noise, just before it disintegrated. 'You talk to me as though I was one of your students, and that is the lecture they want to 'ear. To me, it sounds as though you have a very good job, so why do I detect something else?'

'I don't know, Bernard. I was just thinking about it earlier. I've been a major for four – no, nearly five years now, and going for an instructor's job at this stage of my career could be a bad move – or at best, a sideways one. Of course instructors are always needed, and it can be regarded as a feather in your cap – in that you have gained the top rung in your profession as a pilot. But, if I'm to progress in the army, I really should have gone for a staff appointment – it was my last chance to qualify for entry to Staff College. But... I don't know, I suppose deep down I couldn't stand the thought of it – or maybe I know I'm not cut out to be a general. The instructor's job was the only flying vacancy on offer at the time, and something made me go for it – I suppose a hunch that an instructor's rating could stand me in better stead for whatever lies in the future, rather than the approved career route to Staff College, with precious little flying afterwards...

'But now, having taken that step, I'm beginning to wonder whether I even want to continue flying military helicopters. Sure, they are getting bigger and better all the time and are challenging enough in their own fashion, but the new ones are fast becoming a weapons system rather than a flying machine, and... well, I'm now reaching the age when you start to slow down. You know, the old graph of experience versus reactions? Only youngsters have the reactions to fly the new generation helicopters and old lags like me will be relegated to training machines...'

'Huh, I can give you a few years, and I still fly as well as I always 'ave...'

'Not by military standards, I'm afraid – you're fine flying aeroplanes that you've always flown; you know everything

36

about them, they fit you like a glove and you can cope with any situation. But experienced flyer as you are, I doubt whether even you would find it easy to handle something like a jet fighter? Sure, given enough time you'd be able to get it up and down all right, but would you be able to fly it in combat? Have you seen how quick the kids are at playing computer games? Well, they're like that only a lot more difficult; then add in the physical G forces your body is subjected to – which a young man doesn't even notice; you'd be exhausted in a matter of minutes and the kids would fly rings round you ...' I took a sip of wine, whilst he looked thoughtful, swirling the wine round in his glass and which, I noticed, now had some grains of bread floating in it.

'E-hue, maybe... maybe.'

'You know, I really enjoyed our flight out in the little Twin Comanche this morning,' I continued. 'I really felt at home in it and it was nice to have a proper destination to go to. We normally fly our helicopters tactically – that means just a few feet off the ground, and when based in the field we rarely go further than a few miles. I suppose that's the aspect of flying that I miss. The distances and the *mathematics* of flight – when, say at fifteen thousand feet and a range of fifty miles, to set the aircraft up to descend down an imaginary line, hands-off and without touching power or trim, to hit circuit height of a thousand feet at a range of three miles... to me, that's what real flying is about, and there's not much call for that when flying a helicopter. They are predominantly unstable machines and need keeping in check at all times... although you can trim the later ones to a certain extent. But somehow it's not the same.'

'Don't the army still 'ave some fixed wing aircraft?'

'Yes, we still have a few Beavers left, but helicopters have taken over their tactical role and they've mostly been relegated to photographic work in Ireland now. There's talk of replacing them with a token number of twin-engine Islanders, purely for liaison work – there'll always be a requirement for that, but the mainstream of army aviation will be an all helicopter force from now on... they can do so much more.'

'Eh-hue. The Britten-Norman Islander – that would be a good aeroplane to fly. Do you 'ave a twin rating?'

'Yes I have – I was just thinking about it. After Aden, I flew a Dove in South Africa for the government for a while.'

'A Dove? I did not know that! What engines did it 'ave?'

'Oh, it was one of the early ones – with the original 330 horsepower Gipsy Queen's, which made it somewhat underpowered! They did several upgrades and I believe the later ones – the Dove 7's and 8's had 400hp engines, which would have made them much better. But in spite of that, it was an advanced aeroplane for its day – when you consider it was designed during the war and first flew, I think in 1945! And it was certainly a challenge for me at the time, having just come off Beavers. Although it actually wasn't that much larger than a Beaver, it was a totally different concept. The Beaver was designed as a bush aircraft whereas the Dove was more like a mini airliner, and if you think about it, not a lot different from the concept of today's business jets. But, like many other aircraft of that time, it was an advanced design using old technology; like being powered by those Gipsy Queen engines, which were basically the same engines used in the old Rapide, which the Dove was meant to replace! I suppose there just weren't any suitable engines of that size around at the time. Still, it was a good aeroplane in its day...

'Oh yes, I believe it was in production in one form or another for over twenty years... It was another of De Havilland's masterstrokes and arrived just at the right time! I 'ave never flown one myself, but I believe the later ones were very good aircraft... the Queen's Flight 'ad them for many years – and altogether they must have produced what, five – maybe nearly six 'undred in all? But, I'm not sure I altogether agree with you about being the same as a modern business jet! If you saw one today parked next to a Lear jet, I think you would find it looked very old-fashioned. It's like an old car... Huh, I remember years ago, when they brought out the Jaguar XK150 – you remember it, the model before the E-Type? Well, I thought that was the most beautiful car ever made. I coveted it and 'ow could anyone improve such a pretty car as that? Then, years later I had a chance to buy one – and do you know, the wheels were too thin! Compared with modern cars it looked ridiculous on those thin tyres! So what I am saying, things change all the time without you being aware of it, and I tell you, it certainly shattered that illusion for me! I would not want an old thing like that now. Anyway, your Dove, 'ow come you flew one in South Africa?'

'Oh, it's a long story...'

But in truth, it was a period that even now I had difficulty in recalling. I must have been very tired at the time and just glad of the respite from the heat, the dust and life-sapping humidity of Aden. And away from the war, which no one in Pretoria had even heard about! I remember the weather was glorious and I seemed to spend most of my time sitting by the pool, one lazy day running into another. The aircraft I was meant to be flying was long past its prime and forever going u/s, and understandably not the first priority for the hard-pressed maintenance crew. Each time it was snagged, back it went to the end of their queue whilst they waited for parts and left me once again kicking my heels.

Of course there were certain instances I do remember, most notable being the occasion of one of my first flights with the training captain. We had just lifted off, the engines flat out at takeoff power when there was a loud bang and the starboard engine started to shake itself to bits. (We later learnt that a spark plug had stripped its threads and blown out like a bullet from a rifle.) From years of flying single-engine aircraft my reaction was pure reflex: immediately cut the power, and hope to hell there'll still be enough runway ahead to put it down again. This I did, but compared to what I was used to, the Dove was heavy and fast and as the fence rushed to meet us, I realized it was going to be a close thing. We eventually stopped in a cloud of burning rubber with our nose almost touching the perimeter fence, whilst my instructor calmly informed the tower that we had aborted the take off and would be returning to dispersal. Then he turned to me. Had I considered, he enquired in a mild tone, that one of the main reasons for having two engines on an aeroplane was for safety? Should one engine fail, the aeroplane is designed, and indeed perfectly capable of continuing its flight on the remaining one? So what was that stunt all about? There was no way he could fault my reactions, for I'd been way-ahead of him – and by then it had been too late to take over, especially as it hadn't even entered his head that I might abort the take off! So, wasn't it time I started to *think* and to graduate to the aircraft we were flying? As it was, had we been carrying extra weight by way of passengers or freight, we undoubtedly wouldn't have been able to stop and most likely would have written the aircraft off?

It was another lesson learnt; and one that Mr. Summers had tried to teach me all those years before. 'Think like a bird; become an *aviator*, rather than merely an aeroplane driver...' And thinking about it now, also made me realize the quality of the man who had sat beside me. His calmness and attitude of mind throughout had been admirable, especially as the situation had not been of his making. As training captain he had reached the top of his profession, but would I, as a potential instructor, be able to behave in the same way?

Bernard was still looking at me, a puzzled expression on his face, but then his eyes flicked up and looked beyond me and lit up. 'Eh-hue, I think this is our food arriving.' Whereupon he tucked his napkin under his chin in a manner that discouraged further discussion, and set to.

'So, what 'appened after that?' he said finally, chewing his last mouthful of cheese.

I was about to answer, when a feminine clear-cut English accent cut across the restaurant like a whiplash. 'You are an unspeakable bastard,' the voice drawled, 'and the worst specimen of mankind I have ever had the misfortune to meet...'

No one else noticed, for the French hubbub of voices continued as before; but I did and it stopped me in my tracks, as it did Bernard, who with open mouth swivelled round in his chair to see who the talker was.

It could only come from the couple who were sitting in the opposite corner table near the door. The man had his back to us, but the woman, a well dressed attractive lady in her forties then continued, looking around all the while with an open smile on her face, obviously intended to throw off any suspicion.

'Just look at you, you insignificant little worm! Call yourself a man? My dog has a larger penis than that apology of a thing you support. I *despise* you and everything about you, and I shall make you pay ...' The man mumbled something in reply. 'Do you realize, if you died tonight...' she continued still smiling and glancing around, '...no one would care, nobody even *knows* you are here. Your children have disowned you; not one person would mourn for you and you would not even be missed. You have *nobody* but me. When we get back to our room, I'm going to...'

But what she was going to do, we never did find out. The man mumbled something back to her in an undertone, whilst Bernard hurriedly finalised the bill. 'Come, I think we 'ave 'eard enough about their sexual fantasies – if that is what they are playing at...' he muttered, as we threaded our way towards the door.

We had to pass right by their table. Bernard stopped and then clapped the man on his shoulder.

'Good night, old chap...' he said in his best English accent.

The woman's smile froze on her face and her eyes followed us out.

VI

Something woke me.

It was raining outside, a steady downpour driven by a vicious wind and a window was banging somewhere in the building. I turned and studied the luminous dial of my watch on the bedside table. It was either three o'clock or quarter to six, and I had to feel for the winder on the side of the dial to ascertain which way up it was. That made it three. But my movement made me aware of something else in the room.

I froze, the hairs on the back of my neck standing out and my heart hammering.

Nothing moved, but I could sense an atmosphere all about me. Not the coldness associated with fear, but nevertheless an atmosphere, somehow mingled with a faint aroma: musky, spicy – I couldn't quite place it. Gradually I relaxed, whilst remaining absolutely still. Something was there, but what? It was as before; only this time stronger and somehow more defined. And as before, it was not threatening but almost as if I knew this person or presence – or whatever it was. One thing I was certain about: I was way out of my depth, and this was totally beyond my understanding. Are there such things as ghosts? I don't know; I've never seen one – but I was prepared to concede that other people had; especially if they were in a state of shock, or otherwise psyched up enough to make the subconscious susceptible to psychological projection.

Should I try speaking to it?

No, better not... for last time my voice had shattered the illusion; better to wait and see... I relaxed and quietly lay back on the pillow. If it was a supernatural being, who and why was it here? The first time, one could pass off as a dream or maybe something conjured by a disturbed frame of mind; but to experience it a second time? This not only made it plausible and beyond coincidence, but also the thought that perhaps it was deliberately trying to contact me. But why?

I racked my brain. The only similarity I could think of that came near to my acceptance of a supernatural presence had been the link I had maintained with Mr. Summers after he had died. Mr. Summers had been my mentor in my early flying days: the best instructor a student pilot could have wished for, for he had not only taught me to fly, but also to think about flying, thereby always being ahead of the game. Then, soon after I qualified and left Wallop, he had been killed when one of his pupils had flown into some wires. Yet still he sometimes materialised in moments of stress or when I needed help or encouragement. But that had only happened when I was flying – and besides, subconsciously I'd always triggered it... and it certainly wasn't anything like this. But then, I suppose it *could* be Mr. Summers – although I hadn't called for his help for many years now, and surely he must have long passed on?

'Mr. Summers?' I asked doubtfully, in my mind.

The atmosphere lightened, just as a smile lights the face. Furthermore, I realized my speaking – or concentration of thought hadn't shattered the illusion, and if anything it was more defined and somehow closer.

'I'm in France.' I said quietly to the wall.

'Are you? When I travel, it is to the soul, not to a place...' I sensed the voice, although unspoken, was female and one I knew from some other time in space.

'Are you dead?'

'Good Heavens no! I just like to travel... I'm glad I've found you, even if you are in France. We'll know when we meet...'

I could feel the atmosphere begin to pulse, as though an engine running a dynamo was about to run out of fuel – or in this case, the source of power could no longer sustain the level of concentration; for the presence began to fade.

'Will you come again?' I blurted to the space. The image smiled, I could almost see her face, but I felt the smile and she was gone.

VII

Sleep was now out of the question and listening to the rain outside, I started to think about the flight back to England. Three o'clock in the morning is never a good time to appraise a situation, for this is the time your inner doubts most readily surface, and details that in the light of day you'd consider to be insignificant or merely routine, have a habit of blowing up out of all proportion. Okay, let's look at it logically and take it step by step:

It is an unknown type of aircraft that I haven't flown before...

Fine, you can cope with that: it's a simple machine and all light aircraft behave and perform in much the same way.

Well, it has a low-geared prop, so I don't know what speed it will cruise at, which doesn't help for in-flight planning, especially estimating time and distance...

Come on, you're not a novice! You can map read and you have a watch, so plot your actuals as you go along.

But I don't know anything about this aeroplane. I'm used to flying Service aircraft, with a full service and maintenance record you can trust. The last owner was a farmer, for God's sake?

Bernard has been around aeroplanes all his life; you'll just have to trust him...

Well, even Bernard admitted that it only has basic instrumentation; therefore it's not really equipped for long distance...

Long distance? To a man who has dead-reckoned for hours over the Arabian Empty Quarter with nothing but a watch and a compass? This is a short trip form France, for Heavens sake; Europe, where with a decent radio you can obtain radar coverage all the way. Okay, you'll be restricted to flying visually, so don't even think about climbing above the weather. But Bernard was right when he said this is your sort of flying – you were actually trained to fly like this in the AOP 9! Go on, go and get a map and plan the route...

I went to my flight bag and dug out the 1:500 000 Aéronautique: France Nord-Est chart that Bernard had lent me, together with my kneepad containing blank Flight Plans and my old and trusty Swissair circular computer – that wonderful piece of precision engineering that does everything and I'd first acquired for flying Beavers on airways and now would never be without. It's small enough to fit into the top pocket of your shirt, yet opens up like a book with leaves containing two circular slide-rules set back-to-back, a compass rose, a graduated ruler, every imaginable conversion table and two further half-leaves of instructions and examples to remind you how to find your way about! Whilst flying you can calculate wind angle, drift angle, ground speed, flying time, fuel consumption and all the other things you need to know from the circular slide rules, whilst for planning a route, the nifty little compass rose with its glass centre and piece of string that unwinds, can readily be laid on any map or chart, and is all you'll ever need.

With these basic tools of my trade about me, I set to work.

An hour later I had it buttoned up. A thick line on the chart, following much the same route we had flown down, but more importantly a close study of the map every inch of the way, marking all the topographical features and potential hazards, together with any useful pointers or guides such as line features, on the assumption that if the weather continued as it was now, we'd be low level with restricted visibility. It was like old times, for this is what we used to do before every tactical low-level flight in the old AOP 9 and time spent in preparation and map-work was essential if the sortie was to be a success. Only then we used 1:50 000 Ordnance Survey maps, which show far more detail – so much that the shape of every wood and coppice is clearly outlined, together with buildings, footpaths, power cables et al – the only drawback being, you needed an awful lot of interlinking maps if you wished to travel any distance! At least Bernard's half-million aeronautical chart covered the whole of northern France, including across the Channel to Lydd – and with careful study revealed substantially more detail than was at first apparent. Map reading is easy when you have height and you can see the surrounding terrain, but becomes progressively more demanding the closer you are to the ground, regardless of what else the elements may also have in store for you. Much like driving a car in a fog; but at least in a car – or for that matter a helicopter, you can always slow down or even stop; unlike an aeroplane that needs forward airspeed to fly, and under no circumstance can ever wait.

This done, I then prepared a Flight Plan for submission to the Tower, who would forward it down the appropriate chain, together with a route plan for my knee pad, on which I also listed all the radio frequencies that could be useful during the flight.

Then, in a much happier frame of mind, retired once more to bed.

Chapter 3

I

I stood by the window, nursing a coffee in the small annex they used for a breakfast room and looked out at the rain. Last night's wind had blown itself out and the rain was now a continuous vertical downpour.

'According to the weather map in this paper, the front should pass through later in the day, but eh-hue, with no wind behind it, it could 'ang around...' Bernard said from the table, where, with glasses perched on the end of his nose he was reading *Le Monde*, whilst chomping his way through the last of the croissants.

'Mmm. They'll probably have a better forecast at the field... anyway, it won't keep on like this; it's bound to ease off a bit. What time does it get dark, about eight – or nearer seven-thirty if it's overcast? I prepared a flight plan last night – and assuming the Rallye with its fine prop cruises at what, about ninety knots? So, I reckon about three hours to Le Touquet, then allow an hour on the ground – that's four hours; Le Touquet to Lydd, say twenty minutes, and then allow another hour on the ground to clear Customs and get your paperwork stamped. That's five hours twenty, then about another hour and a quarter home – that makes a total time of six hours, thirty-five minutes. Call it seven, to be on the safe side. So, working back, the latest I can set off is just after twelve noon, that is if the aircraft really has to be back today?'

'Today is the last day, but I hate to ask you – are you still considering to go in weather like this? It's well below the minimum...?

'I've flown in worse – what about fuel?'

'I topped it right up yesterday afternoon and the Rallye has a range of over 600 miles, so you should be okay... and even with the fine prop it will go faster than ninety knots – nearer 'undred and five; but eh-hue, you are right about the time it takes on the ground; maybe even a bit optimistic – you know 'ow long these things take! I'd allow a bit more – say get airborne just after eleven?' He looked at his watch 'I'd better settle up and get my bag... '

'What about your trip to St.Tropez?' I said in the car, as the wipers tried to cope with the downpour.

'I think I'll wait and see what the weather does... I can always stay 'ere another night and go tomorrow.'

We parked outside the Tower and made a run for the door. The Air Traffic Control Centre was essentially a one-man operation, and with nothing flying the controller was pleased to devote all his time to us. He produced the latest weather fax and after a careful study, finally declared much the same as the forecast in *Le Monde:* the front would pass through later in the day to be followed by a strong northerly unstable airstream.

There was nothing for it but to wait, so we made the best of it by settling into two armchairs by a table overflowing with flying magazines in the small restroom at the base of the tower.

'You were going to tell me what 'appened – before that sex-starved woman interrupted our dinner last night?' He suddenly enquired.

'What after South Africa?' I lowered my magazine and looked out at the driving rain. It all seemed a long time ago. 'Well, after that I got roped back into the system again and paid the penance by way of a Staff posting to Verden, in Germany. That was when I married Annie and we set up our first house in a married quarter there. It was all very new for her, and being married put army life in a whole new perspective to for me. It certainly took the sting out of the job, which otherwise would have been deadly boring...'

'Ah yes, I remember Annie. A pity your marriage did not last...'

'Mmm. Well, all that came later and I'd rather not go into it now – but at least we had some very good years. We're still good friends and I'm glad for her sake that she married again...'

'And you never thought of marrying again?'

'Oh I've thought about it, but the right person just hasn't come my way. Once bitten, you know... and anyway, I know enough about life now to realize I'd sooner be on my own than with the wrong person!'

'Ah yes-s...' He drew the word out with a sigh, as though he too had had his share of ups and downs with the fair sex. I lifted an eyebrow, but he didn't respond and instead said: 'So, after your staff job, how old would you have been then?'

'By then I must have been thirty – no, thirty-one, for it was the year the Carabiniers amalgamated with the Greys and sent a shockwave through the whole of the army. All my old cavalry chums began to wonder how severe the cuts would be, and whether their own regiments would survive. By then I'd transferred to the Army Air Corps and was safe from all that; for far from being cut like the rest of the army, army aviation was all set to expand and the future looked pretty bright. But what was also becoming obvious was that a future in army aviation would only be bright if you could fly a helicopter – and it brought home the fact that I was long overdue for a conversion course. So I went back to Wallop as a student and did the helicopter course and after that got posted to Detmold – in Germany again, as a squadron pilot flying Westland Scouts. I had a lot to catch up, especially on the tactical side, for most of my contemporaries had been flying helicopters from the start and had no fixed wing time at all. But Detmold was a good posting: Annie enjoyed the social life and I enjoyed flying the Scout – it was ideal for the European theatre and helicopters totally re-wrote the tactics for the good old BAOR scenario. Then, just before the end of my tour, my promotion to major came through, after which I was considered too imposing a figure to be employed as a mere squadron hack, and the best thing would be to return to Wallop, where they would find me a job.

'Ideally, that would have been the time to have gone to Central Flying School for an instructor's ticket, but unfortunately at the time I hadn't accumulated enough hours on helicopters, so they found an admin job for me instead.

'But at least being at Wallop meant that I was at the centre of things, and eventually I managed to wangle myself onto a Gazelle conversion course – the Gazelle was our latest helicopter and ultimately replaced the Scout. At the time, the Gazelles were cutting their teeth in Northern Ireland, mostly flying close-support to the army on Internal Security duties, so after the course I went to Belfast and joined the flight as second in command and then after I'd learned the ropes, found myself in the hot seat and ran it until April of last year. Annie didn't come to Ireland, for by then things had already started to go wrong between us, and frankly the environment wasn't exactly conducive to mending a shaky marriage...'

He smiled and nodded his head knowingly 'Ah yes-s' he said again. 'You don't 'ave to tell me, my friend.'

By eleven the torrential downpour began to ease, and by eleven-thirty had turned to drizzle and mist. We went upstairs again where I submitted my flight plan to the controller, and then we left him and squelched our way out to the aircraft.

I recognised the Rallye at once, and it was as I'd remembered – as well as being the only other aircraft parked next to the Twin Comanche. It was a chunky all metal four-seater with a low wing, set on a tricycle undercarriage that had heavily faired legs but leaving the wheels free of spats. Access to both front and rear seats was gained by sliding back a large unframed cockpit canopy situated directly over the wing and the whole aircraft was set-off by what at first sight appeared to be an oversize and rather angular tailfin. I stood for a moment gauging its looks and decided I rather liked it: it looked robust and purposeful, a good working aeroplane that didn't pretend to be anything else.

'I told you it was a farmer's machine, not nearly so pretty and sleek as the Robins, eh?'

'Mmm, I can see she wasn't built for speed, but she looks sturdy enough for all that...'

'Huh, if you like an aeroplane that is 'eavy and slow – it is totally the opposite of a Robin! See, the wing is just a *plank*, and then they've added every high-lift device imaginable. As well as flaps, it has leading-edge slots that come out 'ere, like this...' He grasped the front of the wing and pulled, whereby the leading edge, or rather a separate thin-chord aerofoil section, slid up and out some three inches, supported on curved arms that extended to a final position slightly forward and above the main body of the wing. 'When you're flying they're activated by the angle of attack of the airflow and come out automatically, so you do not have to do anything from the cockpit...'

I'd never flown an aircraft with leading-edge slots before and took particular interest. The principle was not only to offer an additional aerofoil for lift – as in the upper wing of a bi-plane, but also to force air through the slot it created, thereby giving additional "forced lift" over the main camber of the wing. It is by no means a new idea, and the same function is achieved by the jib-sail on a sailing boat.

We finished the external pre-flight and then climbed onto the wing and slid back the huge canopy. I settled into the left hand seat and Bernard joined me in the right and then closed the canopy to keep out the drizzle.

The cockpit was large and spacious, offering exceptional all-round visibility and the first thing I noticed was that it had a good old-fashioned joystick, rather than the push-pull wheel normally found in the average American counterpart. But there it ended, for the panel itself consisted mostly of blanked-off holes! I'd never sat in an aeroplane with so few dials, for far from complicating the issue, instruments are there to relay information, be it the in-flight conditions, the health of the engines, aids for navigation etcetera; the more information a pilot has, the better he is able to apply his craft.

'Yes...' was all I could think of saying.

'Master-switch is 'ere, this is the flap lever – you can do a jump takeoff: start your run clean, then yank it up at about forty-five knots and pull the nose up. The slots will bang out of the wing and you go up like a lift! Ignition; Carb 'eat next to the fuel cut-off, this is the new radio I 'ave put in – the headset plugs into the socket there, next to the old one and, and ...' His voice trailed off.

'Well, the less there is, the less there is to worry about, I suppose.'

'I tell you, it is a good aeroplane – very stable and the engine is most reliable – there will be nothing to worry about...'

'Right, well, it's nearly midday... I'd better be off.'

'Are you sure about the weather...?'

'If this aeroplane can fly slowly, I'll be all right. It'll clear once I've passed through the front – which can't be that far off, so don't make me change my mind now! Go on, out you get – I'll see if I can make it go!'

He slid the canopy back. 'I'll telephone you this evening – where will you be, your father's 'ouse?'

'Okay, have a good trip to St.Tropez, and I hope you sell the Comanche!'

He shut the canopy and I sat for a moment collecting my thoughts, then turned the Master-switch on and the aeroplane came to life.

Now, how to start this animal? With no pilot's notes or even a flip card with checklists, I'll have to resort to good old mnemonics – if I can remember them! Flying is full of mnemonics, which are drummed into you parrot-fashion at student level, when you are first confronted with the whole new language of aeronautical terminology and you don't know one end of an aeroplane from another. Or at least that's how they do it in the Service, until such time you graduate to more complicated machines, when it's best to have a flip card at hand. But once you learn the terminology and become familiar with the aeroplane, you find your fingers start to flow through a set pattern round the cockpit on their own – rather like a conductor's baton that becomes an extension of his brain.

So, try shutting your eyes and pretend you're sitting in a Beaver and see if my fingers remember their way round. We used to start at the bottom right, and work right round until you ended with the radios in the roof...

Master switch – done that; Circuit breakers – don't have any of those; Electrics – that was to do with hand-starting and again doesn't apply; Now, up to the three levers that were on the top of the Beaver's facia, M – Mixture rich – where's the mixture? Ah, this knob here, good; P – Propeller, no variable pitch on this aeroplane; T – Throttle, open a crack; F – Friction nuts, only one of those; C – Carb-air, must be that knob there, next to the throttle; I – Instruments, that's a joke! B – Brakes are on and locked; F – Fuel tank selection, there's only one tank, therefore no selection, and F again for Fuel pump. Fuel pump? Where's the... can't find it! Apparently there's no supplementary fuel pump! W – Warning lights, none of those; R – Radios, Aha! Two of those, one old and one new, so turn both on and check the tower frequency from my kneepad. One two-two decimal six, good, the digits on the new radio are already set, so headset on, and plug in the jack. Finally, M is for Magnetos, turn both switches on.

What now? No primer; no inertia reel to wind up; no wobble pump to keep the pressure up – just turn the key, I suppose...

'Clear prop!' The propeller jerked through two revolutions and the engine burst into life.

I let it warm, the propeller-wash blowing the raindrops up

and over the top of the canopy. I used the time to familiarise myself with the cockpit. It was really very simple and perhaps I had over-complicated the start up procedure, especially as it was just a matter of turning the key!

I gave Bernard a final wave, released the brakes and gunned the engine.

'Ah, Darois Tower, Fox Alpha Kilo – taxi instructions?'

The radio sounded strangely dead in my ears. But then, he was manning the tower on his own, so maybe he'd been called away...? No matter, I know the wind direction and where the runway is and there's not likely to be any other traffic. All I need is the barometric pressure to set the altimeter. When operating in the field, we never had the luxury of a control tower and the way we did it was to set the altimeter to the nearest contour from your map, whilst still on the ground. So, Bernard's chart... that shows Darois to be... 1585 feet above sea level. Twiddle the knob to set 1585 feet on the altimeter and in the window below, the corresponding pressure reads 986 millibars. I scribble it onto my pad so I can use it later – or at least until such time I can obtain a more accurate QNH on the radio from Flight Information. But, as I'll be low-level for the next twenty minutes or so, best to reset the altimeter to zero... at least that will give an actual height over the immediate terrain, and I'll re-set 986 when the ground falls away when we reach the plain.

I taxied over the wet grass to the end of the runway, then parked at ninety degrees and increased power to 1750 RPM to check the magnetos. I flipped the left switch off and the RPM dropped 350 and then tried the right and it dropped 400; both within limits with no untoward stuttering or unevenness; then with both magnetos on and the RPM back at 1750, I pulled the carb-air heat knob out and watched the revs drop back to 1650, which showed heat was getting through. Finally, I brought the power right back and checked the RPM at tick-over. Bernard was right; this was a sweet-running engine.

Vital actions for takeoff – try to keep it simple this time for this aeroplane is more akin to a Chipmunk than a Beaver, so think back to then. Christ! It's over twenty years since I sat as a sweating student in the cockpit of a Chipmunk, expecting a bang on my helmet at any time from Mr Avery who sat behind. Mr Avery was a great believer in mnemonics; he had one for every possible aspect of flying – which was as good a way as any for student pilots to familiarise themselves with their new environment, but unless used on a daily basis could also be dangerous, for there were so many of them. He had mnemonics for start-up, taxiing, power-check, takeoff, climbing, levelling off, downwind, aerobatics – that was my favourite, for that was Hazell, whom I fondly imagined as an air-nymph; bare-footed Hazell, with her clear blue eyes and long blond hair blowing in the wind. When called, she would skip out from behind the clouds in her blue summer dress; my fantasy goddess, there to oversee and protect me whilst I nerved myself to start a sequence of solo aerobatics. Her name stood for: Height, Airframe, Zecurity (she came from Devonshire), Lookout and Location. Then there was sourfaced Bill. Bill was an American in a leather jacket and his rhyme went: Bill May Consider Flying Fortresses – Brakes, Mixture, Carb-air, Fuel and Flaps – which were the downwind checks for landing, until that awful day when my brain went dead and I thought it was Harry instead of Bill, and the only 'H' I could think of was Hot-air, which got the whole thing out of sequence and another bonk on the head from Mr. Avery...

Better stay with the fingers around the Beaver routine, until I know my way around...

T – Trims, there's no rudder-trim, so elevator-trim slightly forward; F – Friction nuts, only one of those for the throttle, so set to finger-tight; P – Propeller pitch, okay, strike that off for next time; M- Mixture, that knob – to fully rich; C – Carb-air, cold; Two F's – Fuel, Contents, okay; and Fuel pump, surely there must be a supplementary fuel pump somewhere? Can't see anything labelled, unless it's this switch here! It's the only one left, so it's better on than off... F – is also for Flaps, I won't mess about with Bernard's fancy jump takeoff technique and the standard takeoff setting will do fine; Instruments – engine temperature and pressure both in the green, and set the Direction Indicator... Good God, what's this! It looks as though it was salvaged from a farm sale! Anyway, set this somewhat antiquated gyro-driven instrument to the compass, and keep a wary eye on it to see if it wanders; P – Pitôt heat, ah, got a switch for that, and with this moist air, better have it on. H – Hatches are shut – just double-check the handle on the sliding canopy... and the final H for Harness, which is on and tight.

Time to think like a bird. Mr. Summers first taught me this technique and I have used it ever since without fail before every takeoff. It's all to do with a state of mind – and easy, once you know how. Imagine, he used to tell me, you are standing by the rail of a ship and somehow you slip and fall into the water. What happens? Even if you are a strong swimmer, the odds are that the sudden transition will make you, a land animal, fight for air! Frantically you'll tread water and flail your arms as you try to keep your head above water. Panic will make it worse, for there's no rescue in sight and all too soon you will begin to tire until finally your energy is spent, and you will drown!

Now, take that same land animal and equip him with flippers, a snorkel and a face mask and let him enter the sea. He becomes as a fish; immediately at one with the elements. We used to do it in Aden: hours on end in the Red Sea chasing fish with a spear gun. We did not tire; even in rough conditions when swimming close inshore amongst the rocks, for we were fish, and had no need to fight the waves as they sucked us in and out...

Yet even thinking and behaving as fish, we were ever conscious that we were in an alien element as well as severely handicapped. Our flippers propelled us at a speed relative to that of crawling over the ground, and wearing goggles, our eyes were severely blinkered as well as only being able to see a limited distance ahead. Sometimes you'd catch the blur of a fast moving object out of the corner of your eye – most likely a fish of similar size to yourself; and when you consider a barracuda attacks at a speed of seventy miles per hour...! Once, when snorkelling in the shallow water just off a beach, I came across a discarded beer-can lying on the sand under the waves. It looked huge! To a brain not adjusted to the density of water, the eight-inch beer-can was magnified to the proportions of a three-foot gas cylinder! And as for a lobster, with just its eyes and tentacles showing from the crevice of a rock, it becomes a sea-monster, and it takes a brave snorkeller to winkle one out.

Until you are shown how.

And so it is with flying. If you are forced down by lowering weather to the extent that you finally end up just above the trees, a pilot has every right to begin to fear; and that is only a step away from panic. And once panic sets in, all reason goes and like the flailing swimmer, you will probably crash. Aeroplanes belong in the sky and the more height you have, the safer you are. Lower the ceiling or severely restrict visibility and the sky immediately becomes a different place, and as in the shallow water off the beach, objects become distorted and out of all proportion – and things can happen very fast.

In my early training Mr. Summers attempted to teach me to fly in these conditions, for one day it would become part of my job. The dangers are just as real and are as ever prevalent, but with proper tuition and hours of practice, you can master it. And once mastered, it becomes an invaluable additional flying skill. Always you have to be aware of the dangers, as well as your own handicap; but the most important aspect is the attitude of mind, and this you can only learn from an instructor sitting beside you. 'Birds fly in this weather – that is, if they *have* to, and so can you...' Mr. Summers would say in his quiet voice, showing not the slightest concern for the appalling conditions outside, '...but there are a few – ah, *tricks of the trade* I can show you, that maybe will come in useful someday – or at least, help enhance the odds...'

I looked out to the end of the field and smiled. Could I actually be looking forward to this? The drizzle had stopped and I could just see the trees at the end of the field. And now, suitably psyched-up, it was time to don flippers, face-mask and snorkel and enter the water.

'Darois Tower, Fox Alpha Kilo is ready for takeoff...'

Nothing.

'Darois Tower, Alpha Kilo, do you read?'

Still nothing. Where was the man? Trust him to be away now... still, not to worry, Bernard will catch him and give him my takeoff time. After all, aeroplanes were flying long before radios were ever invented, and many light aircraft still manage without them now... Odd that he's not back though, you'd have thought the noise of my engine would have rallied him to his post. Still, can't hang around here all day, let's see how thick this murk really is...

II

At forty-five knots I eased the nose-wheel up and held the attitude until the aircraft flew itself off the ground. The slots clicked out of the wing, immediately increasing the rate of ascent until I lowered the nose a fraction and with the change of airflow they feathered back into place. They really do work! Now, reduce power early, as we used to do in the AOP 9, and trim for, say, sixty-five with the flaps still lowered at their takeoff setting. We flick over the trees with room to spare, with the aircraft nicely balanced. For this sort of flying, give me a stable farmer's aeroplane any day, rather than a sleek and sensitive high-performance racer!

Next, swing left onto 320 for the first leg to Troyes and how much airspace have we to fly in? The ceiling I guess to be about 250 feet above the trees – but the forward visibility... I peer ahead into the mist... could be anybody's guess. The mist just merges into the canopy of trees, and with no other reference points for perspective, makes it difficult to judge. One thing is certain: we're still travelling too fast for these conditions.

This is not the time nor place to start experimenting with the slow-flying capabilities of an unknown aircraft... but flying is all to do with feel, and although we have only been airborne for a few minutes, already I like the feel of this aeroplane. I inch the power back to 1600 RPM, and as the speed falls off, gradually lift the nose to maintain our present height. The slots emerge hesitantly from the leading edge of the wing and then become fully extended. I hold the attitude and minutely adjust the power until she balances; nose high on the back edge of the power-to-lift curve at 50 knots. Then I trim and take my hand off the stick and wait.

She flies... as she had told me all along that she would.

With hands off, I unfold the chart. My line shows we have thirty-five miles of high ground to cover before it starts to fall away to the plain... at about abeam Chatillon. Chatillon? Wasn't there a Chatillon VOR beacon we used on the way down? I check the chart and sure enough there is, but it's some ninety-five miles further on, near Reims; to avoid confusion you'd have thought they'd have called it Reims, but still... I take a quick look outside. Even at fifty knots the trees are zipping past at an alarming rate. We're just brushing under the base of the overcast and I reckon we have about eighty or maybe a hundred feet clearance over the tallest of the trees. At fifty knots it's going to take an age... I flick open the Swissair navigator and set fifty knots to the One-Hour arrow on the time ring and then read the corresponding time against thirty-five miles. Forty-two minutes! The same distance had only taken us sixteen on the way out... but never mind; fifty knots would see us through, and was plenty fast enough for these conditions.

Now, back to the chart – wasn't there some high ground very near to the airport? Ah yes, there – an 1850 ft. peak about a mile starboard of track, coming up almost immediately – so, swing port ten degrees onto 310 to give it a berth. On the present altimeter setting, the top would register about 300 feet and it could well be in cloud. Allow two minutes on this leg, then double the correction used –

starboard onto 330, and hold for two minutes, then port again onto our original course of 320 and we should be back on track, roughly about there! I wish this chart were a larger scale. Now, what's coming up next? Look for a clearing in the forest where we should cross a minor road or track at right angles... and then there's another peak shown at 1703 feet, dead on track in – check, eight miles, that's – nine and a half minutes. So, plan another detour and an intercept, and from the hatching on the chart the ground looks lower to starboard; so start the detour just after the clearing.

So we wriggled on for forty-two minutes. I was nearly caught out on two occasions, when the ground imperceptibly climbed to meet us and there was barely room to clear the trees. The branches became as tentacles intent upon ensnaring the buzzing intruder in their midst... but the buzzing intruder was fast proving to be the ideal aeroplane for this sort of flying, and in spite of its agricultural label I couldn't have wished for better. But I missed not having an Ordnance Survey map and being able to follow a safe contour line; the half-million aeronautical chart didn't have the contours marked and only showed high ground by hatching – brown for bare hills or green if covered by vegetation. So, having barely cleared the trees for the second time, I decided a better way would be to follow the more obvious lighter-coloured valleys shown on the chart, even though it would mean resorting to larger detours. With each detour I kept a running total of the direction and time taken, so that compensating intercepts could be calculated whenever an opportunity arose. It sounds an over-laborious process, but it's the only way to keep track of where you are, especially when over unknown terrain.

Sure enough, after forty-two minutes – plus another six accrued in detours, the ground at last began to fall away, and with it the final misty tentacles of the Forêt de Chatillon receded and then were left behind.

The body sometimes reacts in strange ways after a period of stress, and suddenly I started to sweat. It poured off me, as though the adrenaline generated over the last forty-eight minutes was now trying to expel itself from every pore in my body. I felt utterly drained – but mingled with the exhaustion was a warm afterglow, a feeling of well being, coupled with satisfaction of a job well done. I hadn't had to fly like that for a very long time – for it's very different in a helicopter, which could have picked its way along at walking pace if necessary, and it was good to know I hadn't lost the touch. For the first time since takeoff, I could afford to relax.

Now, time to take stock of the situation: our in-flight conditions haven't changed; we are still brushing under the cloud overcast with a forward visibility of about two – maybe two and a half miles. But at least the ground has dropped back into its right place and at a guess, was already some five hundred feet below. So, time to reset the altimeter to the QNH – or height above sea level, which was... 986 millibars from my pad, and when twiddled on, makes the altimeter read 1650 feet. This height also tallies with the chart, which shows the elevation of Chatillon to be 905 feet... and then, looking further along our route, Troyes at 394 feet – or in other words, downhill all the way from now on.

Next, where are we?

One of the 'tricks of the trade' Mr. Summers passed on to me was the use of deliberate error. I remember the occasion exactly, for we were returning to Wallop from Detmold in a Beaver and had just descended from the bright sunlit world above, through seventeen long minutes of lumpy dark-grey cloud under the kindly guidance of Boscombe Radar, to emerge into the real world and gloom of a February afternoon. Six hundred feet below, the ground looked dismal and uninviting with waterlogged fields unfolding in a bleak and mottled pattern of browns and greens. I had no idea where we were, but the ADF needle and our Decca track were pointing nicely at Wallop and I was content to follow them home. Casually Mr. Summers leant forward and flicked the switches off. 'People become altogether mesmerized by these things' he said, 'it's like being glued to a television set – let's get home without them, shall we?'

I discarded the airways chart I had been using and rummaged in my bag for an appropriate map. I opened it up and spread it on my knees and looked at it blankly. With no track plotted on it, we could be anywhere... I glanced outside to see if there were any features – a town, village, road, – in fact anything to give me a clue? The pattern of rain-sodden fields rolled endlessly on. Damn! Better tackle it from the other end. Now, what's our heading, 325? So the reciprocal is 145... I unwound the string from the compass rose of my newly acquired Swissair Navigator and extended it over the map on 145 degrees from Wallop and marked it lightly in pencil. Now, our ETA is 1603 – that's in twenty-one minutes and our groundspeed about 120... I set the numbers on the dial... so we are about forty-two miles out, which is... which is off this bloody map, you idiot!

'Why is it you soldiers are so obsessed with map reading all the time?'

'Well, it's the best way I know to find out where we are...'

'Well, stop thinking like a soldier and try thinking like an aviator. This is not a tactical exercise, there's no enemy to take into consideration, all we want to do is to get home in time for tea... look, give it here.' He took the map and put his finger on Middle Wallop. 'This is our destination and we are approaching from the southeast and if our present heading is correct, we know we should arrive at...' he glanced at my knee-pad '...1603, right? That's all you really need to know! Now, even supposing our heading is not quite correct – which could happen for instance if you were still using the calculated drift factor for the upper-air wind that you were using on the Airways, which we know will be different from the wind at ground level...' he gave me a sideways look, which I studiously ignored '... we'll only be a matter of what, five – or at the very worst, ten miles adrift at 1603?'

'Right.'

'Well, which?'

'Which what?'

'Which way will we be, to the left or the right of our destination?'

'Oh I see, well...'

'The point I am *trying* to make...' he put the tips of his fingers together and studied them thoughtfully for a while before continuing. 'I'm not being deliberately old-fashioned, but all these new sophisticated navigational aids – however many you may carry, they're all very well until they either go wrong or somebody turns the system off. Therefore, may I suggest that at all times they should be regarded as their name implies – *Aids*, rather than replacements to normal navigation? Of course they're an enormous step forward and they're getting better every day, as well as being easy to use – I mean anybody can punch in a few waypoints and then follow a needle. *Waypoint*... wherever did they get that awful word from? Anyway, *tempting* as it may be, you must always regard them as supplementary tools to confirm your own navigation, rather than the other way around – or one day you'll be caught out.

'Now, in the days before we had all this new technology, navigators had to rely on their *skill* and their wits. Seamen in their relatively slow moving vessels had to make extremely large allowances for wind and unknown currents, whilst we aviators, although not having to contend with currents, have to cope with an additional dimension as well as the whole process being speeded up. By now, you know yourself there are all sorts of things – apart from the obvious one of *sloppy* flying...' he gave me another sideways look, '...that can affect the accuracy of your intended course. For instance: an unknown wind factor when out of sight of the ground, or when flying over large tracts of featureless terrain like jungle or desert, or trying to map-read in restricted visibility – especially if you are low-level and you have to constantly *hunt* around your course as a result of detours forced by weather or tactical necessity... All these things – and I've only scratched the surface, can affect your true course – with the *inevitable* result that when you finally reach the point you are making for, nothing on the ground will fit the map!

'So how did they do it? For a start, accurate recording of time and distance is essential, for this will eliminate any longitudinal error – thus having flown for the appointed *time*, you'll know that your destination cannot lie ahead, and *hopefully* from observation you'll know you haven't already over-flown it; therefore it must be either to the left or right. A fifty-fifty chance, and if you are low on fuel, you cannot afford to turn the wrong way... so, to *forestall* this eventuality, why not aim-off in the first place? If you add ten degrees of deliberate error to your heading, you know your track will be to starboard of the line, and your destination will lie to port! I've used it time and time again in many different and varied circumstances, for not only is it a sensible safeguard, it also tends to augment your navigational competence in that you never *quite* become lost... you just have to wait for the allotted time and then turn ninety-degrees and hey-presto, your destination will appear...'

Many years after this, I read Sir Francis Chichester's account on how he flew across the Southern Ocean in his open cockpit Gypsy Moth biplane. He had to find an island – a mere pinpoint in the ocean, at the extreme endurance of his fuel. He too, plotted and used a deliberate error!

And now, although not deliberate, chance had decreed that by following the valleys I'd detoured well to the west of my track, and since the visibility ruled out cutting any corners, the prudent thing to do would be to turn ninety degrees to starboard and wait until (hey-presto) the ground once again fitted the line on the chart, which point should be five miles west of Chatillon. If I happened to miss it and over-flew the line, which would be easy enough in this weather, Chatillon would then show up – and is easily recognizable by having a river, a road and a railway all going northwest to Troyes... But before that, there should be some hefty looking overhead cables also going to Troyes... and our track crosses them where they do a bit of a kink to the west, just before Chatillon, after which we need to keep to the west of them... and we'll never get anywhere very fast at this speed, so better clean the aeroplane up!

I ease the nose down and feed in power until the RPM needle settles on 2300, which is the centre of the green sector on the dial. As the airspeed increases, the wing-slots flutter and then trundle back into place, after which I gently raise the flaps.

I nearly missed the pylons. I was looking for a line of them as shown on the chart, but in the limited visibility, just chanced upon one standing starkly on its own. I banked sharply left onto the heading and almost immediately the next two in line swam into sight. Of Chatillon there was no sign... so at what point have we intersected the pylons? The Direction Indicator reads 338 degrees and the bubble compass... swinging either side of... 350! Uh-hu, twelve degrees difference, I thought as much... So, what's the true heading of the pylons shown on the chart? Again I use my Swissair friend and flip it open to the compass rose. The string shows the line of pylons to be 346 Degrees True, then when abeam Chatillon they do a kink to the west onto 330. The True bearing of 346 agrees with the 350 Magnetic shown on the compass, which means we are still south of the point where they kink – and that the ancient D.I. has already wandered, confirming my earlier suspicions. I reset it to 350 to agree with its magnetic brother and then concentrate on following the pylons, as one by one they march towards me out of the mist.

With 2300 RPM set, the airspeed indicates just over 100 knots and if I increase the revs to the top of the green sector, it creeps up to 105 and there it sticks! But 100 knots is plenty fast enough for the visibility, and anyway will be more economical. But even at these reduced revs the noise level in the cockpit is far greater than I would have imagined, and I wouldn't want to fly this aeroplane for more than an hour or two on a regular basis, for above all, noise is the greatest thing that tires you out. Or maybe it's because I'm not wearing my usual soundproofed flying helmet... and certainly these headphones don't help a lot either, for they're pretty basic and uncomfortable and not a patch on those Bernard had in the Twin Comanche that had enclosed the whole ear with snug and soundproofed foam padding. And whilst thinking about headphones, it's high time I obtained an accurate QNH from Reims Information and also officially clocked into the system! I change frequency to 124.1 and listen for a moment before giving them a call. There is none of the usual chatter... I turn the volume up and then fiddle with the squelch knob, but even the usual sudden roar of static is missing. The switches are on and there's a red light glowing, but the radio doesn't offer a squeak.

'Reims Information, Golf Bravo Fox Alpha Kilo, good morning?'

Absolutely dead. I check the lead from the headset and follow it to where the jack pushes into the left-hand and larger of the two sockets. Large socket? Surely, this socket must be for the old radio – modern radio fittings are now only half this size? I feel with my fingers under and behind the fascia and find the two sets of wires leading from behind the sockets. One set – those from the large socket that I'm plugged into, lead off to behind the instruments to be lost in a maze of other wires, but the other set is more traceable and appears to lead to the rear of the new 360-channel set that Bernard recently installed. God, how stupid! No wonder I hadn't heard a squeak so far! I pulled the jack out and tried to insert it into the other socket, but even as I did it, I knew it wouldn't fit. Damn, there must be a different set of headphones for the new radio! You'd have thought Bernard would have... anyway, easily done – now, where would they be stowed, they must be somewhere on board?

But they weren't. I felt under the seats, then undid my harness and knelt on my seat facing backwards and checked as far as my hands would reach. The two pockets on the back of the two front seats were empty, the rear bench seat just had my bag on it and there was nothing underneath. No headsets. The only other place they could be was in the luggage compartment behind the rear seats, which I couldn't reach.

I settled back into my seat and strapped in again. This put a whole new dimension onto things.

III

I suppose I was angry more than anything else.

Angry at myself: here was I, supposedly a professional pilot, who had the temerity to jump into an aeroplane he'd never flown or even seen before, and omitted to check the communications before he took off! Of *course* that controller would have been at his post in the tower at Darois – that was his primary job, especially as mine had been the first aircraft movement of the day; so of *course* he'd have been manning his radio! Flying is a serious business; it also involves a lot of other people on the ground who's job it is to ensure it remains as such, for it is they that have to pick up the pieces. What's more, I'd always prided myself on my professionalism and deplored amateurs or part-timers that either deliberately flaunted, or else through sheer ignorance did not abide by the rules. And now, here I was as one of them; bumbling halfway across France in marginal weather with no one the wiser – unless they'd had time to process and put a query against the Flight Plan I'd filed. They'd more than likely pick me up on radar from time to time and hopefully would be able to warn any low-level military traffic that they had an unidentified intruder in their airspace, but that is not good enough: it should be a two-way team, with the pilot able to report his position and in-flight conditions on request, and more important to be contactable at all times should any change be required.

So, what now? Anger and remorse won't help anything; the situation exists as of now, so how best to retrieve it? First, what frequencies do we carry on the old Mickey Mouse set? There are eight, listed on a card by the radio, and it takes only a moment to crosscheck them with the frequencies on my pad. Only one matches – 120.7, the frequency for Lydd, the Channel airport west of Dover where we have to land to clear Customs and get Bernard's paperwork stamped. At least that's something – but first we have to get across France. I can't turn back; there's little point landing at the first available airfield on route – that would only confuse matters even more, so I may as well press on for now and stick to the Flight Plan.

Hello...? The next pylon isn't in line – this must be where they kink, so we're back on the pencil line on the chart. From this point they swing away to the east by ten degrees, for our course tracks west of Troyes to where the VOR beacon is, whilst the pylons circumvent Troyes to the east. Then, according to the chart they divide, with a double set going off to the northeast, and a single line reverting back to the original heading of 330, to run parallel but roughly five miles east of our course, for a further twenty miles.

I am tempted to follow them, for the chart has already proved to be of too large a scale for close map-work and in this visibility the pylons are a Heaven-sent lifeline that would lead us through the next fifty miles. And in fifty miles, who knows, the weather could lift? I studied their line on the chart again: apart from leading straight through the Seine TMA – which has a lower limit of 2000 feet, which means if we remain under the overcast and at our present height we should be okay – there would appear to be no other obstacles ... except, what if the pylons are no longer there? They could have altered the line, or taken them down and buried the cables ...? I refolded the chart and looked for the date of issue on the front panel – then breathed a sigh of relief: it was this year's.

As the last pylon faded from view, I decided to go for it and changed course to follow them.

And what a lifeline they proved to be! One after another they marched out of the mist, slowly veering to the east until the point where they divided and I knew I was northeast of Troyes. I found the single line, borne by smaller pylons than previously and followed them nearly due west for five miles skirting round the north of Troyes and then, true to the chart, kinked to the right and back onto the original heading of 330. In twenty miles their usefulness would cease for they would then turn north. At this point I planned to turn due west and look for the River Seine, for our track crossed directly over where the river divided into two tributaries just east of Romilly. After that, I would just have to resort to map reading as best as I could.

The smaller pylons were harder to follow and needed my full concentration, so it was some minutes before I became aware out of the corner of my eye that another regular feature was also keeping pace with us on our port side. I glanced out and saw it was the river – and then beyond that was a railway and beyond that a road... and as I watched, the colour of the water changed from black to grey with patches of blue as it began to catch the reflection of the sun. We were through!

As the mist dispersed, so the countryside unfolded all around and with it my lifeline faded into insignificance. Almost immediately ahead I could see where the sagging line of cables turned north, their pylons marching bravely on ahead cutting a swathe through the countryside, until they too became indistinguishable and finally merged into the far distance.

True to the forecast, with the passing of the front came the wind. There was no need to guess its strength or direction; the first indication was a wisp of smoke from a factory chimney at Sézanne, then twenty minutes later, confirmed by a group of tall chimneys that looked as though they belonged to either a cement or maybe a brickworks just south of Soissons, the smoke now streaming back, flat and straight, directly over the path we had just covered! I measured the distance on the chart and worked out our groundspeed to be eighty-five knots, which meant a headwind of around twenty-five knots. It was going to be a long trip, but at least I could now see.

When flying IFR (Instrument Flight Rules) the use of radio is mandatory; whereas when flying VFR (Visual) its use is advisory – and although I still felt uneasy about it, it was quite a novelty to be flying off the rein for once – rather like playing truant!

In the military of course it is an essential tool in order to do your job, whether you are visual or otherwise, and as such we are also governed by a different set of rules in order to fly visually in all weathers however marginal...

Marginal...?

Damn, I hadn't even given that a thought, for I'd been completely focused on my own ability to cope with the situation and had just taken for granted that... but the fact is, I'm not flying a military aircraft under military jurisdiction, but a civilian light aircraft on a private flight. And civilian aircraft are governed by rules set by the International Civilian Air Organisation – whose minimum limits for flying VFR were (rightly) designed for the average private pilot with no instrument rating – and bear no relation to the 'Special VFR' used by my Service. Or in other words, unwittingly or not, I'd been flying illegally, which was another black mark... and even Bernard had remarked on it and I hadn't taken any notice... Ah well, having passed through the front, at least the weather was now officially VMC (Visual Met Conditions), so perhaps it's just as well I was off the leash and unable to answer any awkward questions!

Nevertheless for this sort of flying, a radio can be a mixed blessing. Background chatter can sometimes be irritating, but that is a small price to pay for the reassurance it can offer; for once you have clocked into the system you know you feature as a player on the board, and as such have the comfort of being able to call up at any time. Then, by listening, it doesn't take long to piece together a mental picture of other aircraft movements in your vicinity; so much that should you ever be called to alter course or height to avoid conflicting traffic, it should come as no surprise. On the other hand now, the enforced radio-silence made me appreciate flying for its own sake – something I had taken for granted and not thought about for years. Flying a light aircraft near to the ground is a great leveller, for you see the ground in its correct perspective. You are gloriously remote from the world around, as well as removed from all the mundane frustrations suffered by other earthlings. Cars and traffic-jams become as ants, strung needlessly together within the set confines of a meandering ribbon as you pass overhead. A building site is but a patch of bare earth, with yellow ants this time, nodding their necks and scratching here and there. On the ground there could be bedlam: the concrete delivery could be late; the bricks the wrong specification; the digging machines had struck rock in the excavation and the sub-contract pipe-layers had walked off without completing the manholes... all this is insignificant; it is just another patch of bare earth soon to be left behind.

In spite of the noise, all appears to be right with the aeroplane; with this headwind our progress is slow and we are going to be late, but that can't be helped. We have yet to land at Le Touquet unannounced and without a radio, but nothing can be done about that, so there's no need to think about it until the time comes... and I wonder who or what it is who keeps visiting me in the night?

That makes me sit up and forget about any further feelings of Godliness and the exhilarations of free flight, and focus on what has been at the back of my mind ever since I woke up this morning. Furthermore sitting above the earth is as good a time to think about it as any. It wasn't a dream; of that I'm sure, for not only was I was wide-awake but I actually talked to whatever it was. So what was it, a ghost – a hallucination – a psychological or astral projection? I wished I knew more about these things. I have heard that hallucinations can be experienced from taking drugs – either voluntarily or under medical supervision, and are as a result of chemicals in the brain that heighten perception and enable you to live through an unusual level of reality. Except that hallucinations are strictly a project of your imagination and often create totally bizarre images or features, which although real enough at the time, bear no actual resemblance to reality. And there had been nothing bizarre about my visitor – besides, that can hardly be the case for I hadn't taken any drugs; nor indeed had ever knowingly taken any in my life, let alone experienced bizarre hallucinations as a result!

So, what do I know about ghosts? Although I've never seen one, I remember reading an account in a newspaper about a whole group of people who were visiting a stately home, and they had all witnessed seeing a lady in a grey cloak. The paper labelled the apparition as a "place ghost", for she had materialized at one end of a lawn and then disappeared through a wall at the other end of the garden. When questioned, the staff had said that she frequently appeared and yes, she was always dressed the same and allegedly was the ghost of Lady so-and-so, who had died a century or so before. She always appeared in the same place and walked across the same stretch of lawn before disappearing through the wall, which it turned out, had once had a door there. She never spoke or faltered and the whole thing was rather like an old film that just showed that particular clip over and over again. Apparently, the article went on, there were many other reported instances of similar apparitions appearing in other places and they always conformed to a similar pattern – like a short video that gets repeatedly replayed. So, if this was an accepted fact, backed up by other similar sightings in other locations, as well as being vouched for by whole groups of people who simultaneously had witnessed them, who was I to doubt? But then, these ghosts were clearly attached to certain places, whereas my visitor was somehow linked to me as well as capable of tracking me down in France...

Then, I'd also heard of people who had been visited by the ghost of someone who had just died – especially if they had been particularly close to that person, or the bereavement was sudden or came as a shock. There have been many accounts of people who have experienced seeing or feeling the presence of someone who was dear to them at the instant of their death, or when for instance, they were killed in a war. Sometimes people clearly see a visual projection of the dead person or else they merely feel their presence, which is enough to make them know what had happened. My father once told me that his uncle had actually experienced such a phenomenon during the First World War. He was playing lawn-croquet with other members of the family one afternoon when he suddenly stopped in shock and gasped out that something had happened to Eric, his son. It turned out that that was the very moment his son, an early flier, had been shot down and killed. The difference between a 'place ghost' and this – call it a 'bereavement ghost' being,

71

that the latter phenomenon always revealed a powerful one-to-one connection between the viewer and the viewed and thus related to a person rather than a place.

Which certainly brought it a step closer... but what was it my ghost or apparition had said – something about travelling? That was totally beyond my comprehension and the only practical way I could liken it was to a narrow-band radio wave – a strong transmission or projection from the sender being aimed at a suitably tuned-in receiver – in this case, I suppose my subconscious, which was somehow sympathetic and receptive to the cause. Did that make sense? And isn't that what a medium is? A person who is able to tune in as a go-between in spiritualism and, moreover, does it on a regular basis?

I have never been to a séance, so cannot testify to the powers of a medium, but again it was my father who once told me of an occurrence that directly concerned him, although he was not there to witness it, which fact made it all the more plausible... It was to do with the ram at the village water supply. Before the village was on mains water it had its own supply, which dubious facility was bequeathed to my father by his father before him. Water was collected from various springs and piped to a low-lying pumping house from whence it was pumped up to a high-lying reservoir, before final distribution to the village by gravity. The ram was an automatic pump that relied upon a large head of water to compress in a cylinder, which then forced a jet of water to a greater height by way of a small diameter pipe – much the same principle as a hydraulic press. The time came when the delivery pipe was in urgent need of replacement as segments were rusting though, thereby jeopardizing the working of the whole system; so he decided to replace it with a new plastic pipe on the grounds that plastic would never rust. Unfortunately the only plastic pipes available on the market were of much smaller diameter, which he reasoned would restrict the throughput, but still deliver more than the present leaking iron pipe. In passing, he mentioned this to an old friend of his – an engineer, whom he'd first met at agricultural college years before. His friend, who was generally known by his nickname as Bull, was adamant that the pipe diameter was far too small to allow the system work; he was an engineer and he said the backpressure would be too great. So, in the event my father installed the mile-long length of plastic pipe (which I believe he'd already bought) and instead replaced the hydraulic ram with an electric pump, which arrangement worked perfectly... but his friend Bull never got to know about this, for he was killed in a motor accident the following week.

Some months later my father got a telephone call. It was from an unknown lady who was a medium in London. Several sessions in a row she had been contacted by a man called Bull, who was desperately trying to contact my father. He was extremely worried about a ram – are you a sheep farmer? Something about a ram and a pipe that wouldn't work – does that mean anything to you? Anyway, she was glad she'd got hold of the right person and had been able to pass the message on...

So, another positive step... and this time more than just hearsay, for it happened close to home – and maybe I do know more about this subject than I had realized! But again, that was an incident of a dead person or spirit, trying to contact the living; whereas when I asked my visitor if she was dead, she'd laughed and said certainly not...! Which is a wholly different slant, for I'm not dealing with a spirit but with someone who is very much alive and yet able to project their subconscious. Project – Astral Projection! Isn't that what that is? Anyway, if that's the case, and since I am – for want of a better word – the target of that projection, it's highly likely that it could be somebody I know... or perhaps knew in a previous life... or, maybe a parallel one?

God, now it's getting too complicated and bordering on subjects that are too difficult to even think about, let alone being able to readily accept! So, to keep it simple, assume it is someone I know – hence the familiar feeling I'd felt... but as to the motive? That's the big question and one I cannot answer... so best let it rest there. At least if it happens again I'll be more prepared and ready for it, and maybe then things could become clearer. But it's unsettling – as well as intriguing, for half of me feels eager to exploit the situation further, whilst the other half wants nothing more to do with it and blank the whole thing off – and what's more, it's hardly the sort of thing you can ask anyone, for they'd think you were nuts!

Either way, I have a feeling it's not in my control... for how do you shut your subconscious down?

IV

Three-forty, and I can see the sea and Le Touquet on the nose! The safest way would be to join overhead, which should announce my presence, as well as being able to visually check their signal square and then let down accordingly – and if they're on the ball, they should flash me with a red or green Aldis lamp. That's how it used to happen in the days before radio, though I've never been in this situation before...

I overfly the field and sure enough, there's a white T laid out beside the control tower aligned to show the runway in use. I blip the engine twice for good measure, then let down to 1000 feet running into wind before turning left to join the circuit. There is no sign of any other traffic, nor any red light from the control tower, so I continue downwind and then turn onto base leg, throttle back and apply half-flap. Still no light, and no sign of anybody else dragging in on long-finals, so assume it's clear to continue, and descend to 500 feet and then turn onto short-finals maintaining a trickle of power. Just before touchdown a green light flickers from the tower – perhaps they had trouble in finding it... and then we are down. A car races across the grass and swings round in front of me, so I dutifully follow it to a parking apron, swing into wind and then shut down.

Bernard was right; the forty-five minutes I'd allowed to clear customs stretched to a good hour and a half. Where had I come from? Where was I going? Was I a novice? Nobody flew without a radio these days and it would be out of the question to allow me to takeoff again without one. They asked to see my licenses and logbook (something that in all the years I'd been flying, I'd never been asked for before) and these were taken away to an inner office, whilst I was left to stand and wait.

Eventually the door opened and a fat man wearing a shiny blue suit waddled out. I suppose he was in his mid fifties, but this was belied by his hairstyle, which was pulled severely back into a ponytail and fastened with a twisted rubber band. No doubt it was a relic from his younger days; a forlorn echo to recapture the image when it graced a more sylph-like body, but now it looked totally incongruous and only managed to emphasize his florid and rather paunchy face.

'Je suis le gestionnaire d'aéroport' he announced, handing me back my logbook and papers, 'vous suis un pilote militaire?'

I inclined my head and then tried to explain about the radio.

'Come, we look' he said, and taking me forcibly by the arm, frog-marched me back to the aircraft. I showed him the jack on the headset and how it only fitted the old number-two set. We then checked the cabin and luggage compartment thoroughly to see if there was another set of headphones, but all the cupboards were bare. He then climbed in and studied the frequencies on the card for the number-two set.

'Aha!' he said and asked me to turn the power on. He donned the headset and then clicked to one of the unmarked frequencies.

'It says here Le Touquet is on 118.45' I said, peering over his shoulder and showing him my chart.

'Ah yes, but this is another frequency we sometimes use. Allow me...' he pressed the button '...ici l'avion anglais, me recevez-vous?'

'Parfaitement. La radio fonctionne bien. Que racontait ce pilote?' Boomed back from the tower.

'Ne me demandez pas, ils sont tous pareils. Je vous reçois aussi, c'est formidable! Vous feriez bien de vous en séparer au plus vite.'

'Entendu. Emmenez-le directement à la Douane.'

'So, you see, it works perfectly!' he said in a patronizing voice. 'Bring your bag and papers, and I'll take you to the Officer of Customs'.

I followed him as he waddled back towards the buildings, trying to work out what had been said on the radio. I had a feeling that somehow a u-turn had been executed during the exchange and they were now intent on getting shot of me as quickly as possible – which on reflection would be no bad thing, but it would be nice to fathom out why... His ponytail bobbed ahead, swaying slightly from side to side and seeing it reminded me of the time when a group of visitors from London came into our local pub. One of them had a ponytail rather like his, which immediately became the source of silent speculation from some of our rural residents sitting in their usual corner. The silence stretched, until one local farmer felt obliged to take his pipe out of his mouth and remark in his broad Devonshire accent: 'That there's a proper job... and correct me if I'm wrong, but I always thought a ponytail was to conceal an arsehole...'

But it was Ponytail who finally won the day. He was manning the tower radio when, with documents all stamped, I finally requested permission to takeoff.

'Roger, you are cleared to takeoff, destination Lydd, timed at 1738. I hope you will make it, for Lydd airport closes at 1800! Good day, monsieur...'

I cleared their frequency, then selected 120.7, the only workable channel I had for the whole of the UK. At ten to six I was halfway across the Channel, butting into the same headwind, which if anything had freshened. There were white waves on the sea, and a ship below was plunging its bows into the waves and throwing up sheets of spray. If I called them now, perhaps they'd keep the airfield open...

'Lydd: Golf Bravo Fox Alpha Kilo, good afternoon?'

'Aircraft calling Lydd, say again call-sign?'

'Lydd: Golf Bravo Fox Alpha Kilo is a Rallye light aircraft inbound to your field, mid Channel this time and estimating you at eighteen zero-five.'

'Foxtrot Alpha Kilo, this field closes at eighteen hundred.'

'Lydd: Alpha Kilo... Ah, Roger – can you stretch it by five minutes, yours is the only UK frequency I carry and the only place I can land?'

'Alpha Kilo – we have a facility whereby we can extend the field opening times by prior arrangement – this is subject to a surcharge payable by the minute for time after eighteen hundred; but regret we cannot offer this today as there are no relief crews available. Sorry, the field closes in five minutes. What is your alternative? Lydd over.'

'Lydd: Alpha Kilo is on a VFR Plan with Luton as an alternative, but I'm afraid we have a radio malfunction on our Number-one set, and do not hold the frequency for Luton on our back-up set. The only frequency we can work is 120.7... over.'

'Alpha Kilo, I'm afraid this field closes in three and a half minutes; suggest you re-route to your alternative...'

'Lydd, before you sign off, do you think you could telephone Luton and give them our ETA of – ah, wait...' I fished behind for my Southern England chart and quickly spanned the distance with my hand. About ninety nautical miles – assume the same headwind, so call it one hour '... Lydd, ETA Luton at nineteen hundred on the hour, and would you also advise them we have no radio?'

'Alpha Kilo, we'll try and do that for you. Good day, Lydd Out.'

Things were just not going my way – if the French bureaucracy had only taken five minutes less, I'd have made it! And so much for radio, for if I hadn't had one, I'd have just landed anyway! Ah well, at least they said they'd alert Luton ...but that in itself is a somewhat daunting prospect, and I wish I'd picked a different alternative, for Luton is an extremely busy place with non-stop charter flights going in and out day and night, and they'll want me like a hole in the head! But it's done now; I can't talk to anyone else, let alone change my Flight Plan, so best stick with it. If I map-read my way around the VOR beacons, at least Thames Radar and any others would be able to monitor my progress and hopefully determine my intended route...

I made a landfall at Dungeness and over-flew Lydd at 2000 feet and made for where their VOR was shown on the chart, some four miles to the northwest of the field. When overhead I changed course and leaving Ashford to starboard, closed with the M24, intercepting it just northeast of Maidstone, where the Detling VOR was shown on the chart. Then northwest to cross the Thames at Gravesend and on to the Stapleford VOR, eight miles northwest of Brentwood and safely situated in the corridor between Heathrow and Stanstead Control Zones. Map reading through the spread of London's north suburbia was an exacting business, but wholly necessary to avoid the congestion of controlled airspace that surrounds the city. At Stapleford I turned northwest on a direct course for Luton. The safest place at any busy airport is directly over it, for then all the other traffic will be either on their way in or out, using corridors that are extensions to the runway in use. So, if I approached from the east, it would see me well clear of these corridors and out of harms way... but it was still rather like approaching a beehive, for Luton was the main terminal used by holiday package tours with an unending stream of aircraft approaching on finals, and another queue inching along the taxiways waiting their turn to take off. No way would they be able to fit me in amongst that lot, especially without a radio – and lamp flashing here would be out of the question...

I over-flew directly overhead at 2000 feet and pondered what to do. I had a feeling all my sins were about to catch up with me and in any event I'd be in for a warm reception.

Then I saw the grass. A long strip to the west and just outside one of the main access roads and an open invitation to any farmer's aeroplane! Without further thought I chopped the throttle and started to descend, still heading west and away from the main complex. At a thousand feet and now over the town I did a 180 turn and headed back as though on an extended base leg. I don't know who owns the grass, or indeed whether it is even part of the airport but... about now, drop flap and swing onto finals... and at last we're down!

V

'Ah-ha, the intrepid driver of Fox Alpha Kilo in from Dijon, I presume?' the controller boomed at me in an over-jovial manner that immediately made me wary. I was standing in his office adjoining the tower where I had been asked to report having completed the Customs formalities, and where all the necessary entry stamps had also been affixed to the aircraft documents. This was the meeting I'd been dreading and for the second time that day – and also my flying career, I voluntarily proffered my blue RAF logbook in a wild hope that it might somehow allay the wrath of the rocket I was about to receive.

'Yes, sorry about my unorthodox arrival – did Lydd telephone you and explain?' I countered, whilst thinking that maybe it wouldn't be so simple as a mere rocket; maybe he would be obliged to pass on a report to some disciplinary board convened by the CAA, who then, in the fullness of time, would impose a suitable fine or maybe even revoke my civilian license. That could explain his forced joviality.

'Lydd...? No, they never phoned, but as you didn't land there we were expecting you as it's on the Flight Plan that came through from Darois – and we've also been following you on radar. Why, had a spot of bother?'

This wasn't the frosty reception I'd been expecting at all! I explained about the radio and then apologised for my choice of landing place on the grass, but it had offered the only available area away from all their other traffic.

'Yes, you used the light aircraft landing strip – didn't you know? We tried to call you on the radio to give you instructions, but in the event you did exactly right by over-flying the field and letting down on the dead side. So, no problem – are you going on to your destination this evening, if so, you've only got about an hour of light left – and I take it you'll still be without a radio?'

'Yes – so best if I got off straight away...?' For the first time I allowed myself to believe that I was being let-off the hook – and as such, now couldn't wait to get away. 'I'll take off to the north and clear immediately left, and keep out of your way... if that'll be okay with you?'

'Fine...' he flicked through a few pages of my logbook before handing it back '...are you still in the Army Air Corps – you army flyers are all the same! I went to one of your open-days at Middle Wallop a couple of years ago, I must say it was quite a display. Anyway, if you're all paid up, you'd better be on your way. Have a good flight!'

VI

I tried one of Bernard's jump take-offs on the way out. Wind up full throttle whilst standing on the brakes, then accelerate clean to 45 knots before pulling flap whilst rotating at the same time. As I hauled back the slots banged out of the leading edge and the aircraft literally jumped into the air! I immediately swung left to clear their field and climbed to the west into the setting sun, before turning north overhead Dunstable.

All my previous misgivings together with the build-up of apprehension had evaporated, and this – this was sheer flying again! I'd enjoyed that takeoff and it was another thing that endeared me to the aircraft, in spite of its slow speed and interminable noise! A thought struck me: I wonder how much Bernard would want for this aircraft? In spite of its age and outwardly tatty appearance, the engine was good, and with a few decent instruments it could be a lot of fun, as well as a useful means of transport. I'm sure they'd let me hangar it at Wallop in a corner somewhere – there must be some perks allowed for an instructor, so that would be one major cost taken care of – or alternatively, as it was metal it could always live outside... But it was the short takeoff and landing performance that really appealed; a rugged farmer's aeroplane that you could really use in any weather and operate from almost anywhere. I'd never even considered owning my own aircraft before – especially since I'd been paid to fly by Her Majesty for so long; but then, why not? Other people own aeroplanes, and judging from those I'd met, they can't all be immensely rich!

Evening loomed out of the east like a great silken curtain, my starboard wing cutting through it as it caught and reflected the last of the dying sun. The ground below was fast covering in darkness and already pinpricks of lights, like isolated stars were beginning to appear, as if the earth had been turned upside down. It was one of those moments of suspended animation that somehow never materialises when surrounded by the busyness of flying a helicopter; a sense of freedom and true flight. Here, sitting in your own orb above the earth was eternal peace; a place where you could quietly jettison all reality and responsibility into the depths below. You have never done anything else nor been any other place, for in this exalted situation time itself stood still, and with it a haunting sense of eternity. Are all pilots escapists at heart, I wonder?

I smile and turn on Bernard's navigation lights.

The sweep of the second hand together with the layout of lights from the town below, tell me it is time to descend to earth again. The airfield is an unmanned grass field to the northeast of the town; it borders onto an industrial trading estate that is ablaze with light. Beyond it is a black void where no other lights show, and that is the field. I reduce the power and quietly slip down into the darkness. There will be no other traffic and rather than attempt to find the marked runway, it will be easiest just to land on the grass, straight in from this approach. I reduce the speed to fifty-five knots and drop landing flap. I feel the slots bang out from the wing and then, in a nose high attitude, trim to descend at fifty-five. As I draw near the lights I shut one eye, another trick passed on to me by Mr. Summers years ago, for the closed eye will retain its present night vision that otherwise would be destroyed from the glare of the neon lights. We pass over the lights and into the void beyond and I can open it again, for it's time to ease the power off and feel for the ground. There is no jolt or protest of suspension; instead our main wheels gently kiss the tips of the grass and then quietly settle in. Left alone, this aeroplane will even land itself...

VII

'Eh-hue, you got back in one piece then?' Bernard's voice crackled over the phone.

'Yes, and I got all your papers stamped at Luton, do you want me to drop them off at the shop?'

'Tell me, what about the radio? I found the headsets for the new VHF in the Comanche, just after you'd taken off...'

'Yeah, well – I managed alright without...'

'Luton? What were you doing in Luton? You didn't 'ave a crystal for Luton's frequency on the old set!'

'The only frequency I had on the old set that matched anywhere was Lydd, and by the time I got there they'd closed up shop.'

'I see...' The pause extended as he pieced together the implications. 'And you managed alright? I didn't know they'd let you land at Luton without a radio?'

'Well, I seemed to manage alright, and the Rallye's now tucked up in your hangar. Tell me, what's that aeroplane worth?'

'Why, you want to buy it?'

'Yes, I wouldn't mind... I rather liked it.'

'You don't want a rubbishy old thing like that! If you want

an aeroplane I'll find you a decent one... besides, I would not sell you that one.'

'Oh, why?'

'Because my friend, it is full of rust! The wings inside are full of rust and they need dismantling and taking apart – it needs a proper job doing and will cost a fortune! It is one of the main faults of the Rallye; they all go like it and just rust away if they're left outside! I can get rid of it to a man I know wants one, and I'll find you a decent aeroplane, one that flies properly, just leave it to me!'

My heart sank. Full of rust? I suppose he's right, but what a shame. I thought again about our first testing moments together, skimming the trees of the Forêt de Chatillon in the mist; then her eagerness to fly as we jumped into the air leaving Luton; and finally the beauty and sheer magic of our evening flight together in the gathering dusk and how she'd responded by landing herself in the dark; yes, she was exactly my sort of aeroplane.

Chapter 4

I

'I heard you were coming, and frankly I can't say I'm over-joyed by the prospect of – ah – working with you, let alone having you on my team...'

I looked him in the eye as he sat sprawled behind his desk, puffed-up with his own self-importance and said nothing.

'For that's what we are here' he continued, 'a highly *professional* team doing an important job – and that means total dedication; *teamwork* is the key-word to our success and its absolutely *vital* that we mesh together as well as give each other total support and backing – a *united* front. There's only one standard – and that's *by the book* and there's certainly no room for *mavericks*... furthermore, as the ultimate responsibility rests on my shoulders, I expect total *loyalty* from my team members...'

A varnished board faced outwards on his desk: Lt. Colonel N. Swinford-Hogg A.A.C. it announced, and then another board beside it that said Chief Flying Instructor, as if he needed them there to remind himself who and what he was. Only the joke was, he wasn't the Chief Flying Instructor! He was only there as a stand-in for fifteen weeks whilst the designated CFI was on an extended course in America; but true to form he had readily assumed all the trimmings of office. The same old Nicki-Pig, and the smug little bastard hadn't changed any over the years, as hadn't our mutual dislike for each other. So, he still regarded me as a maverick, did he? Which meant he hadn't forgotten and still bore the same old grudge; the only difference now being that he was the one in the driving seat, albeit on a temporary basis.

'...So, as it appears we are stuck with each other – at least for the *time being*,' he continued with a forced smile, yet managing to put emphasis on the last two words, 'I suggest the way forward for both of us is to bury the hatchet; forget our past differences and start again with a clean sheet...'

'I carry no hatchet Colonel,' I said, still holding his eye. 'I'm here to do a job – and I'll do it to the best of my judgement and ability...'

'*Your* judgement... I think not! Already you seem to have missed the point. Your ability as an instructor is yet to be proven! And as for *judgement*, that does not enter the bounds of your responsibility; if there's any question of judgement it will be made by me and me alone. Do I make myself clear?'

We'd first met twenty years before in Aden when I was a newly qualified Beaver pilot and he was nearing the end of his tour as a helicopter pilot flying Scouts. He was about five years senior to me, for when I joined the Squadron I'd just been made up to Captain, whereas his pips were already tarnished and he was in the slot waiting for his majority. He was a small man and even then running to corpulence, and like many people of his stature had an aggressive nature as well as being highly ambitious. His appearance and mannerisms were unfortunate and matched his name: Nicholas Swinford-Hogg; for with his bristly hair, snout-like nostrils and close-set eyes, together with the way he walked – with head down and swaying from side to side, reminded one exactly of a pig. None of this was of his making – and to be charitable, we are all God's creatures and have an equal place on this earth, to be accepted and cherished by all... but that was not his philosophy; he was not interested in equality or harmonious relationships, let alone any sort of charity, and seemingly went out of his way to cultivate the very opposite. He made his mark by being as obtuse and obnoxious as possible at every opportunity – which, regrettably, was of his own making, as well as being totally insufferable in a small-knit unit such as ours. Not least was his dismissive attitude towards all those his junior, be they brother officers or more importantly, the rank and file, whilst blatantly toadying in the most obsequious manner to anyone and everyone who was his senior.

On first joining, I'd tried to get alongside him in the mess, and although outwardly of equal rank, had rudely been rebuffed – presumably on account of our difference in seniority or the fact that I was the new boy! After that – like most others, I'd steered well clear of him and left him to his toadying. This status quo could well have existed indefinitely, had it not been for an incident that occurred a few months later. He was the duty helicopter pilot and had been called out to fly a casevac (casualty evacuation) from an up-country position that had come under attack. At the time I was inbound in a Beaver from another sortie, and landed just prior to his return. I was in the process of refuelling my aircraft when his helicopter landed on the pad – with no casualty on board.

'Clag' he announced, taking off his helmet after he'd shut down and the rotors stopped turning. 'Couldn't get anywhere near their position; clag right down to the deck and totally below limits.' With that pronouncement, he'd walked back to the crew room, signed off and shortly afterwards was seen driving back to the mess.

Arthur, my Flight Commander came across to the refu-elling bay.

'We've just had, knuff, another signal from Ain – they've had another casualty, so now there are two of them – one's a gunshot wound in the leg and the other has broken his ribs – and they want to know when the chopper's arriving... unusual for cloud to be at Ain at this time of the day – I wonder, do you think, knuff, you could pop up and have a look?'

Arthur was the master of understatement as well as the unspoken word – and once you'd got used his quiet and hesitant manner, interspersed at intervals by his habit of momentarily shutting his eyes whilst blowing down his nose in a reverse sort of sniff – his general demeanour and especially his eyes normally managed to say it all.

'Mmm, well I'm not doing much else, and this aeroplane seems to have plenty of fuel, so I might as well just slip up there and have a look ...' I'd replied in like form, whilst conveying the remainder of the sentence by a lift of the eyebrows.

'Really? Oh good – well, if you do happen to pop into Ain, perhaps it would be best if you took them straight down to Khormaksar and arrange for an ambulance on the radio...' he said, reading my mind. 'In the meantime I'd better sort out some lights here; it'll be, knuff, dark when you get back.'

And so it turned out to be. There were some wisps of low-lying stratus at Ain but nothing much to speak of and I managed to land and pick up the two casualties and then flew them down to Aden, before returning to our base at Falaise where Arthur had prepared a tactical flarepath. This consisted of two Land Rovers parked at an angle so their headlights converged into a pool of light, together with a couple hurricane lamps, one placed at the undershoot and the other at the far end of the runway – and tactical or not, was our only means of lighting.

Arthur was still in his office when I signed off.

'Manage alright?' he asked.

'Mmm, the cloud seemed to have dispersed by the time I got there, so it turned out to be a doddle ... I packed them off in an ambulance at Khormaksar and they'll both be okay.'

'Good, well done ... but – ah, best not to, knuff, mention it to anyone – if you follow my drift? Could be a bit tricky... dangerous bloke to cross, our Nicky – the sort that could bear a grudge, so just...'

But inevitably it didn't take long for the story to get out, and the squadron made a meal of it at Nicki-Pig's expense, his general lack of popularity being what it was. He never confronted me directly with it, but thereafter contrived to make my life as uncomfortable as possible at every opportunity. Fortunately it didn't last too long, for he left a couple of months later, and we then heard through the grapevine that he'd gone off to become an instructor. His fellow Scout pilots couldn't believe it, for by their reckoning he'd always been one to fly strictly by the book, and had never attempted to advance his skills to the levels normally expected of a squadron pilot.

I next ran into him at Detmold, where I was posted straight after my helicopter conversion course and found that he was the station QHI (Qualified Helicopter Instructor). At the time there were two Army Air Corps squadrons at Detmold and the QHI's job was to sustain flying standards and safety procedures for all the pilots on the station, as well as to upgrade new techniques or practices peculiar to that theatre of operation. For instance, should an experienced pilot arrive from, say, the Far East, an hour or two with the QHI brushing up on the use of different weapon systems and the half-forgotten techniques of how to fly tactically in the kind of weather found during an European winter, is wholly necessary as well as mandatory. Likewise, flying standards can deteriorate unless checked on a regular basis and all pilots, regardless of rank, status or experience are subject to a 'periodic check' with the QHI. Rather than regarding it with the dread of an exam, most pilots welcome their periodic check, for this is the occasion when any bad habits can be identified and nipped in the bud, or rusty techniques re-learnt and polished. Most QHI's adopt an easy-going relationship with the pilots under their care, for far from being there to criticise, they are there to help and encourage as well as develop individuals' personal skills.

Being QHI suited Nicki-Pig's temperament admirably, for his automatic interpretation of the job was that it was a requirement to walk alone, lest you be seen to be currying favours or friends; for his was the stick that wielded the ultimate power. The operational efficiency and military prowess of the Squadron's were not his concern, and as such he was not part of them nor expected to fly operationally. Thus removed from the normal hierarchy, allowed him to concentrate solely on the job he was there to do.

He homed in to me the day after my arrival, and seeing his familiar gait approach, my heart sank and I wondered what he'd have in store for me.

'Here's the syllabus for the theatre conversion course all new pilots have to pass' he said handing me a sheaf of foolscap paper. 'Have a look through it, and we'll make a start...' he glanced at his watch '...say one-thirty this afternoon?'

Nonetheless we were both to be in for a surprise. On the one hand I was straight from the conversion course at Wallop and was not only familiar but also well practiced in all the exercises, as well as not having accumulated enough helicopter-time to devise any shortcuts let alone adopt bad habits; and on the other hand, I found him to be an excellent instructor! I remember his fellow pilots in Aden saying he'd always flown by the book, which although not always desirable for operational flying where a certain amount of élan is sometimes called for, as far as handling the machine goes, it is the ultimate quality to strive for. He had flown helicopters from the start (and on seeing my logbook made a point of denigrating my accumulated fixed wing time, saying those hours counted for absolutely nothing...) and knew everything there was to know about them. We'd never flown together before and he didn't give me an easy time, and (no doubt remembering the Aden incident) kept me on an extremely tight rein, lest any previous traces of élan would be resurrected or, heaven forbid, encouraged to surface. But that was his way, and the more exacting his requirements, the more I learned – so much that by the end of the course, in spite of his regrettable manner, I regarded his instructional qualities, and not least the high standards he demanded, with the respect they deserved.

But that respect was to be shattered once again a few years later.

It is strange how Service life it moves in circles: you can have an identical and parallel career with one person, yet never actually serve together and therefore only know of them remotely, whereas others you will run across time and time again. So it was with Nicki-Pig, for the next time we met was when I was commanding the flight in Ireland. We had a fatality – one of our old hands, an experienced staff-sergeant pilot crashed his helicopter into the side of a building one night, whilst supporting a Special Forces operation. A local Board of Enquiry was convened to determine the cause of the accident – and one Major N. Swinford-Hogg was specially flown out to be the specialist adviser to the Board on helicopter operating procedures.

Since I was the officer commanding, I was invited to sit-in during the proceedings, not only as a courtesy but also to be readily at hand to advise upon any matters of a background nature as well as any local anomalies that could otherwise be open to question. As the events of the operation unfolded the members of the Board, all soldiers who had themselves not only held a command but also seen active service, immediately recognised the situation for what it was and were of the view that under combat conditions, unforeseen hazards such as this were part of the overall risk and although regrettable, sometimes unavoidable.

Not so Nicki-Pig, the only person present who had never held a command, yet was the acknowledged expert on helicopter operations. He waited until the Board had assimilated all the facts and were ready to close the proceedings, before standing up to deliver his coup de grâce.

'There is a further factor' he announced, 'and one that sheds an entirely different light on the whole matter.' He paused for greater effect, slowly regarding each member of the Board in turn, before swivelling round to face me. 'And although hitherto unmentioned, one that the Flight Commander here, will be all too familiar and doubtless hoped would pass unnoticed...'

All eyes were now turned on me, whilst I could only stare back mesmerized – and with the others, wait for him to pull whatever rabbit he had out of his hat. Instead, he undid the catches on his briefcase and brought out a blue RAF logbook, which he held in the air for everyone to see.

'This is the pilot's logbook', he announced, '...and as such a vital piece of evidence, for when I examined it, it revealed that the hours of night time logged on the type of helicopter in question, were insufficient to qualify the pilot for operational flying of this nature...'

Having delivered this bombshell he paused, allowing sufficient time for the point to sink in, before continuing in a voice that defied any opposition.

'Had the sortie been flown by a competent pilot who *had* been current on type as well as having the prescribed amount of hours, it's my belief the situation would not have arisen. An *experienced* pilot would not only have been aware of the potential hazards, but would also have been fully conversant and qualified to fly the machine throughout its maximum operating envelope. There would have been no question of his flying either beyond his own capability or in any way exceeding the limitations of the helicopter – for that's what standard operating procedures are all about; their very purpose being to minimise risk – and exactly as illustrated by this regrettable episode. So the first point I would establish is that had the rules been followed, the accident would not have happened.

'This now brings us to the second point that has to be addressed: why it was allowed to happen...?' He turned and levelled his sights squarely at me. 'Although it pains me to have to say this, but as your aviation advisor I feel it my *duty* to bring to your attention that it is the responsibility of the Officer Commanding to ensure that the pilots under his command are at all times fully conversant with their machines – and the only way to achieve this is by establishing an on-going programme of continuation training, so that all pilots are constantly practiced in every situation as well as the likely manoeuvres they may be expected to execute.

'We have already established from the logbook that the pilot only had a limited amount of experience on type – and therefore by definition, had not been qualified to fly the mission. So why did he fly it? There is only one person who's business it should be to know the level of competence of every pilot in the flight, and that's the flight commander! And yet, this is the man who detailed an inexperienced pilot to fly what was obviously a dangerous operational sortie... and that, I'm afraid gentlemen, is the root of the matter, and in my book is tantamount to negligence of duty.

'I therefore submit to the Board that the flight commander's negligence was a major contributory factor to the cause of the accident, and as such, now brings to question whether he is fit to continue in command?'

The Board were immediately out of their depth, for this was strictly a flying matter, the finer rules of which they knew little about, as well as suddenly escalating to a situation that was well beyond their brief: what had started as a routine enquiry was now a serious charge proffered by their appointed aviation adviser, against the flight commander of the unit concerned – and who's presence in the first place had only been there as a supplementary witness. Furthermore, should any mention of possible negligence be made in their report, it would automatically be picked up and become the focus of a further enquiry.

In spite of the mutual respect I thought we had established at Detmold, and where I thought we'd put aside our past differences, Nicky-Pig had reverted to character: he was still gunning for me and here was a golden opportunity to have my head delivered on a plate.

He couldn't quite conceal the smirk on his face as he sat down and it was my turn to take the floor. I faced a row of stony faces, for the seeds of doubt had been planted – by one who was the chosen representative of the Army Air Corps and had been sent as an impartial and reliable expert, against another member of the same Corps whom by implication had now been portrayed as an airy-fairy flyer who didn't take his job seriously, let alone the full responsibilities that went with it. Moreover, as the official representative, could there be more here than meets the eye? Had he perhaps been sent as devil's advocate to exploit the situation – to provoke a further case that would then be subject to further internal investigation? Certainly you don't normally wash your dirty linen in public without very good reason, but...

I stood up slowly, whilst trying to compose myself and hide my anger, as well as giving myself time to assimilate the real situation. He'd played a fast ball and I hadn't come prepared to fight my own corner; for that's what it now amounted to and my back was firmly against the wall. I looked at the faces in front of me and intuitively decided not to rise to Nick-Pig's insidious accusations; it was imperative to defuse any question of personal confrontation as quickly possible and the best way would be to be as dispassionate as possible and relate the facts as I saw them... and trust to the Board's good sense.

'Yes... as flight commander I am responsible for selecting the pilot and authorizing flights – which responsibility and decision is automatic to anyone who has been a commander in the field and difficult or not, comes with the job.' There was a flicker of understanding from two of the members and I decided to expound further on the military theme. 'Also, as with any other unit, training is the key to success and of vital importance if you are to fulfil your role. Just as infantry are initially trained in platoon in the attack in open country and then later taught to modify their tactics to suit the terrain... I don't have to tell anyone here that it takes a lot more training for the same troops to adapt to jungle warfare or the confines of close street fighting – and not least the wholly different disciplines required for long periods of internal security duty?' Their faces weren't so stony now and one or two were nodding. 'And so it is with helicopter operations in this theatre, most of which are in close support to troops operating in built-up areas. All our pilots are taught the basics of these techniques during their initial training, but you cannot expect them to be instantly proficient in a live situation; the only way to learn is to practice under actual conditions. They may be called to deliver an under-slung load to the corner of a balcony at night, or drop a sniper onto a rooftop without hovering or changing the engine note so as not to give the position away – and all this takes a lot of training, for they are no use until they can do these things, and do them faultlessly at the first attempt.

'So when Major Swinford-Hogg said it was part of my job to know the ability of the pilots under my command, he was absolutely right – and I don't have to tell any of you here that knowing your strengths – as well as your weaknesses, is the paramount requirement for any commander...' I had their full attention now and one or two were making notes.

'... And again Major Swinford-Hogg was correct when he said the pilot's logbook is a vital document. It is, for it's the only complete record any pilot has – and by virtue of its layout, can also be used as an on-going reference to assess a pilot's experience and ability. Allow me to explain... I'm not too familiar with the layout of civilian logbooks, but the Service logbook is designed to analyse every minute spent in the air. Each flight is recorded on a separate line that spreads through two pages of columns that itemize every activity. On the left-hand page it starts with the month, date, type of aircraft, its number, the name of the captain or co-pilot and the duty of the flight. The line then follows through to the right-hand page where the actual flight time is broken down and entered into columns for day or night flying, whether as first pilot, second pilot or dual – which in our case usually means under instruction. This breakdown is then added up and shown in the next column as total time and then a further calculation in the following column to show captain time. Then there are further columns to record instrument time – both simulated and actual and also the type and number of actual instrument approaches the pilot has executed.

'Every flight, no matter how long its duration is recorded on a separate line, with the hours and minutes broken down into these categories. At the end of each month a line is ruled under the last entry, and the columns are then added vertically and entered into a box. Thus we now have a monthly summary that analyses the pilot's every activity – and in order to prevent fictitious or exaggerated entries, logbooks are submitted each month to the officer in command of the unit, who then signs it as an authentic record. So now you see the real value a logbook has, for if used correctly, it's the best management tool a unit commander could ever wish for...

'Which now brings me to Major Swinford-Hogg's observation that the pilot in question had only a limited amount of night hours on the Gazelle helicopter...'

I went on to explain that the Gazelle was relatively new to the Flight, and the pilot in question had been one of the last to convert to it. But far from being inexperienced, he had in excess of two thousand hours on Scouts – the Gazelle's immediate predecessor – in which he had executed countless similar night operations on active service in this theatre, as well as being familiar with some of the more exacting demands required by the Special Forces; so much that the unit in question had specifically asked for him by name, which request I had fully endorsed. Far from being unaware of his flying skills, as flight commander I rated him as one of the best pilots in the unit. He had been flying on a regular basis for over twenty years, and prior to helicopters had accumulated over two and a half thousand hours as an army fixed wing pilot, together with the relevant instrument and night ratings. It so happened that I could also vouch for him from that time, as we had been members of the same Flight. All in all, his experience amounted to just under five thousand hours, which is a lot of time when you consider the average duration of a flight is usually under an hour. His experience far surpassed the majority of the other pilots in the Flight, and in my opinion he had been more than qualified to fly the mission – and better than most.

Nicki-Pig immediately jumped up and countered by reiterating that fixed-wing time was not accountable as far as helicopters were concerned, and whatever his prior experience on Scouts, the facts were the facts and were recorded in his logbook, an accountable document, and were therefore irretrievable.

It was impasse and we glared at each other across the table.

The Members of the Board looked at each other in an embarrassed silence, and then the President took a grip and announced that since the proceedings had seemingly degenerated into what amounted to a personal confrontation between two senior officers of the same Corps, a more formal attitude would have to be adopted, and although regrettable, would the two of us now mind leaving the room so the Board could be left to their deliberations?

Needless to say, we didn't speak. We sat in a featureless adjoining room whilst I attempted to do the Telegraph crossword and he became absorbed with the contents of his briefcase, which appeared to contain an unfathomable amount of official looking documents.

Forty-five minutes later we were asked back. The Board sat in silence as we resumed our seats – almost as though we were the ones on trial.

The President sat studying his notes for a moment, and then cleared his throat before stating that he would go through each of his points one by one. He started by relating that the Board had been convened to investigate the loss of a Gazelle helicopter whilst on active service, together with the death of its pilot – who had been the sole occupant at the time. He then went on to say that from statements received from the manufacturers and also other engineering specialists, confirmed that there was no evidence of mechanical or other structural failure, and the accident was clearly a result of the rotor blades striking the building. In view of the hazardous nature of the mission and the fact that it was at night would therefore suggest that in all probability it was a case of misjudgement by the pilot. They had then addressed the question of whether he had been sufficiently qualified to fly the sortie – as brought to their attention by their technical advisor. This they had discussed at length, taking into consideration his accumulated experience as an army pilot together with the testimony proffered by his flight commander, and were in unanimous agreement that in practical terms the pilot had been so qualified. Their finding therefore was that the accident was as a result of pilot error, whilst manoeuvring close to the ground when in close support to ground forces during a night operation. Circumstances such as these inevitably created situations where calculated risks were sometimes called for, and as such deemed to be one of the hazards of war.

Red in the face, Nicki-Pig gathered his papers and without a word to anybody, stomped out.

II

Nevertheless, he had his own command now – and fate had decreed that I was to become part of it. Had I known there would have been any likelihood of his sitting in that chair, even as a stand-in, would have been another compelling reason not to have chosen the route I had embarked upon; but it had happened and the die was now cast.

'So, best let bygones be bygones; start afresh and all that – and we'll just have to see how things develop...' he continued, his steely eyes at contrast to the forced smile on his face. 'As I said, I heard you were coming, and – well, in this job the actual selection of instructors is beyond my jurisdiction – but once here, we work as a team and for as long as I'm in command that is my concern and responsibility. As an instructor you have reached the pinnacle of the flying profession and to do it properly you have to be totally dedicated to the job. It's a serious business... and as I said earlier, not one suited to the casual attitude typically adopted by some of you donkey-wallopers, let alone any sort of lone maverick! So, to start off I'm going to put you with the civilian instructors in Elementary and we'll just see how you get on...'

Although it was rumoured that at some time in the future the basic training for helicopter pilots was likely to be pooled into a central school for all three services, this was still to come, and at Wallop the basic helicopter training was still a legacy from the time when there were few serving army pilots who had an instructor's ticket, and as such was still mostly staffed by civilian instructors who worked on a contract basis. The contract was simple: instructors had a sixty-hour timeframe in which to teach students basic helicopter piloting skills to a recognised and acceptable standard. This, in spite of the fact it was the period of greatest fallout throughout the whole of the twelve-month army-flying course, and on average only about half reached the required standard in the time available. On completion, the successful candidates would then progress to the next stage of their training where they would learn to fly tactically, as well as all the other things expected from an army pilot. This would take a further 120 hours, and in view of its increasing military flavour, instructors were ideally selected from the growing pool of serving pilots who had passed through Central Flying School at RAF Shawbury, and thereby qualified to have the hallowed letters QHI affixed to their names in military records.

One thing Nicki-Pig was right about though, and that was about instructors being a dedicated and select breed; for as well as being able to fly well they also had to have the ability to teach, which is a totally different calling. The latter quality was one I still had to find out about – and thinking about Bernard's astute observation in the French restaurant, couldn't help wondering whether it would suit my temperament? From my experience gained in twenty years of army flying, as well as commanding a flight on active service, I'd have thought my expertise would have been put to better use by imparting the hard-learnt strategies used in Ireland, rather than being relegated to elementary circuit-bashing – but then, someone had to do it, and in any event, it would be a sure way of testing my temperament...

III

'Nobody knows the fullest depths and intricate workings of the human brain.' The Padre smiled at me from his corner of the pew, where we sat at the back of the church. 'From what you have described, I would almost certainly say it was a creation – and I say this carefully, a *figment* of your imagination. Of *course* the Church knows about and accepts the presence of ghosts. We even use the word – Holy Ghost and Holy Spirit in our everyday language – and this usage alone acknowledges our acceptance and understanding of the supernatural. The modern world has bypassed many of the old superstitions; but they are still there, and mankind is just as ignorant about things to which he cannot actually attach a label. The church has always been aware of the powers of good and evil – and also how they can be manipulated...'

'But Padre, it wasn't a dream or a figment of my imagination – I was very much awake and I could actually *feel* the presence. It was a total awareness... it's difficult to explain...'

'Maybe, but dreams are not only about your subconscious recalling *actual* events. More often than not dreams are embroidered by your subconscious – bent into what you want to accept. Let me try to give you a simple example... say you dream about somebody you know – it may be a person you last met ten or fifteen years ago, or it even could be somebody who is now dead. The person – this person whom you know and recall in your dream – let's say it was your bank manager and you only ever met him when he was in his office wearing a dark suit? Yet when you recall him in your dream, he may be wearing a flowery open-neck shirt and Bermudan shorts! In real life you never once saw him dressed so casually, but in your dream you may have met him on the beach and he's now portrayed as such. It's the same person, the same mannerisms, the same smile – you can remember every detail about him, and probably far more than if you had to describe him to somebody in the cold light of day. So why hasn't he come dressed in his normal dark suit? Your subconscious has played with the image! The smile, the mannerisms, maybe even the smell of his after-shave – they are all exact, yet in your dream not only has he different clothes, you can also see he has knobbly knees, hairs on his chest and a golden chain around his neck! And the strange thing is, should you happen to meet him tomorrow, you'd look to see whether the chain made a mark under his white shirt – for you'd know it was there!

'And as for your being awake when you felt your presence – there's also a simple explanation for that, for there are many degrees of wakefulness. You can be wide-awake, you can be drowsy, you can be lightly asleep or you can be deep asleep. In all these instances the mind has different parameters in which to act. How often have you been half asleep sitting in an armchair in front of the fire and the telephone on the table beside you rings? You are awake enough to pick it up, say hello and then recognize the voice as well as visualize the person who is ringing. But your voice and brain are not properly in gear – you know what you want to say, but you can't speak properly, and in all probability mumble something that's totally irrelevant? And the next morning the person who rang you says, "What on earth were you talking about last night?" – and you can't remember a thing!

'Oh yes, the mind can play dangerous tricks, especially when you think you are wide-awake when in fact you're far from it! Does this sound at all familiar – could you have been half asleep and allowed your subconscious to do the rest – just as it put a chain around the bank manager's neck?'

'Mmm. Well yes, I suppose that could be an explanation – but it seemed very real at the time...'

'I don't know enough about you or your background, but I suspect this is a case of your having a deep-rooted anxiety that your subconscious is exploiting. As I said earlier, nobody knows the full depths and intricacies of the human brain... You have come to me as a priest, and as such I can help with – ah, *spiritual* matters – or at least I could put you in touch with someone from the church whose speciality it is, but from what you have said, I think this is more likely to come

100

from within. I'm not trying to fob you off or anything, but have you considered seeing a psychiatrist?'

He got up and smoothed his cassock down, and then changed his mind and knelt down beside me. 'But whilst you are here, join me in a little prayer. In this modern age the power of prayer is often underrated and if you learn to apply your mind, praying can also be an extremely effective way of speaking to your subconscious...'

Outside, as I walked away in the bright sunlight, the protective cloak of the church diminished with each step. It had been good to be able to talk to somebody, but instinctively I knew he was wrong. Undoubtedly there was an element that came from within – or at least as far as being receptive to whatever it was ... but deep down I knew there was more to it than that. And as for seeing a psychiatrist!

Which of course, was the chink my subconscious was looking for.

IV

For the second time that day I set the helicopter down in a disused corner of the airfield and reduced the engine revolutions to idle, leaving the feathered rotor blades to swish round over our heads.

My two students couldn't have been more different. The first had been a boyish twenty-one year old subaltern who had just passed out of Sandhurst – one of the new direct entry officers into the Army Air Corps – who's very shyness and youth, whilst wholly endearing as person, made me inwardly question whether he was mature enough to survive the remainder of the course, let alone cope with the daily rigours of life as a squadron pilot. No matter how well you can fly, senior passengers tend to look for maturity and self-assurance in a pilot – and for that matter, so do a section of infantry when being flown into the attack. In spite of the awe in which he obviously regarded me, his enthusiasm and willingness to learn was boundless as well as infectious and more than made up for his youthful demeanour.

Which could not be said for my other pupil, a thirty-eight year old REME Staff Sergeant who had a life-weary look about him, having seen and done it all. Old by military standards to be accepted as aircrew, the cut-off age normally being thirty-three, he had worked his way up from Craftsman to Staff Sergeant specialising in vehicle electronics and now had reached as far as he could go, and therefore regarded flying as a viable alternative, as well as being a cushy number. Having been a specialist throughout his career, far from being overawed by the status of a flying instructor he soon left me in no doubt that he also regarded most officers with disdain. He paid lip service when necessary, but other than that, officers were a burden and as such had to be carried by people like him. Nonetheless, contrary to his general air of worldliness, his records showed that he had never left the confines of a base workshop, which made me realize he actually knew very little about the army or how it really worked.

'Now Staff, these can be tricky animals until you get to know them, so I find its best to start from basics...'

'I've yet to come across any machine that I can't handle ...'

I decided to ignore him. 'But it's still an aeroplane, and you successfully completed sixty hours on a basic trainer, so tell me, what makes an aeroplane fly?'

'Well, it's got wings...'

I could see this was going to be hard work, so much that I considered shutting the helicopter down – it had been a very different lesson with my young subaltern this morning. 'Okay, it's got wings' I decided to persevere 'and what makes wings fly?'

'Well, you've got to have airspeed to fly.'

'Exactly, or to be more precise airflow over the wings, which in a fixed wing aircraft is achieved by forward motion – and this is where the helicopter differs. The rotors are wings, and by spinning them we ...'

'Look, we've learnt all this in ground school, I know how a chopper works.'

'Don't interrupt, oh, and it's customary to call instructors "sir". No matter what the rank of a flying instructor, even if it is a fellow Sergeant, you will address him as "sir" when you are in an aircraft. It's a courtesy that we all observe, and I'm sure you were advised of that during your preliminary fixed wing training?' He bit his lip and looked out of the window. 'Now, I know you've covered the theory of helicopter flight in the classroom, but I'm giving you an opportunity to try it on a real machine. So, we've got some wings that are now spinning over our heads, and we rev the engine up like this... the throttle is a twist grip, same as a motorcycle and it's on the end of the collective lever – that's the lever that looks like a handbrake down by your side. So, you wind the engine up until the rotor revolutions – they're shown on this dial here – increase, until the needle's in between these two graduated marks on the dial. This is the most important dial on the facia, for if the needle falls below the mark means you have insufficient airflow over the blades to give lift – the same as having insufficient airspeed in a fixed wing aeroplane – and with not enough centrifugal force, the blades will fold up and you'll fall out of the sky.

'At the moment the rotors are flat with negative incidence, so in order to fly we gradually pull up on the collective... and that alters the pitch of the blades until they begin to bite into the air. Listen, you can hear them beginning to whomp, and also note there's a corresponding decrease in rotor revs, so as you pull up, gradually twist on a bit more throttle...

'You can now feel she wants to fly, but before we lift off, just consider what's going to happen the moment she lifts off the ground? As an engineer, I don't have to explain what torque is... so you'll know that the whole machine will want to turn in the opposite direction to the spin of the rotors. To counteract this, we have the small propeller that's set as far back as possible on the tail. This gives sideways thrust to counter the torque, and like the main rotor is controlled by altering the pitch of the blade. So now we have an adjustable

103

means of directional control and just the same as the rudder bar on an aircraft is controlled by your feet – only instead of waggling a rudder, the pedals alter the pitch of the tail rotor. So, I'll just lift her up a foot... and we're now in the hover... and put your feet lightly on the pedals and get the feel of her...'

The helicopter made a sickening lurch to the left as he put his feet on the duplicate set of pedals, completely overriding the pressure of my feet when I tried to correct. I hastily lowered the collective and set it down on the grass again.

'Now, what you've got to remember is that *all* the controls on a helicopter are extremely sensitive. Hardly *any* physical movement is required – and the best way is to *think* the movement through and just let the machine follow. You'll remember from your fixed wing flying that the greater the airspeed, the stiffer the controls become? Then the other extreme, when at a slow airspeed there's less airflow over the control surfaces, so they require larger movements? Well, that doesn't happen on a helicopter because the lift is constant: it's either flying or its not – and that's determined by the needle in between these two marks here, which is why I said it was the most important dial in the cockpit. You've got to develop a real sense of feel for the machine. The other thing to remember is that you've only got one source of power. If you pull up too much on the collective, it will rob power from the tail rotor and it won't be able to hold you straight. *Every* manoeuvre you execute will require a change of power, which is why they placed the throttle readily to hand on the end of the collective. Allow me demonstrate...

'Wind the power up; watch the needle and bring it between the marks, and then gently pull up on the collective. She wants to turn, so a little more pressure on the left pedal... just enough to keep her straight, to counter the torque... and we're nice and steady in the hover again. Now, if I pull up more collective I need more power and more pedal... and then if I pull even more collective – we've now run out of pedal and the machine is starting to pirouette. See what I mean? Peter's robbing Paul – and to stop it turning, just ease off on the collective a touch... and we're in control again.' I lowered the machine back onto the grass.

'So now you know how to go up and down and how to keep her straight, let's look at the last control, which is the cyclic stick and controls horizontal movement. The main rotor is fixed on a pivot, and the cyclic is used to tilt the rotor in the direction you want to go. Push it forward and you go forwards, pull it back and you go backwards – you can stir it like a pudding and the machine will follow the stick... only remember, you only have to *think* your hand into moving.

'So, for the remainder of this lesson, I want you to get the feel of each control in turn. We'll start with the pedals... put your hands and feet on, but only lightly for I'll be looking after the other controls, and I want you to concentrate solely on the pedals. When I lift off, I want you to point the machine at that clump of trees in the corner of the field over there – okay?'

'Right – sir.'

I remembered the first time I took control of a helicopter, and tried to emulate the same degree of patience and understanding that Mr. Roberts, my long-suffering instructor had – even to the point of using the same clump of trees he'd used as a reference point. How the machine had vibrated and tried to tear itself apart and how this was transmitted back through each of the controls. Unlike an aircraft's rudder bar that has a positive feeling, the pedals felt spongy and, connected through their complicated linkage, take time to take effect – only to find that by then it's too late and you'd over-controlled! The trick is to anticipate the time lag. Then there's the cyclic stick, which has a mind of its own. Above all, this transmits the most vibration fed back from the whirling blades overhead. This, Mr. Roberts explained was because of the cyclic action of the blades. By moving the cyclic stick in any direction causes the rotating blades to increase their pitch and move higher on one half of their circle while feathering on the other half. The faster the horizontal speed, the greater the cyclic effect, until you reach the limit that the mechanism can cope with, and again is determined by the upper graduation mark on the all-important rotor-revolutions dial on the facia.

It was he who had taught me to master one control at a time; first the pedals, then the collective and throttle, and finally the cyclic, which meant you then had full control of the machine, whirring and vibrating about you, every part wanting to go in its own direction and the only way to keep them together was by trying to average their various motions.

By the end of half an hour it was a very sweaty and subdued Staff Sergeant who clambered out of the cockpit.

'Not bad Staff – it's always difficult the first time. The trick is to relax and play all the controls together, rather than trying to correct them one at a time. If you only concentrate on one, the others will take over and lead you a merry dance all over the sky... you have to be ambidextrous and work them altogether and then you'll find the machine will begin to behave! Anyway, think it through and we'll give it another go tomorrow...'

V

It was strange to be living in the mess as a bachelor officer again. At least they'd given me a decent room – one, I suppose that befitted my rank and newly acquired status as 'permanent staff'; but there it ended and I felt out of place and almost an intruder amongst the other living-in members, who were mostly subalterns and young captains. I'd last lived-in when I'd been a student myself some twenty years before, but thereafter my brief postings to Wallop had been as a married officer, when you only used the mess at lunchtimes or for the odd formal evening. I sat in a corner armchair in the large anteroom with an unread magazine on my lap and looked about me. The grouping of the chairs and tables were as before, the coffee in the corner smelt the same, the pictures on the wall were all old friends – all in all, the ambience and atmosphere was totally familiar in every aspect, except the people, who were all new.

And this was supposed to be my home Mess!

I imagined it must be rather like being an expatriate, who when abroad fondly talks, thinks and remembers the ethos of a particular place, village, or even England as home; only to find on return that time has moved on. When abroad you are a member of an isolated society, and in order to work and socialise in acceptable harmony, you unwittingly compromise your situation by adopting a common set of values. It therefore comes as a rude shock to realize that you were the one in isolation and your carefully preserved ideals no longer have significance or particular relevance when back in the place you so fondly remembered; for here you are no longer remembered: a stranger seemingly alone in a familiar but otherwise alien environment.

I couldn't help feeling a little sorry for young Stephen Grant – my boyish pupil, whom I noticed standing with a group of other students by the door. Newly commissioned into the Army Air Corps, he would never know what it's like to belong to a regiment, which from its compact size can be likened to a close-knit family, and once accepted, you always remain part of the family and welcomed back as such, no matter where you'd been, or for how long you'd been away. I remember feeling this same sense of loss when I first transferred into the Army Air Corps and realised that unlike the select club-like membership of a regiment, the mess at Middle Wallop was also obliged to embrace members from the numerous arms that were directly or indirectly connected with army aviation, as well as having the overall flexibility to cope with the transitory nature of a training organisation. Stephen Grant's memories of his home mess would be associated with the members of his course, and he would have to pass out and serve with an operational Squadron before he would be able to appreciate the proper aspect of mess life. For then it becomes very different, and like a regiment or any other select organisation, the unit is of a size that can readily absorb and be influenced by the qualities of its Commanding Officer – which is what it is all about...

'Excuse me sir, telephone call for you...'

'Oh...?' It was one of the old retainers, who had been there as a mess steward since my student days, but whom I doubt remembered me.

'Foreign sounding gentleman by the sounds of it' he said with a sniff, 'I've put the call through to the lobby in the 'all, sir.'

I made my way to the door, and gave Stephen Grant a smile as he deferentially opened it for me. The phone in the kiosk was off its hook and I could hear a metallic voice impatiently saying '...'Allo, 'Allo, where is somebody?' as I picked it up.

'Hi, Bernard? – Thought it must be you! The mess steward said it...'

'A-ha, there you are, I 'ave got it for you!'

'Got what?'

'An aeroplane, I said I would find one for you...'

'Oh – well, right; I just hadn't thought...'

'Eh-hue, it is a sweet little thing... you'll love it! I found it at Darois and have had it professionally refurbished in the factory. I've put it on the English register and had it done up. For *you*!'

'But Bernard, I'm sorry if I misled you; it was only an idea – just a thought really, I didn't want you to... How much is it?'

'Never mind that for now, first I show it you – I'll fly it down to Middle Wallop tomorrow...'

'Bernard, wait! – Just hang on a minute. First, what sort of aeroplane is it?'

'I just told you; I found it at Darois, it was traded in for a new one and I have had it 'specially done up...'

'What, a Robin?'

'Yes, yes, of course a Robin. A D100 – the little two-seater, but with a small seat behind, enough for some luggage or a child maybe... it 'as a 105hp Potez engine that 'as been specially tuned, so it cruises at about 'undred and thirty and burns about four and 'alf gallons per hour. This was the aircraft they then developed into the DR250 with a 150hp engine...'

108

'So it's the original tail-wheel model – with air brakes?' remembering my afternoon with Julien at the factory.

'Yes, yes – of course a tail wheel, and no – this one 'as flaps, e-hue, as well as a full panel; a VOR and a 360 channel radio – one that works this time! So you can go anywhere in it. I know you like plenty of knobs to play with. So, I can show it to you tomorrow and...'

'Not so fast! It's Thursday tomorrow and I'm flying all day, and again all day on Friday. What about Saturday – oh, and better fly to Thruxton, it's just up the road from here. I could meet you about midday...?'

'Eh-hue. Saturday? – Let me see... I suppose I could make Saturday' he muttered, as I visualized him thumbing through his diary. 'I'd better ring you before I – eh-hue, tell me what is the best number to get you there, it took an awful time...? No, better still, you ring me! Ring me at nine sharp on Saturday and I'll 'ave the weather... Okay?' Then with a brief 'C'iao', he hung up.

Which gave me a lot to think about before Saturday.

VI

'Right, you seem to have the hover sorted out, it's time we took it off the patch and tried a circuit.' I said to Stephen Grant two days later. 'Call the Tower and ask permission to hover-taxi to the takeoff point and we'll give it a whirl.'

He had progressed well the previous day and was proving to be a promising pupil. 'No need to set her down unless there are others on the approach. Call the Tower again now, and ask permission to lift-off, and then when you reach the point, turn into wind and climb away. We'll do a gentle climb-out, so aim for sixty knots on the cyclic and enough collective to give a rate of climb of three hundred feet per minute. As it's your first time I'll make it easy for you, so climb straight ahead to eight hundred feet, then level-off before turning right into a standard right-hand pattern – okay?'

'Right, sir.' He frowned with concentration as he twitched the controls to maintain the speed with the rate of climb. The helicopter yawed from side to side with the forward speed fluctuating between forty and eighty knots and the corresponding rate of climb alternating between zero and four hundred feet per minute as we waltzed into the sky.

'That's it – try and relax your hold on the controls and just let it flow. Eight hundred feet now, so level off and increase your speed to ninety knots. Now we're moving forward you'll find there's a different feel to her; we're in clean air and also out of the ground-effect... that's it, try and maintain your height and let the speed settle – trade one for the other and adjust the power accordingly. Sort it out and get the feel of straight and level flight, there's plenty of time before we start the turn.'

The familiar countryside slipped by below and not for the first time I wondered whether I was doing the right thing. Buy an aeroplane! But at least I hadn't committed myself yet and could always back out... nonetheless there was an excitement inside me that was forever leading me forward. I hadn't had time to fully exploit the possibilities of keeping it at Wallop, but the few feelers I'd put out had been met with a certain amount of resistance, so I'd decided to tread cautiously on that and had phoned the airport managers at Popham and Thruxton instead. Popham wasn't a real airfield but just a landing strip and the person I'd talked to had said hangar space was limited and most of the aircraft were tied down outside. So I'd discounted Popham and tried Thruxton; after all, a lightweight wood and fabric machine really ought to be kept inside. And yes, they had plenty of hangar space available, but the price varied depending on the amenities and position and it would be best to pop over and have a look. So I'd arranged to meet the manager at eleven o'clock – which would give time to have a look and discuss terms before Bernard flew in at midday...

'Okay, you're getting there, so now let's try a ninety-degree turn to the right – without losing or gaining any height – nothing too violent, just think it through and let the machine follow...'

I must ask Bernard what the actual costs of running an aircraft are. Apart from the purchase price, there were the running costs – Av-gas, what did he say, four? gallons per hour? That seems fairly stringent – especially if she cruises at 130knots – surely it can't be as fast as that, I wonder if he meant mph? Then there'll be hangarage, insurance and of course maintenance... is it on a C of A, which will mean it will have to be stripped down every three years by licensed engineers, and doubtless would cost a fortune; or alternatively it could be on a Permit, which would mean I'd be able to do much of the routine stuff myself? Then, is it the right aeroplane? That's the big question, for Bernard's ideas differed somewhat from mine. Apart from being prone to rust, I rather liked the ruggedness and short-strip perform-ance of that Rallye... although it was very slow and noisy and consumed nine gallons an hour. Compared to the Robin, that's pretty thirsty – in fact it would be double the running cost of the Robin... and no doubt because of its size, hangarage would cost more as well – unless I kept it outside, but then would that only invite more rust? And after all, do I really need the luxury of four full seats? It would make sense if I took paying passengers, but that would never be the case, so a two-plus-two – the same as a sports car, would make a lot more sense...

'Downwind vital actions complete, and the airfield is nicely positioned for a turn onto base leg, just the same as a normal circuit, so start your turn now – keep it nice and gentle, and then start to reduce height to four hundred feet in readiness to turn onto finals...'

So maybe Bernard's choice of an economical yet simple and practicable aircraft isn't so far-out after all? He also said it had a full panel, a decent radio and a VOR, so it'll be able to go anywhere – I wonder what its range is? But most of all would depend on its strip performance... that's my sort of flying and I'll base my decision on that. If it's rugged enough to operate out of fields – to land without bending its under-carriage and has an acceptable takeoff run and climb-out performance, what more do I need?

'Okay, swing round onto finals now, you're doing very well! There's one thing you must watch though, every time you press the radio transmit button, your attitude and revs go to pot! It's a common mistake and means you're gripping the cyclic stick too tightly. Just because you have to press a button on it shouldn't distract you from its proper function. Right, see the end marker on the runway – that's our spot! We fly down a line and then flare the helicopter to kill the remaining forward speed, before setting it down by that first marker. I'll show you what I mean – I have control.'

'You have control, sir.'

'Leave your hands and feet lightly on and follow me through. Speed back initially to fifty-five and set up a steady rate of decent... We're going nicely for the spot now... and about here, begin to flare – cyclic back and cushion the forward momentum with collective – keep the power up, and watch those rotor revs or we'll fall out of the sky. Got it? Nice flowing movement – cyclic and collective together – and here we are back in the hover, three feet above the ground, and we can set it down.'

'Wow! That was great, sir. You made it as though the machine was part of yourself.'

'Don't worry, it soon comes and you're getting the feel of it. By the end of next week you'll be doing the same and wondering what all the fuss was about! Now, I'm going to get out and I want you to hover-taxi back to dispersal on your own. Keep pace with my walk and don't go any faster. Just do as you've been doing, only remember the helicopter will be lighter without my weight, and if you get into difficulties, just set her down.'

I got out and without looking back, began to walk back to the dispersal. I heard the engine note change as the blades began to bite and then felt the downwash as he lifted off. Then like a large dog, he followed me back to dispersal, rising and falling slightly on an invisible sea of air.

VII

The luminous dial on my watch said it was two-twenty and this time I knew straightaway what had woken me. I felt a surge of elation pass through me; maybe now I'd be able to prove something and show that I'd been right all along in spite of what the padre had said – but first, to make sure, am I really awake, or am I still in a state of half-sleep, as he'd suggested?

I reached out for my watch and checked the time again: definitely two-twenty in the morning, so now drop it on the floor! If I can remember that in the morning, it should be real enough. So, what else? The room is still too hot, in spite of my efforts earlier to turn the radiator down; I can pinch my leg and feel the pain; now, close my book that I had left face down – and... and my presence is still there, standing at the foot of the bed! Now, what were all those things I was going to ask...?

'Hello' I said instead.

The atmosphere lightened. 'Hello' she said.

'You managed to find me then?'

'Yes, I know how to look now.'

'You're not dead, are you!' I said, still trying to remember 'you're not a ghost or a lost soul, so why is it you come... why do you come to me? If you're alive, how can you – what did you call it, travel? And how do you know where I am – is it some sort of astral-projection or whatever they call it? And who – who are you?'

'My, all these questions!'

'Well, I've been thinking – and, and well, I'm beginning to come to terms with it – in fact, I was half expecting you, only I thought maybe you couldn't find me. I even tried to will you to come after that time you came to me in France...'

'Did you! Have you been thinking of me?'

'Of course – after all this, what d'you expect!'

'It doesn't matter where you are physically. I can reach you wherever you are...'

'Can you reach me in the day, or do you only travel at night?'

'I don't know – it's difficult and I haven't tried it in the day; there's too much distraction, and anyway, I doubt whether you'd be receptive during the day?'

'Oh – well tell me, have we actually met in real life? I mean, in this life?' I said, remembering another of my questions. Besides, already I could feel the vision beginning to pulse.

She reached out with one of her arms, as though in a gesture of farewell as the pulsations became stronger. 'Shhh! Too many questions and I haven't the strength to stay any longer...'

I quickly sat up to see if I could see her any better, but she was still only a vague outline, coming and going. I stretched my right arm out towards her and immediately felt a slight tingling in my fingers, as though a current flowed between us. 'You'll come again?'

'Of course' she said, and then was no more.

I turned the light on and then got up and went to the writing table. "I am writing this at two twenty-five in the morning, and have just said goodbye to my ghost" I wrote, "she said I asked too many questions!"

There, we'll see if that's there in the morning!

VIII

'Right Staff, it's time we got this hover sorted out. We can't progress until you've mastered it and only *you* can do that! You're still fighting the controls one at a time and you've got to learn to operate them together. Just relax, feel the machine through your bottom and try to *anticipate* what it's going to do. Gentle movements – hardly any at all, just try to *think* the movement through.' We'd been at it for forty minutes and he was no further forward than the day before.

'I know, sir. It's just that – I can't get the hang of doing one thing with one hand and another with the other...'

114

'Never mind, some people find it difficult at first, but it *will* come. So let's try again – just forget I'm here, take your time and think it through.'

The machine lurched into the air and immediately began to pirouette to the left. He jabbed down with his right foot and in doing so yanked up on the collective. The machine reared up like a startled horse and the rotor revs fell beneath the mark. He then pushed down to the point that we almost achieved weightlessness, straining in the straps. 'I have!' I managed to catch it before we hit the ground and then gently brought it back up into the hover at three feet. I held it steady for a while, letting him feel the controls and then gave it back to him. Within two seconds we started to drift backwards. 'I'll not be beaten by any bloody machine' he muttered through gritted teeth, and pushed the cyclic firmly forwards. Our nose dipped and we gathered speed and then crashed onto the grass and slithered forward as he dumped collective, which was the last thing I'd expected and was unable to catch in time.

'Okay, enough for today – I've got her!' The landing had been hard, but the forward motion had cushioned the worst of the shock and I'd witnessed worse landings with overloaded machines on active service. I hover-taxied back, testing the controls as I went and set her down outside the dispersal. 'Right, I want you to shut the engine down and then wait here. I'll be back in a minute...'

David White, the senior instructor was standing by the door of his office and had seen the whole thing. 'David, I hate to admit defeat, but maybe it's me – I'm still new to this game, do you think you could...?'

'Of course, that's what I'm here for. Who is it, Staff Sergeant Wilcox? Let's see if he can give me a better ride!' Without another word he collected his helmet and walked out to the helicopter, which blades were still slowly turning and got in. I watched him buckle-up, don his helmet and then turn to talk to Staff Wilcox. After a while the engine wound up again and the rotors began to turn. I bit my lip and wondered whether I hadn't been too hasty – for I had now put myself in a position whereby I was also under test. Either way David would be scrupulously fair with his judgement. He'd been an instructor for most of his life; first in the RAF and then as a civilian when he'd retired, and he would know instantly whether the student had the makings or whether it was my instructing techniques that were at fault. It was an aspect of the job I hadn't considered – the other side of the penny, for when I'd been a student I'd regarded instructors as being one step away from God: their word was final and they could do no wrong! But now I knew that students were given every possible chance; I hadn't cared for Staff Wilcox's attitude at the start, and perhaps had been too hard on him? Enough to affect the delicate relationship that one strives to achieve between instructor and student, so that they always give of their best? Already I could visualise Nicki-Pig licking his lips and waiting for the kill...

After half an hour the helicopter returned from the corner of the field that David used, paused into the hover and then settled quietly down. There'd been nothing wrong with that landing, so perhaps... I went inside and busied myself by writing up Stephen Grant's notes.

Ten minutes later David White popped his head round the corner and asked me into his office. 'No co-ordination whatsoever' he announced. 'I'm surprised you persevered with him as long as you did – waste of time and taxpayers money. He'll never fly a helicopter as long as he's got a – well, never mind! In fact I'm surprised he managed to pass through his basic fixed wing training: the man's all arms, legs and feet. Especially feet, bloody great clodhoppers! So, I've put him on review and given him an extra hour tuition-time to see if he can get it together – I usually ask Bill to do that; no reflection on you, but it's usual practice to give them a change of instructor. After Bill's had a go, he'll have another check ride with me. If I find there's no improvement – which, frankly I very much doubt, he'll be returned to unit. The system is designed to give them every chance, but my message to you is, don't let it run for so long next time! If you're not sure, wheel 'em in straight away for a second opinion; as I said before, that's what I'm here for. It also gives me a chance to set the wheels turning and keep the process as short as possible. That way it not only saves time and money, but it's better for everyone...

'Right – umm, let me see; Freddie's got three students at the moment, so I'll reallocate one of his to you. There's always a bit of weeding out at the start of a course – yes, here we are, Sergeant Lane, 17/21st Lancers – you're ex-cavalry aren't you, or what our revered Temporary Chief Flying Instructor would call a Donky-Walloper? Never could understand the pecking order of your Pongo regiments – anyway, this chap's a Lancer so you should speak the same language! He should be in the crew room waiting for his lesson now, so you can take him straight away! I'll tell Freddie when he gets down.'

I first went to the filing cabinet where we keep the student reports; extracted Sergeant Lane's file and scanned through the reports on his last two lessons. Most of his ratings were around average or slightly above, and the comments written in the remarks column closely resembled the comments I'd recently written about Stephen Grant.

He was sitting on his own in the student's crew room, a small dapper man who even managed to look neat and well turned-out in the standard issue olive-green flying suit. He got up when I entered the room.

'Hello – Sergeant Lane? I'm your new instructor...'

'Sir!'

'It's alright, it's nothing you've done – we sometimes have a re-shuffle as the course progresses; it's in your best inter-ests – and thinking back to when I was a student, I always found I learned something new whenever I had a change of instructor!' May as well let him know I'm a product from the same stable. 'Besides, at the moment Mr. Freeman's coping with three of you, which means one of you is always waiting around...'

'Excuse me sir, but aren't you Staff Sergeant Wilcox's instruC-tor – does that mean he's off the course?' He had a quaint delivery of speech, stressing the occasional hard syllable either at the end or in the middle of a word, which gave his sentences a certain emphasis as well as a peculiar staccato effect. I'd come across it before and seemed to remember it was a dialect used in parts of Nottinghamshire.

'My, my – I can see you don't miss much! But you're quite right; Staff Wilcox is having a spot of trouble with his co-ordination and has been given an extra hour to sort it out – and to give him every possible chance, it's also policy to change his instructor. But, I've read the notes on your progress and you seem to be up to the mark so far, so let's go and do a circuit and show me what you can do?'

His attitude relaxed once we'd strapped ourselves into the helicopter. It always happens this way and is something I'd noticed so many times before. People who sit in the seats behind are strictly passengers: they become so much weight; a variable factor that affects the performance of the aircraft. But whoever sits in the front beside you (we rarely have the luxury of a co-pilot), be they Private soldier or General, they cannot help but become involved; and as such can be likened as crew. In that seat they share the same set of instruments, hear the same transmissions on the radio and see the same things the instant you see them; it is the ultimate equaliser and there's no place for status or rank; mind and being are totally absorbed, focused on the business in hand – until such time you land again.

'Okay, take her up – sixty knots forward airspeed and rate of climb three hundred feet per minute.' I said as we reached the spot.

'Why that com- bination?' he asked. 'Why not fifty knots and four hundred fee-T per minute?'

In spite of his quaint manner or speech, I liked this man's mind. 'Good question! Unlike a fixed wing aircraft that has a designated "best climbing speed" that's matched to the available power, which then gives the maximum rate of climb, in a helicopter you can vary the combination to whatever you like within the power envelope. You can feed all the power into the collective and go straight up with zero forward speed, or go to the other extreme and use the power for the cyclic to give immediate acceleration whilst accepting only a minimum rate of climb. You can do whatever's best for the circumstances. And don't worry, we'll be practicing all the combinations soon enough! But, in the circuit it's safest for everyone to conform to a set pattern – otherwise you'd get choppers bobbing up and down everywhere and no-one would know who was coming or going! Likewise when on final approach: you could tear down the line and stop with an exaggerated flare – rather like a motorist tearing up to a corner, then jamming on the brakes – or alternatively do a nice gentle approach that requires a minimum of flare to stop. There will be times when its best to zoom in and then stand it on its tail to stop – it could confuse the enemy – or indeed the other extreme, when you may have to lower down vertically! We'll be practicing a lot of that later, when we get on to landing in confined areas – in amongst buildings or clearings surrounded by trees.'

We whined on around the circuit. He was a tidy flyer and I could sense his handling improving by the minute. After a couple of circuits I took over and headed to the corner of the field where we practiced autorotation – or simulated forced landings.

'Now, what's the first question everyone asks a helicopter pilot?'

'What happens should the engine sto-P?'

'Absolutely! And the answer's simple: just like an aeroplane, you glide down! Engines rarely stop – the most likely reason would be to run out of fuel, which I suppose could happen, but whatever, we still have to practice it!

'So here we are flying along and suddenly the engine stops!' I cut the power. 'The first thing you do, before *anything* else is to push the collective lever fully down. This neutralises the pitch and will keep the blades spinning. You *don't* look for the cause, you *don't* look at your map to see where you are – there isn't time; you only have a few seconds and at all cost you *must* keep those rotor-revs up and in-between the lines. So, the helicopter is now descending, and you're using the downward motion to push air up between the blades. Instead of using the engine to spin the blades and then clutching into them to give you lift; now you've got the reverse, and you're sacrificing lift in order to keep those blades spinning – just like a sycamore seed. If a sycamore seed didn't spin, it would plummet straight down to the earth – and the same would happen to you!

'Having done that, now you've got time to do the rest. She'll descend at about 1800 feet per minute, so depending on your height, you know how long you've got. You *should* know where you are, so get your Mayday off whilst you can. You don't have to pick a large field and then plan a circuit as you were taught in a fixed wing aeroplane, just turn into wind and select a suitable patch – anywhere within a forty-five degree arc either side of the centre line. Keep your forward airspeed to fifty-five knots – you're used to that, and it's another reason why we use that speed for final approach in the circuit... and down we go. Can you feel the main rotor acting like a brake now? The sycamore seed? It's the same as a revolving parachute! Next, pick your patch – we'll put down on the grass there, beside that gap in the hedge, so using rudder, over to the left a bit, still keeping your forward speed at fifty-five and the rotor revs up... and we're about on line now, so right rudder and swing her back into wind.

'...Nearing the ground now, so judge your height – remember it will vary according to your speed and weight – and cushion the descent by pulling up on the collective. All helicopters vary – the Scouts used to come down like a brick shithouse and you had to yank the lever fully up and still they'd hit pretty hard, especially if you were heavy; but with this one you can arrest the descent... and then hold her in the hover like this... pause for a moment and if you don't like your spot, you've still got enough rotor-revs in hand to pull her up like this... and put her down over the hedge!

'So that's autorotation and what you can now tell your friends! It's actually a lot safer than dead-stick landing an aeroplane. Remember, engines will *never* stop when it's convenient to you, so you've got to be ready at all times. So from now on, every time we fly I'm going to cut the power at some time. It may be in the hover, or whilst taking off, or landing, or in the cruise – just be ready for it. And when I think you'd be able to survive in a real situation, then you'll be ready to go solo!'

IX

It took twenty-five minutes to drive to Thruxton. I parked outside the offices and went inside, where a smiling girl told me that the manager wasn't in and would be out for the rest of the day.

Good start.

She looked in his diary and tut-tutted when she saw my name, and couldn't *imagine* why he'd seen fit to leave; but never mind: this piece of paper here listed the hangar charges – you see, all according to size and wingspan of the aircraft? And there are spaces available *here* and *here*, pointing to a plan of the airfield on the wall, and if I liked she could get Charlie to show me?

'This is the one you want' Charlie said, selecting a key from the huge bunch he held in his hand. He was a thin wiry man of uncertain age, dressed in what was once a white overall. We'd driven halfway around the airfield to reach the hangar and it stood on its own concealed in a dip, with a short concrete access road leading from the perimeter track. 'It's cheaper than the rest, on account it's furthest away and not part of the main complex. It's small, and there's no electricity, but it's a good hangar – the doors slide easy. You'd have you your own key of course, and the best thing about it is, you can park your car right at the back here!'

'What about security?'

'That's why most people opt for one of the other hangars in the main complex; but take it from me, it's just as secure – in fact it's probably more secure here than over there. We have a guard who drives around and he seems to spend most of his time sitting in his van over at this side, just because it's on its own!' He unlocked the door, gave it a sharp pull to get it moving on its runners and then slipped nimbly into the gap and put his back against it and walked it open the rest of the way, until it finally jarred to a halt when the wheels hit a hidden stop on the rails. 'See, opens easy as pie and much quicker than those others that you have to wind open. I keep it well greased mind...'

As the doors opened, the growing light revealed the intriguing outlines of a variety of aircraft half hidden in the gloom. They were all small and looked fairly elderly, the largest being a Rallye that was right at the back, with one flat tyre and looked as though it hadn't moved for a long time. Next to it, with its high wing slightly overlapping was a Piper Cub, and slotted in front was a diminutive Druine Turbulent. Still in the dark behind the other unopened door, was an elderly Cessna 150, with a nearly-full drip tray on the floor beneath its engine, whilst in front and most accessible of all was a very tidy Bolköw Junior resplendent in dark-blue and white livery.

'What you got, a little Jodel?' Charlie asked. 'Should be alright here – most of the little ones are over this side. Easier to move them about and all. The larger and newer stuff – Spam-cans and the like, are all over the other side. There's a Piper Tri-Pacer that's usually here, but it's being re-covered at the moment, and sometimes an Auster Autocrat, but he seems to keep it mostly over at Popham these days...'

I didn't like to correct him that my proposed purchase was a Robin, but was nonetheless intrigued that he knew about it, as well as already having categorized my intended pride and joy to be with the older and less salubrious collection of aircraft on the field. But at least the hangar rates were good, and a lot less than I had been led to believe. And seeing the other aircraft there also helped to quieten my few remaining misgivings. Other people owned aeroplanes, so perhaps the idea wasn't so outrageous after all!

'Mmm, I think this'll do very well...'

'When are you thinking of bringing the machine over?'

'Well, to tell you the truth I haven't bought it yet, though I'm expecting it to arrive in...' I looked at my watch '...well, any time now. Could you run me over to the tower?'

'Surely. If you do decide, just tell Judy in the office and she'll sign you up and give you a key, and then you can help yourself anytime. We're pretty informal here...'

Halfway there and just before the end of the active runway he stopped the car. 'Better wait a mo', there's an aircraft on approach... Or at least, I thought he was landing, but looks like he's changed his mind!' The red and white Robin flattened out and then did a high speed run a few feet above the ground, before pulling up over our heads in a graceful climb that ended in a turn that put it nicely back on the downwind leg again. 'Very nice – that one yours? Listen to that engine, I've never heard anything so sweet...' He started the car again and by the time we got to the tower, the little aircraft was just touching down in a flawless three-point landing. When it finished its run it turned and started to taxi towards the tower. Charlie got out and waved his arms and marshalled it towards him, and then led it to the visitor's parking area where he swung it round into wind, before drawing his hand across his throat in the universal sign to kill the engine.

'Bernard!' I said, as his bulky form emerged from the cockpit. 'You'll get me a bad reputation – some of us have to live here!'

'Eh-hue, what do you think – I asked permission from the tower first!' he said as he jumped down from the wing. 'Ahh – but she's a sweet little thing to fly – I've a good mind to keep her for myself...'

'You may well be doing that – I don't know if I can afford it yet!'

'Ah, of course you can – a man of your means. It's just like 'aving another car! Let's go and find a cup of coffee and we'll discuss the business.'

There was a coffee machine in the crew room and we took our polystyrene cups to some armchairs in the corner. After thirty minutes I knew all there was to know about owning and operating an aircraft. I'd done a few sums previously and was pleased to discover the net amount fell well within my projected budget – which was a relief, for by now I'd set my heart on it.

'If you've got your chequebook you can fly me back – it only takes thirty-five minutes. Then, if you are wholly satisfied – and I'm sure you will be, you can pay me when we get there... and *voila*, you will be the new proud owner!'

Although it was by far the smallest aeroplane I had ever flown, it was quiet and comfortable and for its small engine, remarkably fast. The takeoff run with two-up took about twice the distance of a Beaver or AOP9, but I reasoned would be acceptable for most fields or farm strips, and Bernard assured me the undercarriage was robust enough to cope with grass fields.

'Aircraft are like women – some you treat gently and some need firm 'andling.' He confided in his chauvinistic yet wholly unpretentious way. 'But I don't 'ave to tell you that! Anyway, this one needs firm 'andling at all times to get the best out of her. You know about the wings – Julien told you at the factory? How the lift works its way in from the bent-up tips as you increase speed? Well, to help the transition you must forcibly push the nose down, quite 'ard – like this... There, now we are flying on the inner stubs only. See the speed increases straightaway, and you then trim well forward so you think you are flying in a nose down attitude. Which you are – it's just an exaggerated way putting it on the step – eh-hue, but she really flies, this little one!'

Thirty minutes later we were ten miles from his home field and he called the tower and asked for a straight in approach.

'Now, while I'm with you, let me show you how she handles at slow speed.' He throttled back and held the nose up as the speed fell off. At sixty knots he applied half-flap and trimmed further back. 'I'm going to hold her back until she stalls...' I watched the airspeed as it hovered around forty knots. There was a slight tremor and he pulled the stick right back. 'There... now she is fully stalled, that's all there is to it!

No vibration, no sudden wing drop – with the exaggerated wing dihedral she's quite stable even when fully stalled. Look, you can even waggle the rudder, and she just swings from side to side – so you can adjust your line like that, and she's quite safe. Now, just apply a trickle of power... and voila, she is flying again!'

We continued down the approach in this manner, on the very back-edge of the curve, adjusting our height by juggling the power. At fifty feet he lowered the nose slightly and held it thus until we touched on all three points. He immediately chopped the power and we rolled a few lengths and then stopped. 'There you are – is that as good as one of your army landings? But she is so docile, she does it all for you! Eh-hue, I think I'd better keep this machine after all, she is a joy to fly...'

But he didn't, and forty minutes later I took off on my own and headed back for Thruxton!

With only my weight, she handled even better – she was light on the controls and unlike so many modern light aircraft, there was not an ounce of sloppiness in them: everything was instantaneous and direct; it felt like being in a fighter. And like a fighter, the cockpit wrapped itself around you, this heightened by the clever positioning of the ancillary instruments which, in order to fit in, were set in a curved facia that arched around on either side.

I climbed to three thousand feet and then tried some steep turns. First, I put her into a left-hand vertical bank with an entry speed of 110 knots. I fed in full throttle and pulled the stick back and felt my cheeks sag as the line of the horizon rotated around the nose. I held it there for 360 degrees and then felt a slight bump as we flew through our own slipstream; with stick and rudder I immediately reversed the turn and did another to the right. I lost fifty feet in that one and there was no bump; then holding the vertical bank, I eased back on the throttle. As our speed reduced, I pulled even further back and felt the outer section of the wings come into play and that was all there was to it. It was rather like doing a tight turn with thirty degrees of flap lowered: the turning radius reduced and my cheeks ceased to sag, but otherwise she went round as though on rails. I held the turn to complete the circle and once again managed to hit our entry slipstream, and then pulled the power right back and waited to see if she would stall and spin-off. I felt the stall, but she didn't spin: she just seemed to flounder and then stabilised herself in the same attitude that Bernard had showed me; descending as though attached on the end of a parachute. 'Eh-hue!' I said to it in my best French accent, as I recovered and once again set course for Thruxton 'Eh-hue, but I like the way you fly, and we're going to get on fine...'

X

I tried a different way back; it was more direct to go through the lanes, and there was one that meandered through Quarley and Grateley and eventually ended up at Wallop. No doubt it would take longer, but there was no rush and anyway, my thoughts were fully engrossed on my new acquisition.

I'd arranged to transfer Bernard's insurance cover to my name and on the strength of that Judy had parted with a hangar key, as well as selling me a book that listed all the farm strips throughout the country. With a bit of planning it would appear you could just about go anywhere: all that was needed was a prior telephone call to let the owner know – and also to give him time to clear the strip of any livestock – and all in all it seemed the perfect arrangement! This way I'd be able to make full use of the Robin and fly everywhere from now on, I decided. I'd then topped-up the tanks at the petrol point, something I always try to do after every flight as it minimises the airspace left in the tanks that can otherwise sweat with condensation, which if left, can contaminate the fuel. I'd omitted to ask Bernard if he'd started with full tanks, but it only took nine gallons – which wasn't bad considering it had flown three flights of thirty-five minutes duration, as well as three take-offs on full power and all the mucking about in between! With full tanks I resisted the temptation to do another circuit, and instead taxied around the perimeter and down the slope to the hidden hangar. Then, by imitating Charlie, I managed to open the doors without too much trouble and wheeled the machine in. I also took the opportunity to have a closer look at the other aircraft in the hangar. As an all-round useful aeroplane I still liked the look of the Rallye, in spite of the neglected appearance of the one in the back of the hangar, but it looked huge and cumbersome beside the sleekness of the Robin. The only other aircraft that took my fancy was the little blue and white Bolköw Junior. It was even smaller than my Robin – strictly a two-seater with only a parcel shelf behind for luggage, but it had the advantage of being all metal and whoever owned it was obviously a serious flyer, for it had all the latest equipment on board. It would be interesting to have a chat with...

A horse and rider suddenly materialised from nowhere.

Fortunately, I hadn't been driving fast – my head still in the clouds, as well as it being a twisty lane and full of blind corners. I stopped the car and waited whilst the rider heeled the horse into the side. There still wasn't enough room to pass, so I waited until she – it was only then I noticed it was a she – looked round. I indicated to a wider patch of road ahead and she nodded and walked on, whilst I trickled along behind. She stopped again and I started to edge my vehicle past. I lent over in my seat and looked up and there was instant recognition.

'Angela!'

I drove on and parked two wheels on the grass verge and got out. 'Angela – it's been ages, how are *you*!' It was Tristan's wife – or rather his ex-wife and I'd been best man at their wedding a lifetime ago. I'd heard she'd married again, but had no idea she lived here.

'Good Lord! You'd better come and have a cup of tea, I'm just round the corner – first on the left!'

'Okay, I'll follow you there.'

Tristan and Angela – now there was another marriage that had gone to waste. They'd been ideally suited – or at least, that's what the rest of the outside world had thought, but their marriage had only lasted a few years. Tristan had left the army and tried his hand at civilian life and maybe that had been their undoing – in fact, come to think of it she'd come from a long military family, and her father had been a general. But that shouldn't break a marriage, so it was probably something else – and anyway, my own marriage had foundered, so who was I to talk?

I hadn't seen either of them for years, although at one time Tristan and I had been very close. We'd been at Sandhurst together, and then served as subalterns in Germany in our respective regiments that had been stationed adjacent to each other in the same Armoured Brigade. Inevitably Army life in Germany is a close-knit community and thereafter we were forever meeting on exercises, training courses or socially at various parties. One February we'd taken leave together and gone skiing – and it was then I'd told Tristan that I was thinking of applying for the army flying course at Middle Wallop. Whether it was the drink or what, but by the end of the evening Tristan said that he too would apply, and he'd be damned if he wouldn't get there first!

We both passed the aircrew selection board, but in the event I got to Wallop about six months before him and so passed-out two courses ahead. On gaining my wings, I'd then transferred to the Army Air Corps and had been flying ever since, whilst Tristan, although a natural pilot, had only flown the one tour and then rejoined his regiment. Maybe that was when his career had started to go wrong, for he left the army shortly after that, then after the break-up of his marriage had gone off to Australia to start a new life.

Seeing Angela brought it all back, as I carefully parked in the yard where she'd just led the horse into a stable. A man, presumably a groom came out and took up some harness that was hanging on a hook and Angela emerged a moment later.

'How lovely to see you, come on in and I'll put the kettle on!'

It was a large farmhouse kitchen, where they obviously lived most of the time. At the business end there was a sink and pine kitchen units under a window full of pot plants that overlooked the yard; whilst an Aga cooker with more pine cupboards and a Welsh dresser took up the whole of another wall. At the other end of the room the wall had been knocked through into what had once been an outhouse, but now formed a cosy annexe with bookshelves all round and a sofa and a couple of battered armchairs facing a television in the corner. The rest of the kitchen was taken up by a large pine table, set in the centre of the room like a roundabout, on which were piles of magazines, bits of harness and an overfull wicker sewing basket spilling out squares of cloth pinned with needles and tail-ends of coloured thread from a half-closed lid. An elderly yellow Labrador bitch lay stretched out on a rug in front of the Aga, and had momentarily lifted her head and thumped her tail by way of welcome. The kitchen was obviously the heart of the house and in spite of the wear and tear and general lived-in feeling, exuded a definite style – and made me wonder what the rest of the house was like!

'What a pity you can't meet Nigel – he's a stockbroker and commutes to the city every day, poor darling! So, tell me, are you married again – and what brings you to this neck of the woods? Oh look, the kettle's already on the Aga, Elizabeth must have done it, I expect she'll be down in a minute.'

'Elizabeth?'

'My baby sister – she only lives down the road, but I must say, she seems to spend more time here than in her own house these days.' Then in a sotto whisper 'I haven't enquired too deeply, but I think she's going through a bad patch, poor dear. Not that I'm at all surprised. She was a frightful rebel when she was a child – well, especially when she was a teenager and of course she got married far too young.' The kettle began to steam and she selected two mugs from a row of hooks. 'It's a job to find two mugs that aren't chipped – I keep meaning to get some new ones – it's just tea-bags I'm afraid! She used to be such a tomboy and the apple of Daddy's eye when she was young, but that all changed when she... but wait a minute, of course, you met her at our

129

wedding; she was one of my bridesmaids! Let me see, she would have been fifteen then, so I don't suppose you remember her. She still wears that lovely necklace – you remember, you gave a matching pair to both the bridesmaids, Elizabeth and my cousin Betty – which reminds me, I must give Betty a ring – she married a farmer and they live in Norfolk, quite near Sandringham actually, but we still keep in close touch. In fact Nigel and I are going on holiday with them later this year – to Greece, but we haven't started to make any arrangements yet! Anyway, what are you doing these days?'

I'd forgotten how Angela never stopped talking! Being married to her had probably driven Tristan round the bend, and I began to have an inkling why he'd done a runner to Australia. Further more, it wouldn't surprise me if her new husband escaped to the office for the very same reason.

'Me? – Well, I'm a flying instructor at Middle Wallop...'

'*Middle Wallop*! That's where Elizabeth lives, in one of the married quarters. I'd forgotten you'd left your regiment and joined the Royal Aeroplane Corps, or whatever it's called. Noisy things, they buzz over the house all day long – and all night too sometimes, I got Nigel to write and complain. It really is too much, and of course plays havoc with the horses...

'What plays havoc with the horses?' Elizabeth said from the door.

It was hard to tell that they were sisters. Whereas Angela was short and dark with a curvaceous figure and thoroughly 'county' both in manner and dress, her younger sister was the complete opposite and looked a mess. She was of medium height with lanky blonde hair that fell down on either side of her face and had a boyish figure – effectively hidden by a coarse-knit old pullover and what appeared to be a pair of army denim trousers, made even baggier by having too many pockets, and an old pair of trainers on her feet. In one hand she held a basket with some freshly cut roses and in the other a broom.

'What plays havoc with the horses?'

'Those *awful* helicopters from Middle Wallop, dear. Oh, what lovely roses! Put them on the table and I'll see to them in just a... I do wish you'd wear some proper clothes instead of slopping about in those awful things all the time. Anyway, come and have a cup of tea. I don't suppose you remember this man – he was Tristan's best man at our wedding?'

She looked at me in a steady gaze. She had a narrow face, made longer by the lankiness of her hair, and it was slightly pitted on one side, the remains of acne from her youth. Her mouth was slightly too large and she had a bruise on one cheek that she had made no effort to hide with makeup... but it was her eyes that were her arresting feature. She seemed to look right through me.

'I knew you would come' she said.

Chapter 5

I

'So, what's the diameter of the rotor?' I asked Stephen Grant who was flying the machine. Sergeant Lane was sitting behind, for we were a helicopter short this morning and I had them both together. Besides, both had gone solo on the same day so they were level pegging, which made life a lot easier.

'Ten and a half meters' he replied.

'Okay – and Sergeant Lane, how much further does the tailfin extend behind the diameter of the rotor?' Unlike most helicopters that have an unguarded tail rotor at the very rear of the fuselage, the Gazelle has a conventional looking swept tailfin – the same as an aircraft, except it has a duct cut into it that houses a thirteen-blade rotor, rather like a kitchen extractor fan. Not only is this extremely efficient, but it also reduces the noise level.

'Ah – I'm afraid you've got me there, sir.'

'Stephen?'

'It extends by another one point seven-five metres, sir.'

'Good – remember that Sergeant Lane, because that's the bit you can't see. Right, Stephen, I want you to fly to the corner of the field – that's it, over there – and you'll see a white circle on the ground. Take her up to 100ft and position so you approach from the downwind side, then hold her in the hover over the circle. That's your clearing – the circle has a diameter of eighteen metres and I then want you to lower down bang in the middle, and remember we are sitting one and three-quarter metres ahead of the rotor mast!'

He made a reasonable approach and then lowered down into the circle. The canopy bubble on a Gazelle wraps right round under your feet so you can actually see vertically down – and a lot easier than the Scout, which only had two small glazed cutouts. Once firmly down, I told him to lock the collective lever in the fully down position and throttle the engine down to minimum idle. I then handed them both a card on which I'd drawn a scale drawing showing the plan view of a Gazelle centred within an eighteen-metre diameter circle. I'd drawn another circle that showed the diameter of the rotors, with the tail protruding 1.75 meters beyond it at the rear, and then three further measurements scaled in from the outside circle: 6.36 meters to the front of the bubble canopy, 2 meters to the rear of the tailfin and 3.75 meters to the rotor diameter.

'That's how it should look if we're centred correctly – I want you both now to unplug and get out and pace these dimensions on the ground, so you can get a feel of the actual distances for yourself.'

They clambered out and began pacing, unnecessarily stooping as all people do when under helicopter blades. I then indicated for them to stand back, and lifted the machine forward a metre and over to the right by two and a half metres and then set it down again. Sergeant Grant gave me a thumbs-up and they both clambered in again.

'That's spot on now, sir!' he said.

'Right, I want you both to sit in the pilot's seat in turn, and fix it in your mind. Don't forget you're sitting to one side, so to start with, try leaning into the centre and you'll find it's easier to gauge an equal distance either side; but the critical one is the 6.36 meters ahead of the canopy. If you get that right, you know you'll have two meters clear behind. So, gauge it by eying it in with the top of the instrument panel — that's what I always do, and as you can see, we're not far out.'

We continued landing into the circle for the remainder of the double lesson, each getting out and pacing the dimensions on foot before handing over to the other. To his annoyance, Stephen Grant's performance gradually deteriorated, his first landing being his best; whilst after an indifferent start, Sergeant Lane's efforts gradually improved.

Whilst I sat and thought about other things.

Elizabeth Lawrence her name was. She was married to a Sergeant Lawrence who was in the RAOC and in charge of one of the stores here at Middle Wallop. She'd met him when she was seventeen — when he was a private soldier at a dance in Aldershot. And her father, who was still a serving general at the time, had objected and they'd fallen out in a big way; so much that the moment she reached her eighteenth birthday she had promptly married him in a registry office. And she'd also been pregnant at the time.

Although she would never admit it to his face, her father had been right. He hadn't objected to the match on social grounds — the fact that she'd married a private soldier, for many a general has come up through the ranks; but with a father's wisdom he could see that they were totally unsuited. Had she been well enough, possibly her mother could have helped heal the rift, but even then she was dying of cancer — and when Elizabeth lost the baby at five weeks, she'd been totally devastated and had died a few weeks later. All this I had learned from Angela who had monopolised the conversation around the kitchen table.

'Hey, hey, Sergeant Lane, that's cheating! It's easy to do a steep approach to regulate your position, but you've got to imagine that circle is surrounded by tall trees, which is why I asked for a vertical descent!'

'Sorry, sir, it's so much easier to hit the jacK-poT this way!'

'Yes, it's a good way to illustrate that helicopters fly much better with some forward airspeed – you get extra lift. Transferring from the hover into forward speed you get – what do you get, Stephen?'

'Er, translational-lift, sir?'

'Exactly – when the rotors start cutting into undisturbed air they become more efficient – you need about twenty knots and then you'll suddenly feel the extra lift and the helicopter begins to fly more like an aeroplane. The faster you go, or rather the more you transfer the available power to the cyclic, the more efficient the blades become, until such time you reach their limit, which is determined by... by what, Sergeant Lane?'

'Er – your maximum forward speed is determined by the speed of the retreating rotor blade, sir.'

'Good; it's fairly obvious if you think about it. Anyway, the point I'm making is that you can use the translational factor to get yourself out of trouble – here, easiest if I show you... I have control!'

I flew them to a clearing in a wood that they would later use in their advanced training. High trees surrounded the clearing, effectively sheltering it from any wind. I emulated what they had been practicing and held the machine in a hover over the centre of the clearing and then slowly lowered down. It was a fairly hot day and I had to use plenty of power to arrest the descent before we entered into ground effect and landed in a cloud of dust.

'Now, hot and high – as I'm sure you know, will effect the density altitude. The hotter and higher you are, the less lift you'll get. Compared to some of the places you'll be flying, today's conditions are tame – it's not particularly hot and we're not that high, but I think it will be enough to demonstrate the point...'

I pulled into the hover and backed the machine until the tailfin was almost touching the trees.

'Ready? I'm going to takeoff straight ahead and try to clear the trees... here goes.' I increased power and gave it all it was worth. We gathered a few knots forward speed and then

I had to transfer maximum power to the collective. The trees grew in the windshield – but it was not enough; we hadn't the power to clear them. I held it for a moment to prove the point, then slowly backed down the line we had come and landed again where we had started. My two students sat silently saying nothing.

'Okay, we've got two options. Either you can both get out and walk home and I'll fly the machine' I glanced at my watch 'and should be back just in time for lunch... or, we can try to get out by using the translational-lift factor. Ready?'

This time I made no attempt to climb, but pushed forward on the cyclic, gaining speed with the machine in a permanent bank around the edge of the clearing. I could have done it in one circuit but held it down for a second full circle, gaining a few extra knots and then when at our start point and twenty-five knots indicated, pulled up into a climb. Once again the trees filled the windscreen... and then slid by underneath with a good twenty foot clearance.

'You have,' I said to Sergeant Lane, 'take us home to lunch!'

II

'Telephone for you again, sir. Young lady this time – I've put it through to the same booth.' The mess steward said with a twinkle in his eye. I put down my paper and followed him out.

'Hello' she said, 'are you busy – but I'd like to see you – can you meet me?'

'Where?'

'I'm phoning from outside the NAAFI...?' Her voice had a slight interrogative lilt, as though seeking confirmation.

'Okay, wait there – I'll pick you up in about five minutes. 'Bye...'

She was waiting by the entrance, this time dressed in jeans, white sweatshirt and with a loose jacket over her shoulder, and looking a lot smarter than when I'd last seen her.

'Take me away – just take me somewhere, anywhere will do...' she said, getting into the car.

I drove out of the camp and turned left onto the Salisbury road. I didn't try to make conversation and we sat in silence: it was as though we both knew. After a few miles I turned left into a lane, which from memory led through a string of villages, in one of which there was rather a good pub. Once or twice I glanced at her through the corner of my eye and was conscious that she was doing the same. Once, our eyes met, and again I experienced that feeling as we swam together and it was difficult to tear my eyes away and back onto the road.

'Now then!' I said as I handed her a glass of red wine and indicated towards a free table in the corner of the lounge bar. She sat down in the pew against the wall and I settled behind my pint of beer opposite. 'Where do we start?'

'I think you know' she said.

'It was you – in the night?'

'Yes of course, silly! You took a long time to join me.'

'It was because I couldn't smell you' I said on an impulse as the realization suddenly hit me, 'or rather now that I've met you I can associate you with the same smell – the same as when you visited me in France. I can smell you now... everything about you – your whole aura... oh, but not that I mean you...' I broke off in confusion.

She laughed. 'Good – that's very good... and I understand. Most humans don't rate the sense of smell any more. Animals do, but humans... I like that very much, I'm glad you can smell me.'

I studied her face, her high cheekbones with the bruise still evident on one side, although she had now made some attempt to cover it. Her mouth was a little too large, but somehow it couldn't have been any different and – and in her own way she was quite beautiful, I decided.

'Did he do that to you?' I asked intuitively. She quickly put her hand up to the bruise and covered it, then slowly lowered it, in a gesture that somehow bared the rest of her body to me.

'Yes, but it doesn't matter... not anymore, and it's by no means the first.'

'I still don't understand any of this' I said, taking a swallow of beer. 'I've never felt... don't you think it's time you told me all about yourself?'

And so she did, in a quiet voice sitting in the pub sipping her wine. How, when she was young, she had envied her sister who was pretty and vivacious and everything she was not. How much she had admired Tristan when he appeared upon the scene, and the knowledge that with her disfigurement – her acne was at its height then, and with the introspective self-consciousness of a teenager, she regarded it as a disfigurement and thought she would never attract someone like him. Then the day of the wedding – the day she first met me, and how Tristan and I had stood together in the church and again afterwards at the reception when we'd made our speeches. And I'd given her that necklace, which she had treasured ever since, and how she had realized then, when she was fifteen that I was to be her chosen soul mate. And how thereafter, through Tristan, she had kept track of my life and when...'

'But I had no idea – I must say I feel very humbled – it's extremely flattering but...'

'Shh – please let me finish, I can only say this once?' The questioning lift in her voice I found totally endearing, like some long forgotten piece of music. I went to the bar and ordered two more drinks, and then with these before us she continued.

The physical hurt she had felt when Tristan told her I was to be married and how she'd then thrown herself at the first man that had come along. And although she knew her father was right, it had been a rebellious act of defiance, to hit out at the people she loved most. Her mother had been gentle and understanding, but the knowledge that she was dying and the void it would leave in her life made her all the more determined to go her own way and stand on her own feet.

Her marriage was a farce – and had been from the start: they were two strangers, poles apart in every conceivable way and she had never been able to adjust. Her husband Ken was basically a small-minded person as well as a bully, who believed the greatest coup in life had been to ensnare the general's daughter. But instead of nurturing the union, he had done the opposite and throughout the marriage had taken every opportunity to parade her as though she were his property, or else publicly denigrate her for his own amusement and self-esteem. At first it had been to his mates; then when he was promoted, to the corporal's club; and now it was the sergeant's mess. This behaviour was totally foreign to both her nature and upbringing and she had not known how to cope with it. Early in the marriage she'd tried to communicate and reason with him, but his automatic response was always a string of shouted abuse, usually followed by physical violence. In the end she had given up and accepted her lot; her saving thought being that the child, so rashly conceived, had never been born. That would have been too much. Then, Tristan and Angela had split up and he'd gone away – although, unknown to Angela, she still corresponded with him on a fairly regular basis.

'Does Tristan know about...?'

'Shhh...?'

Her father then retired and had died within the same year, and with Tristan gone, the only family she had left was Angela – who had promptly remarried and then carried on with her life, including the same social set, as though nothing had happened! Besides, until recently she had never been able to confide totally in Angela, their age difference being just that much too apart.

It was then, when at her lowest point, she found salvation: a chink of light in the darkness that, with concentration, she found could be made to grow. In abject misery she withdrew into herself and began to imagine herself in another life. They were only daydreams, a means to fantasize and escape from reality. She began to look forward to nighttimes so to continue the saga, but soon began to be aware that her daydreams did not end when she fell asleep, for then her subconscious took over – and eagerly she followed. At first she could only remember fragments, a jumble of rubbish that was difficult to unravel. So she started to look for a thread – the tenuous link that had triggered her subconscious to unlock that department of her brain. She found it helped to keep a notepad by her bed and write down what she had dreamt, but it then got to the stage when she wasn't certain whether she was awake or asleep: whether she was daydreaming, over which she still had a modicum of control, or the tangential dimensions of a dream wholly led by her subconscious. Either way, she began to find she could remember more and more detail. And with that came a surprising development. Deep from within she discovered an inner strength that she had not known she had possessed. Once unlocked, it developed to reveal a hitherto unknown set of values that progressively rebuilt her self-confidence.

With this new found strength she became a different person and at last was able to cope with the realities of her marriage. She was able to laugh at her husband; his petty-mindedness and bullying tactics, and get on with her own life – which she immediately set about to change. She began to develop a degree of control over her subconscious, this without consulting outside help or a specialist of any kind, so much that with total concentration she found she could project her subconscious outwards, beyond the chink of light. It was somewhat haphazard at first but with perseverance it began to yield results, although not always those she was seeking. She began to know about things as and when they happened – or what people sometimes call 'second sight'. It didn't always happen, but on the whole she was astounded at how accurate some of her predictions were, although she never publicised the fact and kept them firmly to herself.

'And then I went looking for you!' she said simply, as though it was the most natural thing in the world. 'So now you know – and the fact that you can smell me means that it hasn't all been wasted – you can still smell me, can't you?' she added mischievously, and then looked at her watch. 'Golly, you'd better run me back before I have too much explaining to do?'

We got up from the table and I fetched her coat. She put her hand on my arm and it was though an electric shock went through me.

'There! Did you feel it? That's better than a smell?'

I turned and she came into my arms, our bodies pressing together, united as one; and totally oblivious to all the other people in the bar.

'I can breath you now' I whispered into her neck 'God, what's happening?'

'Don't you think' she said, turning her face up 'it's already happened?'

III

The weather remained fine and we flew every day. Under this uninterrupted regime the students soon mastered the basic eccentricities of the machine until it became second nature, and with this out of the way, their overall powers of absorption suddenly increased – which we immediately countered by increasing the length of their lessons. Thus their hours mounted and soon they were confronted with the second major hurdle of their course, the thirty-hour check. This was to be conducted by David White, and as Stephen Grant and Sergeant Lane were still level pegging, I asked him if he would take them both on the same day. With no pupils to fly, I was asked to checkout our errant helicopter for an air-test. This was an ideal opportunity to set up a simple treasure hunt for them, for subject to their passing, the next exercise on their agenda was a solo cross-country, a triangular course that would take approximately two hours flying. And a treasure hunt thrown in at the end always livened it up – at least, I always used to enjoy them and it simulated the real thing. Strictly speaking, treasure hunts were part of their advanced training, but I thought they were both up to it and anyway, it wouldn't do any harm.

I took off with four large traffic cones in the back and whilst checking the various items on the list, deposited them in various fields within a twenty-mile radius, making careful note of the grid references. The helicopter passed all its checks and it was good to know we were back to full strength again. After landing I spent some time going through the checklist with the maintenance crew and then made my way back to the crew-room.

David saw me from his office window and called me in.

'Both those boys are a credit to you, well done!'

'Oh – thanks David, that's good of you to say so – and I must say I'm fairly pleased with their progress myself...'

'Teaching people to fly is like any other teaching job and the rewards are just the same. But teaching the basic skills of flying a helicopter – over and over again, can be the most boring job on earth and the only job satisfaction you'll ever get is from the results of your pupils. But at least you're in a position now to be able to look back to the quality of your own instruction from when you were learning to fly: you know now which instructors were good and how others just couldn't get it over. So try to compare yourself with them and learn from it! I've been at this game for a long time – too long probably and looking through my logbook all you see is pages and pages of drudgery; circuit-bashing, one student after another. I'm envious of your varied experience: your logbook reads like a novel in comparison! But the point I'm making is, from all those pages of tuition I can now tell *instantly* the quality of instruction a student has received; the little twists that matter and the way they think and approach a problem. Both your lads were good and it was very obvious to me they came out of the same mould.' He paused for a moment to take a sip of coffee, then looked me in the eye.

'The only slight reservation I have... if anything they could be both a trifle over-confident – and as you know that has to be watched! Over-confidence at this stage of their training can be a killer. Give me a cautious student any day – those tagged "prudent-student" are more likely to finish this part of the course, and that's all I'm concerned with! You're an experienced army pilot and you, of all people, know what's ultimately called for at the sharp end. But that comes later in their training; so let others deal with it. They've got to learn to walk before they can run and the fact they're both exude confidence *could* mean you're pushing them too hard, too early. I'm not saying you are, but it's just something to remember. I don't know why you're here really, you ought to be at the other end of the course... but never mind, whilst you are here you're mine, and I just wanted you to know you're doing a good job, so well done and keep up the good work!'

I walked out in a thoughtful mood. Perhaps now wasn't the time to spring a treasure hunt on them – and I'd better collect those cones in sometime... and the truth was, I was bored; of course I'd be better employed teaching the advanced students to fly tactically as well as the multitude of other things they'd have to learn before they'd be fit to pass-out and be of any use in a squadron. But I'd known that all along, and being placed with the civilian instructors teaching basic skills was Nicki-pig's way of reprisal. Maybe if I got a string of good results behind me, at least I'd be on better ground to justify my case. On the other hand, I suppose I *could* go over his head? A lot would depend on how long he'd be in that chair... so, best to mark-time for the moment... or else maybe I could find another way to circumvent the problem?

Like any other job or profession, the longer you're at it the more you learn – and flying is no exception, for there's a lot more to flying than just taking to the air. The longer you fly, the more you learn about the philosophy of flying, which can then be readily adapted to other things in life. For example, should you see a storm ahead, the discerning pilot will know there are six possible options open: you can skirt around it to the left, or to the right, or go over it, or go under it, or turn back, or as a last resort go through it. A lot will depend on the terrain and the performance of the aircraft you're flying – as well as your experience and the fact that you should have analysed the weather from the chart before you set off! So, how to apply this philosophy to the Nicki-pig situation? I know there's a storm ahead, it's just a question of how to tackle it...

But at least the other half of my life had taken a new turn, and one that was far from boring!

My mind had been in a turmoil ever since our meeting. Was she a nut-case or was all that she'd said genuine? And why me? Just because a young teenage girl has a crush on an older man, does it mean they are destined to become soul mates? Whatever a soul-mate means – yes, what exactly is a soul-mate? Of course I'm flattered, anybody would be but... and for some reason, well let's face it, I do find her extremely attractive – both physically and mentally. I'd never known such instant physical attraction – we could have made love over that table in the pub... although to look at, she's no raving beauty. But then, beauty is in the eye of the beholder, and by God, even after a few minutes, she'd certainly got through to me! But there was more to it than *physical* attraction: what about her travelling – when she appeared in France and the other times? I know now that they were real enough, and I remember feeling then that I knew the presence... and there certainly wasn't anything physical then! So, why should there be a mental attraction? I hardly knew anything about her or her mind, other than what she'd told me. And even then she was way ahead of me most of the time, so much that most people would regard her as some kind of witch! And to infer that she'd thrown herself at the first man that had come along because I'd got married... that was a bit rich! I'd known nothing about it... so do I really want to become involved with a witch, who's a scheming little minx as well?

Or, for that matter a sergeant's wife?

That made me stop in my tracks. A sergeant's wife! The implications of that alone could be horrendous – and in the Service was the one big 'no-no'; and rightly so. Although often regarded as quaintly archaic by the outside world, the line between commissioned and other-ranks was quite definite and the very backbone upon which all order and discipline was founded. It was, moreover, respected and observed by both parties and to cross it in anyway, apart from being unthinkable, was an invitation to certain disaster. I smiled as it brought back the memory of Mr. Elliott, my old Regimental Sergeant-Major, and the tactful way he'd reproached one of our newly joined young subalterns, who'd made it rather obvious that he fancied one of the WRAC drivers in the MT pool. 'It has come to my attention, Sir, that you are attempting to cross the Unbridgeable Divide! Take my advice, Sir, don't venture a step further!'

General's daughter or not, Elizabeth was now married to a sergeant and regardless of the moral implications, the system decreed she was therefore untouchable.

I walked on up the drive to the mess. A car passed me and then stopped by the entrance and the Director of Ordnance got out. He stood talking for a moment to a sergeant – a large florid man with a pencil-thin moustache who was making notes on a clipboard, the base of which rested comfortably against his ample stomach. I flipped the colonel a salute and we then walked in together.

'Who was that sergeant, Colonel?' I asked with sudden intuition 'I seem to know him from somewhere...'

'Who, Sergeant Lawrence? He runs a section of the clothing stores.'

'Ah yes, that's probably where it was...'

So that was her husband! That – that red-faced, beer-bellied slob! How *could* she be married to a man like that? I saw her face, and all good sense and logic went out of the window as an ache of longing surged through me – and the system would just have to go to Hell!

IV

I sat in the Control Tower and for the tenth time in the last five minutes looked at my watch and then out to where the windsock had been only a few minutes before. Fog was slowly creeping in and my two students were now both over-due.

'Try calling them again' I said to the controller.

'Charlie Five-Niner; Charlie Six-Seven, Wallop, do you read?' We both looked at the loudspeaker above his head, willing it to answer. Whoever said instructors led a stress-free life?

'Fog often does funny things to VHF, they could be just over the perimeter and still not hear...'

'Yes, I'm aware of that – but just keep trying. This is their first solo cross-country and they're very much alone out there. This powerful transmitter could be getting through and maybe we just can't hear their reply. A friendly voice is what they need right now...'

I sat back and tried to put myself in their place. The visibility hadn't been good when they'd set off, one clockwise and the other anticlockwise around the triangular course. I'd briefed them properly and told them to take no chances; to keep an eye on the weather and to abandon the exercise and head straight back if it started to close. But had they done that, they'd have both been back before now, for the clock had run on to its full two hours and twelve minutes, the time for the full course, and was now three – no, four minutes past their arrival time.

The phone rang and the controller snatched it up. 'Boscombe on the blower, sir.'

'Ah, good... may I?' I'd alerted Boscombe Radar some time previously and asked them to keep a lookout.

'Think we may have one of your fledglings on the screen now' the voice said. 'Approaching from the northeast, range seven miles, height one-thousand feet and a groundspeed of – er – about forty knots?'

'Good, that looks like our Sergeant Lane – many thanks – that just leaves one to come. He's inbound from the south-west – Merryfield, via overhead Yeovilton, any sign of him?'

'Nah – nothing showing – I'll get onto Yeovilton and see if they checked him through.'

146

'Right, much obliged.'

I studied the chart and couldn't help thinking it was history repeating itself, for this was where my old roommate Roger had got fogged in on one of his first solo cross-country flights. As the fog thickened he'd eventually landed his Scout by some remote shepherd's cottage in the middle of the Cranbrook Chase and then spent the night in a chair. But at least he'd managed to walk to a payphone first – even though, when he got there, he could only remember the number of the mess. So with only enough change in his pocket for three minutes conversation, had told the mess sergeant his predicament and who, in his own good time and in between serving drinks, had eventually passed his whereabouts on to the flight! But right now I'd welcome a call from the mess sergeant – or anyone else for that matter. Looking at the chart, Yeovilton's radar keyhole extended east to a line between Henstridge and Wincanton. He'd be low, in the valley between Cranbrook Chase and Salisbury Plain, so maybe there'd been too much clutter for their radar to get a proper fix. But, the main railway line ran smack up the centre of the valley – I remember also mentioning that to Roger when we'd talked about it afterwards, but he'd said he hadn't been able to find it! He must have been a lot further south to have landed in the middle of the Chase; and he'd had more flying hours – at least fifty or sixty more than Stephen Grant had at the moment...

The phone rang again and this time I grabbed it.

'Hello-there Wallop, Boscombe here again! I've just been on to Yeovilton and they say your man – call sign five-niner left their keyhole at 1742 – that's forty-eight minutes ago! There's about a twenty-mile gap between us, and as I say, we've seen nothing of him so far. I've also had a chat with Cotswold Radar and they report nothing. Mind you, they're not very good for low traffic, especially if he's in the valley. Anyway, I'll keep you posted...'

I looked at the chart again and then put a ruler to it. From the eastern edge of Yeovilton's keyhole to Wallop was thirty-four nautical miles. Say, to make the calculation easy, he'd slowed to sixty knots, he should have been back – I glanced at the clock – twenty-one minutes ago! Even if he'd slowed right down to forty knots, it would still make him over ten minutes overdue. Then, Boscombe said they'd had no contact, and their radar extends to – I put the ruler on the chart again – some six miles southwest of Salisbury. So, I reckon he must be down, and if it had been me, I'd say about...

'WalloP, this is Charlie Six-Seven – Christ, I've just realized where I am! Sorry, but I've just crossed the boundary of the field – I've been trying to call you for ages – is it okay to come straight in?' Sergeant Lane's voice boomed out of the speaker.

'Six-Seven is cleared to land and then hover-taxi to your dispersal. No other traffic – and, ah, welcome home!' the controller replied, beaming at me.

I made my mind up. 'I'm going out to look for him – will you be on for, say, another hour?'

'I should have knocked-off half an hour ago, but sure, I'll stay – there's nothing much on television anyway...'

'Right, thanks.'

I went to the crew-room and grabbed my flight bag and helmet and then went out to the dispersal, where the ground crew were about to wheel the last helicopter into the hangar.

'This one ready to go? I think one of my students is down and I'm going out to find him.'

''Bout two and a half hours fuel, sir. Have you signed the 700?'

'No – ah, no I...'

'I'll just nip in and get it sir, whilst you're starting up like?' Sergeant Lane had shut down and was just getting out of his cockpit, so first I went over to him. 'Well done!' I said. 'Sorry, I can't debrief you now, I think Stephen Grant's down somewhere and I'm just going to have a look...'

'Rather you than me, sir. It was alright until about twenty miles bacK, then suddenly it started to set in.'

I threw my bag and helmet into the cockpit and started an abbreviated version of the external checks.

148

'What's going on?' David White said, falling in step beside me.

'Stephen Grant's overdue. I reckon he's down somewhere between Yeovilton and Boscombe. Yeovilton had him on their radar until four-two – but nothing from Boscombe...'

'Mmm. Hang on, I'll just get my hat – two pairs of eyes are better than one, and anyway, if we do find him, he'll be in no fit state to fly.'

We took off and cleared the field, with the radio working beautifully. I dialled up Boscombe Radar and got the same voice that had been on the telephone, and told him our assignment. He came back with the numbers to squawk for our transponder and I'd just entered these in when the radio went dead. Neither of us said anything; there was nothing to say. We just looked at one another and smiled. It was good to be flying with a professional again. I climbed to six hundred feet and reckoned the forward visibility to be about four hundred yards, so kept the speed down to sixty knots and went on to instruments. If you've got them use them: for in fog – or at night for that matter, it's very easy to become disorientated in a helicopter. Sitting in a bubble way out front, there's nothing to relate to – not even a pair of wings; it's like sitting in space. We flew over Salisbury and then picked up the railway line running west out of the city.

'It's the only obvious line feature so if we follow it down to where it crosses over the A350 Shaftesbury to Warminster road, and then on as far as the A357 Henstridge Wincanton road – that's about the edge of Yeovilton's radar coverage and with any luck he'll be along it somewhere...'

'Yes, I agree.' David's quiet voice replied in my headset. 'Did you point the railway feature out to him when he showed you his plan for the cross-country?'

'Yes I did, thank goodness – trouble is, the railway follows the river for most of the way, just where the fog will be thickest...'

'Mmm. That valley is renown for it – there's wet land all around... now, that must be Wilton there, where the track divides... ah yes, there's the one we want, try bringing her down to about four hundred feet to see if it's any better – we're clear of the town now.'

I brought her down to four hundred feet, still flying on instruments, whilst his eyes did the looking.

'No, It's gradually getting worse' he said three minutes later, 'can you slow her down some more?' I glanced up from the panel and all I could see was grey. I looked down and could just about make out the ground. We were passing over a village – from memory, probably Teffont Evias for I could just make out the railway line bearing off to the south. I followed it and then we were in open country.

'Does the chart show any wires?'

'No, no – not that I can see...'

'Poor sod, flying in this on his own with only thirty hours under his belt... I'm coming off instruments and will ease her down to just above the railway line. Apart from bridges, there shouldn't be any other obstructions – and hopefully we'll see any of those in time! If you scan left, I'll scan to the right? This damn weather wasn't forecast – else I'd never have let them go; must have been a sudden change of temperature.'

'Yeah, it can happen at this time of year. Still, at least he's in a chopper, it would have been a lot worse if he'd been caught out in a fixed wing...'

I smiled and thought of my recent Dijon trip, but said nothing.

We followed the parallel lines, now running on a built up embankment over marshy ground. A pair of eyes filtered through the fog and just in time I lifted up. A two-carriage commuter train snaked by underneath, the lights from its windows keeping pace and casting an eerie yellow glow on either side.

'That'll give the driver something to talk about to his mates' David muttered into his microphone 'trouble is, he'll probably lodge a complaint and that'll just mean more paper work... Watch out for a bridge now, the main Shaftesbury Warminster road crosses over the railway, should be coming up any minute...'

I slowed to fifteen knots and a few seconds later made out the dark mass of the bridge ahead. 'Still no sign of the bugger...'

We crossed over the road and carried on.

'Gillingham next – about four miles, a minor road crosses over the railway again...'

'Rog – how far after Gillingham before we meet that other road, the one at the edge of Yeovilton's boundary?'

'Ah – about another six miles. But I'd have thought he'd have got nearer home than that...'

'Mmm. But it was pretty wet back there, he could have turned back...?'

The outskirts of Gillingham ghosted past on our starboard side.

'The line goes through a tunnel any minute now... There! Got it?'

I slowed the machine, then lifted over the gaping hole of the tunnel and cautiously climbed up with the ground. We were in amongst the trees and bushes that grew over the tunnel. 'Shit...!' I slowed to a hover-taxi, and slowly picked a way through the shrubs. Then, I sensed the ground falling away and abruptly the railway line reappeared, leading ever on.

Three minutes later another bridge loomed up – the Henstridge Wincanton road and also the unseen boundary of Yeovilton's radar coverage.

'Not a sign of him – what now?'

'Well, assuming he was following the railway, he'd have either stayed with the machine, or else he could have shut down and left it and be making his way on foot to the nearest village... Either way he'd probably heard us on the way over, in which case he'll expect us back... I reckon all we can do is backtrack – in this soup there's no point in looking away from the line, he could be anywhere...'

'I agree...' I pedalled the aircraft round in the hover and started back.

Just past Gillingham, a strobe light suddenly started to pulse, piercing through the fog from just north of the line.

'There he is!' we both said at the same time and a minute later I gently lowered down beside it.

'Good lad, he was keeping to the line feature' David remarked 'do you want me to hop out and fly him home?'

'No, he's my pupil – I'll do it...' I said as I unbuckled my harness, 'you lead and we'll formate on you – starboard side.'

'Hi Steve!' I said once I'd plugged into the socket 'wind her up, we're going home!'

'Thank God you came back; I tried to call you when you went over the first time, but the radio seems to have gone u/s – I was working Yeovilton but they went out; then I tried Boscombe, as you told me to do – I even tried Wallop, but couldn't raise anyone...' There was a note of panic in his voice.

'Yeah, sometimes happens in fog when you're low – always when you need the radio most! Anyway, you did the right thing...'

'I'd just started to walk back to Gillingham to get to a phone when I heard you, so then I came back and waited, hoping that it was you and that you'd come back...'

'Okay Steve, we're here now and that's all that matters. I'll take her...' I lifted up into a hover and watched as David did the same, then fell back and manoeuvred round to his starboard side. David's machine then dipped its nose and I followed suit and we eased into the climb together.

'You should count yourself lucky' I said to Stephen, 'if you'd been learning to fly in America, you'd never meet this kind of weather! Most of the flying schools there are down in the south where it's one glorious day after another, which is great for building your hours, but you never learn to fly in this sort of muck – at least, not until later! But every serious helicopter pilot will eventually have to fly in this kind of weather, for this is when helicopters come into their own, so it's just as well to learn early. Now, are you able to fly? Good, forget the weather, just concentrate on the machine in front and stay with him, he won't do anything violent. The trick is to pick two reference points on his machine that angle out at about fort-five degrees behind him. On the Gazelle I use the front of the skid furthest away from you – that's his port skid, and line it up through the rear of the skid nearest you. Got it? You can then drop back, like this... or edge in closer like this... until you can hear the buzz of his tail rotor. Can you hear it? Well, when you can hear the buzz means you're about two rotors distant away from him! But always maintain that angle – especially when you're flying in a large formation; everyone then knows their place and what to expect. So, we'll just drop back a bit... to about there, and now register his size through your canopy. If you keep the size the same, and hold the forty-five degree line through his skids, you're holding perfect formation. Okay, ready? nice and easy, you have control!'

It was the age-old remedy to reinstate confidence into a pilot after a bad experience: get them up into the air again as soon as possible; but to teach him formation flying in these conditions was a lot to ask at his low hours, and my hands and feet were never far from the controls. David took us up to 1000 feet on instruments, at which height the radios decided they could work Boscombe, who then took us straight to Wallop. I took over again for the approach and Stephen thankfully sat back and relaxed. I tucked in until I could hear the buzz of David's rotor, and then inched-in some more and we flew down the line together, half a rotor's width between us. Then, still in formation and now in radio contact with Wallop, hover-taxied back to dispersal.

Sergeant Lane was still waiting in the crew room, so I sat them both down with a coffee and debriefed them together, each re-living and learning from the other's experience; whilst I was just thankful to have them both back in the fold.

After they had gone I spent some time writing up their notes and then David and I left together.

'All in the day's work' he said as he locked up. 'But it could have ended very differently – and I've no doubt I'll have some explaining to do to our revered, albeit temporary, CFI when he gets to hear about it! Never mind, best cross that one when it happens...'

V

I took Elizabeth flying the following Saturday.

We arranged to meet at Angela's house at ten-thirty, but when I got there Elizabeth said that Angela was out at some committee meeting in the village, so we left her car in the yard and went on to Thruxton in mine. Her husband, she told me, was out all day at some football match – which, if it followed the usual pattern, would end up in a marathon drinking session, so she would be free all day. We were like a couple of kids on holiday, although ever aware of each other's presence. I could barely restrain myself from touching her and all my previous misgivings had totally vanished.

'Is it a *real* aeroplane?' she asked.

'Yes, but only a little one – I think you'll like it, I think I'm going to call it Marion.'

'*Marion*! That's an *awful* name, most un-aeroplane-like – why Marion?'

'Well, it's a Robin you see, and I couldn't think what a female Robin's called, and Maid Marion was Robin Hood's lover, so...'

'Are you going to be my lover?'

'Yes.' I looked sideways at her 'I think I am already, because I thought of you last night, and if it's in the mind...'

'You *naughty* thing, you – did you really?'

Fortunately I was spared having to answer further, for we'd arrived at Thruxton – or rather the gate at the end of the back lane that Charlie the Mechanic had told me about, so I gave her the key and asked her to unlock it.

We then drove on up the lane to the hidden hangar, and parked in the space at the rear.

'That one!' I said when I'd finally slid open the hangar doors. They'd seemed stiffer than they had the time before.

'Oh, isn't it *sweet*! "Hello Marion!" – no I don't like that name, I think we'll have to call you something else? But it's so small, does it really fly?'

'Yes it does – here, grab hold of it here and help me push it out...'

We pushed it onto the apron outside and I did an external walk-round, pulled the propeller through two revolutions and then opened the cowling and checked the oil-level with the dipstick. Although I knew the tanks were full, I then clambered underneath and pushed the valve to release a jet of fuel from the water-trap, just in case.

I showed her round to the starboard wing 'If you just step up here...'

'Oh but first, could I...?'

'That's it, one foot there – on the black surface; don't tread on the edge – and then one hand here and just swing into your seat.'

'But really, I'd just like to...?'

'These are the seatbelts, they buckle up like this ...' I shut her door and pulled the lever down to lock it and walked round to my side.

I'd studied the pilot's notes – such as they were, the night before and now the pre-start checks fell readily to hand.

'Right, let's see if we can make it go!' The engine stuttered into life.

'Did you really make love to me last night?' she asked with an impish smile. Her eyes crinkled when she laughed and as well as the questioning lilt in her voice, she had a way of lifting her chin.

'Shhh! Not now... I'm busy!'

I taxied up the slope and called the tower. By the time we reached the end of the active runway, the engine temperatures and pressures were up to their marks, so I parked ninety degrees to the runway and did a run-up.

'Where are we going?' she asked.

'Isle of Wight, I thought – we'll go to Bembridge for lunch.'

'Ooh, how lovely!' Her eyes sparkled.

I called the tower, told them our destination and taxied onto the runway. The little aircraft leapt into the air and after a detour over Angela's house, which we circled twice before deciding that she wasn't back, set 145 degrees on the DI for Bembridge.

155

'How long will it take?' she asked timidly.

"Bout twenty-five minutes'.

'Oh.' Then: 'Is there a service-station we can stop at on the way?'

'A service station! We're in an aeroplane for God's sake – anyway, whatever for?'

'Please don't be angry, but I need to... I need to go to the loo?'

'What now? Can't you wait half an hour – we'll be there at 11:45!'

'No, I don't think I honestly can. I'm terribly sorry – *please* don't be cross, but I do need to go, now! I *know* I should have gone before, and I did try to tell you, but then I didn't like to... God, what on earth will you think? I'm not usually like this, I promise! I feel such a *fool*...? But if it's any consolation, I do need to go, now, really!'

'I don't believe this!' We'd just passed over Wallop, which apart from a skeleton crew, was closed down for the weekend and thought for a minute. At least I was over my home stamping ground... then reduced power and headed for a large field some five miles to the south, which Mr. Summers used to use for engine-failure practice in the AOP 9 when I was a student. It was a large pasture and I knew the surface was flat. There was a tractor working in an adjacent field, so not to attract attention, I over-flew the field and then descended to zero feet – we used to do this in Austers and Beavers: it was called a CATO – or Concealed Approach and Take Off, the idea being to conceal the whereabouts of the airstrip from enemy eyes. Only this time the enemy was a tractor driver and I was flying a civilian machine!

I did a one-eighty in a hollow in the ground that Mr. Summers had shown me years before, brought the speed back and lowered the flaps, then with a trickle of power motored back towards the field just a few feet above the ground at about forty knots. The things one does for love... but, if truth be known, I didn't really mind. We'd all been caught out at some time or other, and – well, the fact was, I found the whole thing rather endearing! And what's more, the fog had long gone; the sun was shining; the air was hot and the ground dry – and I was in my own aeroplane with the one person in the world whom I wanted to be with.

We flicked over the hedge and I cut the power and gently pulled back on the stick. We trundled across the grass and I let her roll, then steered towards the edge of the field that bordered onto a small copse. She was out before I had time to stop the engine. I wondered whether to keep it running, then decided to shut down. Now were down, I thought, might as well get out and enjoy the remoteness of a Hampshire field...

She hadn't reached as far as the copse and was only a few paces away, squatting down. I stopped in embarrassment, but she smiled and then stood up with her jeans still around her ankles, unashamedly baring herself. The sky seemed to spin around as I looked into her eyes, then I caught her and carried her back to the shade of the wing.

* * *

'Did you mind?' she said afterwards.

'Mind what?'

'Seeing me like that?'

'Good Lord no! It's perfectly natural – after a few beers I frequently water a hedge! To tell you the truth I found it rather endearing...'

'Oh good, I'm glad you're not a prude! But some people would mind...?'

'Well I don't... and anyway, now we're here, I rather like this Service Station!'

She snuggled down contentedly in my arms. 'Talk to me? Do you really water the hedge?'

'Worse than that. I remember once I was really caught out when I was flying! It was when I was in Aden – I was on detachment in a place called Beihan...'

'How old were you then?'

'Shhh ... in my twenties. Beihan was a place on the edge of the Empty Quarter – that's the Rub'al Khali desert, and it was one of the staging towns on the old spice route. Spices from Arabia – but they actually came from India and then travelled by camel in a caravan across the Arabian deserts to the Mediterranean Sea, where they were then shipped to the Roman Empire...'

'Was Tristan with you then?'

'Yes, but he came out later.'

'Oh good. I like it that you two were together...'

'Shhh. Anyway, I was living in a tented camp with the FRA – that's the Federal Regular Army whom I was working for, and the only place in the camp where you could wash was a sort of tin erection that had a shower heated by the sun. And that was it! It was pretty rudimentary and we had to use a bucket for the rest of our ablutions...'

'Were you the only European there...?'

'Just me and a corporal; he looked after the aeroplane.'

'Gosh! How long were you there for?'

'Well, we used to call in and visit Beihan quite a lot, but on this occasion I was there for about six weeks; flying a Beaver – they needed an aeroplane to re-supply them by parachute when they were in the mountains, and do all sorts of other things.'

'Yes, I remember Tristan telling me about Beavers...'

'Anyway, the Emir – that's the local ruler...'

'Was he a Sheik?'

'No, he was more important than a Sheik – more of a Prince. Anyway, the Emir had two of his boys at Harrow and asked me to fly back to Aden to meet them off the plane, because it was their summer holidays. So I went back and collected them and brought them back to Beihan. They lived in a large white palace that had golden balls on each corner of the roof, and dwarfed all the other houses in the town. So, after we'd landed – it was a nasty trip back, the monsoon had just broken and it was pouring with rain, which only happened once every five years or so, and I had to do find my way down through the cloud with no navigation aids – they didn't have any radios or anything there; anyway, after we'd landed one of the boys asked if I'd like to go back to the palace for some refreshment. So I went and he gave me a guided tour. Do you know, they had a dungeon full of gold bullion? Ever since Roman times they'd been charging a tariff to let the caravan trains through. That mountain of gold was probably hundreds of year's worth... but, even better than that, one of the rooms in the palace was a bathroom!'

'A bathroom? What's so special about that?'

'Well, this was a proper white-tiled bathroom with bidets and showers and all the works. All the other houses only had a sort of angled drainpipe sticking out of the wall, and they had to make do with that! I think the idea was that by the time your business hit the ground, it had turned into dust!'

'Ugh! Really? You are lucky! I'd love to go to go to really ancient places like that.'

'Anyway, that evening the Emir held a fuddle...'

'A fuddle?' She snuggled closer.

'Well, that's what we called it, it's a sort of formal feast when they killed a goat or on special occasions maybe a camel – only I expect it was an old camel, one that couldn't work any longer. Only men were allowed to the feast and first we had to take off our shoes and then water was brought in pitchers so we could wash our hands – there were no knives and forks, and we had to eat with our fingers. Then we sat in a great circle around the dishes of food – great platters of heaped rice and spicy mutton stews all swimming in melted camel-milk butter whilst the host...'

'I thought you said it was a camel?'

'Well there was that as well; the others were just side dishes – and I daresay the mutton was really goat – but as I was saying, the Emir sat at the head of the circle and hacked-off all the tasty bits – that usually meant the fatty lumps or the eyes...'

'Yuk!'

'...With his khanjar – that's the curved dagger they carry in the front of their belts, and then threw the titbit to someone in the ring to eat; it was a sort of symbolic gesture – a kind of peace offering, or a subtle way of showing whom he honoured most. Anyway, after a bit he threw a lump of gristle to me, and they all watched and waited for me to eat it, which I was expected to do with great relish and smacks of enjoyment! I somehow forced it down and he obviously took my anguished expression for one of enjoyment, for he then sawed-off another huge bit that was even more horrible than the first and again threw it at me. Once more they waited, so I shut my eyes and took a bite and then when they'd all started talking again, hid the rest in my pocket. Then it happened! I felt the most terrible twisting pain in my groin and I knew I had to get out of there quickly! I mumbled something, backed out of the circle, found my shoes and made a dash for the bathroom I'd seen. I went round and round the palace, up and down stairs looking into one room after another and at last eventually found it. I managed to lock the door but was only just in time before I literally exploded into the loo!'

'Well, at least you made it...'

'Yes, I was there for ages and felt pretty weak afterwards. We all suffered from the most terrible tummy-bugs from time to time...'

'I don't think I really want to hear this – so, what happened then, did you go back to the fuddle?'

'No – you see, well, what I didn't know was that the whole bathroom was only there as a showpiece – it wasn't connected to anything, no water let alone any sewage outlet!'

'What? You mean – oh my God, how embarrassing! What did you do?' She started to giggle, squirming in my arms.

'Well, all I could do was shut the door and then leg it! Left my visitors card in no uncertain manner...'

'How awful!' she said still trying not to giggle, 'how could you ever face the Emir again?'

'Fortunately we both maintained a dignified silence over the matter and got on with the war in hand. But I was never invited to the palace again!'

I kissed her eyes and the bruises on her cheek. 'It's lovely here, isn't it?' she murmured. Then: 'Can you – I want you to love me again? Only, slowly this time – I want to make sure it's real...?'

We eventually made Bembridge by mid afternoon and instead of lunch, had a cup of lukewarm tea in a plastic carton out of a machine in the clubhouse. We then walked down to the beach and sat on the sand looking out at the sea. We just held hands and talked. She told me her life story and I told her mine, with constant interruptions, each wanting to know all the minute details that only matter to two people who were – well, who were fast falling in love. She was a delight to be with and I couldn't believe it was happening. Love – that overused word that people have written about since pen was first put to paper; not only written, but made poetry, sung songs and acted plays – indeed, everything about life, I suddenly realized, revolved around love. And now it was happening to me – and at this late stage of my life! If you'd asked me yesterday, I'd have said love was an emotion for the young: before the cynicism of life inevitably clouded one's eyes with realism. But yesterday was then; and here on the sands at Bembridge this middle-aged cynic suddenly realized what the true meaning was all about.

It was a shattering revelation. And one that we both felt; humbled by the sheer magnificence of it, together with the realisation of what it meant. Life would never be the same again.

We could have made love again in the sand, but we didn't; there was no need. Instead we just lay close together, complete in our oneness.

'Can you still smell me?' she said.

'No, I can only smell us now...'

* * *

We flew back in the still air of the evening, when all internal combustion engines seem to run at their sweetest.

'I never knew flying could be like this' she said. 'All this – just the two of us flying together! Of course I've been in large aeroplanes before, but then you're cooped up with hundreds of other people and you can't see anything. This – this is just perfect! It's real freedom, better than any dream!'

I smiled and placed my hand on her thigh. She clamped her legs together, imprisoning my hand, sharing her warmth. Then I thought about Hazell, my Devonshire air-nymph. Why not! Height: two thousand; airframe: okay; zecurity: no loose articles; engine: all in the green; location: over the sea and under Solent CTA, Beaulieu River ahead; lookout: I did a lazy 360 turn to the left, and then pushed the nose down.

'What are you doing?'

'I'll show you. Come, fly with me...' Speed: one-twenty and ease back on the stick. The earth fell away and blue evening sky filled our windscreen. Up, up and over, our cheeks slightly sagging; touch of pedal as the speed falls off, then the darker blue of the sea flecked with white, straight down. Ease back on the throttle and don't pinch the circle. The Beaulieu River swam down from the roof and then settled once again straight ahead as it was before.

Her eyes were alight with an intensity I'd never seen before. She leant across and kissed me under my ear. 'Always' she said.

VI

Charlie was still on duty when we got back and I got him to unlock the petrol pumps and top the tanks up before we taxied back to the hangar.

'Where was it you took me? Our handy Service Station – the field where we made love, does it have a name?'

'Well, I don't know its name, although I expect the farmer has a local name for it. It wasn't that far from Ashley Castle, I suppose that would be the nearest place...'

'Ashley! That's a better name for an aeroplane; can we call her Ashley?'

I smiled, 'Ashley would be a perfect name.'

She draped an arm over the cowling and pressed her face against it. 'Thank you Ashley, for letting us make love under your wing' she whispered, 'it was lovely...'

She helped me to slide the hangar doors shut, then ran ahead down the lane to open the gate.

'How are we going to meet?' she said as she got in the car. 'Trust me to fall in love with a man who owns an aeroplane but hasn't got a house!'

'I'll get somewhere. I was thinking of moving out of the mess anyway – if I stay there much longer I'll get fat! There's always cooked breakfast, followed by a large lunch and then dinner on top – if it's put in front of you, you just tend to eat it! Anyway, I'm running out of things to say to all those youngsters... What about your situation?'

'I'm going to leave him' she said simply 'but I don't want you involved. The camp is a small place – I'll work something out.'

But neither of us knew how small a place the camp would prove to be, or the ensuing ricocheting effect that would alter our lives.

VII

'On these bits of paper are two a grid references' I said to Sergeant Lane and Stephen Grant, handing them both a sheet. 'I want you to fly to the grid reference on the paper, and there you'll find a cone – an ordinary red and white traffic cone. Under the cone you'll find another piece of paper with another grid reference; so you then fly to that. In all it should take about an hour and a half, and remember, bring the cones back with you! Okay? Off you go.'

I'd decided to stick to my original plan, for having coped with the weather on their cross-countries, they were both now more than ready for a simple treasure hunt, particularly on a fine sunny Monday morning like today... besides, the cones were still out there and needed bringing back. And it also gave me just enough time to nip into the Estate Agent in

Andover and grab some details about rented flats or houses.

I'd selected the agent from their advert in the Yellow Pages. "The Leading Agency – Rental Properties our Speciality" it had read spreading over half a page. Half a page is quite worthy, I thought, they must be quite some outfit...

I thought I knew Andover pretty well, but still it took some time to find them: a grubby single-room office tucked away in a back street. But at least there was a space to park directly outside.

'I'd like to rent a property' I said to the youth who was manning the shop. He eyed my uniform up and down, looking for signs of chevrons on the sleeves, and detecting none took up a defensive stance. I was wearing normal working dress – a khaki pullover and slacks, which to the uninitiated was fairly nondescript, unless you knew where to look.

'Have you got your references?' He opened a draw and read from a piece of paper 'you need one from your commanding officer, one from your company or squadron commander and one from the barrack officer, or whoever's in charge of accommodation, stating why you can't be allocated a quarter.' He'd obviously come across squaddies before, and to him I was a bad debt waiting to happen.

'Ah, I don't think that's necessary' I said, indicating the crowns on my shirt-epaulettes that were buttoned outside my pullover, 'my rank is major and...'

'I don't know nothing about the army – but it says here, you've got to supply three references...'

'Oh, right – I think I'd better try somewhere else...'

'Yeah, we don't normally take soldiers on our lists – and then only with references...'

I walked out, left the car outside and made my way to the High Street. Was this typical of the sort of person we were expected to fight for? I tried the first Estate Agent I came to, a brightly lit window showing rows of pictures of houses on cards, many with "Sold" pinned diagonally over them.

'Yes, major, can I help you?' This was better. He was a man of about my age, slightly balding and wearing a blue pinstripe suit.

'I'm looking for somewhere to rent – do you do rentals?'

'Of course, sir – what price bracket are you looking at?'

'Oh, ah – I don't really mind...'

His eyes lit up and he walked over to a three-drawer filing cabinet. His stomach, I noticed, hung over the waist of his trousers like a large ball contained by his straining shirt.

'We have a new development – Anton Apartments, undoubtedly the best accommodation in town. Most reputable builders... no expense spared. Insulated walls; double-glazed throughout of course – the sort of windows you can reverse so they can be cleaned from the inside; built in speakers in every room; kitchen plumbed for washing machine, dishwasher, and electronic waste-disposal; underground parking; balconies overlooking the river; electric lift and the whole complex built with security in mind...' He extracted an elaborate looking brochure from a file in the draw. The picture showed an artist's impression of a white modern block of flats set in mature landscaped gardens. Rows of uniform balconies were stacked one on top of another, some with coloured umbrellas. It was the exact stereotype of countless others that have sprouted up in every town in the land.

'Ah, a flat?'

'An *apartment*, sir – these are *superior* in every way. Unfortunately we have only the one remaining. They were simply *snapped* up over night.'

'With a balcony?'

'Ah, no sir, the last remaining one is at the rear of the building, but it has a very warm aspect.'

'Um. I didn't really want...'

'Then of course, you might like to look at these...?' He said quickly, pulling out several more sheets and adding them to the pile with the brochure.

'Mmm. Do you have a house, somewhere small – perhaps an old cottage or something in an outlying village? I don't need anything very large, two bedrooms would be ample...'

'Oh a *cottage*! A cottage with character! *Everyone* wants one of those; they don't very often come onto the market. Let me have a look through...' He went back to a different drawer in his filing cabinet and started to pull one folder out after another, before shaking his head and sliding them back. The very last one at the back of the drawer he pulled out and opened. 'Ah yes, here we are! I knew it was somewhere – it isn't officially on the market yet, so we don't have a full set of details. Another military gentleman like yourself – a captain and his young wife – I believe they're going abroad; let me see... it should become vacant next week. Yes, I remember now, we've had it on before – it's only a small place and it leads straight off the street, but it does have a small garden at the rear.'

'Whereabouts is it?'

'Oh, didn't I say? It's at Nether Wallop – that's a small village not too far from here. In fact it's quite near the army aerodrome – perhaps you know it?'

'Yes, I know it – that sounds fine...' thinking that if a captain and his wife could manage to live there, it would certainly do for me on my own.

'I'll write the address down, and perhaps you'd like to pop over and have a look – then if you like it, come back and we'll sort the agreement out?'

It wasn't until I got back to the car that I realized I hadn't asked the price – but what the Hell, if a captain could afford it on his pay...

I drove back to the field, just in time to see my two students land and then walk back together, both carrying a traffic cone in each hand. Good, they'd obviously completed the course and I could now sneak the cones back from where I'd found them!

I debriefed them in our usual corner. They'd both obviously enjoyed the exercise and were full of enthusiasm, recounting every detail. With David's words in mind, perhaps now would be the time to shorten the rein a little? I thought for a minute about how best to approach it; so far my instructing technique had amounted to either barking or grunting at them... what was it David had said? Think back to your own level of instruction and try to emulate the good ones. Perhaps it would be more effective if I adopted a more subtle approach? That's certainly how Mr. Summers had come over – but then that had been his way about everything and part of his nature. However hard I try, I don't think I'll ever match up to him as a teacher, so for now, best get on with it the only way I know...

'Right gentlemen, I don't in anyway want to dampen your enthusiasm, but it's time we talked about the remainder of your course here – and I mean the next thirty hours with me...' They sat up and regarded me impassively. 'Between now and your sixty-hour check we've got a lot of work to get through. As you know, the Chief Flying Instructor examines you and his standards are extremely high – and rightly so, for that's the only standard there is. You may *think* you can fly a helicopter now, but let me assure you, you are still novices and barely safe! So, before we carry on any further, I want to polish up everything you've learnt so far. We'll be concentrating on accuracy in all the basic manoeuvres, and when I'm satisfied, we'll then progress to the remainder of the course. That will include low-level flying, landing in more difficult restricted areas, basic instrument flying, night flying, as well as fitting in two more navigation exercises and a whole lot more. When – and I say *when* not *if* – *when* you pass your sixty-hour and move on to the advanced flight, you'll be expected to be able to fly a helicopter automatically and without thinking. Unless you can do this, you'll never be able to absorb the military aspects of your training that's still to come. So, learn to fly properly now and it'll make it all the easier. Remember, I can't make you fly straight; it's got to come from within. It's a thought process, so start thinking about it now! I looked at my watch, 'right, time you went off for lunch, see you tomorrow afternoon!'

David beckoned me into his office. 'What's this, the amicable instructor turning the screw? Sorry, I couldn't help overhearing – and, er, may I say I thought that was most timely advice! Now, the new intake's coming in next week and I thought I'd give you these two...' he handed me their files. 'They both did reasonably well with their elementary fixed-wing flying – and anyway, Lane and Grant will be doing more and more solo exercises from now on, so we've got to keep you busy!'

I walked back to the mess for lunch whilst trying to work out how much rent I could actually afford for a cottage, having just bought an aeroplane! I chose a light salad for lunch and when at the table found myself sitting next to the chief ground-school instructor, a colonel who was shortly due to retire.

'You commanded the Belfast Flight until recently, didn't you?'

'Yes I did, but it was only a short tour...'

'Thought so – I've just discovered who you are. What are you doing instructing in basic?'

'Well, I've only just got my ticket, and that's where I was put, Colonel.'

'Hmm. Seems a waste to me – anyway, out of my jurisdiction – but, I'm desperately short of an experienced person to lecture on current tactics, especially Ireland; any chance of helping out – it wouldn't be much, just a period every now and then?'

'Well I don't know, Colonel, I'd have to fit it in – and I've just been given two more new students...'

'I quite understand, and of course I'd clear it with the CFI and David White first; your flying commitments would have to come first – and I dare say we could slide our periods about a bit to fit you in... but it would be dead-handy to know that I'd be able to call on you on occasions? Anyway, perhaps you'd think about it?'

Maybe this chance meeting was the lead I was looking for; the avenue to circumvent the Pig-shaped storm cloud that still loomed ahead?

VIII

That evening I drove to Nether Wallop to have a look at the

168

cottage. As I stopped the car a young captain, still in uniform, staggered out of the door carrying a large black plastic bin liner, full of rubbish.

'Hi!' I said getting out of the car. 'I understand you're moving – the Estate Agent gave me your address...'

'Not a good time to call, I'm afraid – we're in one helluva mess... but I suppose you could stick your head in – there's not much to see!'

'May I? Just to get a general idea?'

'Jennie – visitor!' he shouted, then added 'she'll kill me!'

It was a tiny place. The front door led straight from the road into the front room where his wife sat on a chair surrounded by half-filled dustbin liners. A sofa took up the whole of one wall and there was an open brick fireplace under a large distorted beam opposite. At the back, a door led off to a small lean-to extension that had been divided into a kitchen and bathroom, whilst the stairs led up from behind another door in the corner by the sofa. I poked my head into the kitchen, which although only of galley proportions appeared to contain all the essentials; as likewise did the adjoining bathroom – in which somehow a full bathroom suite had been shoehorned in, as well as an electric shower installed behind a curtain over the bath. Then I tackled the stairs. They were far too steep and narrow to conform to modern building regulations and I wondered how on earth one could get a bed or any other furniture up them. As well as being narrow and extremely steep, they curved round to emerge into a tiny landing that led off to a bedroom on either side. One was completely filled by a large double bed and a kitchen chair, whilst the other contained an old fashioned wardrobe, two chests of drawers and several more kitchen chairs, and was obviously used as a dressing room.

'Told you there wasn't a lot to see', he said with a smile 'we had to bring the bed up in pieces and then build it in situ; there isn't enough room to swing a cat in here! At least we've been promised a quarter in Germany – oh, would you like to see outside?'

The garden consisted of a patch of grass dived by a brick path that led to a brick shed – at one time an outside "privy", but now filled with garden tools and other assorted junk.

'What about furniture, is that included?' I asked.

'No, it's let unfurnished – but what we've got is mostly all junk – we could leave the lot if you want it, it's certainly not worth moving. We bought it all at a second-hand place and it isn't worth anything... I was going to burn most of it!'

'And how about the rent, is that reasonable?'

'Far too much! We pay a couple of hundred a month – that's unfurnished mind you; we've since discovered you can get twice as much for your money in a flat in Andover. I reckon you could screw them down if you tried...'

'Mmm, well it's certainly small, but if the two of you can manage, I'm sure it'll be large enough for... and the location's just right for me. I think it'll do very well' I said, making my mind up. 'I'll tell the agent tomorrow that I'll take it – unfurnished, but just leave whatever you don't want and I can sort it out later.'

'That'll suit us fine – I'll also leave a list pinned on the kitchen board – coalman, plumber, neighbour's names, when to put the dustbins out and all that!'

'Okay, thanks. And thanks again to you and your wife for showing me. And best of luck in Germany...'

So that was that, and I now had a place of my own! And even if it was tiny, once I'd decorated and furnished it with some of my stuff that was still in store, it would do very well. A warm surge went through me, I'll make it so that Elizabeth loves it – it'll be our own place!

IX

There was a telephone message in my pigeonhole when I got back. 'Ring Angela Lawson-Davis it said. And to think, until now I hadn't known her new married name!

'Hello, Angela?' I said, wedged in my usual booth.

'Oh, good of you to ring back so *promptly*' she gushed,

'sorry about the short notice, but Nigel and I are giving a small *cockers-p* on Friday, and we wondered whether you'd be free to come along? Just a few people from the village, nothing too formal, *do* say you'll come?'

Trust Angela to still call it a cockers-p; surely, these day's people just came to drinks?

'I'd love to, Angela, thanks very much...'

'See you about seven then – oh, and perhaps you'd like to stay to supper afterwards? It'll only be *scraps* and leftovers I'm afraid; just Nigel and me and I know he'd love to meet you – oh, and Elizabeth too, I expect...'

'Why thanks, I'd like that even better! Look forward to it – and see you at seven on Friday.'

X

For the remainder of the week I was as good as my word and started over again. We began with the hover: one foot; two feet; three feet above the ground, first into wind, then at ninety degrees crosswind, then tail into wind; at all times remaining stationary over a spot. 'Imagine it's the corner of a flat roof on the top of a building' I said, 'troops have got to get in and out, as well as load or unload weapons and equipment.' When they'd mastered that, I said: 'now imagine its night – pitch black and not a light anywhere as a reference' and I made them do it on instruments. Next, I worked on their takeoff and made them climb out at angles that varied from five to eighty-five degrees, together with the appropriate speeds, exercising the full range of the power envelope. To climb in a straight line at a constant speed is all to do with the smooth transfer of power; each configuration requiring different settings and rates of input. Then, it was time to perfect the circuit. Only accurate rate one turns were acceptable whilst maintaining the exact circuit height and speed throughout. Then, finally to the approach and landing, and as with the climb, with varying angles of descent and forward airspeed, all of which called for different timing and appropriate amounts of flare to enable them to stop before lowering-down onto a spot. Throughout all these manoeuvres I periodically cut the engine, until they could master autorotation from any given situation or height. It was hard and gruelling work, but I had their full attention; both wanted to learn, which made instructing that much easier and not least, rewarding.

'Okay, you've proved you can do it to please me, but from now on I want you to prove it to yourselves! Every time you fly, from now and for evermore, I want you to set your own targets and be your own judge. I won't be there to pull you up, so it's got to come from within. You know what's right and what's acceptable; there's only one standard and nothing less will do. It's easy to flop about all over the sky, but that's not for you. Remember, think about your flying; I do all the time and I've been at it all my life! I even extend this thought process to when I'm driving a car – it all helps – as well as taking some of the boredom out of driving. When you drive to Salisbury next, set yourself a target; try doing it without touching your brakes or using the clutch! You may laugh and I'm sure its against every law in the land; certainly a driving instructor or a police officer wouldn't understand, but think about it – you've got to be at the right speed to enter a corner; you've got to keep your distance from the car in front and you'll also save petrol. How, do I hear you say? Because if you have to brake to slow down means you were going too fast in the first place! Anyway, try it, it will make you think – and that's how you've got to fly!

'When you eventually leave here you'll be awarded a pair of wings. These are not any old pair of wings; they're wings with a crown on top, the emblem of a Service pilot and therefore a professional! So make sure you always live up to them: if you always think and fly as a professional, I promise you, one day those wings will save your life.

'Okay, end of lecture – and end of revision! Next we'll be going on to low flying and for this you'll need a new set of maps. So, before Monday afternoon I want you to make up a set of one-in-fifty-thousand Ordnance Survey maps – the fablon-covered sort are best, so you can draw on them in chinagraph. Get enough to cover the whole of the low flying area, the same as you've marked on your half-million aeronautical charts. Lay them out in order – they should all overlap slightly – and number them. Then, transcribe this pattern and mark it in as a numbered grid onto your aeronautical charts – the idea being that if I ask you to fly from here to Warminster, you'll immediately know you'll need maps One and Four, or whatever. Oh, and from now on, always make sure you've got some black chinagraph pencils on you – best keep them in the little pencil-pockets on the arms of your flying suits, that's what they're there for!

Anyway, I'm pleased with your progress; you both worked hard this week, so well done – and I'll see you on Monday. Have a good weekend!'

I wrote up their notes and then walked back to my room and had a shower and changed out of uniform before going to Angela's cockers-p.

XI

The yard was full of cars when I got there and I could hear a hubbub of voices, pierced by the occasional high-pitched shrill of a woman's laugh spilling out from an open window.

'*Darling!* So glad you could come!' Angela waylaid me by the door. 'Here, let me get you a drink.' Without looking, she reached behind her to a table that had rows of wineglasses with pieces of lemon impaled upon the rims and half-filled with an amber liquid. With a practiced motion, she found the next in line and thrust it into my hand. 'Try one of Nigel's specials – they really make a party go with a zing! Now, let me find you somebody nice to talk to – I don't suppose you know a soul!'

I took a sip and winced. It was a Martini of sorts, mostly gin but with a dash of something sweet. Also it was warm...

'Ah, come and meet Margery...'

'Hang on a sec...' I put the glass back onto the table, and discreetly helped myself to a glass of red wine from an open bottle that was presumably being allowed to breathe.

'Hello Margery!' I took a sip of wine and plunged into the mêlée. The room was full of Angela-sort-of-people all talking ten to the dozen at each other, whilst their eyes constantly roamed to see who was talking to whom, and whether their conversation would be worth eavesdropping or maybe joining. I searched the room to see if Elizabeth was there – and whether her husband was with her. I could see no sign of either of them.

Margery suddenly screeched as she saw somebody across the room, and left me in mid sentence. The void was immediately filled by a red-faced perspiring man carrying a tray of empty glasses.

'Ah, you must be the mysterious man from the past – hello, I'm Nigel.' He was as I'd expected: the very image of a successful stockbroker; late forties, running to fat, exuberating bonhomie from a permanently smiling face and suitably dressed-down for the occasion in yellow trousers, a broad-striped red shirt and a cravat that had red stripes running the opposite way. No doubt fashionable in the stockbroker world, but to my eyes, he looked like a modern replica of the Pied Piper.

We shook hands. 'Hello Nigel – nice of you to ask me... Jolly gathering you've got here' and then added, 'I was just looking to see if Elizabeth and her husband were here?'

'Elizabeth? Yes, she's here somewhere – I don't suppose you know many people... her husband, thank goodness, declined to come...'

'Declined?'

'Yes, we had them both over once, and – er, well it was a bit of a disaster, to say the least! I don't think he was very – ah, comfortable in our company and frankly was quite churlish – even to the extent of upsetting some of our guests. We then had them over again, on a one-to-one basis, but with little better success! At least we tried... funny bloke, I can't think why she ever married him – or for that matter didn't ditch him years ago... oh well, none of my business, but it just goes to show: one never knows what goes on in a marriage! Of course, Elizabeth comes over a lot to see Angela, but she always comes on her own now. I suppose you remember her from when she was a little girl? Funny to think you knew Angela before I did! Ah well, times change... and for the better I hope! Must go and pour some more drinks – look forward to catching you later at supper – you are staying, aren't you?'

So that was Nigel. The absolute opposite of old Tristan, but a good enough bloke and I could see they were eminently suited to each other, and was glad of that.

I suddenly felt her. I knew she was near and swivelled round – there by the door!

She was standing in the doorway; almost like an uncertain child, standing in a defenceless attitude with her arms down by her sides, hands open, palms turned slightly forward. She was dressed in a dark skirt and a white blouse and was wearing the necklace I had given her long ago. Her very simplicity made her stand out and look just... just perfect! But then I would think that. Another woman stopped to talk to her and she inclined her head to listen, in only the way she could. My heart went out to her and an ache of longing surged through me 'God, what is it about you?' I thought. She lifted her head, found me and smiled, then mouthed over the woman's shoulder 'Hello...'

'Hello, where were you?' I asked as I eventually reached her side having fought my way across the room. 'I couldn't see you anywhere...'

'I went out to say hello to the horses' she said, touching my arm. Another electric shock went through it.

'How many horses has Angela got?'

'Three at the moment – only one's mine... well, that's not really true but I think of her as mine and she's the one I look after and ride. The other two are Angela's, but one's for sale?

175

Angela's out riding all day tomorrow, so I was just helping Ted bring them in from the paddock. How are you?'

'Fine...' I breathed, as our minds locked and I swam into her eyes. 'I've managed to get a little house...'

'Ooh!' she clapped her hands and then jumped up and quickly kissed me on the lips. 'Have you really? Somewhere for us?'

I was conscious of Angela watching us from the other side of the room. 'It's only a tiny cottage in Nether Wallop – I sign the lease on Monday. Then I want to decorate it and do a few things and get some of my stuff and pictures, so I expect it'll be a week or two before I actually move in.'

'A week! That's far too long! I'll help you decorate – I could do it when you're at work; when can you show me, then we could plan it together?'

'Well, Monday would be the earliest' I said thoughtfully. 'If I sign the lease and get the keys at lunchtime, we could have a look at it together in the evening if you like?'

'Oh yes! And although you haven't asked, things are beginning to move on my side...' she finished abruptly, as Angela joined us.

'Now then you two! What did he say that made you jump up and kiss him? I saw you! And I must say, it's the first time I've seen you laugh for months... No, no – tell me later, I'd like you both to circulate for now. Elizabeth, would you mind taking some nibbles around?'

The party lasted for another forty minutes and then they all left together. It was as though someone had pressed a hidden bell; they put down their drinks down, some unfinished, and then queued up to where Angela and Nigel had conveniently stationed themselves by the front door.

'See you tomorrow, Angela' from a horsy-looking woman. 'Good bye – jolly nice party and thanks for the tip, Nigel. I'll give you a bell at the office...' and then they were gone.

'Thank goodness people don't smoke anymore' Angela was saying as she gathered a tray and started to load it with glasses. 'Do you remember we actually used to put cigarettes out in small glasses for people to help themselves! And the mess afterwards; people used to stub them out anywhere – all my nice china pieces, just anywhere, as well as flick ash all over the floor!'

I'd been thinking of asking if it would be alright to light my pipe, but decided not to and grabbed another tray instead.

'Ken's going away for the weekend' Elizabeth whispered as we gathered glasses together 'he's taking the car and driving to Sheffield first thing in the morning – to see his parents. I expect he wants some paternal advice after what happened last night...'

'Why, what happened last night?' I whispered back.

'Shhh! Tell you later – it ended in a bit of a fight...'

'Are you okay?'

'Yes, I told him it was the last straw and I was leaving him – are you free this weekend?'

'Yes.'

'He'll be back Sunday night...'

'I can't carry any more' I said out loud as Angela swept past. I followed her with the tray to the kitchen.

With all the glasses gathered, we shut the door and stayed in the kitchen, whilst Angela and Elizabeth loaded the dishwasher.

'Now, you two are being very secretive, what's going on?' Angela said, as we at last sat down around the large table and Nigel started to carve platefuls of cold beef. 'Are you coming riding with me in the morning, Elizabeth – a whole group of us are hacking over to Colonel Bonham's place and then on to that nice little pub for lunch? It should be a splendid day out!'

'Oh! Well...'

'I was thinking of taking Elizabeth flying tomorrow' I interposed.

'He's got the sweetest little aeroplane called Ashley' Elizabeth supplemented, 'we flew to Bembridge in the Isle of Wight for lunch last Saturday...' she caught my foot under the table.

'Oh? You've already been flying together?' Angela lifted

an eyebrow, looking first at Elizabeth, then at me. Suddenly a look of understanding came over her face. 'Oh my God – I just hope you know what you're doing...?'

I looked at Nigel and received a large wink. 'I reckon they know what they're doing' he said, 'after all old thing, we did!'

'Not so much of the old-thing, thank you! Anyway that was different – I was abandoned!'

'Abandoned my foot! You were ready enough at the time...'

'Look!' I said, spreading the fingers of both hands in a sign of peace. 'Elizabeth and I are very new. I'm divorced – and well, I think you both know Elizabeth's got a rotten marriage. Yes, we went flying last Saturday... and – and we found we got on very well! And that's all there is to it – at least for now. But I think I can speak for us both and we both feel the same. Whatever happens down the road is for us to find out – as well as sort out, when the time comes...'

'What about Ken?' Angela asked.

'That's between Ken and me' Elizabeth said quickly, 'and for me alone to handle. I told him last night that I was leaving him and he's going off tomorrow – I think to see his parents in Sheffield.'

'Don't you think he's a bit old to go running back to mummy?' Angela snapped back, 'don't be naïve, you know he couldn't face loosing you, he'll fight to the last ditch – you mark my words!'

'Hey, hey! Whose side are you on?' Nigel interrupted. 'I reckon it's a jolly good thing. Best thing that could have happened – and I mean that to both of you. So if you ask me, I'm delighted – and I think the occasion's certainly worthy a bottle!' He got up and returned with a bottle of champagne from his personal drinks-fridge.

Angela's face cleared slightly. 'Any excuse for you to open a bottle of champagne... but perhaps you're right – and oh darling, just – just do be careful! And you...' she turned to me, '...you, just make sure you look after her! I know we've known each other – or rather about each other for a long time, but I don't know what you're really like! And – and well, she's the only sister I've got, and I won't see her hurt again.'

The champagne popped and we sipped and smiled at each other. In the space of a few minutes, it appeared that Nigel and Angela had already accepted me as a prospective in-law! I thought about mentioning that Elizabeth and I hadn't even discussed the future, and certainly not marriage or the implications of her divorce, but then decided to keep quiet, for deep down I suddenly realized that that was what I wanted.

Elizabeth was the first to break the silence. 'I realize that the immediate future is going to be difficult – especially with Ken, but these things are never easy, and you both went through it and survived... I just hope it won't be too messy.'

'I know you and Ken have had your difficulties – you married him on an impulse, or rather as an act of defiance, and I can't help wondering whether you're being rather impulsive now...?'

'Please, please don't lecture me!' I could see Elizabeth was near to tears. 'Nobody has talked about marriage! All I know is that a pathway has suddenly opened up in my life – a pathway strewn with flowers and a great light at the end. Please try to understand – I don't know what the future holds, but I do know it's at the end of that path, and I've got to go down it. All I ask from you is for some understanding – and maybe a place where I can rest my head?'

Nigel got up and put his arm around her shoulder. 'You know you can always come here' he said gruffly. 'After all, Angela and I are family; you'll always be welcome here... doesn't matter when or for how long – isn't that right, Angie?' He came on to me and put his hand on my shoulder. 'And that goes for you too, old chap. Now, let's not talk about it any more – and anyway, it really is none of our business! So, cheers everybody and let's tackle some of this delicious-looking beef!'

The master of the house had spoken, and silently I thanked him. Maybe Angela didn't wear the trousers – at least, not all the time.

Elizabeth and I left together. I walked her to her car, then got in beside her and put my arms around her.

'Hello!' I said and kissed her cheek. 'I just want you to know that I will be at the end of your path. Just keep coming along it and I'll be there, waiting for you.'

'Oh sweetheart' she said, taking hold of my face in her hands. 'Do you mean it – will you really be there? I'm sorry about this evening; I know we haven't discussed anything, and – and it all happened so quickly; Angela jumping to conclusions and everything, that's just like her! It's different for me – after all I was the one that went looking for you, but God knows what you must think?'

I thought for a moment, and smiled. It was not unlike a theme straight out of a wartime novel: where two people met one day, virtually by chance, and immediately fell in love, for who knew what tomorrow would bring? After all, we hardly knew each other... and there was no need for urgency; there was all the time in the world to get to know each other properly... but then I decided to go with my instincts and throw caution to the winds.

'Elizabeth, we haven't had a chance to talk about anything, but deep down I know it's what I want – and I'm glad it came to a head this evening for they have every right to know. I will be there at the end of your path – for it's my path too, remember? When this is all over and the dust has settled – and it will settle; and when the time is right and only if and when you're ready, I'd be very honoured if you would marry me?'

'Oh darling...' she groped in her handbag for a handkerchief. 'That's the nicest proposal a girl could ever ask for. Yes, of course I'll marry you, you silly thing, it's our destiny... but only if I can come and live with you in the little cottage first! It better not be straight away, but when the time is right?'

'Okay, deal!'

We didn't say anything for a long time after that, we just sat savouring our closeness and the enormity of what was happening.

'Where are you taking me tomorrow?' at last she asked.

'Ah, well – I hadn't really thought. I think the weather's going to be okay, so we can go where we like – when have you got to be back, Sunday evening?'

'Yes, I suppose so, but it doesn't really matter anymore...'

'No, I suppose not, but I think you'd better be there to face the music. The sooner it's tackled, the sooner we'll all know where we are. So, if I pick you up, say at nine-thirty, we could either be at the Channel Isles, France, the Scillies, the Isle of Man or perhaps Ireland – Eire that is, I've seen enough of Northern Ireland – by about lunchtime. That is so long as we don't stop at any Service Stations on the way!'

'Really? Oh you are a lovely man! Can we go to all of them? I love it, I love it and I love little Ashley! No, we'd better not go too far – would it be all right to go to the Channel Isles, I've never been there before. Which Island is best?'

'They're all totally different, and each worth visiting for their own sakes. We'll go to Alderney first, have lunch and then hire a couple of bicycles and bike round the island. It's very small! Then, if we like it we can either stay, or else go on to Guernsey, which is a much larger island and has lots more to see. So we could see all those things on Sunday and then fly back in the evening. Leave Jersey for another day, how does that sound?

'It sounds wonderful! Is life with you always going to be like this?'

'I wouldn't count on it – I'm a grumpy old bugger some-times... where shall we meet?'

'He'll have the car, so you you'll have to pick me up; either from my house – no, better not do that, I'll walk somewhere – the NAAFI's always full of people on a Saturday morning, so it'd better not be there – tell you what, I'll wait at the bus stop outside the main gate. I'll be there at nine-thirty sharp!'

Chapter 6

I

She wasn't there at nine-thirty.

I waited in the car a little way down the road from the bus stop and watched the main gate.

At ten-fifteen I saw what I thought was her car. It came screeching out, turned right and then went haring off down the road towards Andover.

Ought I to follow...? No, better to wait here, maybe it wasn't her car – and this is where we said we'd meet.

I nearly missed her when at last she did come. She came walking up the road from behind and I just spotted her in my mirror before the door opened and she got in. Her face was a mass of red wheals, one eye was puffed up and completely closed and she was holding her side.

'Elizabeth, what...?' I leant across and gently held her in my arms. She pulled away from me and then started to cry.

'The bastard! The rotten, stinking bastard! Why is it he always knows where to hit a girl where it shows most?' She said between sobs. 'I'm not going back. I'm never going back – that's it! Take me away somewhere – oh no, I can't go anywhere with you looking like this. Oh the rotten bastard...'

There was only one place to go, I decided, and that was Angela's. But she was out – maybe Nigel would be there – anyway, it was somewhere to go. I started the car and turned in the road.

'Oh not here!' She said, when she realized where we were going. 'Please, I don't want them involved?'

'They already are – and anyway, there's nowhere else right now. I haven't got my cottage yet... anyway, you know what Nigel said.'

I pulled into the yard and then left her in the car and went to the door. I couldn't hear any bell ringing inside, so after a moment tried the door. It was open. 'Hello...!' I called out, pitching it in my best parade-ground-carrying voice. 'Anyone at home?' I went into the kitchen and then opened the door that led to the garden and tried again.

'Someone there?' Nigel's head appeared bobbing along over the top of a hedge.

'Nigel – it's me! Spot of bother and need your help...' He appeared round the hedge, pushing a wheelbarrow full of logs.

'Hello old man, what's up?'

'Elizabeth – she's been beaten-up, quite badly. She's in the car.' He followed me through the kitchen and out into the yard.

'Oh my God!' He said taking one look at her. 'Here, let me help you...' Elizabeth got out of the car, still clutching her side. I put my arm around her waist to support her. 'I'm going to ring the doctor.' Nigel said going on ahead.

'Oh no, not the doctor, please – I'm all right, really...' But he had already gone.

The doctor arrived forty-five minutes later. Nigel had caught him just as he was about to go out on his rounds and he had to pass the house anyway. By this time we'd put her to bed in the spare room and he examined her there. 'Who did this to you?' he asked.

'Her husband' Nigel replied.

'Husband or not, he needs locking up. I've never seen such a mess. She's got two cracked ribs, which I'll bind up now, and I'll write a prescription for a salve to help the bruising on her face and also some pills to make her sleep. I'll give her one now, she needs as much rest as possible. There's not a lot else I can do – it's just a matter of letting nature run its course. I'll pop in and have a look at her tomorrow. She's also going to have a corker of a black eye. Are you going to prosecute?'

Nigel and I looked at each other, the same thought going through both our minds.

'No, no – not the police!' Elizabeth murmured through bruised lips.

'I think that would be an excellent idea' Nigel said.

'Have you got a camera?' the doctor asked, 'it could be helpful to have some pictures – you never know... and in any event, I'll have to write a report.' He tore off the prescription from his pad and handed it to me. 'You want to get that as soon as possible.'

'Right, I'll go and get it now.'

In the lanes I got held up by a string of horses. I edged slowly past looking up at each one and then, as I'd hoped, spotted Angela on the second horse behind the leader. I pulled ahead and then stopped and walked back.

'Hello, where are you going – I thought you were taking Elizabeth flying?'

I told her what had happened and her lips tightened. 'Right, I'll get straight back' she said, immediately wheeling her horse.

By the time I'd waited half an hour at the chemists for the prescription and then driven back, Angela was already sitting by Elizabeth's bedside. She looked very forlorn, lying there. Her eye had swollen even more and was now completely closed, and the bruises on her face showed in remarked contrast to the whiteness of the pillow, her hair spilling all around. The pill the doctor had given her had already taken effect, for she was very drowsy.

'Elizabeth is going to stay with us – at least for the next few days and until she's better, which will also give us time to sort things out.' Angela said. 'Apparently Ken changed his mind about going to Sheffield, which was what the row was all about, so I'm going round to her house now to get some of her things. I'd like you to come with me, if you wouldn't mind; he doesn't know you and the last thing I need at the moment is a stand-up row with *him*!'

'Angela?' Elizabeth muttered. 'Can you get my diary, I don't want him to find it?'

'Of course, dear, where is it?'

'In my knicker-drawer – buried deep down. Top left-hand side in the bedroom.'

We went in Angela's Range Rover and parked behind their car outside their quarter. Ken was obviously back.

'Oh, it had to be you!' he said with a sneer as he opened the door, 'I suppose the little whore's gone crying to you?' He was dressed in jeans and a stained T-shirt that stretched grotesquely over his stomach and was holding an open beer can.

'Ken, although Elizabeth is my sister, I have no intention of becoming involved in your private marital affairs. I want to make that *quite* clear! Elizabeth is hurt and she needs looking after, so she'll be staying with us until she's better. That's all I have to say and now, with your permission I'd like to collect some of her things?' There was a steel core in Angela that I hadn't known about before.

'Little bitch, serves her right – if she has got a fancy-man, at least he won't fancy her anymore... and who are you?' He said, turning to me.

'Just a friend of the family' I said, holding his eye.

'Good riddance to her, little two-timing bitch. Still, if she's staying with you at least I know where she is, so I suppose you'd better come in and collect what you need... but not you' he said turning to me, 'I'm not having a complete stranger nosing about in my house. You can stay downstairs!'

'Won't be a minute' Angela said to me, pushing past. After a moment's hesitation I followed him into the front room.

185

Or the lion's den.

He had the television on, a huge black affair that dominated the whole room, flanked on either side by a pair of oversize speakers together with a black cabinet containing a stacked stereo system. He had muted the sound when he'd heard the doorbell, and the picture showed a man mouthing something, standing in front of a packed football stadium. An armchair, with an overflowing ashtray of cigarette butts balanced on one arm, had been pulled up to face the television and there was an open six-pack carton of beer on the floor. I wished now that I'd stayed outside.

'Please, don't let me interrupt your game...'

'I've seen you somewhere before, haven't I?'

'Ah – I don't think so; who's playing?'

He sat down, felt under the chair for the TV remote control and pressed a button.

'I'm sure I've seen you somewhere before' he said as the commentator's voice filled the room. 'Never forget a face, I'll think of it in a minute.'

I stood behind his chair and took stock of the surroundings. I knew I shouldn't have been there, but nonetheless I was curious to see how she lived. It wasn't a large room, and my first impression was that it was crammed full of furniture that was incompatible and revealed two conflicting extremes of lifestyles. Opposite the television and stereo complex was a modern self-assembly display cabinet finished in 'antique-pine' that contained cups and small trophies behind a smoked-glass door, whilst on another wall was a matching multi-mirrored drinks cabinet that lit up when you opened it. Yet set amongst these were two traditional winged armchairs and a small sofa, with loose-covers in material that matched the curtains, and a pair of antique mahogany side tables. There was a 'glowing-coal-effect' gas fire, over which hung a large print of a Spanish village – sun-drenched houses with red-tiled roofs and an outside café with striped awning, set against a background of startlingly blue sea under an azure sky; whilst hanging on the only other wall with available space was an original watercolour of two hunting dogs, set in a heavy gold frame. The inner wall was a sliding panel affair that folded like a concertina and led through to an open-plan kitchen/dining area.

'I know where it was', he announced, muting the sound again. 'It was last week, when I drove my colonel to the officers' mess – you went in with him! You're not a friend of the family, you're an officer here!'

'Yes, I am on the staff here, but I'm still a friend of the family; I've known them for a very long time. Look, I'm just here to help Mrs Lawson-Davis... this really is none of my business and I'm sorry to intrude. I – er, do you mind if I wait in here and look at some of the pictures?'

'Help yourself' he said curtly, sitting down and turning the sound on again.

This was obviously more Elizabeth's domain, for here the walls were covered with original paintings, and a large mahogany table with matching chairs and sideboard furnished the remainder of the room. There were flowers in a cut-glass vase on the mahogany sideboard together with cut-glass decanters and numerous photographs in silver frames. A small wicker-backed chair and matching table with a small portable radio on it were positioned by sliding patio doors that led to a terrace outside. Was this where she sat – listening to the radio on her own, whilst her husband drank beer and watched television at the other side of the partition?

I felt rather ashamed of myself. For Elizabeth's sake I should have confronted him; but then, I had no right to be here... but I still felt that somehow I was betraying her. I studied the pictures and wished Angela would hurry up. Then my eyes strayed to the photographs on the sideboard. They were mostly of her parents and family groups taken when she was a small girl. Then I stopped short; there was one of Tristan and me, standing in our cavalry blues in the front porch of the church; groom and best man at Angela's wedding. I remembered Tristan had wanted to get married in morning dress, but Angela had insisted upon a military wedding with archway of swords and the full works. I looked younger and slimmer there – but the fact that I was there at all told me a lot. Poor kid...

Angela came down the stairs dragging a suitcase. 'Can you take this to the car? There's still another one and a holdall to come.'

I was thankful to escape and went through the kitchen area and out through another door that led back into the hall, thereby managing to avoid Ken who was studiously engrossed in his game.

I put the case into the back of the Range Rover and then collected the other two that Angela had brought down, whilst she went in to talk to Ken. I saw them through the window; he was still sitting there with the sound fully up, making no effort to move or acknowledge our departure.

'We're going to have trouble with that one' Angela said on the way back. 'He's been a bastard to her ever since they got married. He's completely perverse; treated her like dirt and ridiculed her in public on every possible occasion, but would-n't dream of ever letting her go. It's as though he enjoys keep-ing her chained up, like some people keep a dog! God knows why Elizabeth put up with him for so long; I told her often enough... maybe this time will be different and she'll have the strength to break away. But he won't give up without a fight – you mark my words!'

'She's lucky to have you so near...'

'Yes, but I can't be there all the time – its not fair on Nigel; he's been very good and understanding, but after all, we have got our own life... how serious is it between you two? I don't want to pry, but she'll need support and I don't know if I can do it all on my own. When Tristan and I broke up it was a mutual thing – but this... this is far more explo-sive; God knows where all the pieces will end up!'

'Well, as I said last night, Elizabeth and I are still very new, but as far as I'm concerned, I'm behind her all the way. I shan't go away and – and when its all over I'd like to marry her – that is, if she'll have me.'

She slowed the car, then stopped and searched my face. 'Gosh, you really are serious! It's funny to think we've known each other all these years – Tristan and now this; our lives really are intertwined! I don't know what to say, except – except...' she suddenly lent across and kissed my cheek '...there! I think that says it all!' She started the car again. 'I couldn't find her diary anywhere though,' she said a little later, 'I just hope he hasn't got it – and also that she's been discreet... but knowing Elizabeth, she'll have written down every thought she ever had...'

When we got back Nigel told us that he'd rung the police and the local community officer would be coming round later to take a statement. I'd always imagined that it was usual for the complainant to go to the police station rather than the other way round, and it made me realize that Nigel obviously pulled considerable weight in this neighbourhood.

'I think it would be better, old man, if you weren't here when he arrives?'

'Why? I'm as much involved as you are – and anyway, I brought her here.'

'We'll get round that somehow – I just think for now, the fewer people involved the better. There'll bound to be repercussions...'

'Did Elizabeth put you up to this?'

'Well, yes, as a matter of fact she did! She said it was her side and she didn't want you involved.'

'I'll just pop up and see her...'

'Better not, old man, I think she's asleep. Give us a call later, and maybe tomorrow...?'

And so I left.

I'd felt guilty at her house, but now I felt doubly so, and suddenly the weekend ahead seemed interminably bleak and empty. I stopped the car a little way down the lane to collect my thoughts. Where now? Then on an impulse decided to drive round to the cottage; it was a good as anywhere.

There was a skip outside half full of rubbish and the front door was open.

'Ah, just the man!' he said as I stopped the car. 'This is just about the last of our lot; do you want to decide what bits and

189

pieces you want to keep? Anything you don't want can then be binned. The skip's only half full!'

So, although officially I had yet to sign the lease, I spent the remainder of the day at the cottage sorting out what would be useful and dumping the rest, as well as assessing what work needed doing. At least it took my mind off things.

I telephoned Nigel that evening. He said the police had been and taken a statement and also a copy of the doctor's report; that Elizabeth's bruises were beginning to come out but otherwise she was much the same, and would I like to come to lunch tomorrow?

I thanked him again for all he'd done and readily accepted the invitation. He was turning out to be a thoroughly good bloke and it made me ashamed to think how very cynical my first impressions had been.

II

I woke early and saw that Sunday morning was sunny and breezy – perfect for flying away with Elizabeth, but instead I consulted the list of decorating materials I'd made and decided to go into Andover to see if the Odd Job Centre was open. I needn't have worried for it certainly was; and when I got there I found the car park virtually full with every other able-bodied male intent on doing the same thing! I grabbed a trolley and joined the queue, shuffling up and down the aisles. In a corner I found a rack that contained assorted self-adhesive letters in various styles, and eventually selected two sets that made-up *Ashley* in a black handwriting script. Elizabeth would like that!

With a boot full of paint tins and brushes, I then drove to Thruxton and wheeled the Robin out of the hangar and took some time making up my mind where best to stick the letter-ing on each side of the cowling. In the end I decided it looked best raked at an angle, rather like a written signature, and stood back and admired my handiwork. The finished effect looked rather good!

Just as I was finishing the owner of the little Bolköw Junior arrived, so I helped push it out and then had a chat with him, as pilots do the world over. After he'd taxied away I tinkered with the aeroplane and gave it a thorough going through, one thing leading to another and in what seemed no time at all it was ten to one and I was going to be late!

Elizabeth was up when I got there. Nigel and Angela melted away somewhere and I held her in my arms. 'Careful! Don't squeeze too hard.'

I kissed her hair and her bad eye and her neck, breathing in her natural scent. I think more than anything it was her smell that excited me and just made me want to eat her. Apart from the unwitting remark I made in the pub when we first met I'd never really thought about it much before, but realized now how important the sense of smell is to binding a relationship. It's extremely personal and very much part of that indefinable 'x-factor' that attracts two people – although has largely been lost, ignored, or more often covered up by scent in humans. Indeed, it made me realise that the reverse also applies, whereby however attractive otherwise, if a person doesn't smell right it can be the greatest repellent!

I held her close and let my hands explore her back and felt the dressings around her ribs. Then I cupped her bottom and she pressed against me; we were one again.

'I think he's got my diary' she whispered.

'Yes, Angela said she couldn't find it in your knicker drawer.'

'I don't like the thought of him going through my knickers – I thought it was safe there. Trouble is, I'd put everything in it – all my thoughts, how I'd found you and then all about us – everything!'

'Doesn't matter, we'll fight it together.'

But that's what I *don't* want – it's not fair to involve you. This is my side and I've got to sort it out on my own...'

'Doesn't matter – we'll fight it together; it's better that

way. Anyway, after beating you up like that he hasn't a leg to stand on.'

'Oh, I only hope you're right! Sweetheart, may I come and live with you in your cottage soon? I can't stay here for ever – and I'm never going back.'

'Shhh. One step at a time. I looked at the pictures in your house – and the photographs; you've got one of me!'

'I know' she breathed, 'that's how I found you.' Then: 'how will I be able to get all my personal things out of the house? He's quite likely to destroy everything I value.'

'I think the next step is for you to get a solicitor – I'll have a word with Nigel. There's a procedure about these things and he'll be able to put a court order on or something. Don't worry; divorce happens all the time – that's what keeps solicitors' in business.'

'Divorce – there's a glorious finality about that word! Only why does it take so long? Once you've made your mind up I think it should happen straight away – what's the point of drawing it out and all the awfulness in between? Now, the sooner I'm divorced the better. Ugh, I feel so dirty! I wish I could come to you as a virgin?'

'You are in your soul and that's all that matters. Besides...' I added mischievously, feeling the heat from her loins, '...we wouldn't have lasted very long! What about the Service Station? Anyway, I was married before – so virginity doesn't really enter into the equation. I love you as you are – black eye an' all...'

'Do you?' she pressed herself even closer. 'I can feel your hard, you naughty man! Will you take me back to our Service Station one day – I want to make love to you there again – under Ashley's other wing?'

'Come on you two, break it up – its lunchtime!' Angela said, poking her head round the door 'besides Elizabeth, I thought you were meant to be ill!'

Lunch over, we sat around the table and talked it through. Elizabeth, they said, was welcome to stay there until such time other arrangements could be made; Nigel would contact a solicitor he knew and start the wheels turning, as well as co-ordinate with the police; Angela would contact Ken later in the week, after he'd received a letter from the solicitor, and arrange for the remainder of Elizabeth's personal effects to be collected; whilst I, – I would do nothing for the time being, except go back to work and move into my cottage!

I went back to the mess much later, in a happier frame of mind.

III

The new course had already assembled in the crew-room by the time I got there. I'd decided to draw a new flying overall from the stores; not that there was anything wrong with my old one, except it showed my rank and was adorned with a couple of squadron badges, which made me stand out from the other civilian instructors who all wore plain flying suits as issued. Maybe, I thought, an unadorned flying overall would be less intimidating to new students at the early stages of their training. They were mostly sergeants or lieutenants, who were still young enough to be rank-conscious, and I didn't want them stamping to attention on the pedals of a helicopter! In the advanced flight it was different, for there most of the instructors were serving officers and NCOs and uniform – or rather wings, badges of rank and other insignia on flying suits was accepted as the norm. Besides, by the time they'd progressed that far, the students could master the basics and were ready to be initiated as an army pilot and it was therefore fitting to be taught by a uniformed instructor!

I bumped into David on the way in. He'd just finished his opening pep talk and the other instructors were busy claiming their new charges. He lifted an eyebrow when he saw me, then nodded and smiled. 'Good idea!' he said and left it at that.

'Paul Courtney and John Barclay?' I announced to the room in general. Two students detached themselves and came over. 'Right-ho, let's find a corner and have a chat!'

I'd memorised their notes and knew that Paul Courtney was a lieutenant in the Royal Artillery and John Barclay, like Stephen Grant, was another direct entry officer straight from Sandhurst, whose commission into the Army Air Corps would only be ratified upon his passing the full flying course. They couldn't have been more different: Paul Courtney already had the mark of a gunner about him, both in mannerisms and speech. It's strange how regiments, albeit unwittingly, put a certain stamp on their officers; I can enter a room full of officers, all from different regiments and dressed in civilian clothes, yet invariably put a regiment or corps to them and Paul Courtney definitely had the stamp of a gunner! He was of average height and build, but walked with the slight stoop of a taller man; his hair was prematurely thin but still strictly cut to regulation length and overall he exuded an air of quiet and neat complacency. In many ways he reminded me of Roger who had also been a gunner and some instinct told me that like Roger, he too would be a stickler for correctness as well as master of the spoken word! There was nothing dashing about Paul Courtney, but with proper tuition he would make a careful and reliable pilot.

Not so Second Lieutenant John Barclay, who was out of a completely different mould. Again he was of average height, but he had a wafer-thin body and in striking contrast to his age, the face of a much older and experienced man. This was possibly accentuated by his hair, which was jet black and brushed straight back with no parting, so that it seemed to stem from a widows peak before falling down on either side of his head. He talked in a lazy drawling voice that matched his suave image and although extremely amiable, I was immediately wary. You cannot approach flying with a casual attitude, especially in the early stages; the two are incompatible and a recipe for disaster. Instinctively I knew Mister Debonair Barclay would need watching!

'So, congratulations on getting this far, and now welcome to helicopters!' I said, as I pulled up a chair facing them. 'You must be feeling somewhat daunted: your first day here – I know I was on my first day here – but if you approach it in the right spirit, it can be a lot of fun!' Poor sods, I thought, little do they know how many buckets of blood and tears they'll shed before they're through... but then, is that really necessary? Do they really need to shed blood and buckets, when it's down to me to set the pace as well as the flavour? Why bark and growl all the time, why not try and make it fun for them; use a carrot instead of the time-honoured stick? Start-off as you mean to go on...

'So let's start-off by thinking positively! It's my job to teach you to fly a helicopter and I'll be your primary instructor for the next fourteen weeks or so. During this time you'll amass the impressive total of sixty flying hours, and subject to your passing the final handling test, you'll then be ready to move on to the Advanced Flight and the start of your military education.' I smiled at them, which only made them squirm in their seats.

'The fact that you've got this far shows that you've got it in you, and from now on its just a question of application and keeping ahead of the game. The pressure's pretty hard and you cannot afford to slack – neither here nor at your ground school studies. If you slack and fall behind, believe me, it's a devil of a job to get back onto stream and the odds are you'll be RTU'd. You'll already know the fallout rate is about seventy-five percent; that's a lot, for our standards are high and we only take the best. But, if you *have* got it in you, but then chuck it all away from lack of application... that's just a waste of rations, and you're not the sort of person we're looking for at all. Now, I promise you, it's as much in my interest to get you through the course as it is in yours, and I'll help in every way I can. Therefore, if you don't understand something or if you feel you're not on top at any time – either with your flying or with your ground school studies, just come and ask and I'll try and help; that's what I'm here for!

'Likewise, I'll be fair with you and tell you straightway if I think you're not up to scratch. Remember, not everyone is suited to being an army pilot and there are many facets to it. If you give it your best but still find you can't get it together, there's no shame attached to it; you're not necessarily a failure as a person, or for that matter an army officer. Many people have left here without wings yet have gone on to highly successful careers – so it's not the end of the world! I remember my instructor, who lived and breathed aeroplanes, likening it to two different aircraft – say a Lear Jet and something like a Twin Otter. Both exceptional aircraft in their own right, of not dissimilar size and powered by two engines – only the Lear Jet is designed as a mini-airliner for fast long-distance travel and can only operate from airports with runways, whereas the Twin Otter is a short-range bush aircraft that can land anywhere. The point being, neither can do the others' job! And so it is with people. Given time, you could teach a monkey to fly a helicopter, but you don't see many of those as army pilots!

'A fellow student on my course RTU'd *himself* just before he was due to get his wings. I've always remembered that – and admired him for it. He could fly an aeroplane all right, but deep down he knew he wasn't *mentally* suited to being an army pilot: or in other words, know thyself – don't push yourself beyond the bounds of your own mental capabilities!' They were both now looking very thoughtful and I got up to get a coffee from the machine, whilst they dwelt upon it.

'Right, I'll just have this coffee and then we'll go out and have a look at a helicopter.' I took a sip, winced and put it down. 'On second thoughts, we may as well go out now...!'

I walked them round and showed them how to pre-flight the helicopter; what to look for, especially all the small things that were so often overlooked or else taken for granted, as well as explaining the reason behind everything. 'Never take *anything* for granted; remember, it's your *life* up there.' We then got in, the stolid Paul Courtney beside me and the dashing John Barclay behind.

'I'm going to take you for a short air-experience ride' I explained as I fired-up the turbine 'many students are frightened of helicopters when they first sit in one – it's an unnatural way of flying after a fixed wing aeroplane, so the object of today's exercise is to introduce you to the machine and show you what it can do – and more importantly what it can't – even helicopters have their limitations! I'll swop you over later so you both get a chance to sit in the front. Don't touch anything, all I want you to do is watch and listen – your turn will soon come!'

I pulled up into the hover, explaining what I was doing over the intercom and then demonstrated the action of each of the controls in turn. I then hover-taxied to the takeoff point, and after clearance from the tower, turned into wind and did a standard takeoff. I cleared to the south and then let Paul Courtney feel the controls in straight and level flight. For the next half hour I demonstrated every manoeuvre a helicopter was able to perform, throwing the Gazelle around the sky as though we were demonstrating it at an air-show. It really is a delightful machine to fly and excels in every way. Paul Courtney sat stoically throughout the whole performance, which I ended with a high-speed torque turn, then landing off it in autorotation with the engine off. The field I had chosen was Elizabeth's Service Station and to enhance the memory, I changed them over at the top edge, where we had made love under Ashley's wing.

With John Barclay now in the front seat, it was time to show them the low-level capabilities of the aircraft. There was a firebreak in some woods that I knew of – I'd once hidden in it in an Auster 9, flying up and down trying to evade the camera-guns of a pair of jet fighters whose job it was to shoot me down. I had a quick look at my map and then lifted off, immediately pushing the cyclic forward and keeping the machine down to a couple of feet above the ground. The wood was about fifteen miles away and we travelled the whole distance at this height, using every contour of the ground, wood and hedge-line as cover. Thirteen minutes later the wood appeared on the skyline and I continued to approach it at 115 knots, then skipped over the fence and entered the main avenue, the trees just a blur on either side before soaring up and out at the other end. John Barclay's eyes were alive with excitement. Maybe I shouldn't have done that with him in the front seat... but then, in a few months he'd be doing it himself, and an introduction to tactical low flying was all part of the demonstration. Nonetheless I then lifted up to 500 feet and made him fly it back to keep his mind fully occupied and then allowed him to follow through with the approach and landing.

'Okay, that's given you a taste' I said after we'd shut down '– as you see, the helicopter is the ideal military vehicle; even in the early days the army tended to regard their Austers as flying jeeps, and the helicopter has advanced that theory in leaps and bounds! Not only is it a flying jeep, it has now progressed to an attack vehicle that can cross the ground using cover at 110 knots – but first you've got to learn to fly it properly, so tomorrow we start in earnest at square one, and that's the hover...'

I packed them off and then walked up to the mess for a quick sandwich. I'd taken to that lately, for I found I couldn't cope with a full-blown lunch if I was flying in the afternoon.

At two o'clock Stephen Grant and Sergeant Lane both arrived together bearing their maps. I made them spread them out on the floor, checked they both had the full coverage and then showed how to fold them: first by halving the map by way of a central horizontal fold leaving the faces out, then folding the doubled map into vertical segments, starting at the right-hand edge, alternatively over and under in six equal parts as a concertina. You can then open it like a book and follow an east-west course through the segments, and should your course turn south, all you have to do is to flip the map over to the underside and continue as before; there is no time, let alone room in a small cockpit to struggle with armfuls of map when you are low flying.

'When you leave here, you'll find the majority of your flying will be conducted at low level. It will always be at low level when you are flying tactically, and in order to do this properly as well as safely, requires a great deal of practice. I would however take this opportunity to point out to you that the Civil Aviation Authority regards low flying as an illegal offence, the penalty being a hefty fine and the probable loss of your license! As military pilots we are exempt from this ruling for operational and training purposes. But that's as far as it goes and I warn you now, it's an extremely thin line. As you can imagine, the school receives numerous complaints from the civilian population – these come at us from all sides: the Police, the Ministry of Defence, the Royal Air Force, the CAA as well as directly to the Headquarters here. Every complaint has to be investigated and justified, and the school will only back you if (a) you are in the designated low flying area, (b) your flight has been properly authorized and (c) that all times you fly with due care and consideration to both the civilian population and livestock!

'So, you have been warned – and if you abuse these facilities, I'll come down on you like a ton of bricks – I just don't need the paperwork!' They both sat and stared at me, poker faced – as I suppose I'd done when my instructor had fired the same shot across my bows. I took a deep breath and decided to plug-on, for however one delivered it, it all needed saying.

'Having said that, low flying is perhaps the most important part of your training, and as such has to be approached in a responsible and recognized manner. It is every pilot's dream – and most pilots would give their back teeth not only to be let off the leash, but to be let off the leash with official blessing! But I tell you now, it's not easy – in fact it's extremely hard work and requires the highest level of concentration at all times; if you relax or take your mind off the job, or allow yourself to be distracted even for a moment, the odds are you won't know anything about it, for it's a killer...' That got through to them, and the glazed look left their eyes and they began to sit up and take notice.

'Ah good, you're with me! Now listen, both of you, for I'm only going to say this once.' I lowered my voice, so they had to lean forward and strain to hear. 'For now, low flying means not below fifty feet – you'll learn how to fly tactically or what the Americans call contour-hugging later in Advanced Flight. But even at fifty feet you'll find things happen extremely quickly, and the most important thing is to know where you are and where you're going! And that means good old-fashioned map reading. Map reading is a doddle when you're at a thousand feet, but at speed and on the deck it's another matter. So, whenever possible, plan your route in advance, even if you can only grab a few minutes before you take off. The main thing to look for are wires – they're the greatest hazard, and have killed more pilots than anything else. So, for a start, this evening I want you to study your new maps, get a feel for the ground and then mark all the power lines you can find in red. You'll be surprised how many there are and if you highlight them now, hopefully you'll see them in time. But power lines are not the only wires– they're the easy ones; the real danger are the hidden ones that are not shown on your map. Consider, every isolated farm or building will have a wire of one sort or another leading to it. Often the posts are hidden, maybe in a clump of trees, so what looks like an inviting gap will in all probability have a near invisible wire running across it. So watch out for them; don't be tempted and always anticipate!'

They were all ears now and I could almost see the cogs turning in their brains as they visualised the real situation.

'And the final thing I have to say to you is this: only you can be the judge of your own capabilities. You'll be doing a lot of solo work and as I said before it's extremely taxing. Everyone has a different level of concentration-span, so if you begin to feel tired, or find you can no longer concentrate, for heavens sake pull up! It's always better to be safe than sorry, so take it at your own pace and don't stretch it. You'll find it will get easier with practice and there's no point in killing yourself – besides, we can't spare the helicopters...

'Okay, Sergeant Lane, I'll take you first, if you'd like to go out and pre-flight the helicopter? Stephen, we'll be about forty minutes; I'd like to do a running change when we get back, so keep an eye open for us... you could perhaps start marking the power lines onto your maps whilst you're waiting!'

By the time I'd filled in the 700 and collected my gear, Sergeant Lane had finished the pre-flight and was half way through the pre-start checks. I gave him a nod and plugged in as the turbine began to whine.

'I tried that business with the brakes' he said as we waited for the temperatures to climb. 'I drove up to Notting-ham at the weekend and only had to use them eight times!'

'You be careful, I don't want to be blamed for causing an accident! How many times did you use them on the way back?'

'Ah, that wasn't so good. There was a lot of traffic and I lost count after a dozen! But you're right sir, it does make you thinK – I find I'm doing it all the time now! I also tried a glide-approach – we live on a hill, so I knocked it out of gear half a mile back and coasted down, using my handbrake one click at a time, as though operating the flaPs!'

I laughed, 'yes, I do that too sometimes! – now, let's see if we can apply the same thinking to your low flying. Take me at five hundred feet to Netheravon and then we'll let down over Salisbury Plain...'

He flew well. I asked him to give me a running commentary on what he was thinking all the time he was flying and it was interesting to see how his mind and reasoning gradually started to reach ahead. At first he was intent upon avoiding the immediate obstacles whilst worrying about his navigation, but after a while he began to assimilate the terrain at the further end of his vision, as well as using his map as a reference, and what had started as a series of uncoordinated zigzags gradually began to flow in harmony with the ground. At one point I made him set down in a clearing and then showed him on the map the route I wanted him to take home. He sat studying it for a moment, then un-sleeved his chinagraph pencil and marked it in, avoiding the high ground and routing around the few towns and settlements on the edge of the Plain.

The way home was opposite to the way we were pointing, and as he lifted up to clear the few sparse trees that surrounded us, he pulled up on the collective without centralising the pedals, allowing the excess torque to turn us through 180 degrees.

'Hey-hey, that's good! Have you done that before?'

'Done what, sir?'

'Used a torque turn to spin you round. You can also prolong that if you want to get out of a tight spot. If you're heavy and there's no room to take a run at it like I once showed you before, try pulling maximum collective and deliberately rob the tail rotor of power. Accept the helicopter will spiral round on its axis, but so what – it may be just enough to get you out! Try it sometime – slowly at first so as not to overdo it, like you did just now, then build up to three or four controlled revolutions, you'll be surprised how much extra lift you'll be able to pull.'

'Huh, and I did it without thinking! It's very logical though – thanks, I'll go off and practice that!'

We flew back and I stayed in my seat with the rotors turning, whilst they changed over. Then, repeated the whole exercise over again.

Stephen Grant was slightly more reticent and took longer to pick it up. I'd noticed his flying had become a lot more cautious since his ordeal in the fog– at least whilst I was sitting next to him, although his overall progress was still roughly on a par with Sergeant Lane, which meant he was making maximum use of his solo sessions to practice on his own. That in itself was no bad thing, but it was interesting to note how the two of them differed. Sergeant Lane would never attempt anything unless he had first been taught and led through step by step, whereas Stephen Grant was more inclined to find things out for himself. Thinking back, I remember I used to fly with far greater panache without the encumbrance of an instructor looking over my shoulder, even though I sometimes scared myself silly during the process! So, each to his own; but my job now was to remember to adjust my teaching techniques accordingly.

By the time I'd finished writing up their notes it was five-fifty and I suddenly realized I was going to be late; today was the day I'd arranged to sign the contract on the cottage and pick up the keys! I found their number in the book and said I was on my way, and would they keep the shop open for me? To which the girl replied in a tired voice that they were always open until at least eight pm every evening and the papers would be ready for me whenever I called!

It's funny how things go like clockwork when you least expect it. I was in and out of that shop in under five minutes.

It was just a matter of signing on the dotted line, handing over a cheque for two months rent in advance and then exiting with a large bunch of keys! So I drove back to the mess, had an early supper, then tried to ring Nigel but there was no reply, so changed into some jeans and set off to view my new abode. Besides, the tins of paint were still rattling around in the boot of my car and at least I could now unload them.

The first thing I saw on entering the village was Angela's Range Rover parked by the church. I drew alongside and then my heart leaped, for instead of Angela, Elizabeth was in the driving seat.

'I couldn't remember which number you said it was' she mouthed through the window.

'Follow me!'

So we arrived at our new house together.

'For Heavens sake don't let the neighbours see me' she said hurrying inside, 'I don't want them to think you're a wife beater!' and then threw herself into my arms.

'Are you sure you're well enough to come out?' I said as I carefully kissed the bruises on her face. The swelling around her eye had gone down a little and was now turning from red to black, as were her other bruises.

'Course I am, silly – I'm a tough old bird you know, and I wouldn't miss this for anything. Besides, we said we'd do it together – anyway, where were you, I've been waiting for ages!'

'I tried to ring, but there was no reply.'

'That's because I was sitting outside the church – Angela said I could use her car; they've gone to the opening of an art exhibition in Salisbury. Oh, isn't this sweet!'

'Do you like it – here, let me show you round; it'll take all of two minutes!' I lifted her off her feet and carried around the room whilst she clung to my neck. 'This is instead of carrying you over the threshold, as you were so keen to enter.'

'I was only trying to preserve your reputation' she murmured into my neck.

In a waltzing movement I half swung her through the door so she could see the kitchen and bathroom, and then in a far less dignified manner staggered up the steep twisting stairs, finally collapsing on the bare mattress of the bed.

'As we seem to be here, I think I need to study the ceiling of this room for quite a while...' she said as she slowly started to unbutton my shirt.

IV

'What have you done to upset our Temporary Chief Flying Instructor?' David White asked, firmly closing the door of his office after me.

Carefully I put my coffee on the corner of his desk before slumping down into the only other available chair. It had been a busy week and I was beginning to feel the effects. With four students, the days had been fully taken up flying and then Elizabeth and I had worked until almost midnight every night on the cottage. The only free period I'd had, had been yesterday afternoon, and that was only because I'd been asked to give my first lecture on tactics to the senior class. It had gone down quite well and at least I'd held their interest throughout, but it had been at the expense of a lot more midnight oil in preparation, so I'd hardly slept at all on Wednesday night. Still, with the preparation now done at least I could use it again – if there was to be a next time.

Then there had been the crash. That too had happened yesterday afternoon, when I was giving my lecture. One of Freddie's students – and thank God not one of mine – had been flying solo and misjudged his climb out of a clearing and had clipped the trees. The helicopter had then proceeded to chop itself to bits but somehow he'd managed to crawl out from the wreckage, despite having broken a leg and an arm; but it had then taken an hour and a half before they'd found him, by which time he was in a bad way. They'd flown him straight to hospital but the word was that he'd also damaged his spine and possibly would never walk again.

And it was to do with this, I suspected, that David had

called me into his office immediately upon his return from a senior instructors meeting with the CFI.

'Oh – it goes back a long way. Why?'

'Well, apart from selecting a board for the accident investigation, it came up in discussion that maybe the curriculum ought to be reviewed and modified; whether some of the techniques and tricks of the trade should be included in their basic training, rather than leaving it to later. I happen to know you've demonstrated to your two how to use translational lift as well as the torque turn, both of which would have got him out of that clearing with no trouble...'

'How do you know that?'

'Well, let's leave it that it's my business to know – besides, we've talked about it before, remember?'

'Mmm. And was it you that put the idea forward?'

'Yes, as a matter of fact it was! And I went as far to say that neither of your two students would have been caught out like that, but at the very mention of your name the man went completely berserk and came down on me like a ton of bricks. He said I'd no business condoning unauthorized tuition in my department! Talk about a red rag to a bull, I've never seen anyone so vehement!'

'So I take it you didn't get your point through?'

'No way – and then of course none of the others backed me up. Just the mention of your name put the kybosh on it! Thank goodness his time's nearly up; Colonel Jimmy should be back the week after next and personally, I can't wait for things to return to normal. But I'm afraid that's not the end of it; he wants to see you in the...'

We were interrupted by the door being flung open and Nicki-pig strode into the office.

'Ah, so you *are* here! I take it, David, you're in the process of passing on my ruling as the result of our meeting?'

'Well we were just beginning to discuss it...'

'Discuss? Who said anything about discussion? I made it perfectly clear at the meeting – it's a direct Order!'

'Hang on, Nicky' I intervened 'of course there's room for discussion! I happen to believe there's a strong case to

205

include some of these techniques at an earlier stage of their training. A student wallowing around in a hover in a clearing is an accident waiting to happen – you know yourself there's always a way to get out, and if this chap had known a bit more, the accident wouldn't have...'

'You'll address me as Colonel, and then only when you are spoken to!'

'Oh for God's sake Nicky, we were captains together, or had you forgotten!' I said, turning in my seat and deliberately not getting up. 'We're not on the parade ground – right now we are three individuals discussing an aspect of our job in the privacy of this office. There's no need to pull rank – we all know who's who... besides, David here was a Wing Commander...'

'Ex-Wing Commander or not, David is an instructor on this base and as such comes under my jurisdiction, as Heaven help me, so do you. And we've had this out before – you are not in a position to think or discuss anything, let alone change the rules.'

'Right, hold it just there!' David slowly stood up and towered over him, his face white with anger. 'You're out of order Colonel and I won't have it! This happens to be my office and *nobody* just bursts in like you've just done. I can't speak for the army, but in the Royal Air Force – or anywhere else for that matter, it would be considered a breach of *elementary good manners*! But since you are now here, why not pull up a chair and the three of us can discuss it in a civilized manner?'

'I'm not here to discuss anything' he snapped back, 'I've given my orders and you will now carry them out.' He turned on his heel and strode back to the door, then swung round to me, 'And as for you, major, I promise *you* this won't be the last you'll hear about the matter...' The door banged shut.

'Jesus' David breathed, sitting down again. 'Do people like him really exist? I've always thought him a bit of an oddball, but that beats... what a nasty piece of work!'

'My old flight commander told me that twenty-three years ago, and he hasn't mellowed an iota since then... the man's a Pratt; always has been!'

'Mmm. He can't touch me so I'm not particularly worried about my position – I can soon square things up with Colonel Jimmy when he gets back. But you – he could do you a lot of harm, so better watch your back!'

'Don't worry, I've crossed swords with him before and managed to survive – and I also know Colonel Jimmy of old... It's my students I'm really worried about. Sergeant Lane and Stephen Grant, they're coming up for their sixty-hour checks; knowing him he's just as likely to fail them on a technicality, just because they are my students.'

'Oh surely, he'd never do that! If they can fly, they can fly... he wouldn't – would he?'

'Well I wouldn't put it past him. He's an evil little bugger.'

'You're happy enough with them, are you?'

'Yes – they're both coming along nicely.'

'Well that's all that matters. Leave it with me – keep their hours down in the meantime and I'll shuffle the schedule so they go in last. Hopefully Colonel Jimmy will be back by then...'

V

That evening we finished the cottage. We sat on the bottom step of the stairs with a glass of red wine each, squirted from a handy wine-box that seemed to fit into the corner of the kitchen worktop as though it had been ready-made for it, and admired our handiwork whilst we waited for the carpet man. The walls and ceiling were all white, in total contrast to the ceiling beams and the beam over the fireplace, which we'd stained in a dark wood stain. The kitchen and bathroom we'd painted light blue, in one of the new kitchen & bathroom paints specially designed for condensation. I'd pulled the old linoleum off the floors and discovered good old-fashioned boards underneath, so I'd sanded and sealed these and then left them bare. With the white bath and sink and white units in the kitchen, it all came together very well in a pleasing Wedgwood effect; fresh and simple. We'd continued the white theme up the stairs and into the small landing, for as Elizabeth pointed out, the area needed as much light as possible. In the two bedrooms we'd tried our hand at papering – nothing too busy, for the rooms were small and the walls far from straight – but the end result wasn't bad for a first attempt, so long as you didn't look too closely. Anyway, we were pleased with our efforts and that was all that mattered.

Angela had put us in touch with the carpet man. She'd used him in the past and he was simply *marvellous*. He bought carpet straight from the warehouse on an 'as required' basis and worked from his van, which cut out all the overheads of running a shop and this was reflected in his prices. Also he was happy to work in the evenings, which, he said, was when everyone was at home and the most sensible time; though Angela had hinted that she thought he really worked for a carpet company during the day and it was best not to enquire too deeply! Anyway, Angela had duly sent him a summons and he'd come round on the evening he said he would, when, under his expert and pointed advice we'd chosen two carpets from the ones he'd marked as 'readily available' in his sample book and he'd then measured up and said he would be back this evening to lay them.

'What do you want to do this weekend?' I asked Elizabeth as I took both our glasses for another squirt of wine.

'Why, what have you got in mind?'

'Well, we've both worked jolly hard and we could give ourselves a bit of a break by flying off in Ashley somewhere ...'

'Mmm. That sounds nice – but I'm not sure my face is ready to be seen outside yet.'

'We needn't go anywhere smart – and anyway, it doesn't matter what other people think!'

'What else could we do where I wouldn't have to show my face?'

'Well, once the carpets are down, the only thing left is to get some of my stuff out of store. We could hire a van and go to Newbury to get it?'

'This must be the carpet man now ...' she put her glass on the floor and took hold of my head in both hands and kissed me on the lips. 'I love you' she whispered. 'So long as I'm with you, it doesn't matter what we do, or where we go! If you don't mind being seen with my face, I'd love to fly away with you in Ashley; or we can go and get your furniture – it doesn't matter; we'd be together and whatever we do will be fun! Listen, it is him, let's talk about it later ...?'

But in spite of our intentions to have an early night, it had still gone midnight by the time I dropped her off at Angela's.

'I deliberately haven't asked' I said, 'but have there been any developments with Ken? Has he been in touch at all?'

'Yes, he got the solicitor's letter and he – well, I'd really rather not talk about it now; it's too late and we've got all weekend?'

'Okay – we'll decide what we're doing in the morning. Have a really good sleep – and I mean sleep and none of your, ah, travelling! I'll give you a ring at about ten?'

'I've no need to travel now' she snuggled in closer and I could breathe her hair. 'I'm glad we've finished our little house ... the carpets look nice don't they? I'm so tired, just hold me for a minute more ...'

VI

As it happened, the weather decided for us in the morning.

I'd checked the forecast in the office and the printout had shown an Atlantic low tracking in towards the north of Iceland which, had it followed the normal summer route would have meant we'd have been well to the south of it and in the clear. But looking out of my window at eight o'clock told a different story; it had obviously changed direction and swung in much further south, for all I could see was blowing rain driving in from the northwest which, judging by the strength of it, would put the centre at around Glasgow. It would more than likely blow through by the evening, but until then it was not a day for flying light aircraft.

So: contingency Plan B, and I consulted the directory for van hire firms and then rang the first number in the book. Yes, a Transit with a Luton body would be the one for me, and yes, they had one and I could pick it up anytime before twelve. They could offer it at their special weekend rate, which meant I needn't return it until first thing Monday morning.

I rang Elizabeth at nine-thirty just before I left and told her she wouldn't be flying today but humping furniture instead and to wear something old, and then set off to collect her.

We left Angela's as soon as we could after a coffee and drove to Andover to pick up the van. It turned out to be a boxy affair with a roll-up door at the rear and an upper platform that extended over the cab. All in all, the interior was deceptively large and would easily swallow the one or two bits of furniture I had in mind. The man said I could leave my car in their car park at the rear, and if I wanted to return the van on Sunday, fill it up with petrol first and then pop the keys through their letterbox.

The weather was awful, and the large windscreen wipers clacked away as we drove north in an unending queue of traffic, all intent on going to Newbury.

'Will the furniture store be open?'

'Should be – it's in one of those warehouse places where you rent a cubicle and you have 24-hour access. There isn't much there, just the remains of my half when we split up. Except that it was by no means half – I think I drew the short straw! In fact, with this van I've a mind to collect the lot and then sell what we don't need to a second-hand shop; if you store furniture too long, it ends up costing twice as much as its replacement value! I can't honestly remember how much there is, so we'll see if we can get the decent stuff in and then maybe ditch the rest.'

'Mmm. Don't forget there's my furniture as well – we'll never be able to get it all into the cottage.'

I smiled at her. 'Yes, I'd thought of that. We'll get mine now so I can close the warehouse account. Then, when we see how much you end up with, you can choose what to keep and we'll have another sort out! I don't want the cottage to end up like your present house, each room divided down the middle with a "his and hers" section; I'd much rather you did it all. Besides, later on I expect we'll want somewhere a bit larger.'

'Oh no, not yet! I love our little cottage – but you're right, I suppose my house did end up a bit like that – there wasn't much give and take in my marriage. It's sweet of you to say that – about me doing it I mean; it makes me feel really wanted. Are your sure you don't mind, I'm so used to dealing with Ken?'

'Well, I'm not Ken and anyway, you'd better see what there is first! Also, I want you to regard it as your house – and so long as you're in it, I don't mind what furniture we have... except I don't want a huge television; just a little one will do!'

So we left it at that – and in the event only loaded the van with the few essential pieces of furniture that we would need, together with three cardboard boxes labelled "glasses", lots of pictures, all of which were old friends, and a few other assorted bits and pieces that were of sentimental value.

With these stowed, the van was still only half full and there just remained the question of what to do with the rest of the stuff. We had a final sort through and were just wondering about it when the situation was neatly solved by none other than the manager of the warehouse himself: realising they had a ready market (from people like us), they had recently started a second-hand furniture department in the corner of the warehouse, and he said he would take the lot! He cast a quick eye over it, named a figure – and that was that!

That done, I closed the account and there was nothing left but to roll down the rear door and head for home.

'All we need now are sheets, pillows, a duvet, some towels, crockery, cooking utensils – oh yes, and some cutlery' Elizabeth said as we sat in our usual place at the bottom of the stairs and admired the room. 'And I've got heaps of stuff at my house – I've still got wedding presents unopened and Ken won't need it all; I'll see if I can persuade Angela or Nigel to go round tomorrow and see what they can get?'

'Well, you know best – so long as the timing's right.

Certainly worth a try, but only if he's agreeable. If not, it's not worth having a row about; we can easily buy them.'

'Huh! We'll see about that! So long as I leave him enough – after all, I've got to live as well; he can't have it all! Anyway, we'll see what Nigel says...'

VII

Once I'd moved into the cottage I felt more settled than I had for years. In spite of the amenities and luxuries of mess life it was still much like living in an hotel, which at best is a temporary existence and the only privacy you can ever find is in your bedroom. But your room is tidied and cleaned every day when you are out, and things like clean sheets appear miraculously every Tuesday – so even that, you cannot really call your own. In spite of its diminutive size and somewhat limited facilities, I soon came to regard the cottage as home; made more so when Elizabeth was there.

At first, mindful of the circumstances and for appearances sake, we agreed she should restrict her visits to the evenings – when she either cooked something or else we went out, ever conscious of keeping a low profile. But after a few weeks of toing and froing, bottles started to accumulate in the bathroom and the wardrobe began to fill with her clothes, until the time came when we realized the situation had undergone a subtle change: instead of living at Angela's and visiting the cottage, Elizabeth now regarded the cottage as home and occasionally popped in to see Angela during the day. This then raised the question of transport. Spending more and more time away, Elizabeth couldn't keep on borrowing Angela's Range Rover, so we decided to make our first joint purchase and bought a second hand Mini. This she loved, and it immediately opened a door to a whole new perspective. For most of her adult life she had been smothered as well as tethered to Ken, and that little car suddenly represented a hitherto unknown freedom: it was something tangible that she could call her own, and an exciting alternative to her previous introspective avenues of escape. She began to look outwards and almost overnight became a different person – or rather, as she put it, the person she used to be long ago. Everything about her blossomed; there was a spring in her step and laughter was never far away. The first thing she did to manifest her newfound freedom was to get a job, something she had never been allowed to do before. This she proudly announced one evening, and that she would now be able to contribute towards the housekeeping. It wasn't much of a job, just temping work for an agency, but it had the advantage of being full or part-time, as well as being able to choose her place of work.

It got better everyday. As the days and nights passed we found ourselves growing closer and closer, as though cast from a common mould. We would wake in the morning and know we had shared the same sleep and then meet in the evening hungry for news of what the other had done and thought throughout the day, whilst individually harbouring our own private and growing joy. By now the difference in age was of no consequence, for the bond that grew between us was stronger than any best matched pair. Lying together it was as though we journeyed to the edge of life itself; where opposites fuse and make new entities, both of the flesh and in spirit; the issue as much of the ceaseless traffic of mind as of the body's pleasure. Soul mate or not, we were content: for we were as one. An old aunt of mine once defined 'love' as being what is left over when being 'in love' has barred the way; and she was exactly right, for love cannot be ruled or stopped, and from these depths we both found a new beginning.

There was nothing we could do to hasten her divorce: that would come; for now we were content to live each day as it came, sublime in our growing awareness.

At work I endeavoured to derive as much job satisfaction as I could by nurturing my pupils and watching them progress; but in spite of giving it my best, deep down I knew there was something lacking. My heart wasn't wholly in it, and I realized I wasn't really cut out to be a primary school teacher. This finally came home to me one Friday evening, as I was about to leave. A Beaver was in the circuit and on hearing its distinctive note, I paused to watch. Originally brought into service as a liaison aircraft, the Beaver soon became the maid of all work, successfully adapting to the majority of roles required by the army, as well as having sufficient power to be able to operate worldwide and in all climatic conditions. It was the ideal stopgap, soldiering-on with no fuss whilst the helicopter became of age, finally to equal its load capacity, range, speed and endurance and not least, its reliability. We hadn't many Beavers left now, for the new generation helicopters had not only caught up but now exceeded their capabilities and those we had left were mostly based in Ireland, equipped with cameras and relegated to photographic reconnaissance duty. They were soon to be phased out and the fixed wing liaison role revived by an individual flight of twin-engine Islanders exclusively formed for that purpose. But the Beaver still held a special place in many army pilots' hearts – mine included. They somehow looked more sinister now than they did in my day, for now they were painted overall in black and dark green camouflage pattern, rather than the lighter brown and green, enhanced by a splash of colour with red, yellow or blue propeller spinners to denote the flight they belonged to. Mentally I followed through with his downwind checks and then reduced power with him as with a sigh he turned onto base leg. The propeller note changed as he fined the pitch and dropped flap before turning onto finals. He continued down at exactly the right speed and angle of descent without having to resort to power. This chap was good – probably one of the multi-thousand-hour Warrant Officer pilots who tended to still fly the Beavers. He held it off, feeling for the ground and then there was that distinct metallic rumble from the undercarriage accompanied by the faint descending whine of the supercharger as it wound down and he held her straight on the landing run whilst cleaning the aircraft up in readiness to taxi to his dispersal. The end of another successful flight – my heart went out to it; what was it that made them so different from helicopters? Little did I know that within the space of a few years I would again be flying a Beaver, only this time it would be on floats and in very different circumstances.

The forecast was good for the weekend and I had a sudden yearning to fly once again to a proper destination, rather than the boredom of endless circuits. What with the house and everything Ashley had been sitting in her hangar for far too long, and it was time Elizabeth and I used her as I'd intended. Besides, I'd bought that book listing all the farm landing strips, which I hadn't even opened it yet!

VIII

Elizabeth was already home when I reached the cottage.

'Darling' she said with that inquiring lilt to her voice 'are you very tired?'

'Tired of what – coming home to you, I'll never get tired of that. Especially on a Friday...'

'No, tired of flying I mean... it's just that I thought – well, could we go away this weekend – fly somewhere in Ashley? You know we were going to fly to the Channel Isles; well I'd still love to do that. If you're not tired, or have anything else planned that is...?'

'Funny, I was just thinking the same when I left work. The forecast's perfect for this weekend. Mmm, the Channel Isles – we were going to Alderney first I seem to remember. What a good idea!'

'Oh good, I'll just quickly change and put something in a grip...'

'What! Go now, do you mean?'

Well, why not! – It's a lovely evening and then we'd wake up tomorrow in Alderney and have the whole weekend ahead of us... unless you're too tired, of course?'

I looked at my watch. Alderney: about ninety nautical miles, if we left straight away we should be able to make it easily before dark. What a girl! 'Okay, we leave in ten minutes.'

It was a glorious evening with still air and about twenty miles visibility that finally petered out in haze. I had two options: I could either remain below two thousand feet, thereby ducking under the Solent CTR and continue across Channel at that height, or else climb up and ask permission to go through. With the imminent seventy-eight mile sea crossing ahead, I decided to do it the professional way and go for altitude, so filed an airborne plan requesting Fight Level 60, being the most convenient height under the quad-rantal rule. Then, as Wallop passed under our port wing I contacted Boscombe and recognized the voice of the friendly controller who had helped that evening when Stephen Grant had got lost in the fog. He obviously recog-nized my voice too, for there was a note of query when he replied to the unfamiliar aircraft registration letters I was using as a call sign; so as an alias I added my personal military call sign, which he then recognized for the doubt cleared from his voice and became jocular and full of warmth. It's funny how these little things mean so much when you're flying. He said he had me on radar (which was hardly surpris-ing, as I was climbing through the edge of his zone at ninety knots) and cleared me to my requested altitude. Six minutes later he passed me on to Solent CTA on 120.225 who then vectored us outbound via Hengistbury Head on a direct course for Alderney.

At six thousand feet with the sea merging into the sky all around it was though we were flying in our own private bubble of reality, suspended in space and totally detached from the rest of the world. No pilot is ever fully at ease crossing tracts of open water in a single engine aeroplane and your eyes never stray far from the engine instruments. But more important is your ear; for those who fly for a living can liken an engine to listening to music – much the same as a driver changing gear in a car, which is normally determined by ear rather than by visual reference to speedometer or rev-counter. The more instruments you have on your panel, the better you can monitor and diagnose the health of an engine – but even with the pressures and temperatures all registering normal, the discerning pilot can usually tell by ear should the engine be slightly sluggish or not pulling the requisite power. There will be a discord in the music – maybe intermittent or half imagined; yet ignore it at your peril.

Today there is no discord; all the engine parts are in perfect harmony as our petite aircraft, trimmed nose down to fly at its greatest efficiency on the inner stubs of its bent wings, sped effortlessly southwards.

'Don't you ever get worried flying over the sea with nowhere to land?' As usual, Elizabeth had been reading my thoughts.

'Lindbergh flew the Atlantic in a single engine aeroplane – and in the days when engines were far less reliable than they are now. Flying eighty miles over the Channel is nothing compared to that... and then, I used to fly every day over the desert, and before that the jungle – both of which can be just as inhospitable as the sea.'

'Mmm. But I'll be glad when we can see some land again.'

Twenty-six minutes from leaving Hengistbury Head we were mid-Channel, or rather at 50° N, the mandatory report-ing point and it was time to give a call. I reported our posi-tion and in-flight conditions and was then told to change frequency to Guernsey CTR on 128.65. I flicked through the frequencies and then called again, asking for a descent and giving my ETA for Alderney in ten minutes time. This was confirmed and they asked me to call again overhead the field, as the airport would likely be unmanned.

'Look, there's your land!' I said moments later, 'see, that smudge to the left of the nose? That's France, the Cap de Hague – and then if you look further on, you can just make out the next headland; that's the Cap de Flamanville.'

'France!' Elizabeth breathed. 'It's so exciting – to travel like this, just the two of us in Ashley!'

I reduced the power by 200 revs and trimmed the nose

further down, maintaining our speed. 'Look, now you can see Alderney directly over the nose.'

'Gosh, but it's tiny! I'd no idea it was so small?'

'Yes it is. It's shaped rather like a miniature Cyprus and tapers off to the northeast, except it's only about three and a half miles long and just over a mile wide at its fattest point. You can bicycle round the whole island in about an hour. But like all islands, it has a magic of its own...'

'You obviously know it well, how many times have you been before?'

'Only once, but I've always remembered it. I've never flown here – I came by boat, in a friend's yacht some years ago... but I thought then that it was special and – well, I know now I've been keeping it for you! It's our sort of place.'

I levelled off at 1000 feet and altered course slightly to fly over Braye, the only harbour, on the north shore of the island. The port consisted of a few houses and a long man-made jetty that jutted out to sea parallel to a natural spit of land, thereby embracing a large deepwater mooring completely sheltered from the prevailing wind. A mile to the south was Saint Anne, the only town, and from what I could remember was just one long main street, with every other house a pub. In fact the island boasted of having something like sixteen pubs all within an area less than a square mile! Just to the west of Saint Anne, in the broadest and flattest part of the island, was the airport – or rather airfield, for it was little more than that: a field where you could land a small aeroplane. I radioed Guernsey and reported overhead and they said they had no other known traffic and bid me "good day". I circled the field at 1000 feet, noted the wind direction from the sock, and set up for landing.

There were three other aircraft lined up facing the prevailing wind. Two were Cessna 150's, which I saw were tethered to the ground and looked as though they belonged there permanently, and the other a red and white open-cockpit biplane with a radial engine, which at first sight I couldn't recognize. I taxied up to the biplane and parked alongside. Bucker Jungmeister was written on the cowling – of course! A rare bird and obviously a visitor to the island, for it was un-tethered and the cockpit had been left uncovered. It was in beautiful condition – and ideal company for Ashley for the night!

We waited for five minutes to see if our arrival would herald any form of officialdom, but nobody came – possibly they were all in one of the many pubs by now, so I strapped the joystick back using the seat harness, retrieved our overnight grips from the rear seat and locked the aircraft up. The landing fee, if any, would have to wait until morning. We set off towards the town in the gathering dusk. As we reached the outskirts, a gaily-painted bungalow had a Bed & Breakfast sign in the window and with unspoken accord we turned and walked up the path. It would be as good as anywhere – and for that matter, anywhere right now would be good.

'What's going to happen to us?' Elizabeth asked, as much later we lay snuggled together in the unfamiliar bed, and then added incongruously 'I can't stand this red-patterned wallpaper, it crowds this little room...'

'What do you mean, what's going to happen to us?' I hadn't noticed the wallpaper.

'Us, the divorce, the army and everything – we haven't really talked about it, will you lose your job?'

'Lose my job? What's that got to do with anything?'

'You forget, I'm a Service Brat – and even I know serving officers can't go around seducing sergeants' wives. The army's still frightfully old-fashioned about that sort of thing...'

'Sergeants wife! You're a general's daughter for heavens sake – and anyway, I thought you seduced me?'

'It doesn't matter who seduced whom, I'm still a sergeant's wife, and it's bound to come out in the divorce – especially with Ken being based at Wallop and... and well, the army can't condone that?'

I did not reply. She raised herself in the bed and lay on an elbow, looking down at me. The moonlight slid over her, making her a thing of silver and shadow, lighting the lovely lines of her temple and cheekbone, throat and breast.

I smiled, tracing the line of her shoulder with a gentle finger. 'How can I think properly when you look like that? Anyway maybe things have changed; everything else has changed in the army. After all, the army's still only made up of people, and values have changed a lot over the last few years. Anyway, seducing is only a part of it, I want to marry you!'

'Oh darling – and I want to marry you, more than anything! But I think there's going to be trouble... just be prepared, that's all.'

I lay and thought for a minute, conscious of her warmth beside me. 'If it comes to choosing between you and the army' I said slowly, 'it's a non-starter. The army have had my best years and I want to devote the rest to being with you. There are plenty of other things I can do...'

She snuggled closer and kissed my ear. Then whispered, so quietly that it was little more than a breath, yet nonetheless penetrated my very being. 'Thank you sweetheart – and I promise, I'll always be at your side.'

But it didn't end there.

I woke up in the early hours of the morning and from her breathing was conscious that Elizabeth was also awake.

'Are you awake? She asked.

'Mmm.'

'I can't sleep. I can't help worrying about what may happen. I know how much you love the army.'

'Well don't. And as I said, I can always do something else... anyway, I don't love the army, I love the sort of people it produces.'

'What do you mean – tell me?'

'Well, for instance there was our old RSM – Mr. Elliott. I used to adore him; he was one of those real characters that only the army can produce, and what's more it worked, for he kept the whole regiment together.'

'Did he; how?'

'Just by being the character he was – for instance, if anyone asked him the time, he would draw himself up to his full height and say in his special RSM voice: "There's only one time, lad – and it's Whaup-tup-three, Whaup-tup-three, Whaup!" as though he was taking arms drill!'

She giggled. 'Daddy used to tell me similar stories – what else did he do?'

'Um – well there was only one man that ever got the better of him. It was during the last days of National Service and we had an Oxford graduate – a tall lanky fellow who couldn't march in step or do anything remotely military. At first, in view of his degree, they thought he might be officer material, but he failed the selection board so they stuck him in the Intelligence Corps instead, and then somehow he got landed on us for the remainder of his time. Anyway, one lunchtime he ambled out of the I.O.'s office, and in spite of all the months spent in the army, absentmindedly cut across the parade ground on his way to the cookhouse.

'There was a colossal roar from the RSM's office and Mr. Elliott came bursting out – for as you know, the square is his province and hallowed ground. Even the Colonel had to walk round it. "You! That MAN! – What are you doing on my square?" he roared, and the poor man looked wildly round, suddenly realizing where he was. The mother and father of dressing-downs followed – the whole regiment heard it, windows opened and people were leaning out to listen! When he had finished, he pointed his pace-stick towards the cookhouse and said: "Right, now cut along or you'll be late for your dinner!" And with great presence of mind, especially for one under fire, our hero calmly looked at his watch and said "My, my – I had no idea, doesn't the day just fly!"

'It went round the whole regiment in no time and kept cropping up at every opportunity "Doesn't the day just fly!" Mr. Elliott knew he'd been taken, but never could quite fathom it out! Mind you, he got his own back...'

By now we were both wide-awake.

'More! How did he get his own back? I do wish I'd met him, he sounds a sweetie!'

'I don't think he'd have liked you calling him that! That wasn't at all the image he was trying to portray. Are you sure

221

you want to hear all this, God knows what time it is?'

'More – do tell me how he got his own back!'

'Well, sometimes on a rainy day the Colonel would assemble everyone who wasn't on essential duty in the canteen for what he called lecturettes. These were short impromptu lectures that had to last for ten-minutes or so, and he would call on any of the senior NCO's or young officers to give them. You had to have one ready, for you never knew when it was going to be your turn. So, one rainy day we were all assembled and he picked on Mr. Elliott. We all breathed a sigh of relief as he marched to the podium, did an immaculate about-turn and stood glaring at us. "Right gentlemen, what we're going on with this morning is wood!" he said in his gravely voice, looking around to embrace the whole audience, "and I don't mean all them himported softwoods what you get these days, but good old Henglish 'ardwood."

'By the way I forgot to tell you, when he was under stress, or thought he ought to be talking 'proper', he tended to get his H's muddled up; he'd either drop them in the wrong place, or else put an extra one in to be on the safe side! Anyway, our newest subaltern immediately cottoned-on to this – he was a product of Harrow and something of a snob as well as always trying to impress the colonel.

"I say, Sarn't-major, don't you mean: English hardwood?" he drawled, with emphasis on the H in hardwood.

"Yus, that's what I said sir: Henglish 'Ardwood! Now then, the first 'ardwood I want to talk about is Helm..."

"I say Sarn't-major, don't you mean Elm?" from the subaltern, glancing smugly at the colonel.

"That's right sir" glaring at him, "Helm! Now it's hunfortunate, but nearly all the Helm trees have been killed by a disease what the Dutch brought over, so our beautiful Henglish landscape is no longer graced by their elegant presence." There was no interruption. "So instead, I'd like to talk about Hash. Now Hash is a very flexible and durable wood and can be used for..."

"Excuse me Sarn't-major, but do you mean Ash?"

"...for furniture or various spars or framework... I do wish you wouldn't keep on hinterrupting, sir. Thank you. Yes, as I was saying, Hash is a very kindly wood, for as well as being strong, it's very light and I'm told very easy for carpenters to work..." He paused, fixing the subaltern with his eye and then continued. "But most of all, I'd like to tell you about the king of our Henglish trees; the mighty Hoak! Now Hoak his an hextremely 'ard wood. Indeed, so 'ard that all the wooden fighting-ships of yesteryear were made from Hoak, because of its himmense durability and strength. And even these days, it's a wood that's still very much in demand in construction – mostly for piles. And before the young gentleman at the back hinterrupts again, I mean the piles that are driven into the ground, and not the 'emorrhoids on the harseoles of the haristocracy!'"

'Darling...! That's a joke, you made it up!'

'Yes, it's a joke; but one that Mr. Elliott used against himself and played up to beautifully. He didn't really drop his H's that much... the whole place collapsed and loved him for it and nobody ever took the mickey out of him again!'

'I can see why you love the army so much. That couldn't happen anywhere else. I do hope everything will be alright...'

'Shhh. Don't worry; everything will be all right. Try and get some sleep now.'

IX

We spent the whole of the next day exploring the island on bicycles.

We picked up a brochure and a tourist map from the bicycle-hire shop, and Elizabeth wanted to see it all.

'I mean, look, sweetheart, we're here now, so we may as well soak in the atmosphere properly! Let's not rush round in an hour just because we've got to get to Guernsey? It says here that as well as sixteen pubs, there are no fewer than *thirteen* old forts scattered around the island, some dating way back – and then there's the Cathedral of the Channel Islands and – oh look, this looks the most scrummy seafood restaurant by the harbour overlooking the beach. Let's stay here, we can always go to Guernsey another day? We could eat seafood tonight and stay another night at the B and B. And that means we could also sample some of the pubs, as you won't have to fly!'

So that's what we did.

We biked back to the B & B and booked in for another night, and asked if we could leave our bags there; then to the airfield, where the office was open and I was able to pay my landing fee. I had a look at Ashley, now standing next to the empty space where the Bucker Jungmeister had been; and then decided to top up with fuel, which took another forty minutes, but at least we'd be able to leave whenever we liked. We then biked to the harbour at Braye, found the restaurant that overlooked the beach and booked a table for eight o'clock that evening.

Whilst there, we walked to the end of the long jetty and looked at all the yachts. I've always been interested in boats and it was interesting to see that no two were the same. The market for private yachts couldn't be that large, but judging from Braye harbour, there was obviously enough demand to offer a livelihood to a great many boat builders, each with their different ideas and input. There were boats there that had been built in Scandinavia, Germany, Britain, France and even two from the east coast of America! Obviously yachting was a leisure activity that was thriving at an International level, unlike my previous observations about the light aircraft industry; or for that matter, and as far as Britain was concerned, our equally lost motorcar and motorcycle industries. Although most of the yachts in the harbour were of uniform white fibreglass, their sizes, shapes, and not least their manner of rig all differed, all of which offered a huge variety of choice to the customer. It made me wonder whether owning a yacht would be preferable to an aeroplane; at least you could go places and live on a yacht...

'No, you can't do both!' Elizabeth said with a smile, once again reading my thoughts. 'Anyway, we couldn't just pop over to France and back for a weekend. We'd need at least a couple of weeks; so don't even think about it until we've got more time. Perhaps when you've retired!'

'Huh, judging from what we were talking about last night, *that* may be sooner than we think! Anyway, we've got thirteen forts to explore, so we'd better get biking!'

By five o'clock we'd only managed four forts, but had explored every beach and promontory along the way. There was a windswept openness to the island that had a unique appeal, together with the proximity of the sea and abundance of wildlife. The sea air and unaccustomed exercise made our faces glow as we followed the coast road – or rather track – eastwards along the northern shore until it curved round the end of the island and we found ourselves pedalling homewards along the southern shore with the sun in our eyes.

'That leaves the rest of the island for tomorrow!' Elizabeth said as we approached Saint Anne from the opposite direction. 'Isn't this fun! I vote we try some of those pubs now – I could murder a long drink, do you suppose they'll be open?'

'I imagine they never shut – French licensing laws, or rather the lack of them are bound to apply here! Anyway, I'm all for that – but first we'd better swing by the bicycle shop and let them know we'll need them for another day.'

But the shop had already closed. In the small island community, obviously the pub and restaurant business had preference over every other activity.

The following day we cycled the remainder of the island and then visited the church – or the Cathedral of the Channel Islands as it was described in the brochure. As we stood for a moment in the entrance allowing our eyes to become accustomed to the relative gloom, a verger approached and thrust a Hymn and Prayer Book into our hands and whispered that we could sit where we liked! We looked at each other and smiled and chose a seat near the back. To join the Islanders at Sunday Matins was a tranquil and fitting way to end our visit.

'Shall we go home now?' Elizabeth asked when we came out an hour later.

'Yes, I agree.'

We had ample time, so we flew home the long way by way of a circular tour. We set off to the northwest and made a landfall at Start Point, just east of Salcombe, and then descended to a 1000 feet and followed the coast around Lyme Bay, over-flying Dartmouth and Exmouth as far as Lyme Regis. There I climbed and cut inland on a direct course for Boscombe Down and so to Thruxton. It was a lovely flight; everything was just right, and made doubly so by being able to share it with Elizabeth.

Having put Ashley away, we drove home through the lanes – and by tacit agreement decided to pass Angela's house by, and instead stopped at the small shop in the village that Elizabeth said remained open until eight pm even on a Sunday, where we bought a few things for supper.

There was a car parked in "my place" outside the cottage next to Elizabeth's Mini.

'Huh, that's unusual' I said, 'I wonder who that is – can't even park outside your own house now. Maybe somebody visiting next door – oh, it's all right, I think he's going...'

I waited whilst the car pulled out, and then slid into the slot.

'Well, here we are – that was the most perfect week... whatever's the matter?'

Elizabeth was sitting silent, staring straight ahead with her lips compressed. 'That' she said, 'was Ken.'

X

Monday morning was the start of the sixty-hour checks; which was timely, for Colonel Jimmy had just returned from America and today was his first day back in the CFI's chair.

I was therefore somewhat surprised to see Nicki-Pig clad in a flying suit, head thrust forward and arms swinging in his porcine way, bearing down on the crew room as I was about to leave to take Sergeant Lane for the first lesson of the day.

'Morning, Colonel' I said giving him a salute, 'Are you flying – I thought Colonel Jimmy was back in the chair?'

'Ah' he said, 'not quite – now, which two are your students, I'd like to check them out first?'

'Better see David, I think he's drawn up a list.'

'Humph, we'll see about that!' he said pushing past and making for David's office. I paused for a moment to see if he would knock before entering and smiled, when true to form, he barged straight in. I just hoped David would be able to defuse him and keep to the schedule we'd drawn up – and that Colonel Jimmy would resume his full duties by Wednesday... otherwise it was going to be a near thing.

Sergeant Lane had already started up and was waiting with the rotors turning.

I put my helmet on and plugged in. 'Morning Sergeant Lane, nice day for it! You're scheduled for your sixty-hour check on Wednesday, so for this and the next two lessons, I thought we'd do a spot of revision. We'll run through the whole syllabus; so if you'd wind her up now and then hover-taxi to the takeoff point?'

He sat there and made no movement, then as though finally making up his mind, he turned towards me.

'Excuse me, sir, but may I talk to you off the record, like?'

'Off the record? – Why yes of course, what's on your mind?'

'Well it's a bit difficult, sir, and well, I just thought you ought to know...'

'Know what?'

'What's going around the sergeants mess. There's a sergeanT – I don't really know him, he's in the Ordnance; Ken Lawrence I think his name is, he's a bit of a loud mouth and tends to throw his weight around a bit. Well, he's putting it around that you've gone off with his wife, and he's going to break you for it. It's none of my business sir, and I'm sorry if... but you've been good to me, and I thought you ought to know...'

The morning suddenly didn't seem so sunny.

'Okay Sergeant Lane, I think I know what it's all about –

and thanks for telling me. You did the right thing – and it can't have been easy. I'll handle it from here – once these things start they're difficult to stop, but at least forewarned is forearmed and – and well, thank you again.'

With that, he wound the revs up and we both did our best to concentrate on the subject in hand. But the clock was running, and for the life of me I couldn't think of a way to stop it. The lull before the storm.

The lull lasted until three o'clock.

I'd just finished debriefing John Barclay when David White put his head around the crew room door.

'Colonel Jimmy would like to see you up at his office... soon as you like.'

'Oh, right.' I finished writing up my report and filed it in its folder in the cabinet. Ought I to first change out of my flying suit? I decided not to; what the hell, I was at work and this was my working dress, so I donned my beret and walked over as I was.

There was a corporal clerk in the outside office. 'Go straight in, sir, he's expecting you'. I nodded, knocked at the door and went in.

Colonel Jimmy was sitting at his desk looking at a file, with Nicki-Pig standing behind looking over his shoulder.

'Colonel' I said giving him a salute, 'welcome home!'

'Ah, thanks for coming over so quickly. Um, bit of a delicate matter this, but it needs nipping in the bud. Colonel Nick here has been approached by a Sergeant Lawrence, who says you have run off with his wife! Is their any truth in this allegation?'

So, the mud was starting to fly and Nicki-Pig was behind the shovel.

'Well, it's not quite like that, Colonel. I knew Elizabeth – that is Mrs Lawrence, long before she was married. This was years ago – she was General Blake's daughter, and I was a friend of the family. Her sister got married to a close friend of mine, and I was best man at their wedding...'

'What, Major General Timothy Blake – a Hussar wasn't he?'

'Yes, they lived – '

'Why are you improperly dressed?' Nicki-Pig interrupted. 'As a serving officer and member of the permanent staff on this establishment, why are you dressed as a civilian? You should be displaying the correct badges of rank and other insignia on your flying suit. I thought I made it quite clear when you joined...'

'Yes, well never mind that for now' Colonel Jimmy interposed. 'Look Nick, I think you'd better leave us. I've got your report, and I think it best if you bow-out now. I'm in the chair and it's my pigeon, so thank you, and I'll keep you informed.'

'This happened when I was in the chair, and I only think it right that I continue to conduct the investigation. After all – '

'There can only be one of us in the chair and I'm here now. So please leave us, there's a good chap?'

Nicki-Pig gave one of his snorts and left the office, slamming the door.

Colonel Jimmy then turned on me. 'Now, what the devil d'you think you're playing at? You're in a right old mess I can tell you! What on *earth* possessed you – surely you know better than to become involved in the domestic affairs of one of our sergeants? Although, I must say I didn't know she was one of General Timothy's daughters – there was no mention of *that* in Nick's report; just that she was the wife of a sergeant currently serving at Wallop... but that, I'm afraid, is all that counts now. I've been looking through your record. It reads well; you did a good job in Ireland and David White thinks very highly of you as an instructor – in fact, with all the tactical experience you have to offer, I don't know why Nick put you down there in the first place; I was going to move you up to the Advanced Flight – but now? Now I don't know what's going to happen. It's too late to put the lid on it; if it had been left with me, I maybe could have kept it in-house; given time, it doubtless would have blown over. But it's gone past that now; Nick has already sent copies of this report to the Brigadier as well as the Director of Ordnance, so it's completely out of my hands. God knows where it will end. All I can say is, you've been a bloody fool!'

'There's a lot more to it than that, Colonel. Sergeant Lawrence had been beating her up, and she'd left home and was staying with her sister...'

'I don't want, or indeed *need* to know any more of the sordid details, thank you. Suffice to say, this report – which I must say is mostly conjecture but nonetheless extremely damning – is now on the Brigadier's desk and a decision will be taken. I'll do what I can, but in the end it will be his decision. And I daresay you'll be hearing from him sooner rather than later. That's all for now, Good Day to you!'

We spent a miserable evening. Colonel Jimmy knew how to pack a good rocket and I was still smarting. Initially I was all for Elizabeth packing her bags and going back to Angela's, in case Sergeant Lawrence took it into his head to burst in and resort to more physical violence. But Elizabeth interpreted this suggestion another way: she was worried that Ken, abetted by a gleeful Nicki-Pig, could be out there with a long-range camera, intent upon collecting hard evidence to augment their damning report in order to blight my career. When we both realized we were trying to protect the other we stopped and started to think as one; maybe for her to leave now wasn't the answer, for it almost amounted to an admission of guilt. We were not trying to hide anything; we had promised to stand by each other, so what use if we fell apart at the first hurdle? The news was out, and the damage already done, so far better to unite and face it together. The fact was, she'd already thought it through and had tried to tell me in Alderney. It was my career that was at stake, and this was now in the hands of the Brigadier. The waiting would be the worst and I only hoped it wouldn't be for too long.

So we had some squirts of wine from the perpetual wine-box, after which the atmosphere lightened and Elizabeth decided to ring Angela and tell her all about it!

'Hello, you!' I said later in bed. 'I dare say we'll know the worst by tomorrow – and whatever happens, at least we'll be able to plan the future. In fact, I'm glad it's out and in the open at last. I was fed up with being furtive and I want to be seen with you on my arm. At least we won't have to go to Alderney to do things openly together...'

XI

'Are you in some sort of trouble?' David asked. 'I've just been told to drop everything and report to the Brigadier, and to bring your logbooks with me – have you got them, by the way?'

'They're in my bag; I'll get them. And yes, there is a fair amount of low-level shit flying around at the moment, so mind you don't get an eyeful!'

'I think I can guess what it's about – ah well, no doubt see you later...'

He was away until eleven. I'd just got in from taking Paul Courtney and was about to take John Barclay who was already out pre-flighting the helicopter.

'Come in a minute? Here are your books – you'd better get changed and cut up to see the Brigadier. I'll take your lesson – who is it, Barclay?'

'Yes – landing into the circle...'

'Right. I'm looking forward to flying with that young gentleman!'

'Oh he's not too bad. Under that suave exterior he has the makings of a steady pilot – it's all a front.'

'Okay, I'll let you know how I get on – and good luck! I think you're going to need it!'

I changed out of flying gear and walked to the Brigadier's office.

I had to wait for forty minutes, then the door opened and Colonel Jimmy and Nicki-Pig came out. Colonel Jimmy flashed me a brief smile and winked, and Nicki-Pig ignored me.

'Ah, come in' the Brigadier said, 'and shut the door behind you.

'You know what this is all about, so I don't intend to make a meal of it.' He said by way of starters. 'You have been indiscreet to say the least, and what's more a bloody fool – not least for being *caught*! And I must say I'm very surprised; it's the last thing I'd have expected from you! You'd expect this sort of behaviour from a young subaltern – but you, an officer of your seniority, surely you must have known this was going to erupt and that you were sitting on a time bomb! You know the army as well as I do and this situation is, is, totally unacceptable – which view I fully endorse on behalf of the Corps – our Corps! It's a bloody *disgrace*! – And heaven forbid if the Sunday tabloids get hold of it; they'd make a real meal of it and would make us all a laughing stock.

'You are a senior instructor and you're here to do an important job. And that job doesn't include mucking about with a sergeant's wife – especially as he's from another Corps on detachment. Do you understand...?'

'Brigadier.' I said, in the age-old army tradition that the least said, the better.

'...And what's more, I've got better things to do than waste a whole morning on the likes of this. – But, having said that, in the limited time I've had available I've also made it my business to furnish myself with as many of the details as possible. Here, you'd better sit down...'

'Thank you, Brigadier.'

'...And it would appear that some of the circumstances are perhaps not entirely of your making. I say this because I had a telephone call from Nigel Lawson-Davis this morning. I know him quite well, and he also told me of his involvement. I didn't realize he was married to Mrs. Lawrence's sister... anyway, from the conversation we had, it would appear that to a certain extent you've been victimized for helping a person in distress. At least, that's how he put it, although personally I'd say your motives could still be highly questionable!' He gave me a piercing look.

'Brigadier' I said as impassively as I could, looking straight ahead.

'Now as you know, on an establishment this size there're bound to be domestic troubles of one sort or another from time to time – it's inevitable and it's why we have a Welfare Department to deal with them. So, I rang Welfare earlier this morning to get their assessment of the situation, and I was surprised to learn that they knew absolutely nothing about it! That leaves me to think they were deliberately bypassed in order for this...' he indicated the report on his desk '...this so-called report to land directly on my desk. It's by no means a balanced document and in my opinion should never have been written, let alone put on my desk. There could be something fishy going on, and I intend to look into it further. Anyway, it's nothing to do with you – and nor does it excuse your indiscreet behaviour, however well intended.'

'I understand, sir.' Did I detect a glimmer of hope? And the Old Man had certainly pulled his finger out, what with contacting Welfare, Colonel Jimmy, Nicki-Pig and David White as well. And then, thank God for Nigel; that was an unexpected bonus...

'But unfortunately the cat's out of the bag and the damage done' he continued, 'so in the interests of this Headquarters, it's my job to defuse the situation as quickly as possible as well as making sure there are no grounds for further scandal. And the only way to do this is to remove the players. I've seen the Director of Ordnance and as of this morning, Sergeant Lawrence has been posted to another unit that's not connected with army aviation in any way. Needless to say, I don't intend to tell you where.

'As for you, I also want you off this Station immediately, and your instructing duties are curtailed forthwith. I've seen David White and he's in the picture. As Wallop is your Regimental Headquarters, your banishment can only be temporary. Say, for the duress of a normal posting, by which time, hopefully it will have all blown over. You have a clean Service record and I do not intend to blemish it by way of any official reprimand. Do you read me?'

'I do, Brigadier – and thank you.'

'Whether you'll thank me remains to be seen. Not many

officers can expect to be kicked out of their job, for what-ever reason, and expect to get away with it – that is without it affecting their career along the way. I don't know how your career structure stands, and frankly I'm not particularly inter-ested right now; all I know is I want you out of here by this evening. Clear?

'Clear, sir!'

'So, what to do with you at short notice? I've had a word with the CFI – Colonel Jimmy that is, and also with your immediate boss, Wing Commander White. Looking at your logbook, I see you are an old fixed wing pilot with some 2500 hours on Beavers?

'Just under, Brigadier.'

'And also looking at your logbook, I see that early in your career you managed a certain amount of twin-engine time? God knows how you wangled that – anyway, it's not for me to comment on now, and it could be quite useful...

'Now as you know the Beaver is being phased-out over the course of the next few years, and we'll be looking for a replacement aircraft for liaison duties? One of the obvious choices is the Britten Norman Islander, but of course there are also others that will have to be evaluated.'

'What about the Twin Otter? I'd have thought that would be the ideal...'

'Yes quite, but there's bound to be a political input and the Twin Otter's a lot more expensive. A lot will depend on whether our budget can embrace this as well as our on-going commitment to the future helicopter force; the liaison role is very much secondary to that. Anyway it's all somewhat premature at the moment, and ultimately we'll have to convene an official board to explore the situation in depth and come up with recommendations.

'But, and this is Colonel Jimmy's idea, if we had a prelimi-nary evaluation already up our sleeves, the whole thing could just slot into place with a lot of the work already done – you understand? That's basically just what he's been doing in the States. So, what do you think? As far as your career prospects go it's a backwater, and one that you may not thank me for. You'll be out of the mainstream, and as you know, army aviation is a fast-moving stream these days. But, there are not many with your qualifications and it could be that you're the right man for the job. And more importantly as far as I'm concerned, it will get you away from Wallop! That's the deal, what do you say?'

'Do I have a choice?'

'No, not really. In fact, no you don't!'

'In that case sir, I'll take it! To whom do I report?'

'Um. Haven't worked that one out yet. Also I'll have to have a quiet word with Britten Norman. Don't want them to think they've already got the order in the bag. Today's Tuesday, you'd better take a week's leave – but for heaven's sake keep your head down, and then give me a ring – say next Tuesday; I should be able to put something together by then. Oh, and give me your home number, somewhere I can get hold of you.'

'What about my – ah, liaison with Elizabeth Lawrence?' I asked as I wrote the number down. 'Because I'd like you to know, sir, that when this is all over I intend to marry her.'

'Mrs Who? I can't recall any Mrs Lawrence at Wallop... and of course I'd be delighted to welcome General Timothy's daughter into the mess if she becomes your wife – and for that matter, welcome her back into the fold!'

'I'm not sure she'd want that! Although she once called herself an Army Brat, she has her own views about some aspects of army life...'

'Well, that remains to be seen; so go and clear your desk and I don't want to see your face again! And take that damn smirk off your face before I change my mind, I'm still not sure if I'm doing the right thing.'

'Right, Brigadier.' I stood up and saluted. 'And thank you, sir.'

I walked back to the crew room in a daze, conscious that only half an hour before I'd walked this same path full of apprehension and dread. But then, does the Wheel of Fortune ever turn slowly?

There wasn't much to pack up and I hung around for another twenty minutes, waiting for David to return.

'Well, I see your head's still attached to your shoulders – you'd better come in' he said when he saw me. 'Oh, and I agree with you about young Barclay' as he shut the door, 'he seems to have steadied up a bit – no doubt under your influence, what did you threaten him with? Anyway, how did it go?'

'I've been sacked' I said as I sat down, 'but I gather you knew that anyway...'

'Did he offer you that other job though – the one that Colonel Jimmy came up with?'

'What, to become an unofficial and unrecognised Lone Ranger; to make a preliminary evaluation on a machine the army may or may not buy? Well, he did mention it – or rather, he said he'd try and fix it. He said to contact him in a week.'

'Believe me, if anyone can fix it, he will! And you've got Colonel Jimmy to thank for coming up with it and bailing you out. He pulled it out of the hat like a conjurer and made a very good case. Of course, it's just what he's been doing in America, which helped, but he needn't have stuck his neck out like he did. I can tell you, your friend Nicki-Pig didn't think much of it! I don't know what happened after that, because I was asked to leave...'

'Well I've been asked to leave too. I'm sorry, it'll be more work for you and I won't be able to see my students through – I hope they do all right.'

He stood up and offered me his hand. 'Everyone has to leave at some time. They'll be all right; I'll keep an eye on them for you. I think you're just right for the job; after all, it's right up your street! And, for what it's worth, I'll miss you – you did a good job here and thank you for that. Ah well, I wonder who they'll give me next? Good luck to you!'

XII

Elizabeth and I were invited to supper 'around the kitchen table' at Angela's that evening.

Nigel had missed his train and was late. Also his car was in for a service, so I offered to drive into Andover and meet him at the station, leaving the two sisters to put the world to rights.

'And just how well do you know my Brigadier?' I asked as he got in.

'Oh the usual thing – had them round for dinner, been there for drinks a few times, you know the form...'

'You spoke to him this morning?'

'It was just a phone call, old boy. Nothing really; only when Angela told me what Elizabeth said and the possible implications, I just thought things might need straightening out a bit, that's all. There are always two sides to every story, and from what Elizabeth said, it struck me it was a bit one-sided. Sorry, perhaps I shouldn't have interfered – I did wonder?'

'Well I'm very glad you did – and extremely grateful. Your phone call saved my bacon! It more than helped swing the pendulum the other way, and couldn't have been timelier. I was on the carpet this morning.'

'Things obviously move pretty fast in military circles – anyway, glad to have been of help – after all, you are virtually family now! You are, aren't you?'

'Oh yes! Very much so. Yesterday the future was somewhat foggy, but now suddenly there's a way ahead for both of us, and as far as I can tell, with everyone's blessing!'

'Oh good, cause for a celebration! I hope Angela hasn't been using my fridge – I've got the perfect bubbly! She chucks it out sometimes you know...'

Chapter 7

I

So, what to do with a week's unexpected leave?

Elizabeth had to get up and go to work, and with nothing planned, I felt at a loose end. Besides, Nigel had been a pressing host last night and we'd managed to make a considerable hole in his fridge before supper and then proceeded to investigate his "other cupboard" until almost midnight, the result of which had left my head as though it didn't belong. 'What you need is fresh air and exercise' Elizabeth said as a parting shot as she drove away, so taking her at her word I walked up to the village and bought a paper from the shop and then retired to the garden to read it from cover to cover – one of the small luxuries of life I normally never have time for.

Helicopters kept whining directly overhead, one after another, for the cottage was less than a mile and immediately upwind of the take off point. I wished now that it had been further away, for each time one went over I couldn't help looking up and wondering whether it was one of my students, and thinking I ought to be up there with them. There was an empty void in my stomach about that; it was unfair on them, especially Stephen Grant and Sergeant Lane at this, the most critical time of their course. But then, David had said he'd keep an eye on them, so perhaps it wasn't so bad. One of the first things you learn in the army is that no one is indispensable. The whole organisation and chain of command is structured to work on a war footing, and as such embraces the realistic fact that every rank, however senior, could be a potential casualty. Organization in depth is therefore essential, as well as clear and practiced delegation, the primary objective always being that the unit must continue to function, whatever the casualties. Nonetheless I still felt bad about it; it was unfinished business and I wished I could have seen them all through. And had I stayed, no doubt I'd have instructed them again in Advanced Flight, if Colonel Jimmy had meant what he'd said. Albeit up to now I'd had mixed feelings about being an instructor, it would have been very different teaching the advanced students. Maybe there would be another opportunity later, and hopefully by then, and after a spell of fixed wing flying, I'd know what I really wanted!

Elizabeth came home at about six o'clock, by which time I was busy preparing a meal for us both.

'Oh how lovely!' she said. 'The ultimate role-reversal; at last I've found a man who can cook! Ken never lifted a finger – you never cease to surprise me!'

'Well I'm not Ken – and you'll probably change your mind when you taste it.'

'No I won't, it smells delicious! *And*, I've got the rest of the week off!'

'Really – how come?'

'Today's job was just a one-dayer, so I told the Agency I was going away and wouldn't be available for the rest of this week, and that I'd work especially hard and do *anything* for them next week! Can't have you hanging around all day kicking your heels and getting all morose. So, we're free! Come on, let's plan something – we've got four full days. They've booked me in at the same place for next Monday– and anyway, I think you ought to be back by then in case the Brigadier rings; has your headache gone?'

During supper we discussed where to go. The possibilities were endless and the more we talked about it the more difficult it became. France was the obvious choice, but then Elizabeth had never been to Scotland and now would be the perfect time of year to go there.

We cleared away and I consulted the book I'd bought on private landing grounds.

'There's one here listed on Islay I said.

'Islay – one of the Hebrides, where they make the whisky? Oh do let's go there!

'I think it's a farm – it gives the co-ordinates and a contact number – a Mr. McDougal.'

'Oh go on, do give him a ring now and let's find out!'

I dialled the number and listened to the quavering ring at the other end. It rang eleven times and just as I was about to hang up, there was a rattle and a soft highland voice said 'Aye?'

'Is that Mr McDougal?'

'Aye.'

'I was ringing up about landing at your farm strip. Are you the farmer?'

'No, that I am not!'

'Oh...'

'But I *am* the person that flies an *aeroplane* from the field. So just' – he pronounced it "chust" – '*when* would it be that you were thinking of coming?'

'Well we haven't made any firm plans yet, but possibly tomorrow?'

'*Tomorrow?*'

'Yes, if that's all right. We'd probably arrive in the evening and just stay the one night.'

'And *where* will it be you'll be staying?'

'Well, we haven't thought that far ahead yet – is there somewhere you can recommend perhaps?'

'Well it all depends on what you want? If it's a hotel you're wanting it's a while away from here. But if it's just bed and breakfast, then you're welcome to stay here. We sometimes do it for the tourists, you know? What *aeroplane* do you have?'

'Oh, it's just a little Robin. If the field's not too rough, I'm sure it'll cope – '

'A *Robin*? That's a new one on me – still, I suggest you fly over the field first – I'll leave my Piper Cub out, you'll see it plain enough. You can then have a look and see what you think; it's a bit hilly but smooth enough – anyway if you don't like it, you can always go to the proper airfield at Port Ellen. I don't know *why* they call it Port Ellen, for it's actually at Glenegadale – about four miles northwest of Port Ellen.'

'Okay, hopefully we'll see you tomorrow evening then...'

'Aye'.

'Tell me, is there anything I ought to know about – '

But the phone gave another rattle and went dead. I looked at Elizabeth.

'I was about to ask him more about the field and the approaches but he hung up! He didn't even want to know my name!'

'Are we going then?'

'Well, it looks like it now! We'd better get the maps out and have a look.'

We planned the route together. Thruxton to Islay was 385 miles non-stop, or about two hours fifty-five minutes flying, so I decided to route via Castletown on the Isle of Man to break the journey and also to refuel. Not that we'd need to, but old habits die hard. I drew a line on the chart.

'What are all these things marked all over it?' Elizabeth asked, 'I thought the sky was empty!'

'Yes, I suppose it does look a bit confusing at first. The areas marked in blue show controlled airspace, and the red corridors are airways – they're the sort of motorways. And then these red ones with hatching around show restricted areas and... and so on. There's a legend on the bottom of the

241

chart that shows what everything is. It's all to do with making the sky a safer place – it can get quite crowded.'

'Telling me! I'd no idea...'

'But it's not quite so bad as it looks. You've got to remember it's three-dimensional; all the boxes are blocks of air and they've all got different height limits. You can either give them a call and ask permission to go through, or else in a light aircraft you can usually go underneath. See, our line starts by going through this blue box here – that's Lyneham CTA and along the edge it's marked 3500 to FL65 together with the radio frequency. That means their block of sky has a bottom level of 3500 feet and goes up to Flight Level 65 – that's 6500 feet on the standard altimeter pressure.'

'Standard altimeter what?'

'Altimeters are set to the regional pressure, which of course varies from day to day depending on the weather. But once above 3000 feet all altimeters are reset to 1013 millibars – that's the standard altimeter pressure – so everyone's the same.

'So now let's have a look at the route and we'll first make a list of all the radio frequencies we may need. Lyneham, that's 123.4; so we could give them a call and let them know we're passing through their box under 3500 feet, to the east of their field. Then over the high ground, that'll be the Cotswolds and on to Gloucester – but first we pass over the motorway, and the airfield's there, see, to the northeast of the city? They're on 125.65, in case we need to call them, so I'll note that down; you never know. After that we're in clear sky for a long way, so we'll work London Information on 124.75 – that's the general frequency for all aircraft west of Airway Amber One.

'So, as you'll be navigating, you'd best now mark in the flying time! Use the ruler and measure off the halfway point between Thruxton and Castletown, and then mark in the quarters.'

She scaled the line on the chart and marked the halfway point just west of Shrewsbury. Then she halved it again and marked the first quarter, which conveniently fell over

Gloucester and then the three-quarter mark, again conveniently falling where we coasted out, just east of Llandudno.

'We'll be cruising at about 130 miles an hour; so the total journey time to the Isle of Man will take about an hour fifty, which makes each quarter – ah, twenty-seven and a half minutes. Call it twenty-eight, although in practice it'll be slightly different because we haven't allowed for any wind yet, but we can compute that tomorrow when we get the forecast – so, for now just make a note of the still-air time in your pad. That'll be what, twenty-eight minutes to Gloucester; fifty-six minutes to Shrewsbury and an hour twenty-four to the coast! Now, having divided it into sections we study each section in turn to see what it holds. By doing this you become totally familiar with the route and know what to expect, which automatically puts you ahead of the game. Then, when it comes to actually flying it, it's a doddle – all the hard work has been done!'

'What are these circles that look a bit like clocks?' she said twenty minutes later.

'What clocks? Oh those, they're VOR beacons. The route you've just planned is strictly a fair-weather route for VFR flying – that's under visual flight rules when we can see the ground to read a map. But, should the weather clamp down, we'll have to climb above it. As you can see we've got to fly over some fairly high ground over Wales. If that happens I'll have to file an IFR plan – the I stands for instruments and then we'd fly from beacon to beacon. For instrument flight we use this other sort of chart' – I delved into my bag – 'see, here are all the beacons, together with their frequencies, and all those lines are the various routes between them, and also show the headings and heights to fly. Then those triangles are reporting points and these dotted lines show the radar coverage around all the airfields... so what with them and the regional radar, the whole of the UK is practically covered; they just pass you from one to another and you can never really get lost!'

'Well you can jolly well navigate if that happens; I'd never be able to thread my way through all those lines – it looks

243

like knitting!'

I studied the chart for a minute and made a few notes of my own.

'If we set off mid-morning, we could have lunch in the Isle of Man and maybe see a bit of the island, and then if the weather's fine, go on to Islay in the evening.' I scaled the chart. 'It's about another hour-five.'

'So, where shall we go after Islay?'

'Well, it depends. Knowing you, you'll want to stay and explore everywhere we land. We'd probably never get further than the Isle of Man! But, instead of that, what we could do is make this trip a sort of reconnaissance. We could have a sniff at a lot of different places and make a note of those we'd like to visit for longer on a later occasion. So, tomorrow we could look at the Isle of Man, and then stay the night on Islay. Then on Friday we could continue up the west coast of Scotland and take in the islands' I traced the route with my finger on the chart, 'and then on around Cape Wrath and the north coast of Scotland, and so on up to Orkney. We could then spend Friday night there and Saturday morning, and then fly south again in the afternoon to somewhere halfway home, say, somewhere in north Wales. Then we'd only be a couple of hours from home, which we could do at our leisure on Sunday?'

'Oh yes, I'd love to go to Orkney. But won't you be tired, flying all that time everyday?'

'I shouldn't think so, you forget I fly every day as it is for a living!'

'Well, couldn't we stay in Orkney for a whole day and then fly all the way home on Sunday – how long would that take?'

I scaled off a straight line and made it 540 miles – and then set 130 knots against it on the Swissair Navigator. 'About four hours ten minutes' and then twisted the computer and read off the fuel consumption, 'and we'd still have enough fuel left to go all the way back again!' This was some little touring aeroplane!

'Come on' she said with a twinkle in her eye, 'I have an urge for an early night! We can always make our minds up when we get there...'

We took off at ten. The forecast was good, with the 3000-foot wind steady from the southwest at fifteen knots. I climbed to 3000 feet and called Lyneham who said they had no other traffic and cleared us up to 4500 feet, my chosen altitude and six minutes later we threaded between Kemble and Cirencester. I leaned the mixture off and then fine-tuned the trim until she flew hands off in the usual nose down attitude. The Cotswolds rose to meet us and then sank down again to reveal the M5 motorway and Gloucester beyond, twenty-nine minutes after take off. The visibility was excellent, to port we could follow the Severn Estuary as it opened up as far as Bristol and to starboard we could just catch glimpses of the river as it wound like a ribbon northwards on its way to Worcester.

Eighteen minutes later we tracked overhead Ludlow, which confirmed the five degrees I'd offset for wind and imperceptibly the ground began to rise again. And with it the air became turbulent. I'd forgotten how susceptible a light aircraft is to even the mildest turbulence, unlike a helicopter, which can just about fly through anything. Even a Beaver would have ironed out the viciousness of most of these bumps, but the little Robin felt every one, like a dinghy in a rough sea. Elizabeth, with the chart on her knees gave me an enquiring glance, to which I replied with a reassuring smile, after which she ignored the bumps and continued to inch her finger along the track she'd drawn yesterday evening.

'That peak down there is 1693 feet high' she remarked a moment later with satisfaction, 'and we'll be at the halfway point in six minutes time. We were two minutes behind at Gloucester but I think we've picked that up now and we're back on time.'

'Good, well done' I gave her a smile, 'navigation can be quite satisfying, can't it! We were two minutes late at Gloucester because of the climb...'

'It's easy when you can see. But I wish you could see those bumps coming; each one takes me by surprise! But look at

Wales! Doesn't it look wonderful; ridge after ridge of hills all waiting to be explored. And oh look, is that the sea, way out on the left?' She scaled the chart, 'that must be about forty miles away! Cardigan Bay...'

'That's Oswestry coming up under the nose' I said, glancing at the stopwatch on the facia. 'That's where the gunners have a camp – we often have to fly there.'

'Oh – that's spoilt it! I wanted to think that this is a flight of exploration for us both, not one of your regular jaunts!'

'Every flight is different, so they never really become regular jaunts. Anyway, after Oswestry it'll be new country for me too, so make sure you keep track of where we are!'

The sky lightened as we approached the sea and at 1123 we coasted out over the sands of Colwyn Bay and into smooth air.

I changed the VOR frequency from Birkenhead to Isle of Man on 112.2 and compared the course on the dial with my heading. The beacon is situated at the southwest tip of the island, some six miles west of Castletown, and so long as the wind remained constant our present heading looked about spot on. I then gave them a call and relayed our in-flight conditions with an ETA of 1149. I also asked if we could remain at FL45, it being the lower level of B3, the inbound airway. They gave me a number to squawk for the transponder and then said they had us on radar and could continue unless otherwise directed.

We touched down as the second hand on the stopwatch swept through 1149: not in itself a remarkable achievement, for that was when we said we'd arrive – but satisfying nonetheless, and what flying is all about.

We walked into town and had a look at the sea and then stopped at a seafood bar and ate queenies – small scallops cooked in a delicate sauce that are the island's speciality. We wondered about catching a bus or maybe taking a taxi to Douglas, but by the time we'd finished lunch, followed by a nap on the sand and then a refreshing coffee in another bar followed by a look around the town, it was quarter to four and the afternoon had gone. But it didn't matter, for we'd seen enough to put a large tick against the Isle of Man for a future visit.

With the tanks once again full, we took off at 1720 for the 116-mile leg to Islay, estimating Mr McDougal's strip in the northeast of the island at 1815. Again I climbed to 4500 feet by which time we could see that great foot of land – or maybe a boot with a long ski attached to it would be a better description – known as the Rinns of Galloway, with the town of Stranraer nestling where the front of the leg meets the boot. Our course ran parallel to it some five miles out to sea and nearly midway in the narrow channel between Scotland and Northern Ireland. Again this was familiar territory for me, for we were only some thirty miles east of Belfast and my old stamping ground. I watched the familiar coastline slide past: Ballyquintin Point, where I'd once landed on the road at Strangford; the Ards Peninsular that opened up to Carrickfergus and Belfast beyond; Larne, where David Simpson had run out of fuel and I'd topped him up from jerry-cans, just enough to get him home. Garron Point, and the background of the Antrim Hills behind; so many memories, but few of them happy, for although seen remotely from a distance Ireland looks a green and pleasant land, for me it is a harsh and unforgiving place. Beyond that coastline the conflict still went on, passed on from generation to generation. My skin felt cold and clammy at the thought and I fervently hoped I'd never have to serve there again.

Elizabeth felt my stillness. 'Ireland?' she said.

'Yes, Ireland.'

I'd lost some good friends there, some going back twenty years. John Applegarth from my regiment and with whom I'd once shared a room. He'd been the first. I could see him now, a tall lanky youth standing hesitant and shy with that lop-sided smile and his hair blowing in the wind. He always wore it too long; his personal vendetta against authority, despite Mr.Elliot's continued pleas that he should set an example. He should never have been a soldier, for he was forever making fun out of the army; but then his troopers loved him and would have followed him anywhere, so who knows, perhaps he was individualistic enough to have made extremely high rank. Had he lived. He was leading a patrol and trod on a mine. He must have heard it click and known that when he lifted his foot he'd be blown sky high. Instead he stayed there with his weight on it and casually waved his men back to safety. I don't think they knew what had happened. I've often wondered how long he stood there before lifting his foot and whether I'd have done the same or called for help. Or maybe help of that kind wasn't at hand and would only have risked more lives. I went to his memorial service in the Chapel at Sandhurst. It was packed – family, brother officers and friends, probably some of them going back to schooldays, and now mostly young executives doing something in the City. They wouldn't have understood; but I did. The cold, the wet, the lack of sleep and above all the tension, day and night with nerves permanently stretched to breaking point. These were the conditions that tested the real quality of leadership, for it was not a clean or simple war. Then, the click of a pressure-switch and you knew your time was up. First, look after your men, then a last look at the sky and lift your foot... Of all the people there I understood all right: I'd been with him only half an hour before; and when he went, he left a space in our room that would forever be empty...

The Antrim Hills receded and with them my friend of twenty years ago, still standing there, arm lifted in farewell. There were others that had followed, some close and others not so close; a steady trickle every year, compounding the futility and waste, but after John Applegarth, I'd allowed my shell to harden.

I looked back to the present and Elizabeth put her hand on my knee. I could feel its warmth and smell her smell.

'I understand' she said, and I knew she'd been with me all the time.

We clipped the tip of Kintyre, another great promontory extending southwards from the Scottish mainland together with its convenient VOR beacon just west of Campbeltown, and then headed out to sea again on the final thirty-five mile leg to Islay.

In a way it felt like running away. In spite of the fact that the Brigadier had literally ordered me to stay clear of Wallop and only to report back to him by telephone after a week, I still felt I should have been near at hand, just in case. And to run away with Elizabeth, the other principal player in the saga, how would that look to the likes of Nicki-Pig and his gang of sleuths if they found out – or for that matter, Ken's solicitor? It certainly wouldn't do anything to enhance the situation... but then, why should they ever know? Better this, than being found together in the cottage, now they knew where we lived. Angela, if asked, would stick to her story that Elizabeth had merely gone away for a few days, and wouldn't elaborate further. Besides, maybe I was worrying unnecessarily, for if the Brigadier was as good as his word and was going to inquire why it hadn't gone through the proper channels, Nicki-Pig & Co could well be doing a lot of explaining or else lying very low themselves by now! At least that was worthy of a smile.

'What are you laughing about?'

'Oh I was just wondering whether we were doing the right thing running away like this together and leaving such a mess – and then about Nicki-Pig's sudden involvement. He's had it in for me for years, and certainly doesn't miss a trick! But maybe he's poked his snout too far this time, because the Brigadier's smelt a rat!'

'Honestly, you and Nicki-Pig! It's not a personal vendetta between the two of you, the real situation is about me – and my marriage to Ken!'

'I know, but as you once told me, it's now also about the army; it's about the behaviour of officers and... and sergeants' wives. It undermines the whole social structure – Mr. Elliot had a good name for it; he once caught one of our subalterns ogling a WRAC driver and quickly nipped it in the bud and told him "he was attempting to cross the unbridgeable divide!" – and he was right, for that's what it's really all about.'

'I do know, darling, and I've known all along... and don't worry about us running away together, I've thought about

249

that too, and believe me it's the best thing we could have done right now. It's not only about Ken and me and the army – it's also about us, and we're the future and need every chance; it's no good pretending just for the likes of Nicki-Pig. We'll survive, you'll see – and I look forward to the day when I can be as sweet as pie to him at a mess function or a dinner party!'

'Really? – I didn't think you... funny, but the Brigadier said something along those lines as well!'

'Sweetheart, I know the army remember? And if that's what you want... I'll be at your side, scarlet woman or not. Anyway, it's only the wives that'll talk, and I can soon handle them! Now is the difficult time for both of us and if we show we're together, people will soon accept it and understand. You once said the army's only people... once we survive this we'll be able to survive anything. It'll blow over, the Brigadier was right, it always does. It may take a little time, but in the end it will be alright; just you see!'

'Spoken like a general's daughter!'

'No, Angela's more of the general's daughter; I'm just me – but I can be as pompous as the rest of them if I have to be! Dear Mr. Elliott; you obviously thought a lot of him – was he in Ireland with you?'

'Yes he was, and yes I did.' It always fascinated me how quickly she could switch to another subject. 'I was at an impressionable age, and in a regimental way he was rather like a father to us – and also the regiment. He retired when we were in Ireland. He must be in his seventies now if he's still about – training roses to grow in straight lines, I expect.'

'You didn't keep in touch with him, then?'

'I didn't personally – I expect the regiment still does, but then I left the regiment.'

'Daddy always kept in touch with his regiment. He was always being invited to their various do's. Right up until he died.'

'It was a bit different for him; once you aspire to full colonel or above, just because you no longer wear regimental badges – collar-dogs and cap badge, it doesn't mean you no longer belong. The regiment is proud of the fact that one of them now wears red collar-tabs and a General Officers' cap badge. But I actually left my regiment and joined the Army Air Corps, and you can't have an allegiance to both.'

'But you talk of your old regiment as though you still belong?'

'I know... some things never quite die – what is it, old schools and old regiments never die, they just fade away! No, I've got that wrong. It's old school friends and old soldiers, but it's the same thing. The longer you're in the army the more you realize it's just one big family, and certainly I'm still labelled as a Lancer by all my contemporaries. In fact, only the other week Nicki-Pig called me a bloody donkey-walloper!'

'I'm tired of hearing about that wretched little man – look, is that Islay? Oh, sorry, I'm supposed to be navigating. Land-Ho, skipper!'

Our course took us along the east coast of the island, leaving the high ground that had peaks rising to 1600 feet to port, and following the narrow channel of sea that divides Islay from Jura. I descended to 1000 feet and continued along our line towards the unknown farm field. We passed over some small lochs and then a road and a larger loch beyond. The road ran northeast/southwest in a valley about three miles wide and there was more high ground beyond. The prevailing wind would funnel through there at a rate of knots...

'Time's up; I reckon we should be there!' Elizabeth said.

I followed the lie of the land, and almost immediately saw a yellow cross, which quickly turned into the wings of a Piper Cub sitting on the ground beside a rusty looking barn. Then I saw the strip, a swathe of lighter mown grass, also running northeast/southwest.

'Okay, got it! We'll just circle around a bit.'

I decided on a conventional left-hand circuit, which would keep us clear of the high ground and joined downwind. The strip was plenty large enough for a Piper Cub – or for that matter a Beaver, but the little Robin was a lot more slippery, and it would need careful judgement. I brought her down to short finals with twenty degrees of flap, then increased power and levelled off at about ten feet off the ground to study the surface. The strip was quite undulating as well as being on the side of a hill, which gave it a cross-slope throughout its length. But it was dead into wind and there was no sideways drift. There were some soft looking patches in the hollows, especially on the downhill side, so I resolved to land as near to the uphill edge as I could. I opened up and went round again.

This time for real. Remembering Bernard's technique I went for a higher and steeper approach and set her up early on a longer finals, nose well up and speed back to forty-five, with 1200 RPM set. I picked a spot, a clump of heather just off the right-hand edge of the strip and powered towards it on the back-end of the curve, maintaining forty-five, as I had been taught in an AOP9 years ago. The wind gradient helped, for it must have been blowing close to twenty knots. As we rounded out by the clump, a final burst of power to cushion the blow and stick hard back. We rolled about four lengths and stopped, the strip stretching out ahead until it disappeared down a dip, to reappear again much further on.

An ancient Land Rover suddenly appeared from nowhere and momentarily pulled up alongside. An arm emerged from the driver's sliding window, waving in a circular motion as though beckoning us to overtake, and then set off again trailing a cloud of blue smoke. I followed, taxiing with the stick held hard back, and at a distance where the blue smoke began to disperse. We went down the hill and then up again and then along another mown strip of grass off to the right, where the Piper Cub was parked by a small corrugated iron hangar.

The door of the Land Rover opened and a man got out. He was dressed for the country, old army pullover, corduroy trousers tucked into calf-length woollen socks and walking boots, but incongruously topped by a bright blue woollen bobble hat, pulled well down over his ears.

'Mr McDougal?' I enquired, jumping down from the wing.

'Aye' he said, looking at Ashley. 'That's a pretty wee aircraft you have there...'

Elizabeth got out and joined us.

'This is Elizabeth, and my name's...'

'Aye, very pretty indeed' he said looking at Elizabeth, but then he went on: '...and such an unusual wing, cranked up like that. *French* is it? Aye, and she stopped all right; most people would have carried on running away down the hill!' His voice was musical, almost like the Welsh and he emphasized 'running' by rolling the R.

'It comes from years of practice...'

'Aye, I don't doubt that. That's how I do it myself, on the back edge of the curve. I think we'd better tie her down – I have some spare tie-downs and ground anchors in the hangar. And then we'll away up to the house. I hope you're hungry for my wife's prepared a right *royal* spread for ye.'

We pushed his Cub back into the hangar and then tied Ashley down facing into wind. He then put our bags into the back of the Land Rover, and as there was only room for two in the cab, I climbed over the tailgate and made myself as comfortable as I could between our bags and a bale of straw. We set off with a lurch and almost immediately the rear filled with blue exhaust smoke, sucked in through the rolled-up rear of the tilt cover.

Fifteen minutes later, and half asphyxiated, we stopped and mercifully the engine turned off. By the time Mr McDougal had got out and walked round to lower the tail-gate, the smoke had all but dispersed. I jumped out, coughing and my eyes streaming.

'Is it a *cold* you have then?' he remarked as he handed out the bags. 'I hope you won't infect us here with your southern germs. Aye, that I do!'

The house was built of stone, and seemed to grow out of the hill. There was a small windswept garden on one side and an assortment of sheds and outhouses on the other. Still wearing his bobble hat, he led the way into the hall, through an avenue of coats and boots, and upstairs to our room where he paused to point out the view that looked over the valley. We left our bags on the bed and followed him along the passageway to the bathroom, and then trooped back again and downstairs to the kitchen.

'My goodness, what a magnificent spread!' Elizabeth exclaimed as we entered.

A beaming Mrs McDougal wiped her hands on the front of her amply filled apron before offering to shake ours, and then bustled around the table pulling out chairs and showing us where to sit. 'You must be starving, poor souls, having come all that way' she said, as though we had walked the whole distance. 'From England was it?' She spoke in the same singsong voice as her husband.

'Well, it didn't take very long' Elizabeth said, sitting down and eyeing the table. 'We had breakfast at home, lunch in the Isle of Man and now all this – it looks simply scrummy!'

'And just where might home be?' Mr McDougal asked, helping himself to ham, cold beef, boiled eggs, salad, potatoes and various pickles before sitting down at the head of the table, completely oblivious to Mrs McDougal's frown.

'McDougal, will you kindly take your hat off and offer some food to our guests first' she said to him sternly, and then in a kinder voice to Elizabeth, 'please help yourselves now, and never mind his dreadful rudeness.'

'We live in a village near Salisbury, in the south of England' Elizabeth continued, carefully watching Mr McDougal's face whilst helping herself to salad. 'Between Salisbury and Andover actually...'

'Oh aye?' Mr McDougal said, getting up and placing his bobble hat carefully on a chair. His head was virtually bald except for a few wisps of white hair above his neck and looked remarkably white in contrast to his weather-beaten face that had a distinct line across where his hat fitted. 'Near *Salisbury* eh? Let me see now, would that be near one of the *Wallops*?'

Elizabeth gave a twitch of a smile and looked down at her plate.

'Why yes!' I said, surprised, 'why, do you know the area?'

'Aye – I know it just fine' he said, going to the

mantelpiece and selecting a framed photograph from one of the many on display. 'I was there myself only a year or two back on my trip south. Army Air Corps Day at Middle Wallop; I'd been promising myself a visit for a very long time...' He put the photograph on the table and I saw a young pilot in a red beret with army wings on his chest, standing in front of a Horsa glider.

'Good Lord! Is that you – you were a glider pilot?'

'Aye, I ended up flying gliders, but before that I learnt on Tiger Moths, and then had a spell flying Austers in Libya, spotting for the artillery.'

'Well I never! That's what I do – I'm still serving; I'm an instructor at Wallop, or rather I was, until a few days ago...'

'Aye, I *guessed* as much when I saw you land! I can usually tell – it was though I was flying it myself!' He poured himself a cup of tea from a large teapot that was covered with a cosy. Mrs McDougal frowned and then with a lift of the eyebrows enquired whether Elizabeth and I would like a cup. 'Aye, I can usually tell' he continued, again oblivious to the exchange, 'and flying is no different from any other skill; a pupil can *only* learn by imitating his master – which in this case is the *army* and the techniques they use. And of course, it's *easily* recognisable if you've been through the same school yourself. And once learnt, you never forget. Aye, it's a funny thing and do you know, somebody once told me it's *exactly* the same with learning to *ski*, although I must say that's something I've never *attempted* myself! I canna mind who it was now, but they said you can *always* tell an army skier on the slopes. Something to do with the way they stand and do it by numbers – like being on *parade*, I suppose? And it's just the same with me watching people fly... So, is it *helicopters* you fly now?'

Mrs McDougal had a sudden coughing fit and I waited whilst she put her cup down and hurriedly excused herself from the table.

'Yes, I started off on Austers – AOP 9's, they were a lot more powerful than the earlier Austers that you flew, and then I went on to Beavers, and latterly helicopters. The army's mostly all helicopters now. And how about you, have you been flying ever since?'

'Certainly! Living here, an aeroplane is essential – even if it's for the *shopping* from the mainland. It takes simply *ages* by boat!'

'Well I'll be damned! – It's very good to know you, Mr McDougal!'

'Aye, it's a small world sure enough – and enough of the Mister, I'd mind it fine if you called me McDougal, or maybe Angus!'

'*Angus* is it? Why, even I call him McDougal!' his wife interjected, wiping her eyes on her apron and sitting down again. 'Now, enough talk about *aeroplanes* and have some more food; I don't want anything left!!'

So McDougal it was. After supper he kindly offered to take Elizabeth and I for a drive around the island. He was about to get into the Land Rover, but then saw the look on my face and changed his mind. Instead he walked to one of the sheds and a moment later backed an old grey Morris Minor out, thus saving me another bout of asphyxiation.

'I don't know why you came here; Jura is a far more *scenic* island to visit?' He said as we rattled our way towards Port Ellen, 'that's where most of the *tourists* go. At this time of year they arrive by the boatload, and then walk *round* and *round* the island...'

'The main reason was, yours was the only landing strip listed in my book. There was nowhere else in this area at all.'

'Aye, that's right enough. And all the years it's been listed, you're the *first* aircraft that has ever visited! How do you like the Robin?'

'I haven't had it that long, but it's a great little touring aeroplane – it gets along at about 130 and only uses four and a half gallons an hour. But perhaps it would be a bit flimsy for general use up here. Your little Cub now would seem to be ideal?'

'Aye, but she's very slow. We get some fairly strong winds here, you know. Sometimes it's difficult to make any headway at all! But for all that, she's extremely economical and simple to maintain. I was thinking maybe of exchanging it for a

Super Cub, but I can never quite afford it and anyway, there don't seem to be many around. One of your old army AOP9's now, that would suit me just fine – are there any of those around?'

'I believe there are a few on the civil register; but you might find spares difficult. With a 180 horsepower engine they're great for strip work, but they're very draggy – they only cruised at about ninety knots. They were never really designed to go any distance. I think you'd be far better off with a Super Cub.'

'Aye, that's what I keep coming back to! Och well, maybe one of these days.'

We stopped for a drink in Port Ellen and managed to buy a bottle of Islay malt whisky by way of a souvenir, and then headed back in the long summer twilight, which at this northern latitude lingers on until almost midnight.

It would linger even further tomorrow, when we reached Orkney.

III

'Fancy him knowing I was an army pilot!' I said as we climbed away the following morning. 'Damned if I'd be able to tell just by watching somebody land! Army or not, there's only one technique for a short landing – and anyway, it was Bernard who demonstrated it to me in this aircraft!'

'Oh you silly thing!' Elizabeth said with a laugh. 'You're so worldly-wise about so many things, but at other times you're utterly naïve! Didn't you realize he was winding you up!'

'What! Winding me up – how?'

'He saw the label on your bag when he put it in the Land Rover! Talk about name, rank and number, it's got Middle Wallop stamped all over it!'

'What! And you knew all the time? Why didn't you tell me?'

'Well, of course at first I wasn't sure, but when he deliberately steered the conversation to Middle Wallop over supper,
then I knew! It wasn't anything to do with the way you flew,
you conceited old ass. He just put two and two together.
Honestly, you men! Mrs McDougal cottoned on, I caught
her eye and we both had a job not to laugh! And then all that
business about army skiers being on parade and doing it by
numbers – you've got to hand it to him, he put it together
very nicely.'

'Why, what do you mean?'

He only read that last week – I read it myself in one of
the Sunday supplements! There was an article about all the
various skiing techniques – Italian, Austrian, French, but
nothing whatsoever about the army! It was sitting on the
table next to you! I really thought Mrs McDougal was going
to burst then. She had to leave the room!'

'Damn me! So you were all in it together?'

'Oh darling, you're really upset! And you sounded so
gloriously pompous: "Years of practice, don't you know!"'

'Huh!'

'Sweetheart, don't take it to heart – I love it when you go
all pompous! And he knew jolly well about the exhaust
fumes in the Land Rover too. "Is it a cold you have?
Infecting us with your southern germs"!'

'Huh!'

But I couldn't help smiling. The wily old devil. I wonder if
he's still there? I dropped the nose, picked up speed and
pulled round in a tight one-eighty. I could see his Land Rover
still parked next to the hangar. I pushed the nose down and
felt the controls harden as the speed built up; an avenging
arrow from the sky. I saw him walk out of the hangar, hand
shielding his eyes against the sun. I flattened out just above
the grass and aimed. He left it until the last the last second
before flinging himself to the ground. Got him! I pulled up
into a vertical climb, throwing in a couple of rolls for good
measure, and then as the speed fell off, pulled back and
rolled-off the top. He was standing again, legs apart and
hands on hips, roaring with laughter. I waggled the wings in a

final farewell and saw him wave, and then snap rigidly to attention with his hand to his bobble hat, palm outwards, in a formal salute. An old soldier, but soldier still, fading away.

At a thousand feet we flew northeast up the length of Jura, then turned north across the Firth of Lorn to Mull and followed the northern shore as far as Tobermory. From there we weaved to take in the islands of Muck, Eigg and Rhum and then on to Skye. The distance from Islay to Skye scaled approximately 100 miles on the chart but apart from one small ship that looked like a ferry plying between the islands and the triangular sail of a yacht butting its way to the north-west, the seas were otherwise empty. And yet these were the waters that every yachtsman I've ever met has waxed lyrically about. This was the cruising man's Mecca, where once visited nowhere else would do. Here you could spend a lifetime exploring the profusion of islands and inlets; passages could be planned so that places of interest were all within an easy day's sail; in the lee of the islands the seas were calm and shelter always near at hand; here there were no crowds and visitors were always made welcome, so much that mooring charges were unheard of; here at a latitude of 58°N palm trees grew on shores ever washed by the Gulf Stream, and by the same token, summer evenings stretched for ever.

Flying at a thousand feet it certainly looked inviting: blue sea under a blue sky, islands dotted everywhere and to the east, deep lochs probing between the mountains of the mainland. But it also made me realize that at a thousand feet we would only ever scratch the surface. Aeroplanes were designed for going places; A to B in a straight line, and the only way to explore an archipelago such as this would be by boat.

'It's lovely' Elizabeth breathed, 'like this it looks idyllic, but I bet it can be a different place under grey skies and blowing rain!'

'No more than anywhere else. But I was just thinking, to see it properly we ought to do it by boat. I think you could soon get bored stuck on one island...'

'McDougal isn't!'

'No, that's a point – but at least he's got his aeroplane and can escape.'

'Well, I think I'd love a holiday on Skye or one of the larger islands. Just walking and sea birds, and maybe catch a ferry to another island for a day. To be one of McDougal's tourists – with an anorak and everything and walk round and round! You pilots think you see the world, but you never know anywhere properly. You are always itching to get on to the next place!'

'Maybe you're right – I'd like to do it by boat though, take our time wandering from place to place, collecting whisky as we go! Anyway, we agreed – this trip is just a reconnaissance remember, and Ashley's just perfect for that!'

After Skye we turned north-northeast and followed the mainland. The sea, which had previously been calm, now became oily-smooth. The further north we ventured the more it came into the lee from the main body of the Outer Hebrides, some twenty-five miles to the west. But although smooth, it had long white streaks on it, suggesting a strong current flowing through the Minch.

I nudged Elizabeth as we saw another yacht, picking its way through the Summer Isles that are scattered around the entrance to Ullapool and Loch Broom. 'See?'

'Yes, I agree; it looks heavenly – all those islands!'

Twenty-two minutes later we reached the furthest north-west tip, Cape Wrath – only today it belied its magnificent name and looked far from angry. We turned east with the coast, Elizabeth's finger still tracing our route: over the sheltered fishing harbour of Durness closely followed by Loch Eriboll and then the Kyle of Tongue, the two great lochs of that northern coast and home to countless seabirds. With the wind behind us we were now covering the ground at 155 miles an hour, romping along and nicely balanced on the step. Four minutes later Strathy Point rushed to meet us, jutting out to sea like an accusing finger pointing now, as it had for the Vikings, the way to the Faeroes and Iceland beyond. Here and there we caught glimpses of the coastal road, sometimes little more than a track, meandering around every headland and inlet, thereby doubling its distance, yet always returning to the sea until it eventually reached Thurso, the capital of the north and ferry terminal for Orkney and the Northern Isles.

Here we turned due north and followed the ferry route that passes west of Hoy, the most westerly island of the Orkneys and final resting place for numerous World War II aircraft, both friendly and otherwise, that lie scattered on its high cloud-topped hill. On past the famous rock, the Old Man of Hoy – which we almost didn't see, for from our vantage it was all but hidden by the backdrop of the towering cliffs behind; and so to Stromness, the main ferry port for the Orkneys, its grey buildings nestling at the western entrance of Scapa Flow.

We were now only a few minutes from Kirkwall, our destination, and it was high time to finish the sightseeing tour and get back to work. I switched from Scottish Information and gave Kirkwall a hurried call and received their landing instructions. Also they said they were quite busy and asked me to hold at 1000feet over Scapa as number four, whilst they handled a British Airways Island flight arriving from Aberdeen, followed by a helicopter from the North Sea oilrigs and another Cessna light aircraft that was short of fuel. It made me smile, for having flown all day without sight or sound of another aircraft; we were now the last in a queue! Scapa Flow, that great natural harbour of two World Wars looked dark and forbidding in the shadow of Hoy. Nearly twenty miles long and up to ten miles wide, no wonder the navy could loose a whole fleet in it! But now it was empty, save the knowledge that under the dark waters lay the scuttled remains of the German Grand Fleet, lying on the bottom in orderly lines, just as they had anchored years ago.

After refuelling we parked in the visitor's park, quite near to the helicopter from the oilrigs, a large grey machine that I couldn't place, but looked as though it was derived from a Sea King or something similar; in any event, there was something distinctly Sikorsky about it! It had passenger windows in the fuselage and obviously worked hard for a living for it was streaked all over with exhaust residue and salt. The oil rig helicopters normally operated from Aberdeen, so what had brought it this far north was anybody's guess. As we climbed out of the cockpit an Islander landed, which naturally caught my interest and made me pause, standing on the wing. It was a pretty twin-engine aircraft with a high wing and the fuselage low to the ground for easy loading, and altogether much smaller than I had envisaged. It was obviously based here for it landed short in order to catch the intersection and then taxied very quickly to its own pickup point. I later learnt that true to its name it was used as the island ferry. Until I'd looked at the chart, I'd had no idea there were so many islands in the Orkney group, let alone inhabited, many of which were working farms. The chart showed landing strips on at least nine of them, and those that had no designated strip could often use the beach, tide permitting! This pleased me, for despite its dainty looks, if the Islander was proving itself to be rugged and reliable enough for this kind of daily work, it could well make an ideal replacement for the Beaver.

I locked the aircraft up and we walked together to the tower to report in and pay for our fuel and landing fee.

The small office was crowded and there were seven people waiting their turn to talk to the harassed clerk behind the counter. We pressed in behind and prepared ourselves for a long wait. Except for the last person in the queue, they all appeared to be wearing the same uniform: that originally adopted by the airlines, and in turn borrowed from the navy; black trousers and white shirt with unbuttoned breast pockets spilling out aviators' sunglasses amongst an assortment of biros, and topped by shoulders heavy with navy-style multibarred golden epaulettes. Presumably they all had jackets to go with the outfit, but by unspoken agreement these were rarely worn and no doubt left permanently hanging in their various aircraft. Maybe I was being unfair, for airline pilots would have to wear the uniform of their company, but nonetheless there seemed to be an awful lot of would-be airline captains in the queue! It made me smile, for in the

Services, where uniforms have to be worn, the only way to express any sort of individuality was to get out of them as soon as possible! Yet here was a room-full of individuals, who all happened to fly a civilian aircraft of one sort or another, yet all striving to look alike! But then, there are many activities where, practical reasons aside, the participants have adopted a quasi-uniform so that they can be seen to belong. Were we standing in a yacht club, the room would be full of people wearing red – or preferably what originally had been red but now washed to faded-pink – trousers, topped by a navy jumper suitably inscribed with an appropriate logo. The same would apply in a golf club, where sturdy thick-sole shoes and bright yellow or pink sweaters, as worn by the professionals, would be the order of the day! And woe betide should you ever wear the wrong uniform – say, pink trousers in a golf club... it would be rather like putting a black ant into a red ant's nest! So, black trousers and white airline shirt was obviously the accepted dress for all those who flew; regardless whether they were captain of a three hundred-seat passenger airliner or a small two-seat training aircraft...

The two pilots at the front of the queue with their heads together and pouring over a document on the counter were, I guessed, from the British Airways flight; the next pair waiting their turn and obviously together, were probably from the oil rig helicopter; one lanky individual on his own, signing a sheaf of papers on a separate table looked as though he was a local and no doubt was the Islander pilot, and the last pair in the queue I knew were the two from the Cessna, for we'd followed them through the refuelling point – most likely an instructor and his pupil, the latter, besides Elizabeth and myself, being the only other person not dressed in a uniform topped by four captain's bars!

One of the oil rig pilots turned as we entered and then did a double take.

'Hello, hello – where have you suddenly sprung from?'

I searched his face. The layers of middle-age flesh dissolved and underneath I saw a face I remembered. 'Why, its Sergeant – ah, Sergeant Willis, isn't it?' He had been a Scout pilot with me in Germany.

'*Captain* now, if you don't mind!' he said tapping the epaulettes on his shoulder. 'Was that you flying that toy aeroplane out there? I thought I recognized your voice on the radio...'

'Captain Willis, I'm sorry. There seems to be a surfeit of Captains in here; never seen so many in my life!' The Captain-Instructor from the Cessna gave me a dismissive look as though dressed in slacks and a jumper I had no right to be here, let alone piloting a toy aeroplane.

At the sound of the exchange one of the British Airways pilots – undoubtedly regarded by all in the room as highest in the pecking order of captains present – turned and looked at me. 'Why, hello sir' he said with a smile, 'how are you?' He pushed his way back through the crowd and clasped my hand in both of his.

'Good lord, another one! David – David Fellows! – We've got half the Army Air Corps in here!' The Cessna instructor looked at me with new interest and then hurriedly cast his eyes down. 'David, of all people – are you driving that great big tub out there?'

''Fraid so – not nearly so much fun as the old days!' David had joined my flight as a young lieutenant in Aden, where he had been my co-pilot for a time whilst learning the ropes. 'What are you doing up here of all places – and are you still serving?'

'Just having a look around – and yes, I'm instructing at Wallop. At least, I was – but I'm about to evaluate the Islander as a replacement for the Beaver. Sorry, do you know Bob Willis here? We flew Scouts together in Germany... ah, and this is Elizabeth!'

We all shook hands and then stood beaming at one another, the years falling away.

'Islander? Did I hear somebody mention an Islander?' the lanky individual exclaimed in an unmistakably Australian accent, and came across to join us.

Not unnaturally the talk was exclusively about flying.

David wanted to know what my little Robin was like, for he was thinking of buying his own aircraft: 'You forget what flying is all about driving an airliner; even on short-haul it's like sitting in an office every day...', Sergeant-Captain Willis wanted to know how the Gazelle compared with the Scout, and then went on to tell us how boring it was flying to and from the oil rigs every day: 'Like driving a bloody great bus!' And I, of course, wanted to know all about the Islander. Elizabeth stood back with a fixed smile on her face, looking somewhat bemused.

After about fifteen minutes of animated talk the Australian said 'Say, are you blokes all staying? Instead of standing here, why don't we go and find a bar?'

That brought us all back to earth with a bump. David looked at his watch and said 'Christ, we're meant to be taking-off in ten minutes – I hope my co-pilot's out there...' and hurriedly shook hands before dashing out. Bob Willis walked to the window and said 'Ah, I see we've nearly finished loading. Picking up fresh meat and vegetables for the rigs – that's why we're up here. I'd better go. Cheese, lovely cheese here – I hope they've remembered it. See you around...!'

Which left the Australian, who shrugged and then offered us a lift into Kirkwall.

I sensed Elizabeth didn't want to be stuck with him all evening, so I extracted as much Islander information as I could on our way into town. He'd started flying them for a small outfit in Brisbane who ran a thriving commuter service between the townships along the Queensland coast, so he knew the aircraft well. The one he was flying here was one of the early ones with the standard 260hp Lycoming engines, but he said the engines were pretty tired and even operating in the cold northern air and mostly at sea level, he rarely flew at the maximum takeoff weight of 5500lbs. Especially on short strip work. Half-loaded it was fine, but anything over that, the performance quickly fell off and you needed a full-length runway. But for all that, they were a great little aircraft, and he'd love to get his hands on the Defender, the military version that had two Allison 250-B17C gas turbine engines driving three-bladed props that were rated up to 425 shaft horsepower, and maximum takeoff weight increased to 7000lbs. He'd give his back teeth to have one of those on these island strips! He then told us his contract here was nearly finished and he was thinking of returning to Australia and hopefully convert to Twin Otters, which his old company were now purchasing for the heavier work, in addition to the Islander.

He dropped us off at the hotel and then excused himself as he had a hot date. So in the end I didn't even have the opportunity of buying him a beer.

IV

As soon as we shut the door behind us in our room Elizabeth turned, dropped her bag and flung herself into my arms. 'Kiss me, kiss me...' she said. We fell back onto the bed and I kicked off my shoes and then slowly started to undress her.

'I've wanted to do that all day' she said afterwards as she lay in my arms. I could smell her hair, which was spread all over my face and feel the warmth of her body, as it lay entwined with mine.

'You wanton woman...'

'Oh yes! Yes please... I always want to be your wanton woman.' Her fingers started to caress me, very lightly, darting from place to place but never quite where I wanted them. I felt myself becoming aroused again. She smiled, looking deep into my eyes. 'This time, love me slowly...'

Later, we sat opposite each other in the huge empty hotel dining room. We were the only people there, which suited us fine. I studied her face and her eyes, which were a dead give-away and had that dreamy look she always had after she had made love. The moment lingered and I swam helplessly into their magnetic depths; the way open and completely unbarred to her very soul. I reached under the table and touched her knee. She gave a start and then covered my hand with hers. 'I know' she whispered. Then, 'I'm so glad we're together at last.'

We were interrupted by the waiter, a young red-haired lad wearing gym shoes beneath his formal trousers and from his manner obviously itching to get off duty. He had come to clear away, but had then seen our half-eaten food, and instead asked if everything was all right.

'Everything's fine' I said, 'we shan't be very long...' and then to Elizabeth as he sidled away, 'I thought at one point we'd be involved in a hard drinking session this evening. The hangar doors were definitely open...'

'I wouldn't have minded. I felt rather... well, I don't want to make your head swell any larger than it already is ... but I felt rather proud of you, I suppose – only that's not really the word I'm looking for, but I can't think of a better one. Those two – David what's-his-name and the other one, the helicopter pilot, they obviously thought the world of you.'

'Huh, I don't know about that! – But it was strange meeting them both like that, here in Kirkwall of all places. It just shows how small the world of aviation is. Mind you, I hardly knew Sergeant Willis, he was just another pilot in the flight in Germany, but I knew David quite well. He goes back a lot further; and come to think of it, he was also a friend of Tristan's.'

'Tristan? Funny, because I was thinking about him earlier too – I was wondering whether that Australian pilot knew him. I'm sure Tristan said he was flying out of Brisbane. I meant to ask in the car, but you two were so busy talking I couldn't get a word in edgeways!'

'Now there's a thought! He most likely does – I wish you'd asked him. Never mind, we'll perhaps bump into him tomorrow. Anyway, going back to the other two, they both seem to have done quite well...'

'That's as maybe, but to hear them talk you wouldn't think so. It sounded as though they were bored to tears in their present jobs; they couldn't wait to talk about the good old days!'

'Yes, but even so, I don't suppose they'd change places and go back. Life moves on you know; it's me – I'm the one stuck in a rut.'

'Well, so long as it's my rut, I don't mind.'

'Elizabeth!'

She coloured. 'Oh, I didn't mean it like that! Trust you...!'

After dinner we arranged with the hotel desk to hire a car for the morning, and then as it was still fully light, walked up the ancient flagged High Street that was only really wide enough to take one car, as far as the Cathedral and the ruins of the Bishop's Palace. We looked around the ruins and imagined the splendour of what had been, and then walked up the steps to the entrance of the red-stoned Cathedral that dominated every other building in the town.

'Can we go in?'

In the half-light of the interior, the cathedral weaved its own spell. Through the stone tombs and effigies, the history of the north was revealed. Ancient Norse Kings with their outlandish names came to life; the struggles for power, easily traceable through the generations, as well as the rapes, murders and pillage that abounded throughout the period– it was all there; a violent history and one that hitherto I had known nothing about.

We called in at a waterfront pub by the harbour on the way back. It was full of men in well-worn Norwegian jerseys drinking pints of 'heavy', as they do in Scotland. But there the similarity ended for they were anything but Scottish. They all talked in the singsong accent of the north, even more heavily pronounced than McDougal's from the Western Isles, and it was only after a little while that I realized that half of them were in fact Norwegian, sailors from a ship, yet were fully able to converse with the locals, each to their own language, purely by intonation alone!

By now it was midnight and nearly dark, so we decided to go back to the hotel and call it a day. We paused on the quayside and watched the lines being taken from a fishing boat.

Whether it was Norwegian or Orcadian I could not tell, but the voices, the place and the manner of making fast, were exactly the same as though it were a Viking ship docking a thousand years before.

Needless to say Elizabeth loved everything about Orkney. It was a strange mixture of not so old, very old and extremely old, with everyday life going on all around notwithstanding. Farmers ploughed around ancient standing stones; cows grazed on the mounds surrounding the ancient and exposed Pict settlement at Skara Brae; sheep huddled about the entrance of an ancient burial mound, in which narrow passage to the long-robbed interior were walls carved with graffiti: ancient runes of the early Teutonic alphabet alongside their modern twentieth century counterpart, yet each bearing the same message: love for a maiden, from a sailor a long way from home. The maidens are all long dead and forgotten, but their names were there; carved in runic lines or under hearts pierced with arrows, spanning the centuries, their message still plain for all to see.

Seagulls nested on the sides of General Kitchener's Memorial: he of pointed-finger fame "The Country Needs You" from the First World War, and erected to commemorate his death by drowning, along with the whole of the ship's company just offshore from the towering cliffs of Yesnaby; which cliffs, those few who managed to struggle to the shore, were then unable to climb and perished nonetheless. Second World War blockhouses and bunkers linked with abandoned gun emplacements abounded, now the home for implements and bags of fertilizer, and anti-submarine nets filled the waters of long worked-out quarries, for where better place to dispose of miles of redundant steel netting?

With an Ordnance Survey map, we drove around in our small hired car and saw it all. Names from all over northern Europe and some from the mists of time sprang out from the map. Ancient Pictish names, Scottish names, English, Scandinavian, Icelandic and names that had travelled with the Vikings: Langskaill, Greenbanks, Mor Stein, Ward Hill, Swart Hellideo, Brockan, Hyval, Mossbank, Burrey Brae,

Horraquoy and Rosehill. And, as with the runes and hearts inscribed in the barrow, they all had their rightful place; all belonged in Orkney.

V

We didn't have a chance to speak to the Australian pilot in the morning, but instead took-off behind him. He, turning north to a hard morning's work of eight or nine strip landings and takeoff's with never more than ten-minutes flight in between; and we turning south, for a single 530 mile straight-line hop that would take us from one end of the British Isles to the other. With the forecast wind I estimated it would take four hours and ten minutes, which coincidently was the same amount of time allowed by the schedule for the Islander to complete its round-the-islands ferry trip.

The weather had changed overnight and we took off under grey skies, the base of which the tower was unable to tell us. Furthermore, the forecast for southern England was not good, with a low-pressure system tracking its way up the Bristol Channel. I wondered whether to File IFR and do the job properly, but Ashley, although fitted with a blind-flying panel, only had one rather basic VOR by way of navigational equipment and for serious work you really needed two in order to take cross-bearings as well as being coupled to an ILS (Instrument Letdown System); let alone the backup of an ADF (Radio Compass) and fan markers. So I filed VFR and climbed to 3500 feet and as we were still VMC, opted to remain at that level. At least further south the radar coverage was good, and I could always file IFR later.

Our True Course of 173 degrees took us straight out to sea, ten miles east of John O'Groats and across the Moray Firth, a surprisingly long sea crossing of eighty-miles to our first landfall at Macduff on the north coast of Aberdeenshire. Our line then ran down through

Aberdeenshire, with the Grampian Mountains under our starboard wing and so into Angus before coasting out once again some twenty miles east of Dundee for the thirty-five mile crossing of the Firth of Forth, now homing to the VOR beacon at St Abb's Head. Sixty-three miles further on we were abeam Newcastle and it was time to change from Scottish Information to London on 125.475. Shortly after that, Pole Hill our next beacon some sixty-five miles ahead, flicked into life. We were now running down the spine of the Pennines and until you've flown over them, you don't realize what a vast area the National Parks of Northumberland, Lake District, Yorkshire Dales and Peak District cover, all of it unspoilt country, and indeed penetrating south right into the heart of industrial Britain.

By the time we reached Pole Hill – which few people have heard of, except those who fly, and they know it to be the central aeronautical roundabout for the whole of middle England – the weather had considerably worsened, and I had already descended to 2000 feet in order to remain VMC. To continue further at this height was now denied, for ahead was the complexity of controlled airspace that surrounds Liverpool and Manchester, through which one cannot blunder. I either had to go up or down: re-file IFR and climb into the cloud to whatever height they decreed; or descend to below 1200 feet and make for the narrow low-level corridor that runs between the two control zones. If I'd been flying a Beaver, or any other fully equipped aircraft, the choice would have been easy – indeed, there would have been no choice for I would have filed IFR at the outset – but now in little Ashley I opted for the latter; to remain VFR and go for the low-level corridor. Besides, I'd never done this before...

I tuned the VOR to Wallasey, which is situated at Birkenhead and then turned starboard onto 245 degrees to home towards it. I then called Manchester and relayed my intentions and asked for their QNH, as all aircraft using the corridor had to be on their common altimeter setting. Had I a second VOR it would have been easy for I could have tuned Shawbury for a cross-bearing; but as it was I had to map read, with Rochdale, Bolton, Wigan and God-know's-where-else all running into one another in the murk. There was only one line feature that I could see from the chart that would be of any use: the M6 motorway, which obligingly wriggled south under the centreline of the corridor towards Warrington, oblivious to the fact that it was supporting an unseen light-aircraft corridor of air above it. But which was the M6? Motorways suddenly appeared from all sides, running in all directions! Together we studied the chart. First we had to ignore the M65, which branched south into the M66; then cross the M61, which also ran south where it joined the M62; and also ignore the M58, the M57 and the M56 as well as numerous other linking dual carriageways that appeared on the ground but were not considered significant to feature on my half-million aeronautical chart. Had we started further north, the M6 would have been easy to find; then it would just have been a question of following it south, but as it was... it was rather like unravelling strands of spaghetti.

'If that was the M66 we just passed over, I reckon that must be Bolton down there. Yes, that fits... at least, I think it does, and then that motorway there must be the M61...?' Elizabeth pronounced.

'It's easy to make the map fit the ground – hang on, I'll try it another way...'

I tuned the VOR to Manchester on 113.55, and the window showed our current bearing to be 340° 'FROM'. I then placed the Swissair compass rose over the VOR beacon on the chart and swung the string to the entrance of the corridor: 305° magnetic. I then swung it further onto 340° and it showed us to be over... Bolton!

'I think you're right! Now, see that number in the box – 340? It will start winding down soon and when it decreases to 305°, we should be at the entrance to the corridor and over the M6. You carry on map reading and see if it still fits then!'

True to forecast the weather continued to deteriorate and now at 1200 feet we were just under the cloud base with rain streaking over the windshield and visibility reduced to about four miles. I carried on, holding the heading for Wallasey but with the VOR tuned to Manchester and watched the numbers as they started to click down.

'Should be coming up any minute' Elizabeth said unperturbed, 'yes, there's the junction where the M58 joins the M6 – I wish they'd stencil the numbers on the motorways, it'd make life so much easier!'

I waited until 305° showed in the box, then called Manchester and turned south into the corridor.

Again with the compass rose on the chart I read-off the bearing from Manchester to the southern exit: 225° magnetic, which should put us overhead Ashcroft, a small civil aerodrome just south of the corridor but directly on its center-line, in... I scaled the distance... eleven and a half minutes.

Right on time Ashcroft loomed up; we were through! We were now clear until the next box, this time a military Air Traffic Zone that surrounding Shawbury and also encompassing three other satellite fields, some fifteen miles ahead. Shawbury also had a VOR, which I now tuned. With Manchester and Liverpool out of the way, it was time to re-plot our course, as well as decide what to do about the weather. Diverting through the corridor had put us considerably west of our original track and closer to the high ground of the Welsh border. Indeed, we were now only approximately twenty miles east of our outbound track of three days ago – but then we'd had altitude, as well as being able to see and now many of the peaks would now be in cloud. It had been different when I'd flown back from France in the Rallye; then I'd had no radio or navigation aids and it was a question of having to fly by the seat of your pants... but now I had these – limited though they were – and as VHF works line of sight, I needed more altitude to make them fully effective. To continue further under the weather with the amount of high ground ahead was just downright stupid!

I called Shawbury and told them my intentions and asked if I could continue through their zone to the beacon, and also if they would monitor my climb to a safe altitude? They told me in familiar military jargon to 'Wait-Out' and then came back a moment later with a number to squawk for the transponder. They then said they had no other traffic, that they had me on radar and I was cleared to climb.

The decision taken, I increased power and eased back on the stick. Unlike most other aircraft, Ashley's instruments were not set out in the standard T layout, which is designed for easy scanning. For one thing, the instrument panel wasn't deep enough and in order to fit at all, the instruments were spread out in a line across the whole width of the facia, and as mentioned before, even curved around to the sides of the cockpit. Normally the flight instruments – Artificial Horizon and Direction Indicator in the centre, flanked by Airspeed and Altimeter on the left and Vertical Speed Indicator and Turn and Slip on the right – are in the T and directly in front of the pilot's eyes, thus minimizing the parallax effect. The next priority are the engine instruments – RPM, Oil Pressures and Temperatures, Fuel gauges, and maybe Cylinder Head and Carburettor Mixture temperatures – and they are placed as centrally as possible and in any event before the remaining ancillaries such as voltmeters and ammeters or the banks of radios and navigation aids – which take last priority, and indeed are often located in the roof or wherever.

With practice, when in the T arrangement, one can virtually read all the flight instruments together and anything unusual is picked-up instantly from the corner of an eye. But the seemingly haphazard arrangement of Ashley's instruments took some getting used to, and I found my head followed my eyes in a repetitive negative shake, scanning each instrument in turn from one side of the cockpit to the other. And Ashley's violent motion didn't help. The interior of clouds can be extremely turbulent, and the little aircraft felt every bump, sometimes in the most alarming way. Perhaps Sergeant-Captain Willis had been right when he described her as a toy aeroplane, for she was not at all happy in these conditions and really too light for serious all-weather flying.

I was conscious of the outside world changing from grey to black and at one time the additional roar of rain above the engine noise, but my eyes could not leave the instruments as we fought our way upward. Occasionally the revs would gradually drop off, the first signs of carburettor icing, and this I countered with a shot of hot-air, which each time brought the needle back to the mark again. I also extended the shake of my head to include the leading edge of the wings, to see if there was any sign of ice building there, but thankfully they remained clean throughout. She was a twitchy aircraft to fly at the best of times, which of course, was what made her such fun – but in these conditions she was nothing short of downright hard work! I'd noticed at the factory that the latest range of four-seat Robins had mostly been fitted with auto-pilots, but it was no use wishing... even a Beaver, with no auto-pilot, would have been a lot easier. I'd many a time flown through a lot worse than this in a Beaver, but then she was the most docile of aircraft and when properly trimmed just flew herself, wherever you took her.

The flag on the VOR flicked from 'TO' to 'FROM' as we passed over Shawbury beacon at 5200 feet, with no sign of the cloud breaking. Ahead, there were no more handy VOR's to tune into, which meant I'd have to stay with Shawbury on a back bearing of 155° for as long as it lasted. Seven minutes later the grey began to lighten, gradually growing to an intense white and then we were through.

It's always a breathtaking experience when you break through to the world above. This especially when you have lived every moment of the ascent, hands-on all the way, in a small wood and fabric aircraft; rather than seen as a casual glance from an airliner's window. It is the pilot's world and shared only with God.

'My God' Elizabeth echoed, 'this makes it all worth it. I thought that cloud was never going to end!' She turned to me, eyes shining, 'are we really meant to be here? It's just – it's just so humbling...'

We were flying above a dazzlingly white carpet of cloud, chasing our shadow that raced ahead, surrounded by a halo of rainbow drops. Mountains of cumulus reared up through the carpet all around, towering ever upwards to vast heights. These were the mighty castles of the Gods, their bastions building and unfolding even as we watched. And she was right, for here we were intruders in another world, dwarfed to the insignificant proportions of a fly, crawling over a vast snowfield surrounded by towering mountains.

I called Shawbury and told them we were VMC on top at 6800 feet, thanked them for their help and that I was continuing to Flight Level 75 on 1013, our nearest quadrantal altitude. They 'Rogered' that and told me to continue on London Information and wished me a 'Good day'.

In the clear air above, the turbulence ceased and Ashley settled down and began to fly. I reduced the power back to cruise configuration, leaned the mixture and as the speed built up, followed it by notching forward on the trim until we were balanced once more in the customary cruising attitude.

Cotswold Radar saw us through the westbound airway G1, by which time the cloud mat beneath us was beginning to break up and there were occasional glimpses of the ground. The weather front, I guessed, had tracked considerably north of the Bristol Channel; more likely across north Wales, which would have put us in the middle of it when we were flying through the low-level corridor. But still the unstable mountains of boiling cumuli persisted, their cotton-wool ramparts occasionally torn asunder to reveal black and forbidding interiors. We threaded our way between them, occasionally darting through a gap between walls, or slicing a wing along a tempting escarpment. Cotswold Radar came on again and asked if we were still VMC and whether we could descend to 6000 feet as they had conflicting traffic climbing out of London, and would I now contact Lyneham on 123.4, as I would be descending beneath the upper level of their zone. I replied affirmative, for the stopwatch said it was time to descend anyway, and at the same time I caught a glimpse of what was probably Swindon through a gap at ten o'clock.

Lyneham confirmed we were eight miles west of Swindon and that we were cleared to continue our descent on a direct heading for Thruxton. I was over familiar country now, running down the eastern edge of the army low-flying area. Wroughton to port, followed by Avebury under the starboard wing, and that'll be Marlborough... all old friends. Pewsey on the railway line and the airfield at Manor Farm; descending through 2500 feet now, and time to call Thruxton and obtain landing instructions. Inbound from the north... I check the watch: four hours fifteen from Orkney; not bad considering all the messing about and diversions! Runway in use, wind strength and QNH noted and reset the altimeter; Tidworth and Ludgershall camp alongside, helicopter on the pad — a Gazelle, the rotors stationary; Thruxton should be about... there, good; left hand circuit he'd said, so jinx starboard a touch and we'll be nicely set-up, downwind at 1000 feet. Toy aeroplane indeed...

VI

There was a bulky OHMS envelope waiting for me at the cottage. I opened it and it was all there: confirmation of my appointment, outline brief; operational parameters; stages of evaluation and requited breakdowns; lines of communication; timings, outline costs and so on. I also discovered that I would still be on Colonel Jimmy's establishment and to report directly to him. Commencement of the job would be subject to my passing a multi-engine refresher course at Kidlington, Oxford, where I should report by midday on Wednesday!

The Brigadier had certainly been busy and had left no stone unturned.

Whilst I was reading this Elizabeth had been on the phone to Angela, which had ended by Angela inviting us to supper around the kitchen table, so they could hear all about our trip! Also, there was a bulky package waiting for her that looked as though it was from her solicitor.

Which suited us fine, for neither of us had given any thought about food.

Nigel greeted us with a large gin and tonic in each hand 'Just a primer — can't beat it on a summer evening...' and we adjourned to seats and a table under an umbrella in the garden. After a while Angela got up and asked Elizabeth if she would help her with the horses, which was Nigel's cue to go back to the kitchen to refresh our glasses – and all in all, it looked as though it was going to turn into another of those evenings. But then, I was still on leave and not flying in the morning, so what the hell?

I told him about the job, and then had to tell it all over again when Angela and Elizabeth returned from putting the horses to bed; and then Elizabeth read her letter aloud from the solicitor, which Nigel proclaimed was a good start and that the wheels were definitely beginning to turn.

'But what's going to happen to you both now?' Angela asked, 'where will you both live?'

'Well, I'd like to think that Elizabeth could continue to live in the cottage, and I'll just turn up whenever I can! I don't know what the set-up's going to be, or the sort of hours I'll be working. I imagine I'll have to get digs of some kind near the airfield – but on the other hand, I might see if I could commute daily in Ashley. After all, it's only a twenty-minute trip ...'

Elizabeth clapped her hands. 'Really? – I thought you'd be away for weeks at a time! Could you really commute in Ashley? What fun – and what an ideal solution, especially working on an aerodrome. Ashley would really justify her existence!'

'Sounds good to me' Nigel said, 'beats the train any day. I wish I could fly to the office every day!'

'Darling, you know you'd hate it!' Angela said, adding more tonic to Nigel's over-generous gin. 'You'd miss grunting at all your chums every morning and reading the paper and doing the crossword. Anyway, what if its dark or the weather's bad?'

'Well, as I said, it's just a thought – and certainly through the summer months it's feasible. Later on, we'll just have to see. Maybe they'll let me bring the Islander back to somewhere like Boscombe. You can get in there any time or weather. Anyway, first I've got to go on this course at Kidlington.'

Later, we drove slowly home in the gathering dusk. 'It would still be light in Orkney' Elizabeth said, snuggling closer to me. 'I did so love it there; promise me we can go again, I'd love to get to know it really properly?'

'I promise.' I gave her a squeeze, 'have you got to go to work tomorrow – I'll miss you.'

'Mmm. What are you going to do?'

'I'll give the Brigadier a ring in the morning, and maybe go and see Colonel Jimmy to sort a few details out...'

'I'll miss you too. It was only a few days, but it feels as though we've been together all our lives. We did so much...'

VII

As I turned the aircraft onto short-finals, the examiner cut the starboard engine.

I'd been expecting something of the sort, but still the sudden loss of power at that critical moment took me by surprise. With the aircraft set up for landing, both engines had only been at twenty-five percent power, but I hadn't reckoned on the severity of the swing to starboard or the amount of rudder needed to counter it. Instinctively I dropped the nose a fraction to maintain airspeed whilst my right hand closed over the levers to feather the dead propeller and increase power to the remaining engine; but already it was too late to save the landing. The crosswind had taken charge and the runway was now away off-line and I knew there was little point in continuing.

'Fox November executing missed approach. Simulated starboard engine failure, going round again on one.'

'Roger, Fox November, call again downwind. Be advised: wind now gusting thirty knots from southeast.'

'Fox November'.

With the port engine bellowing at maximum power away out on a limb, I coaxed the floundering aircraft back into the air, whilst winding on rudder trim to counteract the asymmetric effect, which on this heading was also aided by the viscous crosswind from the same side. I held the nose down to build the speed and at the earliest opportunity flicked the switch to retract the undercarriage. I heard the wheels thump home and then by degrees slowly bled off the flaps, each time countering the sink by inching back on the control column, until at last the aircraft was clean. Finally I trimmed; she was flying again. I momentarily sat back lifted my hands off the wheel in an over-exaggerated gesture to indicate this and that we were climbing out on track, and then followed it by wandering a finger over the one set of engine instruments that were still alive, again to show him that I had their health in mind.

He grinned and looked out of the starboard window. 'Well, you caught that one okay...'

'You're a Machiavellian bastard, and I don't care what they say...' which is hardly the way to endear you to your examiner on your final-handling – but we'd got on well over the last two weeks, and throughout the test, or at least, until he'd pulled that last stunt, the atmosphere in the cockpit had been relaxed and professional. 'She struggles a bit on one – just as well we haven't got a full load...'

'Mmm. But you did right in cleaning her up early; once you've got rid of the drag, she'll cope fine on one engine. She's fairly slippery...' he turned and gave me a brief smile, '...but I don't much like the look of this weather.'

I peered out of my side window at the gathering bank of black cloud, which even as I watched suddenly spat-out a tongue of lightning. 'At least the forecast was right. They gave thunderstorms developing over the whole south of England...'

'Yeah, it'll be on us in about ten minutes. Come on, let's see if you can land this thing on one engine in a thirty-knot crosswind and we'll call it a day...'

I turned the aircraft downwind at eight hundred feet, and we both automatically searched for the windsock at the end of the runway. The light had almost gone, as though

someone had drawn a massive curtain all around and altogether it didn't look good. The last thing I wanted was to be
caught out in a thunderstorm; I'd flown through one once
years ago and once was one-time too many. I could just make
the windsock out: a splash of dirty orange etched against the
indigo-grey landscape. It was standing almost straight-out at
near enough ninety-degrees to the runway, and visual indication of the strength and direction of the crosswind. For
good measure, I turned the aircraft a further ten-degrees into
the wind, away from the line of the runway and gauged the
line of drift whilst completing the downwind vital actions.

'I think I'll leave the flaps as a last minute option' I said.
'On one engine, she handles well enough flying straight and
level, but I didn't like the way she bucked at low speed on full
flap ....'

'Up to you' he grunted, leaning across to peer out of my
window and hopefully noting how our port wing was now
running absolutely parallel to the runway on a perfect reciprocal track. Then, when the trailing edge reached abeam the
threshold of the runway, on impulse I suddenly cut the
remaining engine, pushed the nose down and turned left
ninety-degrees.

This was not at all what he'd anticipated and furthermore
by turning now, I'd committed us.

'Hey, hey – what's this? I'm here to test you on an asymmetric landings! I was looking forward to seeing how you'd
cope with a long final on one engine with a ninety-degree
crosswind working against it!'

'Sorry, but you did say it was up to me... and this is how
I'd do it in a Beaver; old habits die hard... besides, looking at
that belt of rain coming in, I reckon it's high time we were
down – and the quicker the better! A prolonged finals on one
engine would have taken another five minutes... so why don't
you put it in the box for good airmanship?'

He smiled. 'I keep forgetting you're a bloody instructor –
and an army one at that! But at this school we teach pupils to
become airline pilots, not seat-of-the-pants bush flyers. But
go ahead and try it! If you can pull off a dead-stick landing

in these conditions, it'll be an equally good test and I'll take back all I said.'

'Airline pilots... that's not what I'm here for.' I muttered, but even as I said it I wondered whether he was right, for I wasn't flying a bush aircraft but a modern twin executive, deliberately chosen by the school to have similar handling qualities as an airliner. With the strength of this crosswind it was a risky manoeuvre even to consider, let alone accomplish.

I shortened the base leg into a continuous turn onto finals, and then set-up for a glide approach, well upwind of the extended runway line. The trouble was, I'd been flying helicopters for so long I'd forgotten how susceptible a fixed-wing aircraft was to wind effect, even an executive-twin like this; but then, I suppose this was proper flying...

I gauged the remaining height and then fed in thirty-degrees of flap and reduced the speed. With no power, the trick is to weathercock sufficiently into wind to negate any drift, and then back-off a few degrees, thus allowing the wind to drift you in towards the runway at a controlled rate, whilst at the same time co-ordinating a similar rate of descent, so that hopefully you'd end up at zero feet over the centreline of the runway! From the corner of my eye I was aware that the wall of rain had now reached the perimeter of the field, and already had obscured the control tower. I felt for the switch that turned the wipers on, still concentrating on the runway as it sidled into view. Just before touchdown we were plumb in the middle and I held off and felt for the ground, simultaneously correcting the remaining drift with rudder and eased the nose up. The main tyres squeaked one after the other and the aircraft settled with a thump. I lowered the nose and let it run.

'Flash Git!' he said as he re-started the starboard engine. 'I've a good mind to make you go round again and do it properly – but I suppose we'd better call it a day and go and find a coffee. If we can find our way back that is – God, I've never seen rain like this! We'll do the de-brief in my office...'

There would be no flying back in Ashley this evening, so I booked in at the pub and used their payphone to call Elizabeth.

There was no reply from the cottage, so I tried Angela's number. Nigel answered and said they were both out getting the horses in and there was the mother and father of all thunderstorms going on and he could hardly hear. He'd get Elizabeth to ring me back, and what was my number?

I gave it him and went up to my room and watched the storm from the window. Lightning flashed all around and one thunderbolt was simultaneous and shook the whole building. It was a proper storm and totally awe-inspiring – and I was very glad I was watching it from the ground. Suddenly I felt her near and knew that she too was watching the storm and thinking of me. It was a good feeling. To be so close. 'Hello' I said to the sky and I felt her smile. We'd only parted that morning but already I was missing her. 'I shan't be coming home this evening...'

The phone rang. That would be her, right on cue!

The landlady handed me the phone. 'It's for you' she said.

But it wasn't her; it was Nigel. 'I think you'd better come' he said.

And the shutters banged down.

Chapter 8

I

Looking back through my logbook I see it took the best part of a year to fully test and evaluate the Defender for its operational colours. Colonel Jimmy sent me a crib-sheet with boxes to fill in and this was then added to and enlarged upon almost on a weekly basis as more people became involved and more tasks were envisaged, some of them highly improbable. In these situations it's easy to lose sight of the original brief: the army wanted an aircraft to replace the Beaver in its liaison role – but I suspect somebody got hold of the original role-plan for the Beaver when it in turn was being evaluated for service. At that time it was expected to undertake the entire operational role of the AOP9 spotter aircraft, be able to be pushed into a wood and camouflaged as well as being equipped to fly on the airways, carry stretchers, drop parachutes or bombs from wing-racks, and be the maid of all other work!

These continuing demands reminded me of the oft quoted occasion when the army decided to design its own jeep. There was a perfectly good lightweight cross-country vehicle on the market called the Land Rover, but no, the army wanted its own. An all-arms committee was convened and they were all asked to list their priorities and submit them to the manufacturers. Needless to say, by tacit agreement the list was never quite frozen, so allowance could be made should individual committee members be brow-beaten by their respective seniors. 'Don't forget, it's got to have comfortable seats – my piles always play-up like the devil when I'm in the field...' The infantry needed a vehicle that you could get in and out of quickly, so the sills were lowered and the chassis strengthened. The signals people saw the need to be able to operate three different radios at once, so the rear compartment had to be enlarged, extra aerial points fitted and a fancy ring-main to feed everything. It would have to be able to have a machine-gun mounted on the bonnet, so the windscreen was altered to lay flat, the screen-washers had to be done away with and extra mountings had to be fitted under the bonnet as well as the chassis beefed up some more to take the extra weight. Then, it would have to be able to ford a river; to be driven totally submersed. So the engine had to be adapted (major problem; if only you'd told us about this before) the bonnet line raised (and the folding windscreen with it) and a place found to stow the 'easily-fitted snorkel' when it wasn't in use. The medics, who had been quiet up to now, then decided there were too many sharp edges and projections that could cause unnecessary injury, and the whole interior had to be redesigned, and everything rounded-off.

Eventually the vehicle appeared. It was far too heavy for its designed traction and immediately sank to its axles whenever it left the road; the canvas side-panels over the lowered sills were a nightmare in winter, they leaked, they were draughty and the occupants froze; the driver had to stop each time he wanted to clean the windscreen; the vehicle was top-heavy; it couldn't be air-dropped; the multi-fuel engine didn't really work so ordinary petrol had to be used, which it loved and drank copious amounts, which in turn meant the tank wasn't nearly large enough; the snorkel attachment ripped off or was damaged every time you drove through a wood, and nobody dared to drive it underwater anyway, for it always got bogged in – and so on. Apart from the comfortable seats, everyone decided the ordinary Land Rover was a much better vehicle and what's more, they could have told you so at the outset had they been asked.

So, with this in mind I endeavoured to stick to the original brief and based my assessment on that. Time meant nothing any more and I just threw myself into the work, the days running into weeks running into months one after another.

After the funeral I mostly stayed at Bembridge, for it was easier and there was little point in going back. I looked for her at the funeral, but she wasn't there. I thought there might be a sign. But there was nothing. Just empty words and it was as though she'd never existed. Angela was very good and had emptied the cottage of Elizabeth's things, but that only somehow made it worse and the few times I stayed there I kept opening cupboards and looking into drawers to see if there was anything of hers left.

For I had nothing, not even a photograph.

Sometimes I felt anger. To be killed by a horse: Elizabeth, my soul mate, how could you do this to me and leave me behind? That wasn't in the plan; our plan, we had it all mapped out, remember? I believed in you. Surely it wasn't meant to end like this? This, this – nothingness?

And then there was remorse, always remorse: the futility, the misery and – and the waste. The terrible, terrible waste. 'We've done so much' she had said; it was almost as if she had known.

The only way forward was to concentrate on the project. Nothing else mattered and it was the only thing that would see me through the abyss. For that's what it had turned into: an abyss. Then I received a letter – Nigel had kindly offered to act as a Post Office and forward my mail and it was in one of his bundles. It was around Christmas time, for there was also a card enclosed from both of them, asking what I was doing for Christmas and whether I'd like to join them.

I felt a lump forming in my throat and put the card to one side and opened the other letter. It was from Sergeant Lane, saying that he'd passed the course and now had a pair of wings on his chest, and to thank me for all I'd done. Unfortunately Stephen Grant hadn't made it. He'd fallen at the last hurdle, only two weeks before the end, which he thought was a travesty of justice, for all along he'd been the better pilot. He ended by saying he still freewheeled his car and tried not to use the brakes, and that he'd heard about the accident with the horses in the thunderstorm and hoped I was getting on all right.

It was only a note, but it meant a great deal. The ultimate reward – I'm sure any teacher would know what I mean. And it was also kind of Nigel and Angela to invite me for Christmas, but I wrote back and declined. It was too close and I couldn't yet face them. 'You're almost family' he'd once said, but even that wasn't to be.

Six months after that I reported back to Wallop to hand in my final report. The Brigadier welcomed me into his office and thanked me effusively for a job well done, and how useful my report would be when the time was right and Colonel Jimmy then offered me my old job back, only this time instructing the advanced pupils.

But that was my other life; my life before the shutter came down, and I knew I could never go back.

That day was the last day I wore army uniform.

I drove out of the gates, past the bus stop where I had waited for Elizabeth on that fateful morning; and then again as of that morning, followed the familiar route to Nigel and Angela's who once more had asked me to stay with them. Time had dulled some of the pain and this time I'd accepted gratefully. It would be good to see them again and I looked forward to their company. It was high summer; almost a year to the day since that evening we'd arrived back from Orkney and sat drinking gin and tonic in the garden. Only this time we were a subdued gathering, all of us feeling the same loss and not pretending otherwise.

We had supper sitting around the familiar table and, as I

had a year ago, I told them about my new job offer, which I said I had just turned down and furthermore was resigning from the army. They both urged me to stay, to reconsider – but it was no use; she was still everywhere, especially here where we'd been together. Already I'd found myself looking for her car around every familiar corner. There are times when you can't just go back and pick up the reins as if nothing had happened and I knew I had to get away. Nigel said I was being foolish; that one should never make a decision, especially one of this magnitude, when the mind was unbalanced – and that included being emotionally upset. Emotions should never be allowed to rule the head. I knew he was right. Then Angela had a go and was quite forceful, saying that I was running away and would continue to do so until I stopped and faced up to it. And deep down I knew she too was right, and maybe one day I would, but now wasn't the time; it was too soon and I still had to grieve.

That night at Angela's, I tried to contact her. Maybe she was out there and I could reach her in the manner she had first contacted me? I lay in the dark and tried to remember what she'd told me. Empty your mind of everything and focus your subconscious and then just let go... something about finding a passage and following a light?

But it didn't work.

There was no passage and there was no light and instead, I had a confused dream about Tristan living in Australia with his new wife and their two children, one just a baby, but I was unable to see their faces. Tristan I could see all right, he was just the same and he told me he was now flying Twin Otter's with the chap we'd met in Orkney.

The next day I wrote my letter of resignation.

II

I resigned from what was more than a career, but a way of

288

life. I'd always wanted to be soldier ever since I was at school, and had never really considered anything else: Sandhurst; the Regiment; the decision to transfer into the Army Air Corps; the years of my marriage; the first time tested under fire; my friends; the Mr Elliot's'; the Nicki-Pigs and most of all the people who really mattered: those who had depended on me; the soldiers in my first troop, the flight in Belfast and latterly the Sergeant Lanes and the Stephen Grants – and whether I could have helped Stephen to pass, had I been there. All those good times remembered and the bad to be forgotten.

It took but a signature.

The hardest break of all was the day I handed in my Identity Card. Your ID card is more than a passport, for it is never scrutinized or its authenticity doubted, nor is it subjected to a stamp that grants only temporary admittance. It's a Statement; it's your Identity; it's who you are. It opens the gates to every military establishment, both British and foreign throughout the world. I'd once used it to beg a ride on a South African Air Force aircraft from Cape Town to Pretoria. 'Jump aboard, of course there's room...' for I was recognized as one of them; I belonged.

He was a Corporal, just doing his job, but he just threw it in a box and no longer deigned to call me sir.

That hit home. In his eyes I was no longer a field officer, I was nobody; I no longer belonged.

I went out of his office and faced the real world without an ID card, feeling naked. As countless others had before; for it comes to us all – the time when all professional soldiers have to leave the shelter of the military umbrella, and face (in their eyes) the relative disorder and rough and tumble of everyday civilian life. Many find the transition extremely difficult and much depends on your age when you leave, for the longer you leave it the less adaptable you find you are. After all, you'd spent a considerable part of your service learning the ins and outs and which strings to pull in order to get things done, only to find that this knowledge was now totally irrelevant. A different set of rules and values applied. Or, more likely, there were no rules at all. Most ex-soldiers tend to opt for something to do with management, for it is akin to leadership, which the military know about – albeit unaccountable to other related facets such as associated costs, or profit and loss, which they know very little about.

But I was spared this, for all I knew about was flying.

The people at Bembridge were very helpful. Having spent the best part of a year there, at least they knew me to be a proficient Islander pilot, although I must have been a thorn in their flesh at times. They managed to find me a flying job with one of their customers – an international construction company who at the time were working mostly in the Middle East. They operated a couple of Islanders, which they had found invaluable for fetching and carrying, both men and equipment, to and from their various contracts throughout the Gulf. They also had a number of road projects, often crossing large tracts of desert, where an aircraft more than paid its way, especially if it had the ability to takeoff and land from unmade strips or partly constructed sections of road.

So I went back to the desert and did the only thing I knew.

I flew for them for just over two years; hard satisfying work for which the Islander was ideally suited – as I suppose was its pilot, who had little time to think about anything else. Then, when all the current contracts had finished, I flew one of the aircraft for a further three months contracted out to a seismic company whilst my engineer employers looked for new work. This they found, and true to their international market place, the next contract was at Belize in the Caribbean and they asked me if I would go out and fly for them there, only this time they thought they'd need a helicopter as well as an Islander. A spate of smaller ancillary contracts followed and all in all, I was there for just over two years, flying either the Islander, one of which we'd shipped from the Middle East, or their newly acquired Jet Ranger helicopter, which they had leased for the duration of the original contract and then extended accordingly. When these contracts started to draw to a close I wondered where they would send me next, but it wasn't to be; it appeared that their latest crop of contracts had all shifted bias from civil engineering to building construction – oil refineries, sewage works, office complexes and the like, none of which had a requirement for an aeroplane or a helicopter, and least of all a pilot with nothing to fly.

By this time I'd accumulated a fair amount of salary. I'd been flying (or Angela would have said running) virtually every day for five years; a year at Bembridge followed by four years with the construction company, and throughout this time my needs had been pretty frugal.

'Time you had a holiday' they said. 'You've got Godknows how much holiday entitlement owing to you, so why not take a few months off? Now you're on this side of the Atlantic, why not go and see the States – after all, we paid for your trip over – it'd be silly to waste it...'

The trouble was, I still thought like a soldier and didn't realize you could do this sort of thing. But I felt tired and the idea appealed. 'Maybe I will...'

'Great – give us a ring in about six months time and if we've got something or something in the pipeline, we'll negotiate a new contract! If that's what you want, that is; we like the way you operate and so long as we've got the work we'll always be pleased to have you on the team. But should something else turn up in the meantime, just go for it and good luck to you! Don't hesitate to ask us for a reference, and there'll always be another time...'

So we parted company and I headed north.

I bought an old Dodge pickup, mostly engine and cab and very little pickup, and picked my way slowly north. On my own at last, I found myself thinking of Elizabeth and more than anything wishing she could have been with me. She'd have loved it and we'd have had so much fun taking our time and wandering from place to place. I found myself talking to her in the cab and stopping at places she would have liked to have seen. I began to see them through her eyes; for they were better eyes than mine and could see around so many corners.

And with it, the realization that she was still with me.

In spite of my overwhelming grief, I now realized that subconsciously I'd erected a protective barrier – in order, I suppose, to survive. Ever since that night of the thunderstorm, when the shutter had banged down. Wise old Angela had been right; I should have stopped and faced up to it years ago. Running away wasn't the answer, and had only prolonged it. Unwittingly, horrifyingly, I had excluded her.

A wave of happiness mixed with relief surged through me. For the first time since her death I felt a complete person again; we were still soul mates and I now knew we always would be, and nothing could ever take it away... for the soul works in dimensions greater than life. That same evening the word abyss jumped out of a book I was reading, and with it the quote: 'When you look long into an abyss, the abyss also looks into you.' Which made me stop, and think, and finally understand.

America is a huge country, so how do you see it all? I'd driven north through Mexico and now had to decide. I flipped a coin... and then did the opposite, for I knew where I wanted to go! Up the west coast, north to Seattle and then into Canada; Vancouver and British Columbia, for that's where they flew Beavers!

On the road from Tucson to Phoenix – or rather to one side of it, I fell in with a band of crop-sprayers as they worked their way north. Those boys worked hard and also knew how to fly, and as for their aircraft, Middle Wallop would have grounded the lot! I stayed with them for about a fortnight and it was good to have company again – and flying company at that. They let me have a go and it wasn't a lot different from tactical low flying in the army and I soon got the hang of it. By the end of a fortnight I could lay a fairly decent line, but I don't think I'd want to earn a living from it!

After Phoenix they said they were heading northeast for the wheat lands, whereas I wanted to stick to the coast, so after a riotous night's drinking we went our separate ways with me swinging west towards San Diego.

The old pickup trundled along at its own pace, and for

once in my life I was happy to match it, for I was in no hurry and this was the way to see America, or at least, this bit of it. Not to say that we didn't have our moments: a front tyre blew out in the centre lane of the multiple-lane highway leading into San Diego and I somehow managed to pull over, threading through the lanes to the hard shoulder. I was about to get out of the cab when there was a brief 'WEOW' and a black and white Highway patrol car drew up in front of me in a cloud of dust. Two over-weight and black-uniformed Highway police got out, festooned with truncheons, whistles, radios and guns, and demanded to know what the hell I was doing – as if it wasn't obvious. When I tried to explain, they called me a funny guy, pulled me out of the cab and slapped me down over the bonnet and frisked me none too gently; to which, I rather objected and told them so. Maybe the Mexican number-plates on the pickup didn't help and they thought I was an illegal immigrant. So I produced my British Passport and Driving Licence and asked whether they always treated visitors to their beautiful country in this manner. But this only caused more confusion.

'London?' he said looking in my passport, 'London – they got that one wrong buddy, no place called London that I ever heard of! New London now, I heard of New London – that's in Connecticut or someplace round there. You from Connecticut – if so why are you driving a truck with Mexican plates?'

It went on in this vein for some time, the ludicrous barrier growing to un-scaleable proportions. Eventually the other one tried a different tack. 'DO YOU SPEAK ENGLISH?' he shouted at me slowly.

'I am English.'

'I SAID, DO YOU UNDERSTAND ENGLISH?'

I tried nodding.

'RIGHT – I think we're getting somewhere at last' to his partner. 'YOU – YOU GET IN THAT VEHICLE' he pronounced it vee-hick-el 'AND JUST GET GOING. JUST KEEP GOING RIGHT ON OUTTER HERE. Darn foreigners who can't speak English, best to send him on, you

agree?' again to his partner. 'YOU DON'T TURN LEFT
AND YOU DON'T TURN RIGHT – YOU JUST KEEP
GOING, UNNERSTAND?'

And with that, duty done, they swaggered back to their
car, their ponderous buttocks wobbling in unison and the
hanging-down straps from their truncheons slapping against
their outsized thighs. I gave them time to drive away, then
started to change the wheel.

I followed the Santa Fe Railroad up the coast to Los
Angeles. Past acres of dust covered light aircraft standing
unused and baking in the sun, and when I arrived I decided
Los Angeles wasn't my sort of place after all, and to head on
out into the Mohave Desert and have a look at Las Vegas.

The long shimmering empty road began to backup with
traffic, although it kept moving. Eventually I saw the
obstruction: a gaggle of eight or nine motorcyclists, all riding
together and under the direction of a leader. They hogged
the fast lane in a solid block until the leader would suddenly
signal and they'd all pull over together and allow one car
through, before pulling out again. The other drivers were
very patient each humbly accepting the menace for what it
was, and ultra-wary in case they'd be the one that provoked
the gang or give them the excuse they were looking for. One
at a time they tiptoed past, eyes firmly on the road ahead,
until it was my turn at the head of the queue.

I put my foot on the floor and reluctantly the old Dodge
started to creep forward. They were mostly riding two-up
and all on gleaming Harley Davidsons with high handlebars
and sitting well back, legs stretched out in front. No pink
trousers and yellow sweaters here; the uniform was strictly
black leathers with death-defying logos on their backs and
fringes of leather strips blowing from their arms and legs.
Some of them, I noticed, had pistols in holsters strapped to
their legs. Most of the pillion riders were girls – this from the
curvature of their tight fitting leathers, their bodies fitting
like a spoon into the back of their man in front. The leader's
bike was truly magnificent – as was his girl, a long legged
young beauty clasping the waist of a thickset middle-aged

man whose face was hidden by a mass of ginger-grey whiskers out of which peered a pair of rheumy eyes. Which, unfortunately, fleetingly made contact with mine as I inched past.

It was the spark he was waiting for. With a motion of his hand they all pulled out and like hounds after a fox, the chase was on.

I've been in a few tight spots over the years; they've always happened unexpectedly and this was no exception. With that pack breathing down my neck, my mouth went dry and I felt fear on that desert road. The old Dodge wobbled and roared as the speed built up and I started to overtake all the cars that had previously run the gauntlet. The drivers all looked studiously ahead and took no notice; they were minding their own business and I knew there would be no help from that quarter. In my mirror I saw the pack had fanned out, grinning and waving at each other, each leisurely matching my pace.

There was no way that I could outrun them, so somehow I'd have to outwit them.

I could see an incline ahead with a snake of trucks, nose to tail, grinding up in low gear. Perhaps if I could somehow tuck-in amongst them? I took my foot off the accelerator and gradually the pickup slowed to nearer its customary gait. Then I saw my chance, and breaking hard pulled into a gap. It was as though the leader had known all along; he just gathered his jeering gang and rode alongside matching the speed of the convoy and boxed me in, regardless of the growing queue of cars behind. The truck behind me blew a great bellow on his horn; it would have done an ocean liner proud and certainly made me jump; then, having made his protest, he backed off and the gap behind me gradually widened. He too, was having nothing to do with it.

Damned if I would be intimidated by this gang of hoodlums; and where were the Highway Patrol when you needed them? They'd been quick enough to stop and frisk me when I'd had a puncture.

Without warning I pulled out into the fast lane and had

the satisfaction of seeing the hounds put into disarray, frantically braking and wobbling to avoid each other. Why be intimidated? So long as I kept going they couldn't really harm me; my vehicle was a lot sturdier than theirs – and frankly I couldn't care less if it collected a few more dents! True, they carried guns... but even then I doubted they'd actually shoot at me on the public highway. Even if they did, I knew enough about firearms to know it would have to be a very lucky shot to do any harm. You see it on the films all the time, but in practice you have to be pretty good with a handgun to hit a moving target at any distance, especially with one hand and driving a motorbike!

So I carried on at my usual speed; the fox ignoring the hounds. I'd topped up with fuel and at this speed could run for the rest of the day. For the next forty minutes I just ignored them. Occasionally one would roar up alongside or cut in ahead and brake, but I just kept going as if to run them down. Then, when three of them tried it and I still didn't slow and all three nearly went under my bonnet, they realized I was serious. The leader's girl was the first to see sense. I saw her pummelling the man's back and shouting in his ear, and seeing he'd somehow lost the initiative he gathered his gang together and they went roaring past, all jeering and giving me the finger.

I stayed in a small Motel by a Gas Station that night. The first thing I did was to have a cautious look round to see if there was any sign of the bikers, but they had gone. The wind was hot and dry, blowing clumps of tumbleweed before it, bouncing and rolling across the desert to I knew not where. As evening approached the yard – or parking lot, gradually began to fill with long-distance trucks: magnificent well-cared for, almost stately machines, the majority with long square bonnets and two chromium exhaust stacks sticking straight up. The drivers were a cheery lot, many of whom obviously knew each other, this being a regular trucker's halt. If any of them had witnessed the chase on the road, it was not even worthy a mention in their conversation. They all had better things to talk about. Or maybe it happened everyday and they'd seen it all before.

After a trucker's supper I walked across the yard towards my motel room. Then I stopped and listened. There was the faint buzz of an aircraft engine drawing nearer, but I could not see it in the dusk. I heard it throttle back and the whistle of wind through struts and without further preliminaries a Piper Super Cub landed on the main highway before turning off and taxiing up to the pumps behind another car. The pilot filled up, waved to the attendant (presumably he had an account) fired up and took off again on the road, obviously in a hurry to get home before it was completely dark. It struck me as a sensible way of using an aircraft – and one that McDougal in far away Islay would have given his back teeth for!

Needless to say, I lost money in Las Vegas, but it was an enjoyable way to lose it and I told myself worth every cent in entertainment value. Besides I was tired of driving and needed a break and Las Vegas was as good a place as any to walk about and stretch your legs. In fact, there's nowhere else quite like it, which alone makes it worth a visit – and it was good to see that some of the people were winning.

After a couple of days respite I climbed into the truck and headed back towards the coast and San Francisco. By this time I was becoming increasingly bored with my own company and I was looking forward to reaching my goal. Whether things would be any different when I actually got there would remain to be seen, but I'm not a drifter by nature and it's good to have an objective, however vague. I find you can only take in so much sightseeing, especially if you're on your own. I'd heard that Seattle and the Northwest was full of Beavers – so that's where I was going; but it wasn't so much the aircraft – after all, what's in an aircraft, it's still only a lump of metal with an engine at the front and you soon get tired of looking at that! No, it was the people who were around them and what they could make the aircraft do that mattered. Like the crop-sprayers from Phoenix; I'd be among people with a common interest, and who knows, I might even find a job...

So after San Francisco I drove with more purpose; north into Oregon, all the while making for Beaver country.

III

Then came the day when I stood looking at a line of Beavers on floats moored nose to tail on a pontoon, much like an aerial taxi rank. Which is exactly what it was, for this was Seaplanes Northwest, a unique commercial airline that only operates floatplanes. I was at their main terminal and workshops on the shores of Lake Washington, a twenty mile-long sheltered lake, the western shore of which delineated the boundary of the main city of Seattle and the eastern shore the newer satellite town of Bellevue, the two being joined by two mile-and-a-half long bridges that spanned the lake. There was a board outside their office which advertised daily scheduled flights to Victoria, the San Juan Islands and British Columbia's Inside Passage, as well as a Charter Service throughout the whole of the Northwest. In smaller letters underneath it pronounced that this was the centre (spelt center) of the seaplane universe!

I decided to go in and find out more.

A smiling receptionist made me welcome and offered me one of their brochures together with a detailed map that showed their routes and many landing places. No wonder they called it the centre of the seaplane universe for the map listed no fewer than ninety-five regular landing places, most of which had docking facilities. From Seattle I traced the route north to Victoria on the southern shore of Vancouver Island with the San Juan Islands lying offshore to the east, then on into Canada for a stop at Nanaimo before heading north again to the head of the Georgia Straight and a further complex of populated creeks and islands. Here the route turned northwest and followed a narrow passage called the Johnston Straight to where it opens up into the Queen Charlotte Sound where there were another dozen or so islands to serve. Along the whole length of the route the multitude of islands and creeks were in waters sheltered by the massive landmass of Vancouver Island and only accessible by floatplane!

Seeing my interest, the receptionist disappeared into an

inner office and then came out with a member of staff who kindly offered to show me round.

The mainstay of their fleet was the ubiquitous Beaver, which my guide said, would last forever! Not only did they operate them, they also rebuilt them into better-than-new condition to meet the continuing demands of their fleet that numbered twenty or so, as well as having a constant queue of private customers all patiently waiting for one. To this end they also ran a flight school with permanent instructors on hand to convert pilots for their seaplane ticket. He showed me every shop, each in its own separate building: the engine shop, where there were rows of Pratt & Whitney engines in various stages of assembly; the main fuselage shop where there were two partly-built Beavers under construction; the spray shop; the stores complex and so on, one leading on to another. Proudly he told me there were more Beavers flying now than there had been ten years ago, a remarkable fact, considering the last production Beaver came off the line in 1967!

Throughout the tour he was constantly being interrupted by staff who needed his attention, or else called away to the telephone, and since he was obviously a busy man I curtailed the visit at the earliest opportunity and said that I'd like to call again at a more opportune time. To that he gave a brief smile and said 'Some hopes' before dashing away.

Outside again I marvelled at the rows of aircraft standing on the hard. There were Beavers, Turbo Beavers, Otters, Cessnas, Piper Super Cubs and even one Stearman biplane, each to its colour and all stranded on their floats. At the rear of the yard I found carcasses of Beaver fuselages in faded markings from all over the world: crop-sprayers from Australia, Indian Air Force, Gulf Exploration, US Army, you name it, all awaiting refurbishment and to be married to their wings that were stored in long racks alongside.

I walked back to the truck, pausing by the pontoon to watch a Turbo Otter slowly come alongside and then counted ten passengers disembarking.

'They've got four of those now and a fifth on the way', a larger than life American said from behind sunglasses and baseball cap with a picture of a Beaver on it. He turned and walked back towards the truck with me. 'My, you're a long way from home!' he said when he saw the plates. 'Mexico – what are you doing up here?'

'I've come to look at Beavers... it's a long time since I've seen so many together.'

'You'd better come and have a look at mine then; she's the best in the yard! They're about to put her in.'

I walked over with him to where his Beaver was waiting to be picked up by a forklift truck to place it in the water. It was immaculate, with a three-bladed prop behind a gleaming chrome spinner and a paint-job that defied description: white overall, with a dark green nose framed by red and black stripes that somehow all tapered back along the fuselage.

'Yep, I've had her, oh – about eighteen months now. She's a honey; had her totally rebuilt in the shop right here, new engine, the lot!'

'She certainly looks a picture...'

'You ever flown in one of these?'

'Yes, a bit...'

'Say, are you British?'

'Yes I am as a matter of fact!'

'We-ell, that's a coincidence. This airplane used to belong to the British Army before she was rebuilt. Here, I left its number stamped on this plate: XP 778! My name's Rod, by the way...'

We shook hands and I introduced myself, then said 'Just hang on a minute, Rod, I'll be right back.' I went back to the truck and fished out my flying bag and extracted a logbook. XP 778, there – I knew it! She was one of our old Beavers from 15 Flight in Aden! I walked back, thumbing through the pages and mentally adding up the hours I'd logged on her all those years ago.

'At a rough count, Rod, I've flown 250 hours in your aircraft!' I showed him the last entry in the book. 'I used to be an army pilot...'

'Wow! Hey, I don't believe this – you've flown my airplane? I'll be damned! Hell, this calls for a reunion – come

300

on, we'll get her in and you must give her a go!'

Used to be an army pilot... from a different age, but still it made me think. If he'd owned this Beaver for eighteen months, it meant the army must have released it at least two or maybe three years before that; which meant the Islander or rather the Defender would now be in service – and I hadn't known anything about it! It made me realize how out of touch I was, as well as the fact that I hadn't given a thought to the army since the day I'd left! I didn't even know if they'd used my report – unless Nicki-Pig had found it first and buried it somewhere! So much for my earlier doubts and trepidation about leaving the military umbrella, I hadn't missed it one iota! Indeed, I now revelled in the freedom of a society that had little time for petty constraints and certainly no room for the Nicki-Pigs of this world. I remembered the day I left and had actually been upset that the corporal hadn't addressed me as sir! The whole thing seemed totally ludicrous now. I'd moved on and, I believed, was a better person for it. Or if not better, certainly different! 'If that's what you want, I'll stand by you' Elizabeth had said. She'd known – as usual, and now it made me smile. 'If that's what you want' indeed! Bloody woman, but God how I missed her still...

The forklift came and with practiced ease placed Rod's Beaver into the water. There were ropes attached hanging down from under each wing and he grabbed one and manoeuvred the aircraft alongside the pontoon, before making fast.

'You've got to remember she's still a boat at this stage' he said, 'here, climb on round and jump into the right hand seat. Mind that paddle strapped to the float!'

I clambered around the forward bracing strut that held the floats apart, and then up the starboard fore main strut that was V shaped with bars across to use as a ladder, and swung into the right hand seat. There had indeed been a paddle strapped to the float, as well as mooring cleats and fairleads both fore and aft and, I later learned, an anchor stowed in the forward compartment of the port float together with six fathoms of anchor-rope and the prescribed amount of chain. Other compartments held an inflatable dinghy and pump, mooring lines, a manual bilge pump and various other nautical necessities. The floats were nearly as long as the aircraft, with a pair of lifting rudders on their transoms. They were set so they protruded well ahead and either side of the three-bladed propeller, leaving the rear fuselage and tail overhanging at the rear. By fitting a three-bladed propeller instead of the original two-blade, meant the diameter was that much smaller and less likely to pick-up water on takeoff or in rough conditions. It also made the aircraft quieter overall. One of the most endearing qualities about a standard Beaver is the noise it makes on takeoff, for the two-bladed propeller emits a distinctive howl when in fine pitch, this from the tips turning at supersonic speed. With the reduced diameter of the three-blade propeller, the tips no longer became supersonic, but I learned later, also produced less power, so that many owners still preferred to fit the original propeller whilst accepting the reduced water-clearance. Or maybe they just liked the noise...

Rod stood on the front of the port float and pulled the propeller through a couple of turns and then clambered up beside me. 'Two-hundred and fifty hours on this airplane; Hell, I just can't get over that! Do you still fly?'

'Yes, but it's years since I've flown a Beaver, and I never flew one on floats. But they're still one of my favourite aircraft – this is a real treat for me!'

He started to go through the familiar starting drill. 'Yeah, they're just great. I've got a set of wheels as well; usually switch over to them for the winter and back again onto floats for the summer. The only difference about floats is, you've got to do everything on the move. Beavers were originally designed as a floatplane you know, they only put wheels on afterwards, as a sort of afterthought!' The engine coughed into life, and he waved at a lad who had miraculously appeared on the pontoon to cast off.

'What about those ropes under the wings?'

'Oh, they just stay there; they just fly back in the slipstream!

They're nothing compared to the extra drag from the floats. Look, you drop this lever to lower the water-rudders. When its down, you can steer like a boat – they're connected to the main aircraft rudder by a system of pulleys. Only you must remember to pull them up before takeoff.'

We taxied slowly up the lake, waiting for the temperatures to rise. 'They usually just make it into the green by the time we reach that buoy – that's our takeoff point.'

The interior of XP 778's cabin was very different than it had been in her army days. Gone were the windows in the roof with their rear-facing cowled mirrors outside. Gone were the plethora of radios that had lined the roof. Gone was the bomb-arming panel, together with the bomb racks under the wings. Gone was that lovely hanging compass from above the windshield, replaced by a standard US light-aircraft glass-bubble in the facia. Gone was the radio and navaid master selection panel located in the port wing root and in its place was the wing-tip fuel transfer tap, which they had moved from the other side. But I suspect it had been put back to how it was originally, for in our Beavers it was always a pain to have to first un-strap before reaching over in order to transfer fuel. Gone was the heavy inertia-flywheel starting system that you used to clutch into, replaced by a larger battery that they'd moved forward to occupy the hole that had been left. That too made sense, and allowed for more luggage space as well as reducing aft weight from where the batteries used to be located in a separate compartment behind the rear of the cabin. The seats were different; they were fatter and plusher and were colour-coordinated with the headlining and cabin sides. Gone were the two small porthole windows at the rear of the cabin, replaced by larger oblong ones that let in more light and made the rear-seat compartment far less claustrophobic. Then, I noticed the main trapezium-shaped passenger windows were no longer flat, but blown out in a curved bubble-effect that I rather liked as it produced a modern touch to an otherwise dated design, as well as allowing the second-row passengers to look forward. Purists would no doubt disagree, but all in all, the aircraft was far more luxurious and less warlike than it had been in my day. In spite of its British De Havilland origins, the refurbishment had created an atmosphere not unlike that of a classic American car.

Sure enough, at the buoy the temperatures had reached the green. Rod quickly ran through the pre-takeoff vital actions, the very same that I had so laboriously tried to imitate in the Rallye at Dijon, and then with a burst of power, water-ruddered into wind before pulling the lever up to retract them.

'Off we go then...' The old-fashioned (but totally rebuilt) radial engine bellowed as only a radial engine can and we surged forward in a welter of spray. 'Hold the column well back to keep the front of the floats up, and now – there, up she rises onto the step. Ease forward a touch now... and just wait and she'll fly herself off when she's ready. Here, you have her!' as we left the water.

'I have...'

I reduced the manifold pressure and brought the revs back to 2000 and then pumped up the flaps. She felt heavy and slow and it was as though we were flying with a great pendulum hanging underneath. But underneath her mascara, as well as burdened by a pair of floats that together had more surface area than the fuselage, she was still the same old Beaver.

We flew around Seattle and he showed me all the sights. That first time I found her slightly disappointing. She wasn't so docile and predictable as I had remembered. The extra drag from the floats made her very slow – about twenty knots slower in the cruise, as well as cumbersome to handle, taking her time to roll into turns and difficult to trim, especially the rudder trim. They'd added two extra small vertical fins to either end of the tail plane to give better directional stability, but to my mind she was still directionally unstable and not nearly so nice to fly as when she was on wheels. Or maybe it was because I was used to the relative sleekness and better all-round performance of the Islander.

Rod handled her well enough though and I could see he

was one of those people who were a natural with all machines.

'You seem to have got the measure of her...'

'Yeah, but it takes a bit of time. It's always a revelation when I put the wheels back on... but there's something about flying a floatplane. Especially here in the Northwest where you can land just about anywhere and nobody gives a fig! I used to have a Super Cub on floats – that was fun, but you couldn't haul the family and all the wife's luggage like you can in this one! Another time I'll take you up into the mountains, there's a little lake I know, fairly high up and only accessible by Beaver. She's the only one with the right power to weight ratio to get out – say, how long are you staying in Seattle?'

'I hadn't thought, I've only just arrived.'

'Yeah? Where are you staying?'

'I don't know that either yet. I came straight here...'

'You got it! Come and stay with me – I've got plenty of room and if you're here for a month or so, we could have a ball!'

'Well, that's very kind, but I can hardly...'

'Do you sail? I've got a forty-footer and she's just a dream to sail. You'll love her!'

'Well I've done a bit, but...'

'That settles it then! And it would be great for me, make no mistake. I don't often have someone I can go play with; the kids are too young – I'm divorced, by the way – and I've got these toys, as my ex calls them, and it kindda gets boring on your own! Are you married?'

'No – ah no. I used to be but that was a long time ago. Listen, Rod, you don't even know me. It's very kind, but are you sure...?'

'Sure I'm sure! Hell, you used to fly my airplane, that's good enough. You're staying and that's settled. Boy, are we going to have a ball! Come on, let's land this thing and we'll work it out!'

In some trepidation I followed his BMW to the northern outskirts of Seattle. I'd heard about American hospitality, but this was just ridiculous. I'd come here with the hope of finding like-minded company, but this was something else – and what's more, he'd made it virtually impossible for me to refuse. After all, its not everyday that... but then, I must say I liked his style, and I also liked the sound of his 'toys'. Best just take it a step at a time and see...

He pulled into the drive of a pleasant suburban house that overlooked Puget Sound and which an hour before he'd tried to point out from the air. He waited whilst I parked beside his BMW and then we both paused and looked up at the sound of a Beaver flying overhead.

'There she is! About to let down onto Lake Washington. Boy, I never tire of that noise! No matter how often I hear it, it still makes my blood tingle! They go over all the time, and each time I just can't resist looking up! Come on in and I'll show you around – and then it's time for a gin, I'd say. Can't beat a gin and tonic at this time of the day!' Echoing the very words Nigel would have used, so that instinctively I began to warm towards him.

I dumped my bags and wandered onto a wooden veranda that led into the garden. The garden was full of kids, some bouncing up and down on a large circular jumping frame and others squirting each other with a hose that should have been fixed to a lawn sprinkler and all shrieking and dashing about as kids do the world over. Rod came out carrying three gin and tonics on a tray, followed by an attractive girl wearing a blue summer dress.

'Hi, meet my girlfriend Louise – Louise, this is the guy I was telling you about on the phone. He used to fly my airplane when he was in the British Army. He's coming to stay for a while to help me sail the boat and hopefully show me how to fly properly!'

I said Hi, and thankfully discarded one of the doubts I'd harboured in the back of my mind.

'Now, which are my three? Hey, Matt, Sarah, Olive – come over here a minute!'

His three children – Matt the eldest, a sturdy looking lad of fourteen; followed by his sister Sarah, who I learnt was a year younger but looked five years older and already, I suspected, turning the heads of the boys, and Olive, a tousled-haired six year old, who had been setting the pace on the jumping frame, as well as being wet through from the spray – all extracted themselves and politely shook hands with me before tearing back into the fray. I warmed to them too; they looked good kids, well mannered and, for want of any better description, a credit to their parents.

Another Beaver flew over and once again Rod and I looked up at the sky.

I felt at home here; it was rather like sitting in the left hand seat; familiar; and I knew everything was going to be fine.

IV

'You want to keep the speed down' the resident instructor said. 'The engine warms up quicker with less prop-wash over it; being a radial it's got a hell of a frontal area and anyway, you only risk catching a wave-top.'

The same applied when you were taxiing a Beaver on the ground; when cold you always kept the revs down for the very same reason, but I let it go. Once again I was sitting in the left hand seat, and immediately everything had fallen into place. I don't know why it is, but it only takes a few minutes for me to adapt to a car with the steering wheel on the other side and I can fly a helicopter equally well from either seat; but put me in an aeroplane with wings, no matter what its size, and I can only really get the real feel of it from the left hand seat. Sitting on the right, whether as co-pilot or navigator is just not the same. You're still a passenger.

'The temperatures should reach the mark by the time we reach that buoy' he continued, 'so then we turn into wind; we'll then do a run-up, and I'll lead you through the vital actions for takeoff – this, all on the move with the column held well back. Okay? After that we'll be ready to go! You know how to set her up for a run-up?'

'Yes, I believe so...'

'Does he know how to set her up for a run-up!' Rod said from one of the rear seats, 'I tell you, this guy has flown two hundred and fifty hours on this very airplane! And God knows how many hours he's got on a Beaver!'

'That right?' the instructor, a man called Phillip said sceptically. 'How many hours you got on a Beaver then?'

'Enough, I think – but it was some time ago...'

'Yeah, yeah' he said as though he'd heard it all before, 'but this is for now!'

We ploughed up to the buoy and I turned into wind and as he'd predicted, the needles had reached their marks. He pulled a flipchart out from his tip pocket and flicked it through to the run-up section. I held the column back and half closed my eyes and let my hands do the work: Mixture – Rich; Propeller – Fine; RPM – set to the mark; Magnetos – Check one, Check two, both within limits; Propeller Pitch – slowly back to Coarse and note drop in RPM; Back up to Fine and pull up the Carburettor Heat lever by my right calf – and again note the fall in RPM; Heat back to cold and reduce RPM to idle and from the throb of the engine I knew what the revs were without having to look at the dial. This pleased me; I was back in the seat, regardless of the years in between.

Without pause, I then launched straight into the takeoff checks, and for my instructor's benefit recited them out aloud from memory: 'Trims – elevator slightly forward, rudder slightly left; Friction nuts – one, two, three finger tight; Propeller – fully fine; Mixture – rich; Carb-air – cold; Fuel – Front tank, select; Pump – On; Flaps... Flaps set to what, about twenty degrees?' I looked to him for confirmation. Maybe on water he'd want me to takeoff clean... I noticed his flipchart was still open at the run-up section.

'Yeah, twenty-degrees will do fine.'

'Okay, twenty it is; Instruments – check condition, no cracked or damaged glass, they all look okay, and set the DI to the compass... Pitôt heat, we'll leave that off I think; Hatches – are all shut; And Harness' – are tight and front seats locked. You strapped in behind Rod?' I turned in my seat and he winked and grinned at me. 'Oh yes, I nearly forgot: and Water Rudders – Up!' With a lift and a twist I pulled the lever and locked it into place. I was showing off, but I didn't care: "Yeah, yeah, but this is for now", indeed; I'll show him who needs a flipchart! With my right hand caressing the levers, I increased the boost with the heel of my thumb and once again my old aircraft bellowed for me as she had done years before.

'Well... I guess maybe you haven't forgotten' he said in a friendlier tone, sliding the flipchart back into his top pocket. 'Turn onto about one-four-five – no, maybe one-fifty would be better and take her up to five-five, we'll go have a look at that lake...'

I turned onto the heading whilst reaching forward to turn the three-way fuel tap to draw from the rear tank, waited a moment to check the flow and then flicked the auxiliary pump off. I then eased her into a gentle climb. She still felt heavy and cumbersome, but I'd got the feel of her now; I was no longer behind chasing the dials, I was able to lead her. We flew towards the distant line of the Cascade Mountains.

'What's she like carrying ice?' I asked doubtfully looking at the snow-topped mountains ahead. 'With all this surface area...'

'You don't' was the simple answer. 'We always fly under the weather – after all, she's slow enough...'

At five thousand five hundred feet I tried to set her up on the step, but she was reluctant to do so, the drag of the floats taking over each time.

He let me struggle for a minute, then said: 'Try cracking down a couple degrees of flap, you'll find she'll balance that way!'

I tried, and found it was so. It was obvious when you thought about it: to increase the lift ratio even by that small amount countered the drag from underneath. I met his eyes and smiled my thanks; we were beginning to talk the same language.

'Okay, there's the lake' he said half an hour later. Ahead I saw a small ribbon of water trapped between two mountains and held by a dam. 'You'd better let me have it this first time...'

'Okay, you have...'

He hotched forward in his seat and peered ahead. 'The idea is, we do a left hand circuit and descend around that mountain...'

He set up for landing and pushed the nose down, aiming to the right of the mountain and the lake slid out of view. Trees and shrubs swished past underneath; he was taking it awfully low, but then it always seems more hazardous when someone else is flying – a fact well known to anybody who has done any instructing. Even so, I couldn't help readying myself to retrieve the situation, as though our roles were reversed. He dropped half-flap and followed the mountain round onto base leg, the lake still unseen. The trees were just under our floats now and the mountain on the other side of the unseen lake growing ever larger in our windscreen. But I needn't have worried; he judged it to a nicety. At the last minute he banked hard left and dropped landing flap. The lake swam into view nearly a hundred feet below, and I could see now why he'd been scraping the trees, for still we were far too high! If we'd been in a land-plane, I'd have executed a missed approach at this point and overshot, but he continued down towards the foot of the dam at the end of the lake. He pulled back and the rear of the floats chopped into the water and spray was all about.

'It doesn't take much to stop once you hit the water' he was saying as he brought the flaps in, 'it acts just like a speedboat when you cut the engine; the minute you come off the plane, it immediately de-accelerates!' I saw the dam was still a good hundred and fifty yards ahead, and even the wash we'd made would probably never reach it. 'Okay, if you'd drop the water-rudders please, and then taxi back towards that beach...'

I taxied slowly towards the beach and then wondered how we were going to stop. Again I needn't have worried.

'You going to do the honours, Rod?' He said, turning.

'Sure!' Rod took his shoes and socks off and rolled up his trousers. 'Hell, but the water's always mighty cold up here!' He opened his door against the slipstream and climbed barefooted down onto the float, holding onto the wing-strut.

'Okay, throttle right back now and then turn one of the switches off – it'll sound rough, but it's the only way to get the prop to turn slowly enough.'

The large radial banged and missed beats in protest, the propeller now turning at just enough revs to give us headway. Just before we grounded I applied full right rudder and we swung round, parallel to the beach. Rod hopped off, grabbed the trailing rope and waded to the shore.

'Okay, you can shut her down now...'

It was a magic place. The three of us sat on the shore of that remote mountain lake and the stillness descended all around, each aware that we were probably the only humans for miles around. We talked in hushed voices so as not to disturb the environment, despite our recent abrupt and noisy arrival that had probably shattered the peace for miles around.

'You sometimes see bears on that slope over there...'

'Must come up here again for a weekend's fishing. Last time we camped right over there – you can see where our fire was...'

'Do you always reduce the revs like that, by turning off one of the switches? I'd have thought you could have pulled the propeller back into coarse pitch... that would slow you just as much without ruining the engine. All that banging and stuttering; it can't do it any good?'

They looked at each other, then Phillip shrugged. 'Never tried it like that; we always turn one of the switches off...'

'Anybody think of bringing anything to eat or drink?'

Again we all looked at one another. 'Aw shucks, we might as well be getting back then...'

He let me do the takeoff. As we passed over the dam the ground fell abruptly away by hundreds of feet. It was like being catapulted into the sky. I climbed up to altitude, cranked down a crack of flap and turned for home.

Home... and the realization that I could already think of it as such, despite having only been here four weeks! Rod had lived up to his promise and every day we'd had a ball, one way or another. Neither of us could get over how many common interests we shared. He was a man of many different pursuits, the more obvious being aircraft, boats, fast cars, off-road vehicles, motor cycles – in fact just about anything mechanical, as I had perceived that first time we flew together. But it didn't end with his 'toys' as his ex-wife called them, for he was an avid reader and collector of books, classical music and also rare wines. His bookshelves were full of the same books that I had, (although mine once again were in store) and we likewise discovered we shared a love for Bach, Mozart, Vivaldi, and the great choral works; so the house was always full of music.

I then discovered how well-travelled he was. He knew England almost as well as I did. There was a picture of him standing by the display Beaver outside the Army Aviation Museum at Middle Wallop, and he knew of a little shop in the back streets of Putney that sold motorcycle spares at extremely favourable prices. His kippers arrived directly from the smokehouses at Peel, Isle of Man ('Have you been there?' 'Sure, wouldn't buy anything I hadn't tried') and his aftershave came from Trumpers in Curzon Street. He had sailed from Scotland to Nova Scotia in a square-rigged training ship and there were Jerymyn Street labels on his shirts. His two motorcycles in the garage were modern replicas of two classic British bikes from the 1970's and – and yet he only had an old rusty push-lawnmower to cut the grass! I asked him about that:

'Aw hell, I've got to get *some* exercise...'

And so the days passed and I began to relax; the first real holiday I'd had for years. Rob was the ideal host and as we got to know each other he seemed to devote more and more time to make my stay as interesting and enjoyable as possible. He also introduced me to many of his friends, all of whom, in their delightful and openhearted American way, readily accepted me into their circle. Inceasingly I became aware that he must be taking time of work, whatever that was, in order to do this, and one evening I felt obliged to tackle him about it.

'Work? Oh, plenty of time for work later...'

'But what is it you do exactly, Rob?'

'Well, I've got the odd portfolio, and I do own a bit of forest down in Oregon.'

'A forest – so you're into – ah, lumber?' I said, remembering what the American's called timber.

He smiled, 'timber actually; it becomes lumber when it gets cut up into planks.'

'Oh, timber, then?'

'Yeah, got a few square miles. Down in Oregon...'

'Well, that must keep you pretty busy?'

'Hell no! After all, you can only watch a tree growing for about ten minutes a year... anyway, why all this interest? Tell you what: let's take the bikes down to that little restaurant by the waterfront for lunch? Charlie said he might drop by...'

But in spite of this casual dismissal, I realised that generous host as he was, my presence could only be demanding more of his time – both from his business as well as his personal life, which he wouldn't dream of ever mentioning, and I could only hope that Louise and his children hadn't been too resentful about this.

'You got Lake Washington in sight?' Phillip asked. I came out of my reverie with a start.

'Yes, I've got it.' For the last twenty minutes I'd been flying automatically. I checked the boost and revs and saw that I'd set them as Mr Summers had taught me long ago, to give a gradual 200-foot per minute descent in a straight line from the altitude of the mountain lake down to sea level. If I left everything alone we would continue down that line to a point just south of Lake Washington when we'd be at a thousand feet. I'd then turn north onto long finals for the seaplane base on the northern shore. Three-dimensional time and distance, the mathematics of flying that to my mind give more satisfaction than anything else and the element I'd missed most when flying helicopters.

313

'Well, if you position for a long approach from the south, then let down onto short finals when you're over the second bridge – so reduce the boost now and bring the revs up to...'

'Okay, Phil – do you mind if I do it my way?'

'Why sure; I keep forgetting. Just do your own thing. Bring her in any way you like. It's just that I thought...'

'Thanks Phil.'

I continued down the line.

No, much as I felt at home here, I knew it was now time to move on. I'd really taken to the Northwest, the country and especially the people. They were far removed from the cops I'd encountered outside San Diego, and the motorcycle gang on the desert road to Las Vegas. It was my sort of place and they were my sort of people, and I could easily settle here. Rod had opened many doors for me and maybe I'd come back. But first I had to go to England and square up a lot of loose ends. Staying with Rod had helped far more than he'd ever know. It had brought back a sense of propriety; an awareness that unwittingly had been cut-off when – well, when the shutter had come down. That's what I'd found at the end of what I'd thought was the Beaver-trail. I'd stopped running. But I couldn't bear the thought of outstaying my hospitality; even with someone as generous as Rod, whom by now I knew well enough to know that we'd always remain friends and that he'd understand.

As the altimeter passed through a thousand feet I turned XP778 onto finals, right over my imaginary mark. Mr Summers couldn't have judged it better himself. I took my time going through the landing checks and then partially dropped the flaps to the climb setting. We rumbled on down, and intuitively I knew this would be my last flight in a Beaver. She had played her part; more than played it, for she had been my aeronautical idol for more years than I cared to remember. She was a unique aeroplane, but now destined to be a classic: frozen in her own time warp. In their day Beaver's had been the best bush aircraft in the world, but now I realized that that too was in the past; they were too expensive to run and were already outclassed by the new generation Islanders and whatever else would follow. Here in the Northwest there was still a place for them; here they would linger on for as long as the people at Seaplanes Northwest and a few others like them would continue to rebuild them and find them commercially viable. I felt inexplicably sad and yet at the same time grateful; sad that this was the last time I would fly her, yet grateful for all she had taught me, the times we'd shared together and most of all, the countless occasions she had looked after me when I'd least deserved it. Who said aeroplanes had no soul?

Over the second bridge I dropped a further fifteen degrees of flap and set the propeller to fully fine, whilst dropping the nose a fraction to compensate for the additional braking effect. For some reason Ashley suddenly came to mind. Ashley, my little toy aeroplane that had been so much part of my life with Elizabeth; lightweight, fast and responsive and the complete opposite of this robust radial-engined workhorse – of which I was so fond. After Elizabeth I hadn't wanted to use or even see Ashley again, but at the same time had been reluctant to part with her, as it was the only thing... anyway, I'd stored her with Bernard all these years and now it was high time she flew again, for the sky was where she belonged. Also it would be good to see Bernard again and little did I know our story was still to come...

I reduced the boost and levelled out over the water, then, as the speed fell off, inched the column back. The underside V of the floats slit the surface like a surgeon's knife. I held it there, tiny droplets hissing out behind. Still we were flying, and still I held it, in the void between ground effect and surface tension of the water. The moment stood still and seemed to last for an eternity, as though the aeroplane knew and was trying to tell me something. Then she settled quietly in and was a boat once more.

'Wow!' Phillip broke the silence. 'If that's doing your own thing, as far as I'm concerned you can do it whenever you like, and you sure don't need me!'

V

Tristan was waiting by the checkout at Brisbane airport as I had hoped he would be. He was in airline uniform – black trousers, white shirt etc., and standing next to another pilot dressed the same. I dropped my bags and we embraced, the years melting; a couple of subalterns again.

'Very, very good to see you, old man.' His manner of speech and voice was exactly the same as when we were at Sandhurst; and I was glad. I thought that maybe living in Australia all these years he could have picked up an Australian inflection, but I should have known better. 'May I introduce George, a friend of mine. We fly for the same outfit...'

'Yes I – I know. Hello George... we've met before, although I never knew your name! I don't suppose you'd remember...'

He gave a start and then looked at me long and hard, recognition slowly dawning in his face. 'Yeah, I remember you! Up in Orkney, you flew up in that little two-seater. I gave you and your wife a lift into town?'

He'd put on some weight, but was as Australian as ever. 'Yes you did; only she – she wasn't my wife. We were going to be married, but – well, she died... in an accident, not long after we got back from Orkney...'

'Ah Jesus, I'm sorry to hear that, man. She was such a lovely lady – and a good sport too. A really lovely lady, I remember thinking that at the time. A real English Sheila. Jesus, I'm so sorry...'

'It's all right; you weren't to know.'

But I had known we'd been destined to meet, and had almost expected him to be there with Tristan.

'Anyway, what brings you here?' he went on. 'You seem to have a habit of dropping in everywhere!'

I laughed. 'I'm actually on my way back to England; only I'm going the long way round. I've just come from Seattle. Thought I'd check up on my old mate here, to see what he's been up to all these years!'

I couldn't begin to understand it, and I didn't attempt to try. It was just some inner feeling, as though I'd known that this man, whom I'd only met briefly once before at the other side of the world, and then not long enough to find out his name, was part of the jigsaw and would be there. I put the thought aside. Maybe I was just tired from the flight.

Tristan picked up one of my bags. 'Come on; the next thing is to see if we can find the car! George left his at my place this morning. We find it's easier to dump one car and travel in together when we're on the same shift; the parking here's just a nightmare!'

We found the car in one of the far car parks that bordered the airfield. It had been sitting in the sun all day so Tristan turned the air conditioning on and let it run for a minute before we got in. Then, as with every other airport in the world, we followed the signs that took us by a circuitous route to the exit, eventually to join the busy traffic stream of the main airport road. This we followed for a couple of miles until the junction of the Arterial Way, which we then joined and headed north.

'I live at Sandgate; it's a village just a few miles north of here so it's quite convenient to nip into work – although the traffic tends to get a bit thick at rush hours. It's a nice enough place – huh, village! – I sound like one of the locals; they always refer to it as the village, but it's hardly that anymore; like everywhere else it's all joined up now and very much part of the suburbs. But Maggie and I like it; we bought the house when we got married – it's got a lovely view overlooking Moreton Bay. George here, lives further on at a place called Redcliffe...'

'It all sounds frightfully English.'

'Yes, I suppose it does. Hadn't thought about it really... you know how it is when you live in a place.'

'How long have you two known each other?' I asked the question that Elizabeth was going to ask six years ago.

George answered, leaning forward from the rear seat. 'Well, we go back a fair way, but nothing nearly like as far as you two blokes! But long enough, I guess; long enough to

317

know he's a rotten pilot at any rate! How long since I got back from Orkney, Tris? About five, maybe six years? Jesus, time flies! Anyway, I was away for just over a year, and we knew each other before that. When did you join the line, Tris? Must have been a year, maybe two before I went to Europe? But it was only after I got back that we became mates...'

So, Elizabeth had been right; they had known each other when we'd met him in Orkney.

Although I'd slept in the aircraft I still felt tired and jet travel being what it is, my mind was still back in America. As Tristan drove I closed my eyes and tried to put the jumble of thoughts that had been nagging at the back of my brain into some semblance of order.

I suppose it started soon after I left Belize, when, for the first time in years I was no longer fully occupied or otherwise engrossed in work. There'd been a lot more to my job than just driving an aeroplane, for I'd also been responsible for planning the maintenance and servicing, which takes up a good part of an aeroplane's life, whilst constantly juggling the workload to suit. This, as well as trying to keep everyone happy, which I'd found a lot more difficult than the actual flying! Then suddenly I found myself grounded, nothing to fly, nothing to plan or otherwise preoccupy me. Moreover, I was completely on my own, which again I wasn't used to and I'd almost had to force myself to relax. They said I needed a holiday, and perhaps they'd been right and I had the whole of America stretching before me.

Then came that day in Mexico, the day when I flipped the coin to decide whether to turn left or right, and I'd known even as it was spinning that it didn't matter whether it landed heads or tails, for I knew where I had to go. Almost from that moment, it was as though my future was predestined. Like the Wise Men of old, I had a star to follow. That was the day I finally lowered the barrier, started to talk to Elizabeth in the cab and with it the realization that she was still there; the day I looked into my abyss. The Beaver trail was only part of it; that was just a lure to appease the practical side of my nature. So, try thinking along those lines... did that mean I was meant to meet Rob in Seattle, that that too was predestined? Or perhaps it was something connected with his busy life; or maybe some other event or person that I'd met there, did that figure? Then there was that last memorable and poignant flight in the Beaver, when I realized what was past was past and it was time to move on. Was that part of being led by a mythological star?

Rob, bless him, hadn't wanted me to go at all. 'Hell, I'm just getting used to having a playmate around! We've still yet to sail to Barkley Sound and up the west coast of Vancouver Island; maybe take a couple of weeks off and go look at some whales! You sure you got to go?' But I had been adamant. So he sold the truck for me and managed to get nearly as much as I'd paid for it, Mexican plates and all, and the following day had driven me to the airport. 'Going westbound, via Australia? Sure is a long way to get back to England! Still, you take care now, and mind you come back real soon!'

I'd bought the ticket without giving it a thought: westbound to Australia. Of course it would be good to see Tristan again, but what had prompted the decision? It wasn't exactly what I'd originally intended... and finally there was George. None of it made any sense.

'Nearly home now, look you can see the bay!'

I opened my eyes and focussed on Australia.

I was here now, so just take it as it comes. I was probably being paranoid; it was just a normal chain of events and the hidden implications were all of my own making, the product of an overtired mind.

The first thing I saw as Tristan pulled into the drive was a small girl jumping up and down on a large circular trampoline.

When she saw the car she did a final bounce onto the grass and came running towards us. I did a double take, it could have been Rob's little Olive out of the garden in Seattle, but of course it wasn't. 'Hi dad!' she said in passing and flung herself into George's arms.

George threw her up into the air and then made as if to drop her amid much squealing.

'Well, my little sweetheart, my little Sheila, how are today – and what a welcome!'

Tristan laughed and opened the boot to get the bags. 'This is Jasmine, our little mistake, but what a mistake; she's a ball of fire! She's got a huge crush on George, in spite of the fact he's her Godfather – it's positively incestuous! She's – how old are you today Jasmine?'

'Um, now let me see' the little girl said primly. 'Today's Tuesday, so...' she started to count on her fingers '...I'm five years, ten months and twenty-three – no, twenty-four days old! It will soon be my birthday and Mummy says I can have a party. Do you want to come to my party Uncle George, there'll be lots of cakes and crisps! Do say yes?'

'Crisps! How could I refuse an invitation like that!' said George. 'Just try keeping me away; I'd love to come to your party! Now, here comes Peter so I'm going to put you down. He's a big boy, so I've got to shake his hand! Then I must get on home else Aunty Lil will want to know what's happened to me! Hi Pete, how're you going?'

'Hi Uncle George. Hi Dad!'

Peter was a tall fresh-faced lad, who looked remarkably like Tristan and indeed, at fourteen, was only five years younger than when I had first met his father. He had the same hair, the same open face with blue eyes that looked straight at you and even the same hesitant carriage. He put an arm round his father's waist and then looked shyly at me, waiting to be introduced. Jasmine, meanwhile, had run straight back to the trampoline and was busy jumping again.

'I've got to get going' George said, 'Hi Maggie, can't stop, catch you later!' This to Tristan's wife who had just come out of the house to join us in the drive. She was beautiful; tall and graceful, wearing lose-fitting slacks with a white silk shirt and long silver-blonde hair held back with a simple clip. She had wide-set grey eyes framed by high cheekbones that fell to a delicate mouth and – well, all in all, she was one of the most beautiful women I'd ever met.

Tristan laughed when he saw my confusion and put his arm around her.

'Maggie, Peter, I want you to meet one of my oldest – no, my oldest friend.'

Which simple statement said it all, and despite my previous misgivings, was reason enough to be here.

We didn't sit in the garden, for although it was early evening the unfiltered Australian sun was still strong enough to burn. Instead, we sat in the shade of the veranda, which was not unlike Rob's in Seattle. Nor did we drink gin, for in true cavalry fashion and without asking, Tristan pulled a bottle of champagne from an ice bucket.

I took a sip and then looked at the label on the bottle. 'Good Lord, there's an old friend!'

Tristan smiled and raised his glass 'Yes, I managed to find a source; we're not all heathens in Australia – we were weaned on this stuff in Germany' he added to Maggie. 'Cheers old friend, it's very good to see you...'

There was a lot to catch up from both sides. The talk ranged from Sandhurst, to Germany; to the time we'd served together in Aden, old friends and instances galore. His son Peter then went to a side table and picked up a photograph in a silver frame. 'Is this you?'

It was the photograph of Tristan and me standing in our cavalry blues in the front porch of the church: groom and best man.

The talk went on with Peter now sitting on the floor hugging his knees taking it all in, whilst his sister Jasmine was busy watching 'her programme' on television. At some time Maggie got up and set a salad on the table, to which we then helped ourselves and ate on our knees, watching the fading light die over the sea. He told me about his job in Australia, how he'd progressed from Islanders to Twin Otters and the type of flying they did, which he said was rarely dull. In turn I told him about my career, to the point I'd left it at Belize, to which he immediately suggested that I joined them, for they were always looking for experienced pilots. Peter, by this time was doing his school homework and Jasmine's television programme finished.

'Come on, young madam, time for bed!' Maggie said.

'Story, story – it's story-time now, mummy!'

'Well, perhaps a very quick one then.'

She ran out and came back a moment later with a dog-eared picture book.

'Will you read me a story?' she asked, her shyness at last overcome.

'Yes, of course I will.'

She started to clamber onto my knee, all bones and elbows, and then thrust the book at me and jumped down.

'Ashley, I must have Ashley – he needs a story too!'

She dashed to a chair and retrieved a soft toy that had once been a mouse, and immediately started to suck its dilapidated nose. The room darkened and the walls started to close in.

'This is Ashley' she said, taking its nose out of her mouth. 'He's my friend, he *always* listens to the story!'

'Yes, I know.'

I could hear the rain thundering on the concrete of the apron as she settled back onto my lap, wriggling as only a girl can, as if to make a nest. The blackness of the sky was suddenly pierced by lightning all around and I knew she too was watching the storm and thinking of me.

'I knew you'd come' she whispered and then, 'can you smell me?'